"GRAND
INTRIGUE, VIO

'As the world's most opulent train streaks across the breadth of Russia, the American doctor Alex Cousins finds himself plunged into conspiracy, nuclear intrigue, and a passionate affair with a beautiful Soviet agent.

"Adler qualifies as a successor to Agatha Christie."　　　　　　　　　*—Indianapolis News*

"In the Alistair MacLean vein . . . reminiscent of Arthur Hailey."　　　　　　　*—Denver Post*

"HARROWING SUSPENSE"
—Nashville Banner

"Brutal murder, bittersweet love, and a massive power struggle fill the pages of this supremely engrossing and vividly evocative novel. . . . It will grab you tight at the outset, hold you securely through page after page and set you down with a dramatic thump at the end."　　*—Cleveland Press*

"ENGROSSING,
GRIPPING, ABSORBING"
—West Coast Review of Books

TRANS-SIBERIAN EXPRESS

WARREN ADLER

A KANGAROO BOOK
PUBLISHED BY POCKET BOOKS NEW YORK

Distributed in Canada by PaperJacks Ltd., a Licensee
of the trademarks of Simon & Schuster, a division of
Gulf+Western Corporation.

POCKET BOOKS, a Simon & Schuster division of
GULF & WESTERN CORPORATION
1230 Avenue of the Americas, New York, N.Y. 10020
In Canada distributed by PaperJacks Ltd.,
330 Steelcase Road, Markham, Ontario.

Published by arrangement with G. P. Putnam's Sons
Library of Congress Catalog Card Number: 76-30634

ISBN: 0-671-81736-1

First Pocket Books printing July, 1978

Trademarks registered in the United States and other countries.

Printed in Canada

To my three sons
David, Jonathan, and Michael

LIST OF CHARACTERS

NIKOLAI ANDREYIVICH BOGACH, *Chief of the Guards Directorate of the KGB*

MARSHALL BULGAKOV, *Supreme Commander of the Red Army*

CARLYLE, *Secretary of State of the United States*

DR. ALEX COUSINS, *an American doctor*

VIKTOR MOISEYEVICH DIMITROV, *General Secretary of the Communist Party of the Soviet Union*

ALBERT FARMER, *British diplomat with the British Embassy in Ulan Bator, Outer Mongolia*

MIKHAIL MOISEYEVICH GINZBURG, *a Jewish engineer*

VERA DANILOVNA GINZBURG, *his non-Jewish wife*

IVAN VASILYEVICH GODOROV, *a Georgian and former prisoner under Stalin*

MAXIM SERGEYEVICH GRIVETSKY, *General in the Red Army, Soviet missile expert*

KATRINA IVANOV, *train attendant*

KISHKIN, *a Ukrainian engineer; Ginzburg's boss*

KENNETH MACBAREN, *an Australian traveler*

NATASHA, *Godorov's former fiancée*

COLONEL PATUSHKIN, *Tania's first lover*

MARY PETERSON, *American tourist and retired librarian*

PLATINOV, *a friend of Godorov's*

PRESIDENT OF THE UNITED STATES

TANIA REVEKKA ROMORAN, *train attendant*

SHMIOT, *a former prison inmate with Godorov*

SOKOLOVICH, *a senior inspector of the railway*

MR. AND MRS. TRUBETSKOI, *a Communist Party official, and his wife*

VLADIMIR TRUBETSKOI, *their son*

ANNA PETROVNA VALENTINOV, *Professor of History, resident of Irkutsk*

VOIKOV, *officer of the railway police*

IVAN LEONIDOVITCH YASHENKO, *a red-haired KGB agent, Zeldovich's assistant*

FYODOR PETROVICH ZELDOVICH, *KGB agent and confidant of Dimitrov*

1

An early spring sun, all light and no warmth, was slipping behind the gargoyled, columned mass of the Yaroslav station as the black Zil pulled smoothly up to its main entrance. The policeman posted there stiffened as he noticed the large, official-looking car.

The driver and his companion in the front seat, both small-eyed, high-cheekboned Slavs, got out and talked briefly with the policeman. Then they returned, pulled several pieces of baggage from the trunk and strode swiftly inside the station. Immediately the second car, a Chyka, pulled up. Five tall, dark-suited, somber men quickly emerged and fanned out. Two positioned themselves on either side of the entrance, conspicuous in their alertness, while the others walked through the station entrance and disappeared into the converging crowd of people.

Inside the Zil, Alex Cousins glanced at his watch. It was 4:15. The train was scheduled to leave at five, precisely five, Zeldovich had said confidently.

"They will take care of the details," Zeldovich assured him.

"Thank you," Alex responded in Russian. He had no illusions about Zeldovich.

It had been an uneventful trip from the dacha near Barvikla. Viktor Moiseyevich Dimitrov, the sixty-nine-year-old General Secretary of the Communist Party of the Soviet Union, had been expansive at lunch. His appetite had returned along with his color, and he had stuffed himself with huge portions of black bread and globs of sour cream heaped on top of deep bowls of borscht. The chemotherapy was working, Alex had observed, his doctor's pride expanding as he reviewed the charted progress and the past six weeks of endless diagnosis, observation and treatment. At best, the disease was tricky, and as cunning as a jungle beast. Acute myeloblastic leukemia was a microscopic war between the proliferating white cells and the rapidly weakening red cells in Dimitrov's blood. And the reds had been losing. Now Dimitrov, alert again, was no longer in the depressed manic state Alex had initially encountered.

At lunch a waiter had brought a fat bass, broiled brown and dripping with butter. Dimitrov had watched its arrival, smiling broadly with boyish pride. Alex had been allowing him out to fish again in the Moscow River, which meandered a few yards from the rear of the dacha. Fishing was Dimitrov's one passion, aside from the exercise of power, and returning to it had restored the General Secretary's buoyancy, reassuring him that he had been snatched, however temporarily, from the grave.

Alex had only picked at the fish. Despite his anxiety, he was excited by the prospect of this Siberian journey. Although, under different circumstances, he now would have been searching back in time, with all the emotion that nostalgia engenders, to prepare his mind for the mystique of the adventure. "It is a legacy of the soul," his grandfather, that old Siberian fox, would have said. But to begin such a journey under duress seemed, somehow, incongruous, against the grain. He looked down at the fish, runny with butter, the skin crisp and shiny, wondering if he could force his appetite.

"Delicious, Kuznetsov. Eat!" Dimitrov commanded, jabbing his knife forward, a trickle of butter escaping along the side of his mouth. Despite himself, despite what he suspected, Alex felt satisfaction in Dimitrov's enjoyment. It was the damnedest personal sensation, this dichotomy within himself, this raging war between his odd affection for the man and the knowledge of his impending act that had, somehow, seeped into his brain. Could it be possible he was mistaken, that all the comings and goings, the odd bits of information, the strange admissions and little confessions of Dimitrov himself, were only a distorted view through some faulty prism? I am a doctor. I am apolitical. You had no right to draw me into this, he wanted to shout across the table, trapped now like a fly that has fatally touched the flypaper with the tip of one wing.

"Why the long Siberian exit?" he had asked. "A flight would be much faster."

"Nonsense," Dimitrov had said blandly, as if he were persuading him merely to have another glass of brandy. "How could you deprive yourself? How many chances do you get in life? Whoever heard of a Russian with no curiosity about his past? You're here. Don't be foolish. I insist."

"But my wife—" Alex had answered mildly, not able to bring himself to even the first plateau of protest. His wife was certainly no reason to return. He might have been more accurate to say, "My life."

"Take a look at where you began," Dimitrov persisted, knowing that there was truth there, a match to dry tinder, for Alex had often longed to see the place from which his grandfather had escaped. But his escape had been merely physical. In the old man's mind and heart, he had never really left Siberia.

"I'll come back," Alex mumbled. "I'll do it another time."

"Nonsense," Dimitrov said. "It is my gift. Consider what you have given me."

Another old fox, Alex thought. Why don't you tell me the truth? I know too much. Perhaps you'll never let me out.

"One more week. What will it matter?"

He had been gone six weeks.

"The Politburo meets in seven weeks," the American Secretary of State had repeated again and again. "You must keep Dimitrov alive until that meeting," he might have said if he had not been so well schooled in obliqueness. Alex had, of course, received the message and had done his duty. How naive and ineffective the president and the secretary now looked in retrospect. Dimitrov had outmaneuvered them both. Still worse, he, Alex, could be characterized as a co-conspirator. And this trip was his fat reward for success. Let me put you in a rolling prison across the wastes of Siberia while I prepare a holocaust. Did they think he had the brains of a pea? Suddenly the idea of seeing his wife again—dear, bland, irritating, unaffectionate Janice— seemed almost attractive.

How they must have chuckled over their good fortune in discovering him, a Russian-speaking doctor who was an expert on leukemia. And he had been right under their noses at the National Institutes of Health. He had been very unreceptive. Couldn't they find someone else for this job? He was beyond politics, disgusted with their silly little power games. The preservation of human life, the alleviation of suffering, was the bedrock of his motivation. He had actually willed himself to be apolitical, dismissing everything that was not within the confines of his expertise. In his stupidity, man inflicted so much misery on himself. He could not seem to organize society for his own benefit. But that was the politicians' problem. One could not bleed over uncontrollable factors. At least in his field he could focus on a recognizable enemy. All else was trivia, he had convinced himself. Now, in

Moscow, the events of the last six weeks had effectively demolished that self-delusion.

As Dimitrov's strength returned, so did his cunning. He had struck exactly the right chord for a Russian—antecedents, roots. Russians and their damned ancestor fixation. To this day, every child born was given two names—his own and his father's. "Aleksandr Aleksandrovich Kuznetsov" was the name which appeared on Alex's original birth certificate. He had changed it to Alexander Cousins, in spite of his father's passionate opposition, since the practical advantages for his career were obvious. But he could not change the heritage that had been programed into his fantasies from birth. Siberia—a myth weathered and matured by repetitive storms of memory.

His grandfather had been caught in the Czar's penal machinery as a boy and sent to Siberia as punishment. He had helped build the Trans-Siberian Railroad, and his labor shortened his sentence. He landed in Irkutsk, which those given to sentimental exaggeration had dubbed the "Paris of Siberia." After several years there, his grandfather took his wife and young son and escaped to America. It was with these stories of youth, hardship, despair, danger and escape that Alex's ancient gnarled grandfather had mesmerized him, ever since he was old enough to understand. As he grew older he could pick Siberia out on a map, roughly along the 55th degree of latitude. He learned that it was an area of five million square miles that could encompass all of the United States, including Alaska, and all of western Europe, and still have hundreds of thousands of square miles left over.

When his grandfather eventually escaped from Siberia, the route took the family through farms and cattle ranches, through trackless virgin forests, around the earth's deepest lake, to heights where the sky is fair for all but sixteen days of the year, down to places where insects swarmed to torture men and animals, through pockets scourged by unspeakable disease and Manchurian tigers. During those interminable first days with Dimitrov, Alex had, of course, dwelt on the stories with relish, especially after seeing Dimitrov's enchanted reaction. It was all part of the treatment. Who could have expected it to be flung back at him like a weapon?

Alex's father had actually returned to Siberia years later, where he served as an interpreter with General Graves' American expeditionary force in Vladivostok. So it had passed down through the blood, a genetic yearning to rediscover some link to the beginning. Now Dimitrov was using his roots to put him on ice, literally, to keep him under their thumb until the time came, perhaps, to blow him out like a candle. He would be Dimitrov's health insurance until the meeting. And then? What would it matter by then? *Fait accompli!* A few million Chinks atomized, the China question solved. Even Dimitrov would not want to live beyond that. Only a dying man could bring himself to such a decision. If only Alex could wash his suspicions from his mind. But even that would not help. Dimitrov sensed his knowledge, and that was enough.

"Siberia is a great immensity," Dimitrov had said at lunch, his eyes peering from under thick, shaggy eyebrows. "Cold, wonderfully cold."

"I'll wear the fur-collared coat and hat that you gave me," Alex said stupidly. Perhaps he should have insisted more forcefully on flying home. Or demanded that they let him talk to the President. But that would have confirmed what Dimitrov suspected. They would never let him go. Not now! Maybe not ever.

"And keep your balls warm," Dimitrov warned with mock seriousness, his eyes twinkling, his famous charm called into action.

Still, Alex could detect in Dimitrov's manner the usual anxieties aroused by the departure of a trusted doctor.

"I could stay longer if you wish," Alex had said when Dimitrov had first suggested the trip. He was deliberately trying to frighten his patient, a lapse of ethics that he would not have thought possible a few weeks before.

"But you have already said I am in remission," Dimitrov said, with great seriousness, almost a trace of alarm. Alex watched the deep eyes above the high cheekbones, seeing the fear.

"At the moment."

"So I am still a time bomb?"

"Let's not talk of bombs," Alex had replied, regretting it instantly. If Dimitrov understood, his expression did not reveal it. But Alex knew that the information had been transmitted.

"Well then," Dimitrov said, clearing his throat. "What is your best guess?"

"I have told you"—Alex paused—"I do not guess."

"Days, weeks, months?"

Alex sighed. Again this interrogation about time. But he could not bring himself to lie despite his own sudden thirst for survival.

"The average is six to nine months, but some have lived as long as five years." He watched Dimitrov's eyebrows twitch.

"And the short side?"

"Days. Perhaps weeks."

"Days?"

"I am not God," Alex said testily. It could spring anytime, this leopard of a disease, he thought. It could spring from behind a rock and sink its teeth into the jugular.

Dimitrov was silent for a long time.

"Well, I will know where to find you," he said at last.

"No doubt about that," Alex said cautiously. "That is, if your trains run on time."

"You will be amazed at what you will see," Dimitrov said, his spirits brightening for a moment, then faltering again. "But Siberia is also a dangerous place. Like your West years ago."

"Now you're worrying about my health."

"It is of some importance," Dimitrov said grudgingly, averting his eyes. "You are, after all, the medical magician. I have a vested interest."

"What can happen to me in a week on your great Trans-Siberian Railroad? Your tourist brochures are quite ecstatic about it," Alex taunted.

"Anything can happen." Dimitrov's eyes narrowed.

"I'll watch out for the food and the cockroaches," Alex said.

"And the jackals."

"On the train?"

"They are everywhere," Dimitrov said quietly.

"I shall be as close as your phone, Comrade Dimitrov," Alex said, tired of sparring.

"There is no phone on the train," Dimitrov said, brightening again. "But there are eighty stops." He smiled and shook his head, tapping a finger on his desk.

"It is too close to the Chinks," he said. "They are like a fish bone in the throat."

"Who?"

"The Chinks."

The older man stroked his chin, then seemed to notice Alex again.

"You will enjoy it."

"If you say so."

When Alex had detected the first signs of a remission of the disease, confirmed both in tests and in the sudden explosion of energy in Dimitrov, he had noted an immediate surge of comings and goings in the dacha. When officials and military men were with Dimitrov, Alex was politely accompanied to other parts of the dacha, usually to the medical facility which had been installed in one wing. At first he was only mildly curious about the sleek Chykas pulling up the frozen gravel road, the sudden beefing up of the military, the appearance of increasing numbers of heavyset men in civilian dress, tense and alert, looming in every corner. It was of no concern to him, he told himself. His business was only with Dimitrov's bloodstream.

"You are pushing too hard," he told Dimitrov in his bedroom one night. Alex had almost pushed his way in insisting on admittance. Exhausted, Dimitrov was propped against the pillows.

"It is a question of time," he had replied weakly.

"Don't think about it."

"That is all I think about."

"Even if you were well, all this activity would exhaust you," Alex had said sternly.

"There is something I must do before I—" The words trailed off. Remembering what he had heard at the White House, Alex felt the sense of imposed deadline, so incongruous, even demeaning. He watched the gray-faced older man fight the heaviness in his lids, then finally slip into a deep sleep. Papers and maps slid to the floor beside the bed. Bending, Alex caught the designations on them—"People's Republic of China."

In the light of the bedlamp, the details of the map were clearly visible in a circle of yellow light. "Missile Disposition," he read. The words were written across the white edge of the map. Not without a tug of guilt, he puzzled over a series of random "X" marks on the China side, then, bending to explore further, he read the words, scrawled in pencil, but quite legible: "First strike potential destruct." Then he shrugged, turned off the light and tiptoed from the room, past the brawny, expressionless guards who eyed him with contempt.

That had been the beginning of his suspicions. But what did I do to betray my knowledge? he had wondered, sitting in the soft interior of the big Zil. "How do they know that I know?"

"We must go," Zeldovich said.

Alex grabbed his bookbag of medical journals and followed. The brief blast of biting cold that cut through them as they left the car subsided quickly as they entered the crowded room where a loudspeaker crackled. He could barely make out the words: "Trans-Siberian, 'The Russiya'—" The crowd—old men with deeply rutted faces, huge-bosomed mothers in thick coarse coats with children clustered around them, men squatting over outsized bundles—stirred and gathered their belongings. Then they began to line up at the gates where a hard-eyed train agent looked over their papers.

"Please wait here," Zeldovich ordered, leaving Alex standing near a snack counter where a red-faced woman dispensed an unappetizing variety of chicken and a greenish beer.

The loudspeaker crackled again, barely audible over the sudden whistle of the wind outside: "Trans-Siberian Express, Track Four, leaving—"

Alex strained to hear, then looked at his watch. It was 4:30. The train was scheduled to leave in half an hour.

Watching the line as it threaded its way slowly through the checkpoint, Alex noticed the arrogance of the train agent, a ruddy-faced Slav who looked over the papers contemptuously, sneering into each person's face. Seated on either side of him two of the men who had been in the Chyka also reviewed the papers, checking information against lists on clipboards. To one side Alex saw Zeldovich and the station master in close conversation, looking toward him.

The line moved ponderously. The heavy winter clothing everyone wore made the group look nondescript, an amorphous glob with sexual and class distinctions blurred. Most of the passengers accepted the agent's intimidation with resignation and humility. Alex could see the fear in their eyes as they stepped forward. One couple was shunted aside and interrogated by one of the men from the Chyka. Others stepped forward and would not be stared down. An attractive young woman actually opened her heavy coat, putting her hand on her hip and straightening to show her breasts, subtly challenging the power of the three men. Even from a distance, Alex could see she was forcing the men into a special kind of submission. She passed through, dignity intact, the long coat flowing behind her as she walked toward the train.

"When the others have moved through, you will go," Zeldovich's flat voice said. Alex hadn't seen the man come up behind him.

"This is one big pain in the ass," Alex said in English, knowing it would annoy Zeldovich, who spoke only Russian. The past six weeks had made them mutually antagonistic. Zeldovich, the fawning flunky, disgusted him.

They stood for a while watching the line. Suddenly a deep voice boomed out over the din. A tall man was confronting the train agent, pulling rank, demanding speed. He seemed vaguely familiar. Alex had seen him at Dimitrov's dacha.

"Yes, General," he heard the train agent say, his voice high-pitched and suddenly obsequious. The agent clicked his heels, indicating that he had once been a soldier. Satisfied that he had won his point, the tall general slowly lit a cigar, surely a Havana, and passed through the gate.

"General Grivetsky," Zeldovich mused, his forehead lined with a frown. He seemed momentarily confused, surprised at the general's presence.

"I saw him at the dacha," Alex said, hoping to contribute to his displeasure.

"You are mistaken," Zeldovich mumbled.

"Bullshit," Alex said in English, under his breath.

He had grown used to their odd little lies by now, their automatic need to mask the obvious.

"He is a great hero of the Red Army," Zeldovich said suddenly, recovering his Russian sense of hyperbole. It was part of their syndrome to create celebrities. Worker heroes were everywhere, decorated for making cheese well or sweeping streets thoroughly. Even the train agent wore a medal. Railway work was quite an important profession in the Soviet Union, Dimitrov had said, cataloguing all the benefits—higher pay, early retirement, and a string of enviable privileges.

His encounter with the general had served only to increase the train agent's arrogance toward those still in line. Next was a smallish man, squat, who moved with a pronounced waddle. Alex watched, his doctor's mind suddenly analytical. The man's shoulders and arms were too big for his stumpy torso. He had probably developed them to compensate for the lower parts of his body, the muscles of which seemed badly atrophied. But the power in the shoulders and arms was unmistakable. The man could surely crush the train agent's head like an overripe melon.

When the man did not produce his papers fast enough, the agent railed at him in an obvious attempt to reassert his importance.

"Goddammit, you slow nitwit, you're holding up the line."

Unruffled, the squat man moved deliberately, taking out his wallet in his own good time. For once the train agent had chosen someone who was not easily intimidated, someone used to little pyrrhic victories and silent rebellions.

The train agent took the passport angrily, shouted out the man's name, "Godorov," then let the passport drop to the stone floor at his feet.

The squat man looked at it for a moment, then slowly—painfully, Alex was certain—bent to retrieve it. As the man knelt at the train agent's feet, reaching with gnarled stubby fingers for the passport, Alex suddenly expected the train agent to kick the man in the head. But the blow did not come. The agent, perhaps conscious that his intimidation had failed, turned his venom on the next in line. A couple in their middle thirties, whose fear seemed to sweat through their heavy clothing, sprang forward, cringing and obsequious. The agent smiled tightly as he looked at their papers. Grist for his mill, Alex thought, noting that the man had a Semitic look about him.

The train agent brushed the couple to one side as he threw their papers on the table and called for the next passenger. The couple, their faces ashen now, stood nervously watching the papers.

Alex turned away in disgust and saw that Zeldovich was no longer watching the line but scanning the interior of the station. The men who had accompanied them from Dimitrov's dacha were ranged around the edges of the waiting room. Hard-eyed and constantly on the alert, they made clumsy attempts at casualness that could not conceal their professionalism.

"Dimitrov takes no chances," Alex said.

"Not with you."

Turning back to the line, Alex searched among the faces for Westerners. A little woman, wearing a pink coat and an absurd white bunny hat, stood talking nonstop to a tall man in a bowler hat. He had bent slightly to catch her words, and had been trapped in the endless stream. Alex smiled. She was the only bit of brightness in the drab scene.

A tall sandy-haired man reached the checkpoint. He tapped his foot impatiently while his papers were scrutinized. When he had been cleared, he started toward the train, turning once to lift his fist in what Alex suspected was an obscure obscenity.

The line continued to move forward and the loud-speaker crackled additional warnings. Crowds of babush-kas, strong, dull-eyed older women carrying brooms, moved ponderously toward the tracks. They were every-where, these grandmotherly types in heavy shoes and bulky clothing, breathing vapor, their heads swathed with faded kerchiefs. They were visible all over the Soviet Union, sweeping the streets, repairing the high-ways, working around Dimitrov's dacha, sprouting everywhere like ancient weeds.

The last couple, fat Russians dragging a small boy, passed through the gateway.

"Now," Zeldovich said.

Alex picked up his bookbag of medical journals. The rest of his baggage was already loaded onto the train. The station master waved Alex through the gate while the train agent turned back to the tearful Jewish couple who cowered, eyes lowered, beside the table. Up close, the agent's cruelty was almost tangible, and Alex stared at his heavy back, the thick neck muscles, the skin red as borscht. The woman's eyes met Alex's briefly, then darted away, perhaps frightened by his foreignness. For a foreigner to appear sympathetic, he surmised, would only make matters worse.

2

Alex and Zeldovich strode past the rows of glistening green railway cars. They were strikingly clean and shiny after the gloom of the waiting room. The carriages seemed taller than the American variety and certainly wider, since the Russian railroad track gauge was the widest in the world. Excited faces peered from the windows as he passed and he could see people already on their bunks in the "hard" class carriages, the cheap sections which housed four in each compartment.

Zeldovich clattered up the metal stairs of a carriage near the front of the train. A woman in a linen smock met them at the passageway entrance and quietly exchanged words with Zeldovich. She was a large woman, big-breasted. When she opened her mouth in a half smile, a stainless-steel eyetooth glistened.

"I am pleased to meet you, Dr. Cousins," the woman said, holding out her hand.

"She is the attendant in this carriage," Zeldovich said, poking his head beyond her to see into the passageway. "I know she will make your trip very comfortable."

"I'm sure," Alex said politely.

Zeldovich turned and pulled off his glove, a deliberate act of courtesy, and held out his hand. Alex was surprised. He had hardly expected Zeldovich to let him out of his sight. Could he have been wrong? he wondered.

"I hope you have a pleasant journey," Zeldovich said, his little eyes blank as he pumped Alex's hand vigorously in the heavy Russian way. Then he clattered down the metal steps, leaving Alex to ponder his unexpected retreat. They are giving me a false sense of security, he thought. Or throwing me to the jackals.

Following the attendant down the passageway, over an Oriental patterned carpet, Alex peered into each compartment as he passed. By American standards, they were commodious. Two bunks were ranged along one side of the wall. Over each bunk was a net catchall. There was also a table, covered with a cloth, on which stood a lamp with a tasseled shade. An Oriental rug covered the floor and red velvet curtains hung at either side of the window. The walls were done in deep-toned mahogany. There was a hint of the Victorian in the decor and, after the bleakness at the station, Alex found it particularly inviting.

Looking down the passageway, he could see a shiny metal samovar, laid on a faintly glowing bed of charcoal. Large pails of charcoal stood on the floor beneath it. A small metal scoop was sticking up from one of them. Apparently this apparatus was meant to be the principal source of heat for the train.

At the entrance to compartment four, the attendant turned and took Alex's bookbag from him. As she carried it inside, Alex could not resist glancing into the next compartment down the hall. Sitting there was the general Alex had seen in the station. He had already usurped the only chair and was staring out of the window, his head bathed in heavy clouds of cigar smoke.

The attendant returned to the passageway. "If there

is anything you wish, ring the buzzer inside," she said. Then she whispered, almost conspiratorially, "My name is Tania."

The moment Alex stepped into the compartment, he felt a decided change in atmosphere. A heavy smell of perfume hung in the air, Russian perfume. It was the same overpowering scent worn by the nurses in Dimitrov's dacha. It smelled as if it had been made in one gigantic vat of strawberries.

Someone had already arrived and opted for the lower bunk. It was obviously a woman. This, Alex had already learned, was another quirk of the Russians, who championed sexual equality to the point of arranging accommodations with stubborn disregard for the sex of the passengers. Alex felt a tug of excitement. Except for a brief unsatisfactory episode with one of Dimitrov's heavy-thighed nurses, he had been celibate for the past six weeks.

A suitcase lay open revealing feminine underthings, unusually frilly for a Russian—pink panties, a garter belt, brassiere with a dainty little ribbon between the cups. There were dresses too, hanging on a bar at one end of the compartment. Alex flung his bookbag on the upper bunk and hoisted himself up two steps of the wooden ladder to feel the mattress. It was firm, and the pillow seemed well stuffed. Alex smiled with relief. At least his nights on the train would not be as uncomfortable as he'd feared.

He noted that both his suitcases had been placed neatly under the lower bunk. He slid them out. They were heavy, difficult to swing to the upper bunk. As he did so, he accidentally bumped the woman's suitcase, disarranging a scarf. His eye caught a gleaming bottle of vodka stuck in one corner of her suitcase. He looked around, not without a twinge of guilt, then carefully covered it with the scarf again.

Opening one of his own suitcases, he felt under his pajamas for his leather toiletry case. It wasn't there. Pushing down with his palms, he could feel its outlines under layers of clothing. Someone had searched his belongings. He shrugged, feeling a surge of paranoia, his brief sense of freedom at Zeldovich's departure dissipated. They were watching, after all.

He removed the toilet kit, placing it in the net bag over his bunk. He hung his two suits in the open closet next to the dresses and felt a sudden intimacy. Like home, he thought, although Janice and he had separate closets. He felt the material of one of the dresses, jersey, smooth. As he moved toward his suitcase again, he glanced into the passageway and saw the squat man whom the train agent had tried to humiliate. He waddled past, looking quickly at Alex, in a sudden movement, then looking forward again.

Removing his pajamas and robe, he hung them on a hook next to the flowered robe of the anonymous woman. His long coat and fur hat he hung next to his suits, embarrassed that he had taken up so much room. When he had finished with all the details of settling down, his ear began to register an undercurrent of music, faintly audible. Following the direction of the sound, he saw the perforated disc of a speaker built into the wall and beside it the volume knob.

He turned the knob to the right, but the volume did not change. The knob had to be broken. He was in for it now, he thought, making a note to call the attendant. He knew the music could become an annoying sound, like the maddening drip-drip of water from a loose spigot.

With great creaking noises, as the coupling strained and the wheels rolled on the wide-gauged track, the train began to move. It gained momentum slowly, picking its way cautiously through the railyards. Peering out through the grayness, he watched the swarm of babushkas sweeping under harsh floodlights. Beyond, on the edge of the light, Alex could see the decaying boilers of aged steam locomotives and the rusting hulks of old carriages ready for the scrap heap. He pressed his head sideways against the cold glass and watched the train station recede. Behind him was the darkening, barely visible skyline of Moscow.

"The tea is lovely," a woman's voice said in English. He turned quickly, embarrassed at being caught in such an odd position. She was standing inside the compartment, holding a glass of tea held gracefully in her long, graceful fingers. The glass was fitted into a silver-filigreed metal container. He watched her settle into the single chair of red velvet. She crossed long, well-muscled legs and watched him through her brown lashes. He recognized her as the woman who had intimidated the train agent with her sexuality. He was not immune to it himself, he discovered.

"The tea in this car is excellent," she said. "Just press the buzzer. The Petrovina will get you a glass."

She had meant to be charming, he realized, but instead he felt slightly intimidated. He pressed the buzzer, more to recover his calm, than out of a desire for tea.

"I speak Russian," he said. Was it meant to be a lion's roar? It came out as a bleat.

"Wonderful," she said, in English again.

She leaned her head back, smiling broadly, showing a line of gold fillings. He calculated she was somewhere in her mid-thirties. It was her size that must have caused this sudden anxiety. She was close to six feet, he reckoned, with a figure that was beautifully proportioned to her size, but was extraordinary compared to those of other females. She was the ideal of Russian beauty, like the painting of sturdy peasant girls smiling in the wheatfields that were hung everywhere in Dimitrov's dacha.

"Well then, what shall it be?" she asked. Her voice had depth and timbre. It was her aggressiveness, too, that had caught him by surprise.

"Russian train. Russian tongue," he said, slipping onto the lower bunk, which obviously served as the only other seat in the compartment.

"Okay," she said in English, then laughed and switched to Russian. "I wanted to practice my English," she said. "Perhaps later, okay?" She laughed again, raised her tea and touched her full lips to the edge of the glass.

Tania appeared in the doorway, waiting for orders.

"Tea, please," Alex said. She nodded, departing.

"I am Anna Petrovna Valentinov," the blonde woman said, extending her hand. He took the long fingers in his, feeling their heat and strength.

"Alex Cousins." She probably knew that already.

"I'm going to Irkutsk," she volunteered.

"The Paris of Siberia," he commented, suddenly cautious, remembering Dimitrov's odd warning. "Be discreet," he had urged, repeating it over and over in the last days. Why discreet? Alex had wondered. Dimitrov held all the cards. And this woman was probably his agent.

"My husband has an important post with the university in Irkutsk," she said. He imagined he caught a slight sigh. "I myself am a Professor of History there."

Alex was not surprised. If they were going to vest her with a profession, why not choose one that was esoteric? Or was it? Everywhere in the Soviet Union there were women in professions dominated by men in America—doctors, lawyers, trainmen, construction workers, professors. There was, he had learned, a surplus of twenty million women in the Soviet Union, the result of long years of war. He studied Mrs. Valentinov. Underneath the sexuality, which he could not erase from his mind or his senses, he detected a hard earnestness and intellectual power. She was certainly different from his wife, Janice, the archetypal American housewife, who was motivated by acquisitiveness and all the anxieties and insecurities it created. Not that this Russian woman was without her little vanities. He noted how carefully she applied her mascara; the light, artistic rouging of the high cheekbones; the delicate painting of her lips. He remembered the lacy underwear he had seen in her suitcase. They are outflanking us everywhere, he thought with some amusement.

Tania appeared in the compartment again with a glass of tea on a small tray. Alex removed two unwrapped lumps of sugar from the steel bowl Tania offered, then watched her depart. Blowing on the tea, he peered out of the window. They were passing through a tunnel. The total blackness beyond the window created a dark mirror in which he could see himself and Mrs. Valentinov. They looked like a contented Victorian couple ensconced in their cozy living room.

"It's been two months." Mrs. Valentinov sighed. "I had to attend an important seminar at Moscow University. They are redoing the Russian encyclopedia, a mammoth task. The mass of details is enormous."

He had been watching the woman, but listening only peripherally. The train was picking up speed now, the sensation of bouncing becoming more pronounced. On one bounce the tea slopped over his fingers. The woman laughed.

"The roadbed," she said. "Roadbeds in other countries, they say, make the trains sway. Ours bounce. They put the tracks together in an odd way." There was a very long pause.

"The Russians have to be different," he said, filling the vacuum with an expected response.

"You notice that about us?"

"Is the Pope Catholic?"

He was sorry he had said it, wondering if the wisecrack would be misinterpreted as sarcasm. His experience with Russians had discouraged his propensity for wisecracks. At Dimitrov's dacha he had discovered that each casual one-liner needed further explanation, until by the end, the humor was gone. But the woman seated across from him had blinked her eyes and nodded with a wry smile, as if she had understood. Did she, he wondered, or was she simply trying to be ingratiating?

Through the open compartment door he watched the parade of people. Most took sly little looks inside, then turned away. One well-dressed gentleman turned and smiled. A little boy was dragged past. He stuck his tongue out at Alex.

"Vladimir!" The sharp, dominating voice of his mother rang through the passageway.

A man passed wearing striped pajamas. Alex stared, and Mrs. Valentinov laughed.

"It's a Russian traveling costume," she said.

"Pajamas?"

"It's quite practical. Very comfortable and saves wear and tear on the clothes." She paused. "It's quite respectable, really."

Perhaps it was the use of the word respectable. Suddenly Alex's thoughts took an odd turn as he watched the woman, larger than life, slumped in her chair, her long legs crossed, a bit of white skin showing where the garters met the top of her stockings. His imagination followed the whiteness up her thighs, beyond, and he could feel himself stiffen. It was one of those male fantasies come true, he thought. How many times had he wished that chance would create opportunity? Like now. This beautiful Amazon dropping from heaven less than a yard from him.

"My husband prefers to fly," she went on. "He can't understand why I'd want to spend four nights on a bouncing train when the jet trip takes only seven hours."

Alex sensed that she was deliberately explaining her presence. Yet, despite his suspicions, he could understand the compelling sense of isolated time and space that a train journey induced, a suspension, an interruption of the life cycle. He could define his feelings about it quite accurately, and yet he had only slept on a train once before in his life, when he had first taken the sleeper down from New York to Washington. He had had an upper berth then, but even after twenty years he could still recall the excitement of finding himself tucked into the cozy shelf while the wheels churned somewhere below, moving him securely over a mysterious road to nowhere.

However calculated her intent, Mrs. Valentinov's comment had served to eliminate her husband from this experience, and, despite his caution, he felt a commonality between them, a sharing of more than space.

The train was picking up speed. He finished the dregs of his tea and looked at his watch.

"That won't do you any good," she said, smiling broadly. He felt like a small boy caught with his hand in the cookie jar. He must have frowned, looking confused.

"The train runs on Moscow time, despite the fact that we travel through five time zones between here and Irkutsk. I always just take off my watch." To prove the point, she undid her wristwatch and tossed it into her open suitcase. "The human clock"—she pointed to her stomach—"will be more accurate."

The suggestion triggered his hunger.

"Don't worry, the restaurant car is open from nine in the morning to eleven at night." She seemed alert to every one of his responses.

"My clock is ringing now," he said, getting up. "Would you care to join me?"

"I'm afraid our clocks are not synchronized," she said.

"I didn't eat much for lunch," he explained, embarrassed by his own banality. Sliding his bookbag from under her bunk, he pulled out a medical journal to take with him. He looked toward Mrs. Valentinov, but she had already turned away, and was staring into the darkness outside the moving train.

3

In the passageway Alex looked in either direction and saw Tania step out of one of the compartments and move toward the samovar. He walked toward her, passing some open compartments. In one of them, the fat Russian couple he had seen in the queue were munching sausages from a makeshift plate of oily paper. A bottle of vodka stood on the table. Seeing Alex watching, the man kicked the door shut. Alex shrugged, determined not to look inside the other compartments as he passed, although his eye quickly took in the layout of the carriage. There were twelve compartments and, along the outside wall of the passageway, a number of little pull-out seats which were now pushed tightly against the wall. At either end of the carriage were lighted signs reading "Toilet." In the passageway he recognized the music that was playing in some of the compartments. It was "The Yellow Rose of Texas." Dimitrov, too, had a propensity for American popular music, and the dacha had rung with the familiar sounds.

25

"The restaurant car is in the other direction," Tania said, wiping her hands on her smock.

"Thank you," he said, retracing his steps, peeking into his own compartment again. The woman had not moved. Her eyes were still fixed on the window though nothing was visible except her own reflection. As Alex passed the door marked "Toilet," a neatly dressed man he had seen on the queue emerged. He had discarded his bowler hat, but he was quite obviously British.

"Bloody awful," the man said. He seemed to be in his late fifties, thin, with a network of little red veins spread over his cheeks and nose. "The bloody thing's stuck. I'll have to tell the attendant."

"Will they fix it?" Alex asked with vague concern, remembering the faulty loudspeaker in his compartment.

"They're not much for fix-its." The Englishman lowered his voice and winked. "Sometimes they do it deliberately, you know. It's all part of their grand design."

"Grand design?"

"To test the outer limits of our ability to tolerate hardship. A broken toilet provides an excellent model."

"Well then, we must fight back." Alex smiled.

"How?"

"Shit in the corridors. Pee in the tea glasses."

The Englishman coughed and cleared his throat. "You're American," he said.

"We're all a bit uncouth."

"We'll have to chat a bit. I have a sister in San Francisco." He turned abruptly and passed Alex in the direction of Tania, who was now shoveling chunks of charcoal into the brazier. Had he been too rude, Alex thought. The man could be a conduit for what he knew. He filed away the idea. Had he the right to destroy the man's innocence? It was a new moral question.

Pulling open the heavy steel door, Alex felt the blast of icy air as it poured through the rips in the rubber coupling protectors. After the warmth of the corridor, he felt as if he had just walked into a refrigerator. He reached for the handle of the opposite door, feeling his fingers stick to the cold metal as he struggled to open it. Before he could pull the latch free, he heard a door open behind him, felt the sudden whoosh of air and the clang of heels on the metal flooring. He turned and saw the somber face and tight-cropped red hair of one of the security men who had ridden in the Chyka from Dimitrov's dacha. The place must be crawling with them. Could he have believed they would let him go free? Dimitrov was hardly a fool, he thought, deliberately squeezing through the door quickly and letting it slip back in the spy's face. He would not think about it, he told himself, knowing that it was getting increasingly difficult to put up with the signs of Dimitrov's surveillance. In the restaurant car, he ducked into the toilet and listened, his ear cocked against the door, until the red-haired man passed.

The restaurant car had the same old-fashioned look as his compartment. Heavyset women wearing brown aprons and a kind of cloth tiara moved about, serving the diners in the half-filled car. Toward the far end Alex spotted the red-haired man, his nose buried in the large menu. Vaguely uncomfortable and disoriented, Alex wondered if he was supposed to wait or to seat himself. Finally, a small, officious man came up and tapped him on the shoulder. Alex held up a single finger and the man led him to a table in the center of the car where a man in striped pajamas was drinking borscht from a stainless-steel bowl. A drop of red juice was hanging from his chin.

Alex smiled politely. "Is it good?" he asked in Russian.

"*Nyet,*" the man said with some annoyance.

Picking up the lacquered menu, Alex began to thumb through it. It was fifteen pages thick. Hundreds of items were listed, a compendium of every conceivable dish available in the Soviet Union. His eye picked out the word *"Pilmenis,"* and he suddenly remembered his grandmother's specialty, minced meat in envelopes of dough, which he had eaten with huge globs of cream and dabs of mustard sauce.

He could feel the yearning in his stomach as the waitress arrived.

"*Nyet*," she said flatly when he asked for the dish.

He was disappointed. Like a stone-thrown into a well, the *pilmenis* had stirred the deep waters of nostalgia. Many of the dishes listed were part of his grandfather's stories. Salmon caviar covered with cream and honey and sprinkled with bilberries; bear steak; cream of reindeer milk with wild raspberries laced with *Kvas; kissel*, a liquid jam made of cranberries. He was sure he had tasted that, eaten it with a spoon.

"I'll have the herring with vegetables," he told the waitress.

"*Nyet*," she said.

"And the roast pork?"

"*Nyet*." She seemed to be enjoying herself.

"And the fried liver?"

"*Nyet*."

He was perversely tempted to read the entire fifteen-page menu.

"*Nyet* seems to be the operative word," he said.

A woman giggled behind him. Turning, he saw the little woman who had worn the pink coat and the bunny hat. Her blue eyes sparkled with laughter behind rimless wire glasses. Her hair was gray with a liberal coloring of blue rinse, giving it a peculiar sheen in the yellow lit car. She wore a primly cut, high-collared black dress with a single strand of pearls. She must have been about sixty, the perfect maiden lady. Beside her on the table was a book entitled *Eurail*.

"They do have borscht and stew," she said in American-accented English.

Alex looked about the restaurant car as if to confirm her observation. Across the aisle he observed the large-faced man whom Zeldovich had identified as General Grivetsky. He was eating a slightly burned omelet and drinking great quantities of red wine from a water tumbler.

"And omelets," the woman said.

"I'll start with the borscht," Alex said. The waitress sneered and walked away slowly, her big haunches packed firmly beneath her tight smock.

"The Eurail book offers subtle forewarning," the little woman said. Alex turned to her again. She was sitting alone, drinking a cup of tea. "The trains run on time," she continued, "but the restaurant car is beyond hope."

"That's why it's so empty?" he asked, marveling at the easy way Americans befriended each other.

"Most of the Russians supposedly eat in their compartments, except these brave fellows. And us."

"May I join you?" Alex asked, suddenly eager for the company of an American, feeling his foreignness in what he had begun to regard as the hostile environment of the restaurant car. He moved to her table and noticed the red haired man's eyes flicker at his movement.

"Alex Cousins," he said, putting out his hand.

"Mary Peterson, Miss Peterson," she responded, smiling primly, putting a delicate cool palm in his. "Youngstown, Ohio."

"Bethesda, Maryland."

"First trip on the Trans-Sib?" she asked, the shortened version indicating a possessive familiarity.

"Yes."

"Second time for me. I did it in 1960 on the way to Australia. It was all steam then. Now we don't get steam, even after Lake Baikal."

The waitress arrived with the borscht, annoyed that Alex had changed his table. He began to eat. The borscht was good. Why not? he thought. They invented it.

"Exciting, isn't it?" Miss Peterson said, looking out of the window. He followed her eyes, seeing nothing but her reflection. She watched his mirror image, then directed her conversation toward it, as if it were a wholly different person.

"I'm getting off at Khabarovsk, going just for the

ride. Then I'm flying back to Moscow. Foreigners have to change there for Nakhodka. They don't let us go to Vladivostok."

"Yes, I know." He sipped his borsch.

"The line goes five-thousand-seven-hundred-seventy-eight miles to the Pacific. That's a general term, since technically it's the Sea of Japan. Imagine, nearly six thousand miles. We pass through eight time zones and, if we stayed the whole way, we'd be making eighty-three stops and go an average speed of thirty-seven miles per hour."

"My God," Alex said, "you're a walking encyclopedia."

"I'm a travel freak," she whispered, obviously proud of her knowledge. "When you work in a library, you take many journeys in your mind." Her eyes sparkled with alertness.

Alex eyed her coolly. Perhaps she might be persuaded—He checked the thought. Had he the right to create new victims?

"You must be a doctor," she said, looking at the medical journal that lay unopened beside the plate of black bread that had come with the borsch.

"Yes," he answered.

"You must be here on some medical meeting."

He wondered if Dimitrov's admonition to be cautious extended to nice gray-haired American ladies traveling alone. He decided again to defy their paranoia, at least in this instance. Or was she one of them?

"I was," he lied. "This leg is strictly for pleasure. My grandfather helped build this railroad; then he settled in Irkutsk. My grandparents came to the States just before World War I. My father came back as an interpreter for General Graves." He marveled at his own explanation. It all fit so beautifully.

"So that accounts for your Russian?" No, she was an innocent, he decided. They could hardly have manufactured her.

The little man in charge of the restaurant car eyed them curiously. Alex saw him talk to the red-haired man, then move toward their table. Standing over them, he quickly wrote out a check and put it before the gray-haired woman, who ignored it. But the stocky man continued to stand over them. The sweat was gathering on his upper lip.

"I'm terribly sorry," he said in Russian. "We expect a large crowd. Would you pay the check please?"

"What did he say?" the woman asked pleasantly.

"He said you should pay the check. They need the space." Alex looked around the half-empty restaurant car. No one was waiting.

"I'll be happy to make room when the parties come," Miss Peterson said politely.

Putting down his spoon, Alex looked up at the man, who lowered his eyes. He appeared frightened.

"The lady said she'd be happy to leave when your people come," Alex said, dipping his spoon again into the thick mixture before him.

"I need the space now," the man said. His voice had a whining, pleading tone. "It requires preparation."

"What did he say?" the woman asked again. She opened her large pocketbook, pulled out a Russian dictionary, and began thumbing pages.

"He says you should leave now," Alex said. He watched the resolve grow in her face, the chin rise, the lines tighten.

"I'll do nothing of the kind."

"Of course you won't," Alex said. He turned toward the red-haired man, who was eying them impassively, and jabbed his middle finger in the air. The man stopped chewing for a moment, his eyes narrowing.

"What are you looking for?" Alex asked the restaurant manager. "Bug off."

Then he translated it for Miss Peterson.

"Bug off," she repeated.

The man apparently did not understand the idiom, but he could not mistake the tone. Turning angrily, he walked back to the red-haired man, who stopped chewing again to listen. The general turned toward them, his mouth filled with omelet. The man in pajamas at the table in front of him continued to slurp borscht with unconcerned abandon.

"They're usually quite rude to each other, but rarely to foreigners," Miss Peterson whispered.

"Pay no attention to it," Alex said, understanding why they were being intimidated.

He continued to eat his borscht. The train had apparently reached a stable speed and the bouncing splattered the borscht on the tablecloth with steady regularity.

"When they built the railroad, they didn't stagger the fittings but made them parallel instead. That's why we bounce instead of sway," Miss Peterson volunteered, proud of her knowledge. Across the aisle the general drained the dregs of his glass.

"You seem to know a great deal about railroads," Alex said.

He was nearly finished with his borscht and was ready to order a main dish, the inevitable stew. Where was the waitress? She had been out of sight for at least ten minutes.

"I travel the rails whenever I can," Miss Peterson said proudly. "People who don't travel trains miss all the fun."

"Waitress," the general's voice boomed out. "Where is the waitress?" He stood up, a big, heavyset man, his face flushed as he looked in either direction and made his way to the kitchen. "What kind of a train is this?" he shouted.

The manager emerged, the surly waitress behind him. "This is a disgrace," the general's voice boomed. "I want more wine."

"Good for him," Miss Peterson said. "The squeaky wheel gets the most oil."

With a frightened look at the red-haired man, the harassed manager responded quickly to the general's obvious authority, rushing toward him with another bottle of wine. With a shaking hand, he pulled out the cork and poured a tumblerful of wine into the general's glass. The general nodded, picked up the filled glass and lifted it in Alex's direction.

"And take care of those Americans," he said. "What kind of hospitality do you offer here? You are a disgrace to the country, to the railroad." He drank the glass off in one swallow.

The little man came closer, nodding obsequiously, as Alex rattled out orders for more tea and a plate of stew. The waitress went to the kitchen and was back with the food almost immediately.

"And a bottle of wine," Alex added.

In a moment the wine had been opened and poured.

"I drink to you, sir," Alex said to the general.

"By all means," Miss Peterson said, lifting her tea glass.

"And to you," Alex called to the red-haired man, who looked up, scowling. Alex drank the wine quickly. It was too sweet, but he was grateful for the way it soothed him. The waitress had put a wine glass in front of Miss Peterson, but when he attempted to fill it, the American woman covered it with her hands and smiled benignly.

"Dear no," she said, with the innate primness of the maiden lady, although there seemed in her an uncharacteristic streak of toughness. He felt drawn to Miss Peterson, whose sheer innocent enthusiastic Americanness was like a whiff of freedom in the paranoid Russian atmosphere. Even her quotations from Baedecker were oddly refreshing.

"The Trans-Siberian Railroad was begun in 1891, in the time of Alexander the Third; Nicholas the Second turned the first shovelful of earth in Vladivostok. I always believe in knowing about the history of things when I travel. Don't you agree?"

He hesitated, wondering if he would be triggering an endless history lesson. "Yes," he said finally, sipping his wine.

"Are you going all the way to Nakhodka, Dr. Cousins?" she asked.

"Yes," he whispered, trying to swallow his answer.

He had wanted to say, "Hopefully." Would they ever let him reach that destination? he wondered.

"Then you'll be taking the boat to Yokohama."

"Yes." Please, yes, he thought.

"I took it in 1960. The *Khaborousk* it was called. Same name as the city, both named for a man, actually. He was a fur trapper and trader, quite ruthless." She sipped her tea. "But I'm more at home on trains than on boats. On this trip I've gone straight through from Victoria Station."

Alex stole a quick glance at the red-haired man. His long conversation with Miss Peterson might be putting her in danger. But he felt incapable of rudeness.

"The silliest thing is their wide-gauged track. They actually thought it would save them from invasion. So now, when you cross their borders, giant cranes have to change the axles of your train. Quite ridiculous, don't you think?"

"Typically Russian," he mumbled, remembering Dimitrov.

"They didn't foresee airplanes," she continued. But Alex was no longer listening.

The restaurant car was beginning to fill up now, although all the seats were still not taken. He noticed that the man who ran the car seemed to be deliberately leaving the two seats at their table empty. The man in pajamas finally rose and disappeared through the exit. The din increased as more people crowded into the car. Relaxed by the wine, Alex watched the faces.

In the Yaroslav railroad station, under their heavy coats, all the people had seemed nondescript. But now he could read in their faces evidence of the vast spectrum of peoples that occupied the Siberian land mass. Skin tones varied from the pinkness of the European White Russian to the reddish-darkness of the Mongol, the olive tones of the Armenian, and all the variations in between. He saw eye shapes varying from the Caucasian through the Tartar to the Oriental; round heads, flat heads, wide fleshless noses, some delicate aquiline noses. It was the oddest assortment of humans he had ever observed in a single place. He marveled at the diversity, remembering Dimitrov's boast: "If we can control this hodgepodge, we can control anything."

"The Americans are not too bad at it, either," Alex had replied.

"You melt; we paste," Dimitrov had responded cryptically. Alex had not understood until now.

"Oh dear," Miss Peterson said suddenly, looking anxiously toward the group of waiting people. "Now I *am* taking up room." She looked at the check and fished an Intourist food coupon from her bag, placing it carefully on top of the check.

"You will see that it gets into the proper hands, Dr. Cousins?"

"Of course," he said, relieved that she was leaving. He stood up to make way. She was remarkably small at full height, slender and compact. She held out her hand.

"I am sure we will see each other again," she said. "We should have plenty of time for a nice long chat."

"It would be my pleasure," Alex said, conscious of his insincerity. Watching her move down the aisle, he felt mildly disturbed. The food lay like lead in his stomach. He looked quickly at the red-haired man, who averted his eyes.

Damn, Alex mumbled, throwing some kopecks on the table. He started toward the door of the restaurant car, pausing briefly to confirm that the red-haired man was following him. "Beware of the jackals," Dimitrov had said. But wasn't it he who had set them on Alex in the first place?

4

Pushing open the door of his compartment, Alex found Mrs. Valentinov lying across the bottom bunk. She had changed to a long dressing gown and hung her dress next to one of his suits. She had also pinned her hair in an upsweep, revealing a long stretch of soft pink neck. She lay on her side, supporting her head in her palm. The pose had disarranged the top of her robe, revealing the upper portion of her large breasts.

Beside her on the table was an open bottle of vodka and an empty tea glass. The scene had a calming effect on him, a sense of coming home. She had taken off her makeup and when she looked up at him, her eyes had an innocent girlish look.

"Satisfy the human clock?" she asked, flashing a wide smile.

"Satisfy is hardly the correct word," he said. He threw the medical journal onto the top bunk and sat down heavily on the chair.

"I should have warned you." She laughed and he felt their tension ease.

"Where are we?" He looked at his watch. It was 7:30 Moscow time.

"You sound like Pyotor," she said.

"Who's that?"

"My son. Whenever we take him on the train, he asks every five minutes where we are." Then, pointing to the vodka bottle, she asked, "Can I offer you a drink? What good is it being Russian if one has to drink by oneself?"

He nodded, wondering if her friendliness was sincere. What does it matter? he asked himself. He got up and opened the washroom door. Inside was a tiny sink with a gleaming shower attachment hooked on the wall. He found a glass on a shelf above. Reaching for it he glanced at himself in the mirror, noting the flush along his cheeks and nose. His eyes were bloodshot and under them dark hollows had deepened. He looked exhausted. He went back to his chair and poured himself a drink.

"To answer your question, I'd say we were an hour or so from Yaroslav; we cross the Volga during the night. And late tomorrow we will be in Asia."

He sipped the vodka, feeling the spreading inner warmth.

"I've never been there," he said, lifting his glass. "To Asia."

"We make that vodka in Irkutsk," Mrs. Valentinov said, rolling over so that she lay on her stomach facing him, her breasts flattened under her. Irkutsk! He hesitated for a moment, feeling the urge to explain his own vision of that city, the dream that sprang from his grandfather's recollections. He rolled the vodka on his tongue, feeling in its warmth the compelling link of the generations, Russian to Russian, grandfather to father to son.

Irkutsk! The very name could send shivers up his back and straighten the hairs on his neck. He envisioned a jumble of wooden houses, log cabins and stretches of plank sidewalks. His grandfather had told him tales of lurking thieves, who had escaped from the penal colony outside the village. The strong ones had lived off the villagers, pillaging, robbing to survive. The weaker ones, miscalculating the brutality of the Siberian wastes, had attempted to make it back to European Russia. They rarely, if ever, succeeded; their corpses were found the following spring, perfectly preserved in the ice. "Spring flowers" his grandfather had said they were called. It was remarkable, Alex thought, the power of the old man's recollections and the effect on his own sense of reality. Even now!

But he did not speak of this to Mrs. Valentinov, inhibited, perhaps, by Dimitrov's strange admonitions: "Tell them nothing. Give them no information."

"What is it like in Irkutsk now?" he asked, wondering if his use of the word "now" might provoke her curiosity. But, he reasoned, if she was one of them, she would know all that.

"It is beautiful," she whispered. He strained to hear. "We are more than three hundred years old, but we are a young city. Young people are everywhere. That is the way you must think of our city—young, fresh, strong. Like the Angarra itself."

"Angarra?" he repeated, remembering the mention of it somewhere in his own past.

"The beautiful daughter of Lake Baikal. You know Lake Baikal?" It was the first question she had put to him.

He nodded. "One of the most ancient lakes on earth. Deepest fresh water body in the world—" He checked himself.

"It is fed by more than three hundred rivers, but only one, the Angarra, flows from it." She had the same force, the same yearning as his grandfather. It was an aberration, he thought, this passionate territoriality that afflicted the Russian psyche.

"We are a city of half a million souls living on the edge of death," she went on. Could she know? But she was speaking of the rock tremors that could unleash the waters of Lake Baikal.

"Your family has a long history in Irkutsk?" It was

half statement, half question. Was he taking some bait?
But it was tantalizing, irresistible.

"We have found evidence of five generations in the
cemeteries on my mother's side. My father was a
soldier who arrived in the thirties. He was a Russian."
Alex thought he detected a slight curl of contempt on
her full lips. "On my mother's side we are mixed up—
Yakut, Evenkis, Buryat blood." She pointed to her eyes,
the high cheekbones, the almond shape. "Can you see
the hint of Genghis Khan?"

Her glass was empty and he refilled it as well as his
own. Lulled by the vodka, the voice of the woman, and
the rhythm of the train, Alex felt a strong need to tell
the story of his grandfather and to explain the reasons
for this pilgrimage across Siberia. Certainly the tales
were harmless, his caution and suspicion irrational.
But still he hesitated to speak.

"People from Irkutsk were explorers and fur traders,"
she continued. "Did you know that it was men from
Irkutsk that crossed the Aleutians, claimed Alaska and
put a Russian flag in California?" She had been watching him. Was he being overly cautious? he asked himself. Was he expected to stay alone and keep his mouth
shut for eight days? Despite his suspicions he felt
drawn to Mrs. Valentinov. She lay on her stomach,
her large breasts ballooning beneath her, her body
deliciously relaxed, languid. He was surprised at his
own awkwardness as he turned his eyes from hers,
assailed by a youthful shyness he hadn't felt in years.

"You're not going to eat?" he asked, feeling the
banality of the question.

She reached for her glass of vodka and lifted it to
her lips.

"Quite enough caloric content in this," she said with
a smile, her eyes glistening as she sipped while watching him.

"Very bad for the brain cells," he said. "The alcohol
destroys them."

He felt increasingly silly, bantering with her, wondering if she would respond to his cautious overtures. His

comparative celibacy and the tension of the last six weeks was reawakening his lust. Seduction had always been difficult for him and now his old fear of rejection was bubbling upward, eroding his self-assurance. The episode at Dimitrov's dacha with the chubby nurse had been furtive, a quick groping in the dark. His disappointing performance had made the woman irritable, bitchy, and he had finally maneuvered her transfer, though not without guilt.

And yet, he had been strong and authoritative in his medical dealings with Dimitrov. Imperious, in fact, and Dimitrov had allowed it, believing that Alex held his life in his hands. Did Mrs. Valentinov understand her effect on him, the intimacy, the privacy of their surroundings as the train chugged its way into the mysterious land mass of Siberia? Of course, he thought. It is all orchestrated. But why? To what end?

He stood up suddenly, balancing himself against the edge of the upper berth, feeling a bit dizzy. He sensed her eyes on him, following his face. The vodka had made him looser, unguarded. He wondered if she could detect the bulge in his pants as he returned the medical journal to his bookbag that lay on his bunk.

But as he reached into the bookbag, alertness suddenly returned. His head cleared. The bag had been tampered with, he was certain, the journals removed and thumbed through. Again he remembered Dimitrov's warning. The jackals are everywhere. Or was his imagination playing tricks with him? Had the vodka turned his head?

"How much time?" Dimitrov had asked again and again.

"I'm not God," he would reply.

"That is the point," Dimitrov chuckled. "They will want to know, and no one can answer." He had slapped Alex on the back. "They will try everything to find out. It is precisely the bit of information they will require. We will fool them, Kuznetsov."

From the beginning he had insisted on using the old

family name. Alex had long since stopped correcting him.

"Who is 'they'?" he had asked innocently, but by then it was a pose. He had been drawn in, had begun to piece things together like a detective trying to un- ravel a mystery. At first, he had tried to characterize it as merely an intellectual exercise, a scientific pursuit of truth. Then it all came together, and the information had cascaded into his consciousness like molten lava, covering all doubts. He knew! The old bastard was going to die, but he was going to take along with him a few million Chinese, Chinks as he called them. This was not the dream of a wild visionary. It was the will of Viktor Moiseyevich Dimitrov, General Secretary of the Communist Party of the Soviet Union.

Alex shivered lightly as he opened a medical book. But he couldn't concentrate. Mrs. Valentinov had closed her eyes, perhaps on the verge of sleep. Alex watched her. She looked so innocent, virginal. But the image of Dimitrov kept returning, keeping him from pleasanter thoughts.

"It must be settled once and for all," Dimitrov had said. And the President of the United States and that self-proclaimed genius of a Secretary of State. Did they actually believe he had meant to achieve a nonviolent solution? How little they knew of Dimitrov. How little they knew of the Russians.

5

The call had come in from the director of the Institute, routinely, almost casually.

"We've been invited to be present at the signing of the new research bill," the director had said. "The usual political show. Frankly, it's a lousy bill. But every little bit helps."

At first, Alex had tried to decline, but it was made quite clear that this was a command performance. Actually, most civil servants might have considered it a plum, to be in the ritual photograph of the doctors standing behind the President as he signed the bill. But Alex had never enjoyed such occasions.

About thirty senior men from the various Institutes had driven downtown in an agency bus.

The East Room had been converted to an auditorium, complete with podium and microphones. It was, Alex had thought, hardly a bill warranting such fanfare and the President himself seemed halting and preoccupied as he recited a series of platitudes about the "necessity of unlocking the secrets of man's destroyers." Then the President had signed the bill and they all adjourned across the marbled vestibule to the Green Room for coffee and cakes.

A receiving line had formed and Alex had taken his place obediently in line.

"Dr. Alex Cousins," an aide next to the President announced and he had found himself facing the tall, clear-eyed man. He felt the pressure of a strong hand-shake and watched the smile break evenly as the eyes narrowed.

"Dr. Cousins," the President had replied, and then, in a whisper, "Would you please stay on?" He was still smiling, and looked so casual that Alex glanced over his shoulder, thinking that the remark was directed at someone behind him.

"I must see you later. Make some excuse to hang back," the President whispered again, noting Alex's confusion. He felt his heart begin to quicken its pace. Was he hearing things? The President turned away quickly and stretched out his hand to the man next in line as Alex moved toward the coffee cups. His hand shook as he lifted one and he quickly put it down. There must be some mistake, he had thought, although the President's conspiratorial manner had been obvious. He put his shaking hands in his pockets, annoyed by his sudden lack of control.

"I promised my wife I'd pick something up for her at Garfinckel's," he told one of his colleagues. "I'll get a taxi back."

He hung back as the crowd began to thin and his group began to file downstairs. Watching them, he reached over to pick a little cake from a paper doily on the table when a tap on his shoulder startled him.

"Follow me," a tall man said. Alex popped the cake into his mouth and followed. The President was already gone; he had left the room as soon as the receiving line had finished. The tall man suddenly stopped, waved Alex into a small elevator, and stepped in after him. Motors whirred and in a few seconds the elevator door opened again and the man led him to a thick white door, knocked softly, then admitted him without waiting for a response.

He found himself in a cheerful, quite comfortable living room, obviously the President's private quarters. On a piano in a corner, directly in his field of vision, stood a forest of family photographs. The President stood up, grabbing Alex by the forearm and directing him to face a man who was sitting quietly in a wing chair. It was the Secretary of State.

"Dr. Cousins. This is Secretary Carlyle."

"Mr. Secretary," Alex mumbled.

Secretary Carlyle nodded. The President directed Alex to a couch and sat down beside him.

"You've got to believe we're all a little touched in the head," the President began. "All this hocus-pocus. All this subterfuge."

"Well, it is a bit out of the ordinary," Alex said, feeling surprisingly calm. He appreciated the President's attempt to put him at ease.

"I assure you, Dr. Cousins, that your visit here is purely professional," the President said.

Alex searched the two faces before him for signs of the weakness that accompanies leukemia.

"Neither of us," the President said, reading Alex's thoughts. "Thank God."

Alex remained silent, watching the President fidget, uncross his legs and stand up. He walked toward a table and picked up a heavy large envelope, which he tossed on the couch next to Alex.

"The patient's records," the President said. Alex reached over for it instinctively. "Not yet," the President said gently, looking toward his Secretary of State, who raised his head and began to speak.

"The balance of foreign affairs is as tenuous as life itself," Secretary Carlyle said. He seemed tired, his voice strained, betraying fatigue. He removed his glasses and wiped them clear with a handkerchief, his pale blue eyes squinting into Alex's face. "We reach agreements, sign treaties, most of which are only as good as the man in power at the moment." He paused. The President squirmed beside him.

"I've just come back from Russia," Secretary Carlyle said. The statement had the quality of a revelation which, indeed, it was. Alex had not read of any such trip in the Washington papers.

"I didn't know," he said innocently, thinking that perhaps he had overlooked it. He was, after all, locked into his own occupations, his research, his writings for journals. Politics, foreign affairs, were unimportant to him and what he knew was sopped up with the morning coffee and the idle chatter of colleagues at lunch. He was indifferent, as Janice had charged, to most things outside the intense, all-absorbing orbit of his own medical pursuits.

"It has been the most secret operation since Kissinger went to China," the President pointed out. "And probably under the oddest set of circumstances in the history of foreign affairs."

"Without boring you with the gritty details of global geopolitics, Dr. Cousins," Secretary Carlyle said, "the fact is that our carefully wrought policy of détente with the Russians is now in serious danger. Détente is the underpinning of everything we have striven for in the past few years. It represents one of the last hopes of mankind to move backward from the brink of nuclear annihilation." Secretary Carlyle's eyes seemed to grow wide with despair. "I know that sounds a bit frightening, but you must accept that statement. The danger is acute. Our intelligence has revealed that now there are men in positions of power in the Soviet Union who would like to carry out the final act of Lenin's revolution—global hegemony."

What has all this got to do with me? Alex wondered, looking at the large envelope beside him on the couch. He had heard enough about Lenin's revolution as a boy.

"When you are dealing with an oligarchy," Secretary Carlyle continued, "your position is far more vulnerable than when you are dealing with a single ruler.

You cannot predict the dynamics of a small group interacting with each other. It is actually easier to deal with a dictator."

"Few understand it," the President interrupted. "You make a deal with one man, who represents the group, then you wonder how long the group will support the deal."

"In a nutshell, Dr. Cousins," Secretary Carlyle said, "the concept of détente rests in the hands of a single man—Viktor Moiseyevich Dimitrov, General Secretary of the Communist Party, one of the sixteen members of the Politburo. He is its architect and, within the Politburo, the guiding spirit." Secretary Carlyle paused and rewiped his glasses, replacing them with a one-handed gesture. "It is no secret that our policy, by the very nature of the democratic process, is one of reaction. The Soviets always make the first move. We react. They move again. We react again. Dimitrov has apparently managed to consolidate a great deal of power within the Politburo. He has the most dominant, persuasive personality; he keeps the others frightened and divided and has convinced them that their greatest leverage lies in pursuing a policy of détente. To the Soviets, China is the real enemy. The United States can wait. But it is in China where the problem lies. The Chinese will never bend until the Russians give back most of the land they took from them in the past. And then there is the vital ideological question: Who shall lead the revolution?"

As Alex listened, he could recall his grandfather talking contemptuously about the "Chinks" and their sneaky ways. He thought he understood what Secretary Carlyle was trying to say.

"The Russians have been trying to dominate the Chinese since the seventeenth century," the Secretary continued. "You know that the Russians are the most notorious racial bigots in the world. For years, they have treated the Chinese as vassals, and from the Chinese point of view, the Russians still control great pieces of China. There have been pitched battles along the five-thousand-mile border. Today, hundreds of thousands of men face each other across these borders, and missiles with nuclear warheads are poised to strike in either direction."

"It is a powder keg," the President said. "At the moment, the Russians have the advantage of range. They can send their missiles deep into China. They can knock out major cities, bases, ports, while the Chinese missiles cannot yet reach beyond the cities of Eastern Siberia. The land mass in that part of the world is incredible. The Russians could lose all of Asian Siberia through nuclear destruction and still have a huge population. Their big cities are concentrated far to the west. The Chinese, on the other hand, have vast populations within easy reach of Soviet missiles."

"Under that kind of pressure," Secretary Carlyle continued, "one would think that the Chinese might work for some kind of détente with the Russians. The fact is, the Chinese are not to be intimidated by words. Mao himself publicly expressed the opinion that nuclear war would still leave the Chinese with more manpower than the Soviets, enough to reproduce and eventually swallow the Russians, even if it takes another thousand years."

"Ghoulish," Alex mumbled. At the mention of Siberia, his heartbeat had quickened. Was it merely nostalgia or did he feel some strange genetic pull, as his grandfather had always claimed he would.

"There are those in the Politburo," Secretary Carlyle said, "who might opt for a quick strike now, a massive blow. They do not intend to occupy China. Their gamble is that, after the destruction. the Chinese would turn against the Maoists and turn over the rebuilding of China to Russian-oriented revolutionaries. Then China would become what it was always meant to be in Russia's eyes—a puppet state, like Outer Mongolia, like Hungary, Czechoslovakia, East Germany."

"Now, one would think," the President said, "that the United States would be happy to stand by while the two great superpowers of the Communist world bludgeon themselves to death. Not at all. Our own scientific people have told us that a huge nuclear strike in either direction would mean immense nuclear fallout, certainly over Alaska and parts of Canada, and very likely over the continental United States. The odd thing is, with the prevailing configuration of winds across the surface of the earth, we would get more fallout than European Russia."

They had now crossed into Alex's own field. He was a member of the "Special Task Force on Evaluation of Nuclear Destruction," which studied the projected kill potential of radiation fallouts from dirty bombs. It would destroy the blood as quickly and ruthlessly as any form of leukemia. But these studies had always been an unemotional exercise in probabilities, a game of bureaucrats. Alex had attended sessions of the Task Force for ten years, evaluating kill-ratios, radiation intensity, the effect on the human machine. But it had only been theoretical, make-work, time away from his basic research. He watched the two men in the quiet room, the family pictures on the piano, the pleasant afternoon light through the tall windows. Faintly, from the distance, he could hear the rumble of cars and the occasional honk of a horn.

"So you see," Secretary Carlyle said. Alex seemed to have missed something. Had his attention strayed? "It all boils down to time. In time the Chinese will develop a nuclear capability to reach into the cities of European Russia, complicating Soviet strategy. And Mao's death, of course, has a great deal of impact on the situation. He was one of the most implacable opponents of Stalin, and of the Russian brand of Communism. Now that he's dead, some experts think the Chinese might come back into the fold, good little Communists under Russian control."

"Now we are faced with a new question of time," the President said. "It is no secret that Dimitrov is committed to détente with us. He is also committed, apparently, to a more moderate stance toward the Chinese. Considering all the dangers and possibilities, his is the approach we favor. Dimitrov, Dr. Cousins, is our man in the Kremlin and he will be meeting in approximately seven weeks with the Politburo"—the President cleared his throat—"to recommend immediate negotiation with the Chinese to resolve all differences."

"Is that what we want?" Alex said thoughtfully. He had always assumed the opposite.

"Considering the alternatives"—the Secretary of State paused—"yes." He hesitated for a moment. Alex would remember that pause later, in the light of his own knowledge of events. "He has assured me that he will act at the next Politburo meeting, that he will put the stamp of consensus on it."

"He is the man," the President said. "He controls. They may intrigue against him. They may rant and rave, but he is the dominating force. Dimitrov gets what he wants." The President shook his head and stood up, then pointed to the envelope.

"The problem is in there. His time is running out."

"I see." Alex nodded.

"What I saw," Secretary Carlyle said, "was an exhausted man, weakened to the point of total collapse. I was driven to his dacha, where he lives literally in a state of self-imposed siege, both mentally and physically. Add that to the traditional paranoia of Soviet rulers and you can imagine his mental state. The dacha has been fitted with a complete medical facility and all tests have been conducted with elaborate subterfuge. Luckily I speak Russian and he was able to convey his fears."

"I don't understand," Alex said, eying the envelope.

"He trusts us more than his own people. That's not so strange. Many Russians are the first to admit that they don't trust each other," Secretary Carlyle said. "Oh, Dimitrov was quite frank about it. He said they were waiting like vultures to pick his carcass and he has warned us that his death will bring down the whole structure of our mutual policy.

"At this point he trusts no one," the Secretary continued. "He claims that there is a faction in the KGB working against him, but he has managed so far to keep them at bay. He also assures us that he still has the other members of the Politburo and the Army under his control. The only thing he has not been able to keep at bay is this." He pointed to the envelope. "Although he has maintained massive security about his illness, his secret enemies in the Politburo, the KGB and elsewhere suspect he is suffering from some form of terminal disease. He distrusts Soviet doctors in the political sense. He also distrusts the state of the medical art in his own country."

"He should," Alex said. "It is definitely well behind us."

"He knows this," Secretary Carlyle repeated. "And he asked me to convey his medical records to the President, in the hope that we could prolong his life. We have, of course, a vested interest in it. At least until the Politburo meeting."

"And then?" Alex asked.

Secretary Carlyle shrugged, obviously sidestepping the question.

"I told him that we would submit his records to the foremost leukemia specialist in the country. I also told him that I would get word back to him within seventy-two hours. He is quite realistic about his condition, a most interesting man. Even he points out that it is a question of time. 'You must find a way to buy me time,' he pleaded, the implication being that time would allow him to cleanse the oligarchy of adventurers and hand-pick his successor."

Alex could feel both men looking at him, waiting. He felt inadequate to the sudden barrage of information. As he struggled to assess the incoming details, the quick lesson in geopolitical realities, the Machiavellian scheming, so foreign to his experience, he still felt reluctant to become involved.

"I do admit some expertise in the field of leukemia," Alex said. "But the study of this disease is still in its infancy. We have made progress. We have managed to achieve some remission with chemotherapy. But we can never promise recovery. In science, gentlemen, you are never an authority. You are always in a state of transition. There are others surely that are equally qualified for this job."

"You're being modest," the Secretary said. "Besides, we need someone who speaks Russian. We couldn't have manufactured a better candidate."

"So I've popped up on the computer," Alex said.

"You put it quaintly, Dr. Cousins," the President said, detecting his annoyance. "When it comes to Russian ancestry the CIA is ridiculously efficient. We know your grandfather was a Czarist exile, who just beat the Bolsheviks out of Siberia. We know your father was with Graves. We were looking for you, Dr. Cousins."

"May I?" Alex asked, pointing to the envelope.

The President nodded. Alex broke the seal as they watched him. He pulled out the pile of papers, forms, X rays. All of the notations were written in Russian.

I must stay detached, he told himself, concentrating on the reports and documents, as his mind clicked into the Russian language. Russian had been his first language. His mother had barely learned English by the time he was born. She had come from Vladivostok, where his father had met her in 1919. Only a schoolgirl then, she and the young officer had become correspondents. Ten years later he had brought her to America to become his wife. Alex had actually entered kindergarten knowing only a few words of English.

As he reviewed the documents, the President stood up and spoke to someone on the telephone. He then nodded to Alex and left the room. Secretary Carlyle also reached for a phone and began talking in hushed tones. It was obvious to Alex that somehow their meeting with him had been the top priority of the day. When Secretary Carlyle had completed his phone call, he walked to a sideboard and poured himself a drink.

"Brandy?"

"Thank you," Alex said. He could use one. He noted that the Secretary's hand shook as he poured. Sipping, he continued to read.

"It is an efficient presentation," he said, after absorbing the information in the documents.

The Secretary had dozed. Clearing his throat deliberately, Alex roused him.

"You should get some rest," he said. The man looked wan and exhausted.

"Normally, I sleep on the plane," Secretary Carlyle said. "But Dimitrov disturbed me. I couldn't get him out of my mind." He removed his glasses and rubbed his eyes. "What does that tell you?" he asked, pointing to the documents which Alex had replaced in the envelope.

"From the information in these reports, I'd say the diagnosis of the Russian doctors was quite correct. Acute myeloblastic leukemia."

"Which means?"

"His condition is tenuous."

"How much time does he have?"

Alex sighed.

"With chemotherapy, perhaps some. I could hardly give you a complete evaluation from this." He pointed to the envelope on his knees. "In any event the problem is that the chemotherapy must be carefully monitored. It could set off all sorts of debilitating reactions and, even under optimum circumstances, it is quite chancy. Unfortunately, Russian medicine is not sophisticated in its administration, but I'm sure that I can provide adequate instruction—"

"Dr. Cousins," the Secretary interrupted, "I don't think we've made ourselves clear."

"I don't understand," Alex said, merely to prolong the inevitable.

"Dr. Cousins, Dimitrov wants you. At his side. In Russia. We're expecting you to fly to the Soviet Union within the next twelve hours. You'll have to wind up your affairs at home and keep your destination a secret. It won't be easy, Dr. Cousins, I know that, but, as you now know, this is a matter of the gravest national security."

Alex knew. He had been waiting for this announcement and his mind had been turning over various methods of refusal. It was quite possible for the chemotherapy to be administered by a reasonably competent Russian doctor who was given precise instructions over the phone. Why did he have to be part of their political intriguing? He had, long ago, reached his own conclusions about the basic immorality of politicians and all their games. Besides, despite the careful arguments of the Secretary, he remained skeptical. The whole scenario was too fantastic to be believed.

"I would be less than honest," the Secretary continued, "if I didn't tell you that this assignment may involve some physical danger."

Such a possibility had also occurred to Alex, who had never felt himself to be particularly courageous. He knew the low threshold of his own tolerance for pain.

"They will watch you constantly, listen to your conversation, follow you everywhere. They will minutely search your possessions. The loyal intelligence under Dimitrov's direction will watch you and the potentially disloyal intelligence will watch you. Dimitrov's enemies will want to know his condition. They will try anything to find out. After all, you will have in your possession the most important piece of information in the Soviet Union."

Alex wanted to laugh. It was absurd. He wondered if he was not dreaming this; if he would not soon awaken in his own bed and discover the whole episode was simply the result of too many Swiss cheese sandwiches before retiring. But the Secretary was quite real. Alex watched him clean the mist again from his glasses.

"Really, Mr. Secretary!" he said finally. He had determined to show his skepticism in its mildest form.

"I assure you, Dr. Cousins, this is not speculation. I am merely paraphrasing Dimitrov."

"And you believe this?"

"Yes."

"You know, of course, that a terminal disease affects

a man's logic. His mental state might be drastically impaired. He could easily slip into paranoia."

"I commented earlier on his mental state. He was depressed, but quite lucid. And I assure you that, as ridiculous as all this may sound, it is believable and probable. In the game of nations such activities are commonplace."

Suddenly impatient, Alex tossed aside the medical documents.

"Well, it's not my game. I'm a doctor. That's all I know. All I care about."

"And that's all we're expecting you to be."

"It can be done long distance."

"I'm afraid not. Dimitrov would not trust your instructions coming through third persons."

"You can't force me to do this. Not in this country," Alex said, surprised by his sudden outburst of belligerence.

"I know," the Secretary said calmly. "It's your choice."

Alex stood up, feeling hesitant. Damn them, he thought. He disliked being forced into anything, especially decisions outside the scientific realm of abstraction. He could be bold and courageous when dealing with theoretical conclusions amid the clutter of his charts, test tubes and animals. But he had steeled himself against the cries of human suffering. He had seen too many men and women die, and he hoped it had hardened him. The process had taken years of discipline, years of controlling himself as he watched the human body wither under the onslaught of mysterious forces. But even as he pursued his scientific endeavors, he knew what he was sacrificing. He could see it in the faces of those who lived close to him—Janice, their daughter Sonia, his father. He felt isolated, blocked, cut off from humanness, as if he had forgotten its language.

He felt a shiver of that isolation now. Was there some mystical force that had sent this message to him halfway across the world, mysteriously pulling him back to his roots? No. It was just a crazy coincidence, nothing more. To believe anything else one would have to believe in fate and that was surely unscientific, beyond the limits of logic. What did he care about all this intrigue, these political stupidities wrapped in academic explanations? Even the prospect of nuclear war was an abstraction. He had speculated on its results too often not to see it as an interesting abstraction. What did he care about Dimitrov, the besieged leader, the manipulator, the keeper of the flame of all their silly dialectics? Nothing. Politics was an annoyance, a babble of words that filled newspapers. But the giant land that Dimitrov governed was very real. It was the land that called him.

"At least until the Politburo meeting," Secretary Carlyle pleaded.

"I can promise nothing," Alex said. He was thinking about his roots, not Dimitrov.

6

Ivan Vasilyevich Godorov waddled along the passageway, his fingers balancing his ungainly body against the steel panels. He stopped to look at "The Russiya's" timetable, which was posted under glass and screwed to the far wall of the carriage. He had memorized it, knew every line, every variation of every train that traversed the ribbon of track which snaked its way back into the black pit of his own private nightmare. Kirov, 596 miles; Sverdlovsk, 1,130 miles; Omsk, 1,688 miles; Novosibirsk, 2,077 miles and Krasnoyarsk—Krasnoyarsk!

He smiled inwardly, although his hard thick features expressed only perpetual contempt. Krasnoyarsk! It meant "beautiful." His fist clenched, as a wave of pain shot through his deformed spine. The train was bucking like a horse. Not a single moment of his life had passed during the past thirty years without the feel, the sound, the detestable click of train wheels continually present in his mind.

Scratching his chin, he pondered again the seventeen-

57

minute stopover in Krasnoyarsk. He had estimated that the third car from the end, a hard class, would stop at the exact position at the end of the station where the station manager's office was located. According to Platinov, the office would be a small whitewashed room, with one desk and a chair, charts and timetables on the wall, two wooden benches facing the desk. He had forced it all from Platinov, innocent foolish Platinov, who had stared wide-eyed and dull-faced, his nose running in the cold Moscow afternoon, as the two of them sat on a hillock overlooking the Lenin stadium.

"I knew it was Shmiot instantly," Platinov had said, "even before I saw his name on a little plaque outside the office."

"Did he recognize you?"

"Shmiot?"

"Who else, you ass?" Godorov calmed himself down. He must not betray his single-mindedness, he thought, fighting back the hatred that had festered inside of him for twenty years. Could Platinov know he had searched every face that had crossed his path since his release, seeking Shmiot? Every time he thought of that name, he rubbed the small of his back, digging his fingers into his pain, which condemned him never to be able to stay in one position for more than ten minutes at a time.

"But are you sure?"

"Of course I'm sure." He jabbed Godorov in the hard muscles of his stomach. "Do you think any one of us could forget him?" He had actually smiled as he said it, as if it no longer mattered.

"He is, of course, older," Platinov continued. "Still very tall with that thick bull neck and those hamlike hands. It was very odd seeing him looking so respectable in his railway uniform." Platinov paused to rub the snot off his sleeve. "It was odd seeing him out of a convict's uniform, and the hair grown back on his head. But the eyes are still ice cold, as cruel as ever."

"And you are certain? Repeat it, please, Platinov."

"He is the train manager at the Krasnoyarsk station. I saw him. I spoke to him."

"You spoke to him?"

"Yes. I asked him if there was a Moscow train on Thursday morning."

"Did he recognize you?"

"No."

Not to be recognized. That would be the final blow. He must be recognized, Godorov thought. That was essential. He had gone over it in his mind a thousand times. The confrontation. The instant recognition, the sound of his own name: "Godorov! You!" Then he would grasp Shmiot simultaneously by the windpipe and the testicles and draw his body into a kneeling position.

"You remember me, Shmiot?"

Of course he would remember and the terror that would come with recognition would be the sweetest moment of Godorov's life, the one flicker of light in the bleak landscape of all those wasted years.

"There is no mistaking it, Platinov?"

He had grasped the poor man by the collar of his coat, shaking him. It was only then that Platinov had realized what Godorov planned, and his pale eyes opened wide.

"You're crazy," he hissed. "You're crazy, Ivan Vasilyevich." He wrenched himself free of Godorov's grasp. "It's over. What can it matter now?"

But it had never been over. Not if a person was reminded of it every moment of his life by the perpetual gnawing of the raw nerves, the hot flashes of pain. Platinov knew. Why else had he sought out Godorov immediately on his return, the very day that the train had pulled into the Sverdlovsk station? He pretended to be innocent, but Platinov understood. Why else had he noticed all the little details? How could he have dredged them up, if he had merely observed them casually? He had been a deliberate observer. And that idea softened Godorov toward the man who had been his old cellmate with whom he had lived in the special hell of those days, the Gulag. He squeezed Platinov's arm.

As he stood up to go, Godorov saw the glint of the morning sunlight on the windows of Stalin's gingerbread university. He remembered the first glimpse of Shmiot's hated face, the imperious snarl, the cold eyes which blinked at the sudden light as the door opened and Godorov, the new prisoner, was thrust inside. The railway compartment had been specially constructed to house eight men in two tiers of shelf-like bunks. Instead, Godorov found twenty-eight men there, including himself. He was the last to enter, the last man to be pressed into the tiny metal cage by the guard who jabbed his buttocks as if he were the last pickle to be squeezed into a jar.

He had been delivered by the black maria from the Taganka jail. People often turned away from the sight of the black maria cars, those sealed, rolling prisons which moved, always deep in the night, from place to place in the crazy-quilt pattern of the mad prison bureaucracy. As hard as Godorov tried, as they all tried, he could never discover a logic to the strange movements, the transporting of convicts sometimes across the entire length of the Soviet Union. The prison bureaucracy used the black marias and the hated Stolypin—the specially constructed railroad cars—to carry the Zaks, the prisoners, through to the endless chain of prisons, mines and farms that snaked across the face of Stalin's terrain.

Godorov had been in various cages of the system for two weeks and had somehow managed to keep his civilian suit, which his father had bought him to replace his lieutenant's uniform after he had been released from the Army. He had been an artillery officer at Stalingrad; wounded and decorated, which made his parents proud. Their whole village in Georgia had turned out to welcome him home. Often in the cages of the Gulag he would remember that homecoming, the singing and dancing until the early morning, and the sweetness of Natasha's body as it yielded its softness to him on that very first night, so wonderful a gift that he had actually shed tears of joy.

If he had been guilty of any crime, it was the crime of temper, for he had lost his self-control when confronted with the long delay in getting his work card. It was a silly thing really, and all he had done was break a few chairs and call the clerk an ass-kisser. Not that that was a special crime in itself, except that he had specified whose ass—Stalin's—which sent the office into paroxysms of patriotic zeal. He was a criminal against the State. He went through the whole ordeal of administrative trial and sentence, as if it were some terrible nightmare from which he would soon awaken. Of course, he never had.

They had given him a "fiver," five years, and he had learned quickly that they could easily tack on another five years for good measure. He had determined, therefore, to be as inconspicuous as possible, to move silently through the Gulag until the time had passed. He was only twenty-two. Surely Natasha would wait. What was five years? My God, five years! It would be endless.

He had jumped from the black maria to the metal step of the Stolypin that would transport him to the prison camp. Briefly, he felt the clean icy air of the night. Then he was inside the compartment, and the crush of bodies was unbearable. Clutching the paper bag that contained his civilian suit, he managed to squeeze into a spot near the closed compartment door. Looking up, he discovered a strange thing. Convicts were crammed into the bottom rung of bunks, arms, heads, legs, stuffed together like cast-off dolls in a garbage can. Even the baggage rack near the ceiling was lined with convicts. But on the top tier below the baggage, one man lay stretched out in comparative comfort. Shmiot! It was Godorov's first view of him. His head was propped up on his palm and he was looking blankly into space, munching a carrot. A carrot! Godorov had looked at the man curiously, hardly comprehending why he should have the luxury of so much room, while the others were cramped together like sardines.

He felt the train move under him, felt it pick up

speed, heard the clanking of the metal as the train strained against its couplings. He tried to sleep, but the surroundings were too uncomfortable and unfamiliar. It could have been hours or minutes later—he could never remember—except that at the first light of dawn he had seen Shmiot's gaze alight on him. Then he pointed his finger at Godorov.

"The bag," he said, smiling. Stupidly Godorov had turned his head around, as if the man might be addressing someone behind him. He felt a poke in his ribs, and turning, saw the round and innocent face of Platinov for the first time.

"He means you."

"Me?"

"The bag," Shmiot repeated.

"What does he mean?" Godorov whispered.

"He wants to see what's in the bag."

"That's none of his business," Godorov hissed.

"You'd better tell him."

"Why?"

Platinov shrugged. "Because."

"Show me the bag," Shmiot repeated. Godorov noticed that the men in the compartment stirred. Some jumped from their high perches to take positions on either side of Godorov. Since there was no room, they landed on top of the men below them. He is a prisoner like me, Godorov thought. But before he could protect his package, two grim prisoners had grabbed it from his hands and offered it to Shmiot.

"Goddammit, that's mine," he shouted, trying to stand up. One of the men kicked him down again and placed a heavy knee on his chest, pinning him to the floor.

"I'll call the guard."

"Well, well," Shmiot said loudly, looking about the crammed compartment. "Call away."

"Guard," Godorov shouted, feeling his temper strain, the anger rise within him like the rumbling of a volcano. "Guard," he shouted, "I am being robbed." He watched as eyes turned away from him. "Help me," he cried, struggling to free himself from the knee.

"Beautiful," he heard Shmiot say. "It is a suit. Look, gentlemen, we have here a suit. Quite a tradable commodity, wouldn't you say?" Shmiot's eyes turned toward him, cold as flint.

"You bastard," Godorov shouted. All this was still beyond his comprehension. He had not yet learned the pecking order of the prisons, the power of the thieves and murderers over the "white collar" convicts. What could he possibly know of such a life?

"Leave it alone," Platinov said in his ear. "It won't do you any good."

Instead of quieting him, the whisper fed his anger. He managed to remove one arm that was pinned under him and, concentrating his energy into a tight balling of his fist, he moved his arm upward and smashed it into the softness of his captor's unprotected crotch. The man's agonized scream echoed in the compartment. Springing loose from the man's weight, Godorov scrambled to where Shmiot sat, displaying the suit. He managed to get a grasp on Shmiot's arm, but it was futile. He felt himself grabbed from behind and his arms were pinioned behind him.

"Nasty. Nasty," Shmiot said, kicking Godorov in the stomach. He doubled up in pain. He could never remember whether it was the sudden loss of breath or his own will that caused him to remain silent. Again he gathered his energy as he recovered from the blow, then, head down, he lunged at Shmiot like a bull. His skull pounded into the man's iron-hard torso, laying Shmiot flat against the outer wall of the bunk.

He felt hands tear at him harshly, pulling his body down to the floor again. Perhaps a half-dozen men held him now, as Shmiot stood up and watched him sullenly in the half-light.

"Strip him," Shmiot said.

Godorov felt hands mauling his clothes, unbuttoning, pulling off his shirt and pants. He struggled, twisted, screamed. Suddenly the convicts began to sing, yell, stamp their feet and clap their hands, drowning out his cries. But it was the humiliation of his exposed body that finally subdued his spirit. He felt degraded, broken. His courage drained from him. They held his body down on the cold metal floor, pinning it to the iciness as they spread-eagled him and piled their bodies over him until he could not move a single muscle. His brain was alert to the terror of it.

"Think of yourself as a pillow," he heard Shmiot say. "A nice comfortable pillow. A man that does not share with his fellows is no longer a human being, just an object. Right?"

Godorov heard the chorus of affirmative replies, and tried a last lunge to free himself, but it was impossible. He could do nothing but surrender to Shmiot's authority. It was impossible to fight them on both sides of the iron grating. There was simply no place to hide. He cursed his weakness, the uncontrollable temper that had landed him in this hell.

"Please," he heard himself bleat. "Let me up. You can have my suit. Give me back my clothes." The icy metal had already begun to eat into his spine and the bouncing of the train was torture to every nerve.

"Please," he begged. The only response was a kick in the face from Shmiot's heavy shoe.

"Save me," he remembered crying repeatedly, and then silently, as he fell into a state of semiconsciousness.

It was only later that he could reconstruct the scene, as bits and pieces of it floated up from his subconscious. He never determined how many hours or days they kept him pinioned to the metal floor. Someone had blindfolded him and stuck a gag, a filthy sock, in his mouth. The sound of metal clanging was the opening of the compartment door as a small group of convicts filed out to the toilet. There were also smells of food and strange chewing sounds.

He was too numb with pain to feel hunger. He knew

even then that if he survived—and many times on that dark journey he longed for the peace of death—he would remember Shmiot as he had first seen him, munching arrogantly on a carrot.

He was not even sure of the exact moment when they released him, since his body had finally lost all power of feeling. Platinov told him later that the men had simply moved to one side, one at a time, as if they had finally become bored with the game. It was Platinov who had propped his frozen body up into a sitting position, rubbing his back in an effort to start the blood circulating again. Platinov dressed him in what was left of his clothes. Someone had stolen his coat.

Platinov had described the journey later, the endless delays, the long days along the sidings waiting for another train to hook on to, then the interminable vibrations again as the train crawled over the track, a relentless nightmare of moving and never arriving. Platinov had counted ten days and nine nights.

Finally, they reached their destination. The compartment door was opened and the guards clubbed the prisoners on the shins to get them to move out of the train.

"You," they screamed at Godorov. He remembered their cries of frustration at his inability to move, and the sound of their clubs against his shins as they prodded him to stand. When they discovered that he could not get up, they lifted him and were annoyed at his inability to stay on his feet. It would have been much easier to deal with a dead man.

It took him months, in a substandard prison hospital, to regain even partial movement, but when he was fit enough to stand and move one leg in front of the other, he was sent back to the work prison. By then, of course, it was apparent that he would never regain full use of his once-strong body.

"I thought you were dead," Platinov had told him, when he had come back. Godorov was assigned to kitchen work.

"See how lucky you are," Platinov told him cheerfully, his round boyish face still innocent under layers of grime and coal dust. "You might have been assigned to the mines."

"I was born under a lucky star," Godorov had sneered, rubbing the small of his back, as if the gesture would stop the constant pain. The pain will help me never to forget, he told himself.

Even then he knew that hatred had kept him alive and that hatred would give his life a sense of mission. I will find him and kill him, he had vowed, feeling the beginning of the obsession that would dominate the rest of his life.

Nature did its work of compensation well. His hands and arms siphoned off the lost strength of his legs and back until he could crush a melon with a squeeze of one hand.

"Shmiot's head," he had said to Platinov. "I will crush his head like this."

"Leave it alone, Ivan Vasilyevich," Platinov pleaded.

"Never!"

At first, when he had been returned to the work prison, he had been disappointed that Shmiot was no longer there. It was odd, he thought, that he felt no animosity toward the faceless, foul-smelling men who had tortured him. They were mere instruments, following the protocol of the Gulag, where the thieves and murderers held sway with the cooperation of the guards with whom they did business. No form of protest would ever crack the system, he had learned. It had been that way from the earliest days of the Czars, and the best way to get along was to submit. Which he did, outwardly, while inside he nurtured and cherished the hatred that sustained him. And now he actually felt joyful, although his face had long ago lost its ability to smile. At last he was on the last leg of the journey, traveling toward the final glory, the culmination of his life's yearning, the moment for which destiny had spared him.

In the meantime, he had, somehow, to get through

the next four days on the train. Due to his affliction, it was impossible for him to sit or lie in one place for more than ten minutes at a time. How many room-mates had he lost because of this agonizing restlessness? People were always moving out, complaining bitterly about "Crazy Godorov" with ants in his pants, the stupid fellow who simply could not stay still.

He had deliberately chosen the soft class, despite the expense, so that he would only have to share the com-partment with one person, rather than with three others in hard class. There was also the off chance that the other bunk might remain empty. It hadn't, and he found himself rooming with a middle-aged sports en-thusiast who had instantly changed into a gym outfit and begun an interminable series of complicated ex-ercises.

"Good for the circulation," he would mumble, after each series. Godorov ignored him.

He had been tempted to ask the train attendant if he could be transferred, noting that the florid-faced man who smoked a big cigar had a whole compartment to himself. Probably bribed someone, he thought en-viously. He himself had spent his last ruble to buy his round-trip ticket.

He had pored over timetables for weeks, allowing the plan to form slowly in his mind. It was a special joy to go over it again and again. At Krasnoyarsk he would slip off the train and in the seventeen-minute stopover, he would perform. That was exactly the way he saw it in his mind, a performance: he and Shmiot. He allowed himself the special luxury of contemplating a wide variety of acts, even though he knew that he would not make rigid plans, but would play it exactly as it came to him in the final seconds. Over and over again, for the past thirty years, he had imagined how it would be done, in all its delicious varieties. The important thing would be to get the man on his stomach so that he could somehow dig his heel into the lower spine, feeling the bones give, hearing the sweet crunching sound as the vertebrae were crushed, while he watched the eyes bugging out in pain, as his own had done. Such a vision had sustained him over the years and surely could sustain him four days more.

7

General Maxim Sergeyevich Grivetsky lay on the bottom bunk of his compartment puffing angrily on his cigar. He could not afford such carelessness on this mission. He knew that he had had too much to drink and was quite annoyed with himself for letting it happen. But it had been the only way to quiet his excitement. He had been agitated over the inefficiency and stupidity of the attendants in the dining car. He simply could not abide the arrogance of underlings, a quality that had enhanced his reputation as a cruel general. This reputation angered him, because deep inside he believed that he was a gentle man. Anyone who questioned his behavior obviously had no understanding of the responsibilities of command.

It was a general's task to reach an objective by whatever means necessary; to hold that objective until it came under civilian control, and then to engineer an orderly withdrawal. It was truly a science. Men and equipment were simply the raw materials of the equation, the x's and y's of the elaborate formulas of defense and attack. Emotion, anger or compassion had no place.

It was precisely this emotional discipline that gave Grivetsky a special edge over his fellow officers. It had propelled him up the ladder, until finally he had won the complete confidence of the General Secretary. Dimitrov would have trusted no one else with this crucial, most dangerous assignment. Grivetsky was proud of the fact that he had reached this position without the usual intriguing or ass-kissing. He was, first and foremost, a military scientist, with special expertise in the field of nuclear armaments. This specialty immunized him from political considerations. Politics was for them—not for him. He paid little attention to ideology. Marx and Lenin were simply names on the lips of party flunkies. He was concerned only with competence, with developing a nuclear strategy that would function under all foreseeable circumstances. Grivetsky did not deal in issues and decision-making. He did not choose objectives, he reached them. Grivetsky followed orders.

"We must teach them a lesson," Dimitrov had said, grinding a stubby forefinger into the area of the map designated the People's Republic of China. The map denoted all the Russian missile batteries, some poised to knock out every confirmed and suspected missile battery that the Chinese had erected, while others pointed directly into the heart of every major Chinese city.

"We cannot count on knocking out every Chinese battery in a first strike. There is every likelihood that they could get off a few retaliatory missiles," Grivetsky told him, "mostly from their Manchurian sites."

"How many?"

"Maybe five. Maybe six."

"And a year from now?"

"Possibly double that number as their range increases. They are moving quickly." Grivetsky watched Dimitrov concentrating on the map. "At the moment they could very probably destroy the Trans-Baikal area,

Irkutsk, Ulan-Ude, Chita and, of course, Vladivostok and Nakhodka. I can more or less guarantee that European Russia will be safe. But I'm afraid that parts of Asian Siberia would be in very bad shape indeed."

Dimitrov's eyes narrowed. He shook his head.

"Our poor Siberian orphan," he said. "She has been raped so many times, what is one more sacrifice?" He sighed. "If only those Chinks would be reasonable. If only Stalin had been a little more considerate of Mao's feelings, all might have been different."

He remained silent for a long time, then shook himself awake. "Nonsense. It was inevitable from the beginning. There is simply no room for the two of us. Without hegemony our leadership will disintegrate in time." He opened one hand and began to tick off a list of treaties.

"The Americans want us to compromise. They can't understand that the Chinks will never settle with us unless they are forced to do so. They cannot swallow what we have done to them for a hundred years. The Treaty of Aigun, in 1858, giving us the territory north of the Amur and west of the Sungari." As he ticked off each treaty, he pointed to the territory on the map. "The Treaty of Peking, by which we acquired the lands east of the Sungari and Ussuri; the Tehcheng Protocol, where we claimed additional areas in western China; and the Treaty of Ili, where we picked up this land in Sinkiang. Now they want all that back and, to boot, Outer Mongolia." Dimitrov had grown agitated, jabbing his finger into the map, his temper rising. "And here, and here, and here—five and a half million kilometers. And, of course, there can be no dealing with them. No compromise will suit them until we've handed over all the lands east of Lake Baikal, including Vladivostok, Khabarovsk and Kamchatka."

Grivetsky had listened in silence to this lesson in political geography. It was not his domain. What did it matter? All these claims and counterclaims. They only confused the real issue, the true objective, which was the neutralization of the Chinese nuclear capability.

"This is our last chance to get away so cheap," Dimitrov had said, his energy increasing as his argument warmed. He seemed to be pleading, asking for understanding of his motives. But Grivetsky's mind was wandering. What would happen if the Americans responded with an aggressive strike of their own? That, of course, was the major risk. His mind raced over the compendium of options that had been worked out by his military planners. An American response would be a holocaust, a no-win draw, with no one left to crawl out of the ruins.

"Don't worry about the Americans," Dimitrov had said, as if reading his mind. "It will all be a *fait accompli*. We will, of course, have to answer to them. They will accuse us of duplicity. Oh, they will beat their breasts and vilify us. But, in the end, they will only bluster."

Grivetsky watched as Dimitrov's energy waned, his face grew pale, his eyes sank deeper in their sockets. He spoke more slowly, more deliberately.

"You will be given total command of the entire Sino-Soviet front, Maxim Sergeyevich. You will proceed to Red Banner Headquarters in Chita under the guise of a routine inspection. Once you are on the spot, I will give the order."

Dimitrov watched his reactions. "You think I am throwing you to the wolves, Maxim Sergeyevich?"

"There is Bulgakov," Grivetsky had stammered. An image of the strong, broad face of the Marshall floated into his mind.

"Bulgakov will bend. The Politburo will bend. We must give them no time to intrigue, no time to second-guess." Dimitrov paused. "I have your trust?"

"Without question, Comrade."

"Good."

Little more explanation was needed, Grivetsky thought. He had no illusions about the dangers of his position, which he assessed with his usual coolness.

Dimitrov's time frame, Grivetsky reasoned, had been compressed by his own illness, which was quite obviously serious. He had been forced to move his time-table forward by months, perhaps years. Dimitrov's mysterious affliction was causing ripples of confusion and uncertainty. The various bureaucratic factions that intrigued around the seat of power were nervous. They could no longer predict their own futures and they were totally unprepared for change. The major issue was: Was Dimitrov dying? If so, how long did he have to live?

Grivetsky could imagine the whispers going on behind the scenes, the furtive conferences and social calls outside official orbits. He could imagine, too, the activities of the intelligence service. It was as if the whole world was waiting for the other shoe to drop, and Dimitrov surely knew it.

For Grivetsky himself, every question suggested another, revealing still more questions to be studied. Suppose Dimitrov died before Grivetsky's mission was accomplished? Suppose opposing factions within the KGB discovered Dimitrov's plan? Suppose the Chinese got wind of it? Suppose this entire plan was the dream of a madman, of a paranoid on the brink of death, of a desperate megalomaniac who wished to leave his mark on the world? Suppose? But it was not Grivetsky's job to suppose. Above anything else, Grivetsky knew that Dimitrov was correct in at least one assumption. He had chosen the right man in Grivetsky.

Sitting now in the privacy and comfort of his compartment, he felt his fingers burn with the heat of the dwindling nub of his cigar. He smashed it out quickly in the ashtray and looked at his watch. It was past eleven. The dining car would be closed now and his mind was too agitated for sleep. Standing up, he brushed back his ruffled hair and surveyed his image in the black window of the train. He needed a shave.

Before he had left Dimitrov's dacha, the Secretary had assured him that their meeting would be confidential. The general's visit would not be considered unusual, since Dimitrov was accustomed to ask Grivetsky for periodical briefings and the Supreme Commander, Marshall Bulgakov, welcomed the opportunity for his protégé. After all, they were all comrades, dependent on each other's trust and good will. And Grivetsky, in Bulgakov's mind, could never—would never—be disloyal. Hadn't he been godfather to Bulgakov's second child? And Dimitrov himself had been godfather to the Marshall's firstborn.

Grivetsky had not been back in his Moscow office thirty seconds before the phone rang. Of course it was Bulgakov. So they were watching him, he thought. Bulgakov requested that the general come to his office.

"So tell me, Maxim Sergeyevich," the Marshall said, after the door had been closed behind Grivetsky. "How does he look?"

"Better," Grivetsky had replied.

"Better than last time?" They had been together a month before for a working luncheon at the dacha.

"He is better. But he tires," Grivetsky had said, feeling Bulgakov's big brown eyes probing him. "He is definitely not a well man."

"Did he tell you what's wrong?"

"A flu, I suppose."

"But did he tell you that himself?"

"No." Grivetsky paused. "I thought I shouldn't ask. That would be indelicate."

"You don't think he was acting strangely?"

Grivetsky felt the pressure of the inquiry. I must not appear suspicious, he told himself.

"Perhaps a bit more guarded," Grivetsky said. "The security surrounding him was more intense than usual, but he seemed cheerful."

"Did he ask you anything specific?" Bulgakov asked, betraying his own suspicions.

"No, just the usual. General questions about the dispositions."

Bulgakov turned his eyes away and looked out of the window.

"They say he is dying," Bulgakov said abruptly,

without taking his eyes from the window. "He is alleged to have leukemia."

"My God!"

"Did you see the American doctor at the dacha?"

"No."

"He is an expert on blood diseases. Apparently the Secretary doesn't trust Russian medical science." He turned to face Grivetsky. "I can't say that I blame him."

"How do you know all this?" Grivetsky asked, wondering if he was being incautious.

"The vultures are picking at the carcass while it is still warm. They are starting to kiss my ass with ever-increasing zeal. The KGB bastards are planting the biggest kisses."

"It may just be a ruse," Grivetsky said. "From what I observed last night, I'd say the Secretary's mind was quite intact." He paused a moment, observing Bulgakov. They had come a long way together. "He mentioned something about wanting me to look over the Far Eastern situation. I assumed he meant personally. I'm sure he will talk to you about it."

He watched Bulgakov's face for any signs of hesitation. Instead, it was apparent that Bulgakov was thinking in a totally different direction.

"But, if he is as sick as they say, we must watch him carefully. A man at the end of his rope has little to lose." Bulgakov seemed to be talking to himself. Then he lifted his tunic and brought out a silver flask from his rear pocket. "Brandy?"

"No, thanks."

"Good to have you back, Maxim Sergeyevich," Bulgakov said, taking a deep swallow from the flask.

Grivetsky took this as a signal that he had been dismissed.

When he heard nothing for a week, he became irritated. Maybe the man is dying, he thought. Finally, he was summoned to Bulgakov's office. It was at the end of the day and the Marshall had already set up the nightly buffet of fish, caviar, vodka and brandy. He poured Grivetsky some vodka.

"Well, I heard from the old man today," Bulgakov said. "He was positively buoyant. Haven't heard him in such good spirits for years. He's invited me down in a couple of weeks. Says his flu is clearing up."

He smeared a gob of caviar on a sliver of toast and stuffed it into his mouth. "Oh, yes," he said, his mouth still full, "he wants you to tour the Far Eastern bases." Grivetsky felt his stomach tighten. "Look things over. Wants it to be low-key. No boat rocking. Just a hard look."

"Did he give any special reason?" Grivetsky asked casually.

"He said he'd talk to us in a couple of weeks about some ideas he was having. After you get back."

"I'd better make arrangements immediately."

"Oh, yes—he said you should take the train."

"The train?"

"He wants to emphasize the low-key. And between you and me, Maxim Sergeyevich, I think he wants to telescope the message that his illness is not as bad as all that. He didn't say that, but I know how his mind works."

"It's a waste of time," Grivetsky said. "I hate trains. I'll be bored to death."

And now it was only the first night, and already he was climbing the walls. He was sorry that he had arranged for a private compartment. It was nerve-wracking, the isolation, the loneliness. He opened the door of his compartment. Its smallness was making him claustrophobic, and yet he could not abide all those staring eyes poking into the room as people moved along the passageway. One strange waddling man was particularly offensive, walking up and down like some wounded homeless dog.

Poking his head out of the door, he looked down the passageway in either direction, then stepped out, a bottle of vodka tucked under his jacket and held in place by the crook of his arm. He passed through the soft-class carriage, through the darkened restaurant car. The little man in charge sat in a corner going over his accounts. Grivetsky glared at the man and, without stopping, passed through the darkened car, through the freezing vestibule to the hard sections.

The carriage door slid heavily behind him, in a great crashing sound that carried with it a message of finality. Here in the hard class the scent of less-privileged humanity hung in the air like the smell of rotting fish. Clothes dangled from ropes strung out along the ceiling. Young soldiers sprawled on hard bunks in their underwear, playing cards or sipping from open bottles of wine. In the din of voices and train sounds, Grivetsky could pick out the heavy snores of those who managed to sleep regularly amid the confusion. But despite the general disarray, he sensed the camaraderie, a kind of happy infectious resignation, which made an adventure out of the discomfort.

A crowd had gathered in one of the compartments, spilling over into the passageway. He stood on his toes to peer over the heads of the spectators. He could see men leaning precariously from the upper bunks, while others literally hung by their arms from the mesh of the baggage racks. The center of their attention was two men, sitting opposite each other on the hard bunks. One was an old, unkempt man with a patch over one eye and deep ridges in his forehead. His opponent was a heavyset man with a pushed-in hog's face. They were playing chess, oblivious to the crowd that milled around them.

"He is an old champion and he has already beaten all comers," a little man whispered to the general. "It's two rubles a game."

"He makes his living that way," another man snickered. "All he does is ride the Trans-Siberian. He never sleeps, plays day and night." The man looked at his watch. "This is only the beginning."

Grivetsky watched the game, holding tightly to the vodka in the crook of his arm. The old man was expressionless, hardly blinking his one good eye as he studied the board, while the other man's lips moved with the tension of mental exertion. Grivetsky felt his agitation subside, as he insinuated himself into the little crowd.

The spectators were deep in sympathetic concentration, as the sweating, hog-faced challenger opened his clenched fist and placed a finger lightly on his knight. No, you fool, Grivetsky shouted within himself, knowing that others in the room were feeling the same frustration at the man's denseness. Almost in defiance of their unspoken commands, he moved the knight, exposing the king. It was all over in a moment, a swift move of the bishop and the king had no escape route. Grivetsky counted the moves. Eight!

"Are you ready for another opponent, Father?" Grivetsky boomed, pulling out the vodka bottle and passing it over to the old man. The crowd made way and Grivetsky sat himself on the bunk opposite.

"I am always ready," the old man said quietly, removing the cork of the vodka bottle with his teeth and taking a swallow without moving his one good eye from Grivetsky's face. But the general had already begun to lose himself in concentration, studying the chessboard, calculating the old man's previous moves. He felt completely calm now, back in his element, the anticipation of the game drawing his mind together, focusing his concentration on the abstractions of move and countermove. He took the vodka bottle from the old man, drank deeply and began to set up his pieces.

8

Tania Revekka Romoran lay on the lower bunk in her compartment. As she massaged her feet, she calculated the amount of work she would bestow on her assistant, to keep the old thick-headed crone out of her hair for most of the night. Tania decided to have her clean and polish the samovar, reload the coal fires, polish the brass window protectors in the corridor, vacuum the drapes and carpeting, clean the toilets, and polish both the windows and the interior paneling.

The old woman's body odor lingered in the compartment. Tania got up with a sigh. She knew she would have to spray the room, although the medicinal stench of the spray was equally unpleasant. Cleanliness was a key ingredient to her peace of mind, not only because it was important in her work, but because it had been ingrained in her from childhood. "Wash, Tania. Brush, Tania. Scrub, Tania." Her mother had been a chambermaid in a Leningrad hotel, and Tania never forgot her railing against the sloppiness of the guests, their disgusting slovenly habits, which not only increased her work load but filled her with everlasting contempt.

"They use the towels as toilet paper, then they drop them all over the carpets. You can't imagine their disgusting habits."

Tania was even more obsessed than her mother had been. She was particularly sensitive to smells, and could differentiate the odors of a person's mouth, armpits and crotch. Sniffing at an unmade bed, she could form an opinion of its occupant's character from both the odor and the way in which the sheets had been ruffled. She evaluated her passengers according to how they treated their compartment, and she had formed an unfavorable opinion of humanity from her ten years as a sleeping-car attendant, a Petrovina, on the Trans-Siberian Railroad.

Naturally, as befitted her profession, all her judgments were private. This was her 415th run from Moscow to Vladivostok as Petrovina in soft class. The train, she knew, had become her real home, her life. It was no accident that she had won no fewer than five medals for zealousness and industry. Vacations on the Black Sea at the huge railroad workers' resort were boring. Worst of all, she could not sleep in stationary beds and she always returned to her little compartment with the joy of a homecoming. For Tania, life began as the great wheels rolled and bounced over the square joints of the rails.

She had never married. How could one in such transient circumstances? Not that sex was unavailable to the train attendants. When she had started her career on the railroad at the age of twenty-one, the older women had warned her.

"It's the vibrations," she had been told. "It makes them sexy. And the drinking and boredom unhinges them. But be careful. You never know who might be an inspector."

There were, of course, all sorts of horror stories about attendants who had been caught with men, or raped by drunks, or mauled by peasant soldiers, who copulated like pigs in a barnyard. But she prided herself on her ability to fend those types off. There were times, though, when a man's advances somehow coincided with her own desires. She remembered Colonel Patushkin vividly, a tall, spare man, wearing an immaculate uniform with shiny insignia and red epaulets. He had walked toward her on the platform, his lips fixed in a confident half-smile. She was surprised at her own interest, since she was used to seeing Russian military officers on their way to some base in Siberia. There was a special aura about him, she decided, feeling a kind of electricity as she shook his hand.

"I am Colonel Patushkin," he said, his warm deepblue eyes looking into hers. She looked up at him dumbfounded, suddenly losing track of time and place and the demands of her other passengers. It occurred to her after he had been shown to his compartment, that he might have mistaken her attitude for rudeness. Determined to correct that impression, she found herself giving the colonel special attention. When he and his fellow officer left their compartment for the restaurant carriage, she rushed in with a mind to tidying up, dusting the curtains, rubbing the brass fittings to a pretty shine, fluffing up the bedclothes, cleaning the ashtrays and vacuuming the rug. Instead, she found herself fingering the colonel's pressed and brushed uniform, putting the material to her nose and smelling deeply, wondering at the uncommonly clean masculine smell.

During the first two days of the journey she could barely get the colonel out of her mind. One night she burst in as he emerged from the adjoining washroom, a towel in a perfect arc around his neck and his curly black hair still damp from combing. Once, toward evening, she had come in quietly with a glass of tea and had seen him in his underwear, white neatly starched shorts and soft ribbed undershirt. He was alone in the compartment, standing with his back toward her, and she let her eyes wash over him, taking in his tall smooth body, and across the center of him the neat white underwear.

Later she realized that it had been reckless of her, especially since she was sure he had seen her reflection in the darkened window. When he had finally turned, taking the tea glass from her, she imagined that his eyes had lingered over her face longer than usual.

"Thank you, Tania," he said, and she imagined that he returned her admiration. Later, lying in her upper bunk, her mind was assailed by a jumble of uncommon thoughts and images, involving the colonel and his deliciously white body. She imagined that her hands were his and performed acts upon herself that made her breath come in short gasps and filled her body with wonderfully exquisite feelings.

During most of the next day, she used every possible subterfuge to enter his compartment, providing him and his companion with an excess of service. She was certain, too, that he was being extra attentive to her actions, watching her coolly as he sat in the one easy chair, his long legs crossed, a book open on his lap, his shirt collar open at his white throat. She was taking particular care about her appearance and her clothes and, when the train stopped briefly at Novosibirsk, she dashed into a station store to buy a lipstick. Later, she coated her lips lightly with it and smeared some into the skin over her cheeks. Then, admiring herself in the mirror, she brushed her chestnut hair, pinning it up with particular care.

The senior attendant, a large chunky woman with a brooding expression, rarely talked to her, except to bark an order or smirk when something had not been done to her satisfaction. But seeing Tania so freshly turned out caught her attention.

"What are you painting yourself up for?" she hissed. "Got some man giving you the eye?"

"Of course not," Tania had replied, blushing.

"Better watch out," the senior hissed.

Tania knew she was under surveillance now, but could not help herself. She worked harder too, approaching her chores with remarkable zeal to prove to her superior that she was only interested in improving her job performance. It was only when the senior attendant had gone off to eat or sleep that she moved closer to the colonel's compartment, keeping close to the door, like a starved puppy, peering in to catch his eye.

As the journey had progressed, she began to feel the pressure of time. In just twenty-four hours they would arrive at Chita and the colonel would depart. She began to grow anxious, wondering how she could possibly cope with the farewell, as if they had been lovers for years. The fact was, as she later remembered, they had exchanged no more than a few polite words, she of inquiry, he of casual response, mostly "Yes, thank yous" or "No, thank yous."

But she was now certain that somehow she had gained his attention. She entered the compartment while the other soldier was in the restaurant car and began tidying the upper bunk. She was quite conscious of her own movements, stretching upward to puff pillows and smooth the linen dust cover. It was then that he stood up and, politely waiting for her to descend, touched her shoulder, and spoke the only complete sentence that she was ever to remember.

"You are a remarkably dedicated comrade," he said. She felt the weight of his hand on her shoulder and, blushing deeply, she placed a hand over his. Then, overcome by the gesture, she had run out of the compartment and rushed into her own, to douse her face with cool water. Luckily, the senior attendant was stretched on the lower bunk, her face to the wall, and she was snoring noisily as usual.

Later, when the train stopped at the Irkutsk station, Tania stood beside the car breathing gulps of fresh air and feeling the impending sadness of the colonel's imminent departure. Chita was next. A bright moon hung in the distance, unreachable and mysterious, like her relationship with the handsome dark man. Her melancholy was intense. It was only after she had climbed up onto the metal step again that she felt her depression ease, for she saw in the window the face of the colonel, who had apparently been watching her.

When the train began to move again, she waited near the samovar, watching the doors close, and some of the passengers, including the colonel's companion, walked unsteadily toward the restaurant carriage. When the passageway was empty, she poured out a glassful of tea and placed it in the filigreed container, then, watching it shake in her hands, opened the door of the colonel's compartment.

He had drawn the curtains and the room was dark except for the occasional pinpoints of light along the track. She put down the tea on the table, as usual, and almost immediately felt the colonel's hard body against hers, his mouth searching out her lips, digging deeply between them with his tongue. The crush of his body against hers seemed a culmination, a release from pain, and the feel of his mouth on hers seemed to trigger an enormous wellspring in the depths of her body. She felt her own hunger to touch his flesh, his clean white pure delicious-smelling flesh. She felt the melting of her body, and the pleasure of an inner warmth that she had never experienced before.

They stood locked in this embrace for a few moments, their hearts pounding against each other, the colonel's breath and her own coming heavily through their nostrils. She felt the colonel's hands, his clean white hands, roam over her body, playing with her erect nipples through her tight brassiere. Then she felt him reach under her dress and roll down the elastic of her panties, stepping backward so that she could kick them free, which she did instinctively. She felt her nakedness against the length of his trousers; then he stepped back again and fumbled with his pants. With her eyes closed, she felt him return to the standing embrace, his mouth against her ear, breathing heavily, while his fingers reached downward, searching for and finding what she had always termed her secret place. Then she felt herself being guided so that her back was buttressed against the ladder to the upper bunk; his body arched and somehow he was entering her secret place, and suddenly she screamed as a sharp pain ripped through her, filling her body with a kind of hysteria.

He ignored her protest, and pressed his lips against hers as if to smother a scream, his tongue reaching deep into her mouth. Without mercy he battered her body in a staccato motion, like the relentless thrust of pistons on the wheels of the train, and then his breath was coming in deep gasps, until there was a final choking sound and the shiver of his pleasure.

Then he was quiet. Her back ached and her thighs burned with the friction of the material of his pants. He slipped from her body and she felt a wetness in her crotch which offended her sense of cleanliness. He said nothing and before she could raise her aching body to a fully standing position he had moved into the adjoining washroom, leaving her alone in the darkened compartment.

She smoothed her dress down and sought in the semidarkness for her panties. She picked them up and put them in the pocket of her smock, looked around the compartment briefly, force of habit requiring that she check its condition. The bunks, of course, were in perfect order, since they had not used them. It crossed her mind that perhaps some drops of blood or moisture had fallen on the rug, but she could explore that later.

She felt a sharp pain inside her as she moved toward the door and opened it a crack. The passageway was, thankfully, empty. Then she let herself out, hearing behind her the rush of water in the sink. He was a clean fastidious man, she remembered saying to herself as she moved quickly to her own quarters. She washed herself carefully, and then her panties, which she hung across a string to dry, and climbed wearily up to her bunk, knowing that she was neglecting her duties, but feeling weak and somewhat shaky from her new experience.

But she had no frame of reference, only her expectations. He is my first love, she told herself, and blamed her disappointment on the tight quarters and their need for secrecy. And yet, the experience conditioned her for all future couplings, which always took place in similar circumstances—in darkened compartments, with fastidious men who barely spoke. She learned how to position herself against the lower bunk so as to avoid the bruises of her first experience, and she boasted to herself that she had never spent more than twenty minutes in a man's embrace. To disappear any longer would be unfair to the other passengers and might be noticed by her superiors. To lose her job, to have to leave the railroad, was unthinkable.

The railroad made her important. Aside from her general duties, she was often singled out for special assignments by the dour, official-looking men who sometimes rode the trains asking for specific information about certain passengers. She had learned that zealousness in those assignments would always earn her special commendations from her superiors. Beside her bunk she kept a clipboard with the diagram of the train and the names of the passengers neatly penciled in over each of the nine compartments entrusted to her care. She picked up the clipboard now and went over the list, mentally impressing a picture of each passenger in her mind. In the compartment next to her was the strange-looking cripple and the middle-aged gymnast, an odd combination, she thought. Both men were beefy and bull-like and, worst of all in her lexicon of horrors, dirty-looking. In the next compartment were the red-headed KGB agent and another man, whom she had not yet seen. When she came into the compartment he was always out of sight, hiding, she knew, in the washroom. She could not imagine how he had gotten on the train without her knowledge, but she did not question the KGB. She knew that they watched her carefully as she tidied up their compartment. And she knew that the big box they had shoved under the bottom bunk was filled with electronic eavesdropping equipment.

She also knew whom they were watching—that American doctor, who shared the next compartment with a big attractive blonde whom she recognized from previous journeys. On the other side of the doctor was the tall distinguished gentleman—a general, she would say, judging from the two uniforms on the clothes bar. Experience had taught her to recognize the ranks of the Red Army, but it was most unusual for a general to be traveling in civilian clothes. Perhaps she should tell the KGB men. But the general was very polite and distinguished, not unlike Colonel Patushkin.

Two English-speaking gentlemen shared the compartment next to General Grivetsky. She squinted at the clipboard to read their names, wondering if the phonetics were correct. Albert Farmer, nationality British. She supposed that was the thin gentleman with the amusing sparkle in his eyes, always making little jokes in English. He was carrying a British diplomatic passport and was with the British Embassy in Ulan Bator, Outer Mongolia. She made a mental note to remind him that he must be ready to change at Ulan-Ude, where the Trans-Mongolian Railroad intersected with the Trans-Siberian.

The big, sandy-haired, forever-complaining Australian was Kenneth MacBaren. She had met lots of Australians and New Zealanders in her time, big-boned men and women who took the Siberian route to the Pacific as a kind of exotic short cut to their own continent. They seemed to laugh a lot, like Americans, although they weren't quite as noisy. MacBaren, however, was on the surly side.

In the next compartment were those slobs of a Russian couple on their way to Khabarovsk with their bratty son. They had filled their compartment with smelly foods, most of which would stink in three days' time, and they were constantly leaving bits of sausage and cheese all over the place, grinding some of the garbage into the carpet. What were their names? She squinted again at the clipboard. Mr. and Mrs. Trubetskoi. The wife was fat and Tania knew from experience that people like this would rarely leave the compartment. They would loll about, she in her torn flowered house coat, he in his soiled pajamas, eating their way across Siberia and leaving their dirty nest only to empty their bowels and bladders.

But the worst part would be the little brat, Vladimir. He had already made a mess of the toilet, and she had discovered bubble gum stuck to the underside of the upper bunk. She positively hated all little boys, most of whom could not cope with the boredom of the long journey. Little Vladimir had arrived in a state of hysteria and, she knew, he would only get worse as time wore on. But Comrade Trubetskoi was a high-ranking Party official, so Tania dared not be too open about her disgust.

In the compartment next to the Trubetskois' was the gray-haired American lady. Fortunately, Tania knew little English, so the talkative lady would present no problems. Her roommate was an elderly Mongol woman who spoke no Russian and spent most of her time drowsing on her bunk.

In the last compartment were the young couple Ginzburg, probably on their way to Birobidjan, that little jerkwater town in the Jewish area. Tania resented that town, not because it was supposedly reserved for Jews, a subject on which she was ambivalent, but because the Express stopped there for only one minute. Then she would have to scramble, usually at some ungodly hour, to see that the passengers ticketed for that miserable place got off in time. They stopped at Birobidjan so briefly one had barely time to jump off the metal steps before the train picked up speed again. Passengers for Birobidjan had been more numerous lately, probably because Moscow had increased the pressure on Jews. It was not a subject that particularly interested her. As far as she was concerned, Jews were just the same as all the other passengers, to be treated with equal care. She had noticed, though, that the Ginzburg couple seemed particularly frightened, especially the woman.

When Tania had finally finished the catalogue and fixed her impressions in her mind, she clicked off the little light over her bunk and settled her body comfortably. She could feel the movement of the train beneath her, the rolling of the great metal wheels, a rhythm occasionally broken by the strike of metal on a faulty joint. She knew every joint on each stretch of track, every tie, every dip of the roadbed and could sense every subtle change in the rhythm, as if it were her own heartbeat.

"They have just fixed this stretch of rail," she told herself drowsily as she slipped with quiet confidence into a well-earned sleep.

9

It had been a wild, impulsive idea, Mikhail Moiseyevich Ginzburg thought as he lay in the upper bunk, knowing that Vera was below him, also unable to sleep. Three years ago he had presented himself to the authorities and declared his intention to go to Israel. He knew he was taking a chance, rolling dice with their lives, but some people were actually getting out and things were getting worse. It had become obvious, over the last five years, that neither of them would ever get a promotion again. And Vera Danilovna wasn't even Jewish.

He remembered how he had argued for a promotion with the head engineer, Kishkin, a warmhearted, good-natured man, who had been one class ahead of him at Kiev University. Kishkin was far from brilliant and Mikhail had spent long school nights cramming Kishkin's head with the details of aeronautical engineering. They were both students trying to get ahead in the only way they knew, by educating themselves in a useful profession. Engineers were always in demand in the

Soviet Union and they knew that, if they graduated in the top ten percent of the class, they would have a shot at the best jobs.

They had started together. Now Kishkin was the boss. Mikhail had tried not to be jealous. He was smarter than Kishkin, but that was not what the higher-ups considered an essential characteristic of leadership. At first, Mikhail had refused to believe that his Jewishness was a factor. How could that matter?

It did matter, he learned later. It began to matter a great deal. This was no subtle campaign to hold down Jewish advancement. It was government policy. Others began to be advanced over him.

"What the hell can I do?" Kishkin had said. They were walking along one of the streets in a deserted old section of Moscow. Kishkin had chosen the meeting place. After all, there was no point in being conspicuous. And the head engineer's office might even be bugged.

"But you know I deserve that promotion."

"Yes."

"There is no question at all about my competence?"

"None."

"The bastards."

"I did fight for you, Mikhail Moiseyevich. I did not go down without a fight." Mikhail believed him, but could not believe that Kishkin had pressed the argument. They walked along the deserted streets, faces sunk deep into the high collars of their overcoats.

"Did you really make a stand?" Mikhail spluttered.

"Within the limits of what any reasonable man could expect," Kishkin said gently.

"It's a question of moral courage," Mikhail shot back.

"Bullshit," Kishkin said swiftly. "My choice was no promotion for Ginzburg or no job for Kishkin. Well, Kishkin has a wife and two children. At least Ginzburg still has a job. And everybody knows that anti-Semitism is cyclical. It will pass." Kishkin put his arm around Ginzburg's shoulders. "This burst will pass, Mikhail."

"I've got to get the hell out of this rotten country," Mikhail said suddenly, feeling the genuine sympathy of his friend, knowing that nothing could be done.

"That'll cook your goose for sure," Kishkin said, stopping and grabbing Mikhail by both shoulders. "They'll fire you. You won't get a job anywhere."

"It's only a matter of time anyway."

"You Jews," Kishkin said angrily. "Why can't you ever be satisfied with anything?"

Mikhail paused; his own anger seemed to disappear. Is he talking about me, he wondered? Me? A Jew? There had never been the slightest hint of religion in his upbringing. You couldn't find a more dedicated Bolshevik than his father, who often ridiculed the bent and pious Jews, in their strange beards and odd clothing, walking to their broken-down synagogue. And he, Mikhail, had married a non-Jew; hardly given it a thought, since the only reminder of his antecedents was a word on his passport. And now Kishkin, his friend, was flinging that ancestry in his face.

"You're right, Kishkin." He could feel the tendons in his throat tighten, the blood rushing to his head. "Why do you put up with us? If we are so impossible, why don't you let us the hell out of this great Soviet paradise? Why keep the parasite inside the walls?" He could feel the cutting edge of his hysteria now, as his voice echoed and reechoed in the deserted street. He watched Kishkin stiffen.

"For crying out loud," Kishkin hissed. "Can't you lower your voice?"

"Jew. Jew. Jew," Mikhail screamed, his voice echoing in the empty streets.

"You crazy bastard," Kishkin cried, as he turned and walked, then ran into the darkness.

"Run away from the Jew, Kishkin," Mikhail shouted, starting to run after him, then slowing as Kishkin disappeared. Exhausted, Mikhail sat down on the curb and buried his head in his hands, feeling the anger turn to bitterness. Then tears came, tears of pity for himself.

The next day, he had presented himself to the immigration authorities and applied for a visa to Israel. The clerks were surly and officious and he had to wait for hours before anyone would see him. Then they handed him a long, impossibly detailed application and a battery of forms. When he returned to their apartment, Vera was waiting for him with tears in her eyes.

"They called me from the plant."

"So."

"They said you were fired, that you had applied for a visa to Israel."

"I also applied for you."

"Are you crazy?"

"This whole country is crazy."

Vera sat down on the couch, her face pale, her eyes flickering as if she were in physical pain.

"I'll lose my job soon, too."

"I know."

"And none of this bothers you?"

"We're going to get the hell out of here."

"To Israel? What is Israel? It is a foreign place."

"Not to me."

"I'm a Russian."

"I thought I was too."

"You know what I mean."

"Well, then stay."

He could see the big tears roll down her cheeks. She was warm and decent, and she had come to the marriage bed supremely innocent in every way. As he had then, he held her gently in his arms, kissing away the tears, feeling the salt against his lips, hearing her soft sobs as she buried her head in his chest.

"It's a gamble," he said. "But it's really pointless to stay. Here we'll simply survive. There we might have a better chance."

"Chance for what?"

"We'll be free."

"What does that mean?"

"I'm not really sure," he responded, feeling for the first time his own doubt.

Vera did lose her job and soon they had to give up

their apartment and move in with another Jewish family in the same circumstances. Days stretched into weeks and their savings dwindled. They heard rumors that others were getting out, mostly older people, and Mikhail began to haunt the immigration bureau. Vera became paler, thinner, the pressure telling as she dissolved into tears at the least provocation. At night, in the bedroom they shared with the children of the other Jewish family, he would hold her in his arms and feel her thinness while they made furtive, soundless love.

"I can't take this anymore, Mikhail," she would whisper. "It is consuming me."

"Maybe tomorrow."

"You know they'll never let us out."

By then they had told him that skilled engineers, especially aeronautical engineers who had worked in sensitive priority industries, would be put on the bottom of the list. "What list?" he had asked. But the clerks never deigned to answer him.

Finally he told Vera, "I'll withdraw the application."

But they both knew it was too late for that.

"They won't let us out and they won't let us back in," he cried.

"Maybe if you threw yourself on their mercy," Vera had suggested.

"How do you do that? They have no mercy."

But despite his pride, he wrote a series of letters to his old employers and to the immigration authorities, withdrawing his application for immigration to Israel.

"Everything will be fine again, you'll see," Vera assured him. For the first time in months, he saw the color return to her cheeks.

But then came more weeks of uncertainty, more waiting, more haunting the mailbox. When no answer came, Mikhail appeared one day outside the plant, waiting for Kishkin. He stood near the gate, watching his former co-workers turn their eyes from him, more in pity than in fear. This was how it felt to be a pariah.

Kishkin saw him and went back inside. But Mikhail

would not be daunted. He returned to the plant day after day, but Kishkin avoided him.

Finally, after weeks of fruitless waiting, Mikhail made a frontal assault, showing up at Kishkin's apartment at dinner time. Kishkin's wife treated him politely, like a stranger, and told him that Kishkin was at a meeting, although he saw his old friend's familiar coat lying on a nearby chair.

"Please," he said, as Kishkin's wife began to shut the door. He shoved his foot between the door and the jamb. The woman looked at him with fear.

"You must leave us alone," she whispered. "He will have to report you."

"I know."

Kishkin's big form emerged from behind his wife. He opened the door wider and stood looking fiercely at Mikhail.

"They're killing me, Kishkin," he said.

"I warned you."

"All right, I know. I'm not asking you to understand. Just for your help."

"I can't," Kishkin said, his expression showing some of the pain he felt. "Your shit will slop on me." He looked into Mikhail's eyes. "I've been warned," he whispered. "You've got to leave me alone. I can't do a damned thing."

"I've withdrawn my application for a visa. I'll renounce anything I have to renounce. I'll sign anything, do anything. I won't be proud. Just say it. Whatever I have to do I'll do."

"It's beyond any hope, Mikhail Moiseyevich," Kishkin said, shaking his head, his big eyes misting. "You must go, please."

Mikhail ran down the stairs and went to the river. He walked the streets for hours, cursing his lack of courage for not being able to throw himself into the murky waters.

He spent days haunting the immigration office, urging the arrogant clerks for an interview with the person in charge, whoever he was.

"I'm not a dissident," he cried. "I am not one of them." His arm swept the shabby waiting room, crowded with Jews of varying ages, waiting patiently, the mark of hopelessness engraved on their faces.

"They are deliberately trying to drive me mad," he told Vera. He was extremely nervous and tense by then, easily thrown out of control, on the edge of total paranoia.

The apartment house in which they lived was occupied only by Jewish families, as if they had been corralled there on purpose by government decree. The atmosphere was strained, since most of the tenants had applied for visas to Israel and all were living as if they were suspended in space and time. But unlike Mikhail, most of them took comfort in their Jewishness. They formed Hebrew classes for the children and discussion groups for themselves, all somehow related to achieving a greater sense of identity after two generations of alienation. Mikhail had attended one of the discussions, making himself thoroughly disagreeable by challenging their motives.

"All this attempt at retribalizing is bullshit. The only reason you want to get out is that you can't make it in this society anymore."

"That's only part of it," someone said. "The persecution, the harassment, they have taught us the meaning of our Jewishness. We were wrong to think of ourselves as Soviets. We must think of ourselves as they think of us, as Jews."

"But as soon as they stop the harassment," Mikhail said, feeling his face flush, "you'll forget about all this Jewishness and go back to being good Soviet citizens."

"Never again," someone shouted.

"Being a Jew is not worth the hardship," Mikhail hissed. "You're all fooling yourselves."

Storming out of the room, he came back to the apartment where Vera, pale and wan, was sewing. She was not good at the work, but it did earn them a few rubles.

"They're all pricks," he said loudly, running into the bedroom and slamming the door behind him.

He got the idea quite by accident. He had been standing in front of the immigration office, milling around in the crowd, aimlessly reading a newspaper. By then he was totally indifferent to his appearance. He looked like an unshaven bum and he knew he had become a kind of character, an object of comic relief.

Someone had come out of an inner office and walked into the street. It was the habit of the crowd to surround anyone who had come out of the office, to see if they had learned some great piece of news. The man in question was about sixty, bearded, bull-faced, with an air of stubbornness that made him look more like a predator than the victim.

"The bastard said he'd give me a visa."

"That's wonderful!"

The man now had the attention of the entire crowd.

"You think so?" the bull-faced man replied. "The visa was to Birobidjan."

"That hellhole," someone said.

"I told him to shove it," the bull-faced man said.

"It's the worst place on earth," a woman whispered beside him.

The crowd broke up in disgust, but Mikhail was curious. Stopping by the library, he looked up Birobidjan. It was located at the very edge of Eastern Siberia, a few miles from the Chinese border. In 1934, Stalin had declared it a Jewish Autonomous Region. It now had a population of 40,000 people, about half of whom were Jewish, and it was still described as a Jewish Autonomous Region.

"You don't believe that shit, do you?" his fellow tenant said, when he had returned to the apartment.

"What shit?"

"In the first place, it's a hellhole. You freeze your ass off for six months out of the year and the other six months are a nightmare of insects and disease. Some

Jewish suckers did help settle the place back in the thirties, but they came back to the cities like flies after honey."

It was too late. The idea had begun to soak into Mikhail's mind that here was an opportunity to escape from limbo, to prove to "them" that he was really a Soviet, like a Ukrainian, a Georgian, an Armenian. He began to write carefully composed letters to the immigration authorities, explaining that some Jews had fastened upon Israel as "their place" only because they had no piece of Soviet territory for their own. The authorities had not followed through on their original idea of giving the Jews "their place of territorial dignity within the confines of this great socialist state." He worked on the letters for weeks in the reading room of the main Moscow library, polishing each sentence, changing, cutting, reworking.

"You stupid ass," one of his fellow tenants told him one day, after he had attempted to proselytize the idea. "Stalin declared that place for the Jews to get them out of European Russia. It was another form of exile, a special place for Jews to freeze their balls off."

"Jewish paranoia," Mikhail responded. "Siberia is coming into its own. It's rich with resources. Cities are growing by leaps and bounds. What's wrong with it? Think of the dignity it will give us, a place of our own; a land of our own within the Soviet Union. We'd be proud to have 'Jew' stamped on our passports."

He sent the letters off with a real feeling of optimism.

"You'll see. I have found a solution," he told Vera, who was no longer fighting him. She was passive now, brittle as a dry leaf, barely communicative. He knew the authorities would respond. It was just a matter of time.

When the letter came, he ran up the three flights and threw it on the table in front of Vera.

"See," he said, waving it in front of her. "You thought I was crazy." The letter was from the Chief of the Bureau of Jewish Affairs in Moscow. It was polite, oddly expansive and committal for a Soviet bureaucrat. The real meat was in the last paragraph, which Mikhail read over and over again until he had committed it to memory:

"We have been considering reactivating the resettlement program in the eastern territory of Birobidjan, which, quite obviously, could provide an excellent solution to the terrible problem now confronting certain gullible Jewish people within the Soviet Union. These misguided people have succumbed to the lies of Zionist imperialists and anti-Soviet internationalists in the capitalist countries. We welcome your application for resettlement and are hopeful that it will serve as an example of the historic respect that the Soviet Union has had for the Jewish people."

"Can't you see what that means, Vera?" Mikhail pointed out, trying to break through her indifference. "They will let us lead an honorable life. They want us to settle in our own place." He felt his face flush and his eyes begin to mist. "We are saved, my darling," he said, taking her frail body in his arms and kissing her cheek. "Trust me," he said. "You'll see."

With remarkable ease, he received permission to depart and he bought two "soft" tickets on the Trans-Siberian Express. He wondered if Vera was up to the journey. Her strength had continued to wane and she had begun to spend a great deal of time in bed, as if sleep had become an escape. But he would not let himself become discouraged. The authorities had even found him a job in an aluminum extrusion plant. It wasn't in his chosen field, but at least it was a start and the wages were actually higher than for similar work in other Soviet factories.

There had been a few bad moments. Their interrogation at the Yaroslav station had brought Vera to the verge of fainting. The train agent had been intimidating and Mikhail had been too frightened, he admitted, to stand up to him. He lay on the upper bunk, feeling the bounce of the train along the tracks. It was nice and cozy living in this way, as if he were in a warm cocoon. Vera now seemed to be asleep, for which he was thankful. He had brushed back her hair and kissed her on the forehead, covering her with an extra blanket that the attendant had kindly delivered. At Birobidjan, he was certain he would be able to get adequate medical care for her.

Tomorrow they would start having their dinners in the dining car and he would buy a bottle of wine each night in celebration. It was extravagant, he knew, but it was the least he could do for having been the cause of her ordeal. He felt the tension ooze out of his body, and a sense of well-being crept over him as he began to picture their new life.

10

Alex's eyes popped open. It was dark and it took him some time to rediscover his sense of place. Someone was moving about in the compartment. Moving his head, he caught Mrs. Valentinov in his field of vision and remembered instantly. Her back was turned and she was in the process of dressing or undressing, he could not tell which, only that the entire length of her body was naked. She was stepping into her underpants, the curve of hard buttocks outlined as she pulled up the pants and half-turned. He dropped his eyelids quickly, then raised them slightly as she fitted her breasts into the cups of her brassiere. He felt his penis harden and rise between his spread legs. As she turned, his eyelids fluttered closed again, but he imagined her putting on her slip, the sound of her movements increasing his excitement. Then he heard her close the door to the washroom, the swish of water in the sink, and the sound of her brushing her teeth.

Sitting up quickly, he squinted at the face of his watch. Despite the darkness, it was eight o'clock in the morning, Moscow time. It wouldn't be long, he thought, as the train crossed the various time zones, before night would become day and he would be having dinner at dawn and breakfast at bedtime. He quickly removed his shirt and pants and poked in his suitcase for fresh clothes. Quickly, he zipped up his slacks and began to work his loafers over his feet. He noted that the bottle of vodka was nearly empty.

Standing up again, he began to button his shirt, goaded by some strange sense of modesty, feeling the pressure to be dressed by the time Mrs. Valentinov returned. Then the door opened and she stood in front of him, wearing only a half slip. His eyes went immediately to her pugnacious breasts which seemed about to burst from their brassiere.

"I hope I didn't wake you," she said.

"Not at all. I'm programmed to wake up at this hour anyway."

"The ingrained habits die hard, although you will find that it will be more and more difficult to maintain them on this journey."

"I can imagine."

"That's part of the adventure," she said, pulling a blouse from her suitcase and putting it on. Then she took a gray skirt from a hanger and stepped into it. He marveled at her nonchalance, dressing before a total stranger. It seemed as natural as if he were at home with Janice.

She patted her stomach. "I'm hungry," she said.

"You should be."

"The tendency on these trips is to eat too much."

"And drink too much," he said, pointing to the vodka bottle.

"So," she said, laughing. "We have a moralist on board."

"No. Just a doctor," he said quickly, and immediately regretted it. He had tried so hard to be guarded and discreet, to offer nothing about himself. But Dimitrov and all his problems seemed far away now, and his suspicions about Dimitrov's plans seemed absurd, impossible. I imagined it all, he told himself.

"A doctor?" she said easily, as if it were mildly interesting. "How secure. I can outline my ailments for the next few days."

"From the look of you that would hardly take more than a few minutes." My God, he was being flirtatious.

"I'll make some up," she said, coquettish, promising.

She put her hand on the handle of the compartment door. "I'll save you a seat in the restaurant car," she said. "Breakfast is always a bit of a scramble and Russians are quite voracious in the morning."

"Great," he responded, going into the washroom.

But before he could put a ribbon of toothpaste on his brush, he heard a great commotion in the passageway. He opened the compartment door and peeked out. The small boy was kicking furiously at one of the toilet doors. Heads poked out of doors and Tania came running down the passageway, her lips pressed together. She grabbed the boy by the shoulders and tried to draw him away. But he broke free and began bashing the door again.

"What the bloody hell is going on?" MacBaren, the sandy-haired Australian, cried as he looked into the passageway, his face still heavy with sleep.

"I want to go to the toilet," the boy shouted, grappling with Tania, who had pulled him finally from the door.

Another head popped out from the compartment next to Alex's. It was the red-haired agent, his "protector." So they put him right next door, Alex observed with some annoyance.

"I want to go to the toilet," the boy shouted.

Tania dragged the boy toward his parents' compartment and knocked on the door, banging with the heel of her fist.

"I'll pee in my pants," the boy shouted, his arms lashing out at Tania's stomach. Finally, the door to the compartment opened and the bloated man in filthy striped pajamas stood there blinking into the attendant's face.

"You had better teach this young man some manners," Tania said.

The Australian shook his head, shrugged and slammed the door to his compartment.

"You leave that boy alone," the bloated man hissed, suddenly comprehending the situation. The boy smirked and broke free from Tania's grip.

"He was kicking the door, making a racket, annoying the pasengers," Tania explained to Trubetskoi.

"Listen, you bitch," he said imperiously, the model of stern Communist authority, in spite of his incongruous costume. "You do this again and I'll have your job."

He looked toward the locked door of the toilet and walked out into the passageway. "Who the devil is in there, anyway?" he said between clenched teeth, obviously enjoying the exercise of his authority. Alex watched with some curiosity, feeling a suggestive pressure on his own bladder. Maybe the kid's got a case, he thought.

The boy's father strode to the door of the toilet and banged against it. "Who is in there?" he shouted.

But before he could bang again, the red-haired man, as agile as a big cat, had moved behind him to hold back his hand.

"I wouldn't," he whispered.

"Who the hell are you?" the fat man asked, still flaunting his authority.

Instead of answering the red-haired man twisted Trubetskoi's arm behind him and moved him swiftly back to his compartment.

Tania, left in the passageway alone, looked at Alex and smiled thinly, shrugging, as if such activity were all part of a normal day's work. Then she moved down the passageway to her own quarters.

Alex stepped back into his compartment, keeping the door open a sliver and pressing his eye to the crack. His curiosity was aroused. Why had there been no response from the toilet? The train bounced and he pressed his body against the wall, holding the compartment handle to keep the door from opening wider. Then he saw the toilet door move, first slightly, then quickly. A man emerged, moving swiftly down the passageway, and deftly letting himself into the compartment next to Alex's. Zeldovich! Alex shut the compartment door and stood with his back against it. So Zeldovich was on the train after all. How silly he had been earlier to think that all that had gone before was a mad dream.

Anna Petrovna, he whispered, as if she were in the room. Was she really one of them? he wondered. The memory of Zeldovich's face jabbed him. "Don't be a fool, Kuznetsov," he said aloud, and walked into the washroom.

When he had washed and shaved, he made his way to the restaurant carriage, where Mrs. Valentinov was already eating a big plate of eggs and a small mound of caviar. As she had predicted, the restaurant was crowded, with lines waiting at either end, but she had obviously protected his seat with great determination, much to the annoyance of the little manager. They were seated opposite the British gentleman whom he had shocked the night before. So they were letting him communicate without harassment, he thought.

"Albert Farmer," the man said, putting out a delicate white hand.

"Alex Cousins. And this is Mrs. Valentinov." Alex paused. "Anna Petrovna," he said boldly.

"Very good," she said, winking at Alex and smiling at Farmer.

"A pleasure," he responded.

"She's my roommate," Alex said, feeling an odd sense of possessiveness, perhaps a bit of macho. He remembered her strong, tall body as she dressed that morning.

"I must say you're luckier than me. I've got a snoring Australian."

The waitress came and dropped the fifteen-page menu on the table before him.

"I won't go through that again," said Alex. "Eggs and caviar," he said in Russian, pointing to Mrs. Valentinov's plate. The waitress nodded and started toward the kitchen. As he watched her depart, he noted a familiar face in the crowd, the red-haired man, waiting patiently, big sleepy eyes trying to look indifferent. Poor Zeldovich, Alex thought maliciously, doomed to sucking sausages in his compartment and making surreptitious trips to the john.

Mrs. Valentinov spread caviar on a piece of toast and stuffed it into her mouth with relish. Alex watched her, caught by the sensuality of the act. Would they have a brief future together? Why not? he thought, his confidence soaring. He looked beyond Farmer at the sky lightening over the low hills, a layer of glistening frost covering everything with a blanket of spangles, like a tranquil Christmas scene.

"We are in Asia now," Mrs. Valentinov said. She sounded wistful, almost sad.

"We must have passed the Monument of Tears," Alex said, still watching the passing scene. Beyond that marker, his grandfather had told him, was the unknown —Asian Siberia, a vast waste, from which few returned. "You were entering the gates of hell," his grandfather had said. "What was there to do but wash the earth around this marker with your tears?"

Albert Farmer looked nervously at his watch.

"We will be in Kirov soon."

"Where are you headed?" Alex asked.

"Ulan Bator," Farmer said. "I'm with the British Embassy there."

"Oh." Alex's interest quickened. Ulan Bator was the capital of Mongolia. It was the edge of the world. Ghengis Khan's capital. "I didn't know the British maintained an embassy there."

Again he wondered if this mild-mannered man could carry his information.

"Ah, yes. The residents of our little island always had their bit of wanderlust."

"So I've heard. Anyway, it sounds quite gloomy."

"Quite the contrary. It's rather exciting." Farmer looked furtively around, then continued. "Just take a peek at any map. It's rather in the middle of things."

Alex was, of course, quite familiar with the location of Ulan Bator. He had seen it on the map of China at Dimitrov's dacha. I must be careful, he warned himself.

"You know Mongolia, Mrs. Valentinov?" Farmer asked.

"When you live in Irkutsk, Mongolia is not as exotic as you might imagine. We're very neighborly." She spoke pleasantly, but Alex sensed a certain tenseness that hadn't been there before.

"Irkutsk. Lovely city. Been there many times. I rather am fond of music and Ulan Bator is, well, not exactly a cultural mecca. But in Irkutsk, you have a superb symphony orchestra."

"You see," Mrs. Valentinov said to Alex, jiggling his elbow with a child's exuberance. "That's my town."

The waitress brought his eggs and caviar and Alex began to eat.

"And you, Mr. Cousins," Farmer said blandly, breaking the silence. "What are you doing on the Trans-Siberian?"

The inquiry came too suddenly, like a spear thrust. Chewing hard, Alex held up one finger to signal that the answer would be forthcoming, while his mind raced to prepare a safe response.

"A private visit to ancestral haunts," he said, smiling at his choice of words, suspecting that he had encouraged Farmer's curiosity. He felt Mrs. Valentinov stir beside him.

"So, your people are also from Siberia." She spoke the words with a raised eyebrow, and he suddenly remembered. The night before, he had listened silently as she talked about Irkutsk, holding back his natural responses, feeling the tension of resisting his own inclination to talk. She must think I'm an idiot, he thought. He was suddenly angered by his caution.

"As a matter of fact, Mrs. Valentinov," he said, relieved to be speaking at last, "our grandparents came from the same town."

"No," she said in disbelief, her eyes glistening in excitement. Then she ran her fingers through her hair.

Could she be acting? And so successfully?

"Cousins," she mused, a fingertip on her cheek.

"Kuznetsov."

"Ah ah." She laughed, then turned to Albert Farmer. "He is traveling under false pretenses and a false name."

"Nobody in America could pronounce the damned thing," Alex said in English.

He washed the last of his eggs down with tea, savoring the warmth. He was enjoying this easy bonding of relationships, particularly with Mrs. Valentinov. He turned and looked at her over his uplifted cup, studied her high cheekbones and the deep-blue eyes set wide apart. Her natural blond hair fell softly to her shoulders. There was a fullness, a sensual richness, in her lips that he had not noticed before. His eyes met hers. She did not turn away. Again he felt a twinge of possessiveness.

"Soon we'll be seeing nothing but the taiga," Albert Farmer said, as he looked out of the window. "The endless white birch forest."

The train seemed to be slowing.

"Kirov," he said, looking at his watch. "And right on time. That's the most fascinating thing about Russian trains. They are always on time, to the minute. It's astonishing, considering the Russians' lack of efficiency everywhere else." He flushed suddenly, remembering Mrs. Valentinov. "A ten-minute stop," he said briskly, refolding his private timetable.

Out on the station platform people huddled in overcoats, their faces red with cold as they watched anxiously for the train to stop. A line of women near the tracks suddenly came to life as the train finally ground to a halt. Older women in their babushkas, young flat-faced girls carrying baskets stocked with foodstuffs and strange-looking bottles of a milky substance, which Alex later learned was *kvas,* packages of sunflower seeds and little bouquets of flowers. A motley assortment of people in pajamas, housecoats, jogging suits, overcoats and uniforms swarmed around the women purchasing their wares.

Alex paid his check and stood up.

"I think I'll pop out to the terra firma," he said. "Anybody like something?" He had to test them.

Both Mr. Farmer and Mrs. Valentinov shook their heads. Alex moved into the aisle, stopping by Miss Peterson's table.

"Would you like something?" he asked politely.

"Are those sunflower seeds?" she said, pointing at one of the baskets.

"If they are, I'll get you some."

He moved through the crowd, brushing past the red-haired man, who was still pretending to wait for a table. Bounding down the metal stairs, Alex felt the cold bite through his jacket. Looking down the length of the train, he noted the long line of carriages, including one tacked on at the end that seemed different from the others. Beside it, clusters of armed troops stood around smoking cigarettes, automatic weapons slung over their shoulders. Alex gave a quick backward glance toward the restaurant car and picked out the lumbering red-haired man.

Alex smiled to himself and stood aloof from the crowd around the sunflower-seed vendor, patiently waiting his turn. When it came, he made his purchase and stuffed the bags of seeds into his pockets. Starting back to the train, he passed the flower vendor and bought a little bouquet, then grabbed the hand support and lifted himself aboard. The red-haired man had kept a respectful distance, but the string seemed to have little slack.

Alex felt a tug at his trouser leg and, turning, saw the moon face of little Vladimir. He was apparently too small to get a grip on the hand support and was using Alex's trouser leg to hoist himself up. Alex could feel the tension in the fabric, then the giving way as his pants began to rip.

"For crying out loud," he shouted in English, kicking his leg to shake the boy loose. The boy screamed but held on.

"Leave the boy alone!" Trubetskoi had appeared on the platform, his face red with cold.

"Get the damned brat off my leg," Alex shouted, letting go of the handrail and gripping the waist of his trousers, barely keeping his balance. The father reached out and lifted the boy onto the first step, but not before Vladimir had lashed out and punched his father in his big belly.

"Are you all right?" Alex asked.

"You bastard," the fat man said, still gasping.

The red-haired man had moved near them, observing the scene. Trubetskoi struggled to gain his composure.

"Somebody should lock that brat up," a woman said. It was Tania.

"And his father," Alex mumbled.

"They are a menace," Tania said, moving back into the carriage.

Alex followed her and behind him he could hear the ubiquitous red-haired man moving in his wake.

Back in the compartment, Mrs. Valentinov was sitting in the chair thumbing through the pages of a Russian magazine.

"I was attacked by a four-foot monster," Alex said, rubbing his hands together and emptying his pockets of the bags of sunflower seeds. He felt along the waistband of his trousers and discovered that two of the belt loops had been torn.

"I have some sewing things," Mrs. Valentinov said, standing up and moving past him to her suitcase.

The train began to move, haltingly at first, then with gathering speed. Outside Alex saw the army of grandmothers, brooms in hand, sweeping the tracks, ignoring the moving train as it slid smoothly past them.

"I was about to kick the brat in the face," he said, remembering the flowers, which he had thrown onto his bunk along with the sunflower seeds. They were slightly crushed. Looking at them he felt his old boyish shyness return.

"I bought you this," he mumbled, his heart pounding. My God, I am clumsy, he told himself.

"A bouquet," she said, smiling broadly. She took the flowers and arranged them in an empty tea glass.

"Everybody in Siberia is passionate about flowers," she said. "These were grown in hothouses. But in the summer Siberia is a forest of flowers." She opened the sewing kit and, squinting, threaded a needle. Crooking a finger, she slipped it beneath his belt and drew him toward her.

"Now let us see." She surveyed the loose loops, pressed one torn loop to the material and began to sew.

Alex turned his head, and looking down, watched her with interest.

"So, we are neighbors in spirit," she said, drawing the needle in and out through the material.

"In a way," he agreed. "Although we're a generation or so removed."

"And this journey is a pilgrimage?" she asked abstractedly.

"I hadn't thought of it quite that way," he answered. He knew he was throwing caution to the winds now, feeling the sluices within him unlock.

"Then why?" she asked, her busy fingers pausing.

How much did she really know, he wondered.

"Pilgrimage seems so ponderous. Call it curiosity," he said, watching her bite off the thread with her even white teeth. She re-threaded the needle, preparing to repair the other loop.

"Or putting it another way," he said, drawing a deep breath, "I'm searching backwards in time within myself to understand my antecedents." He shook his head and smiled. "What an insufferable pedant I am."

When she didn't respond, he went on. "My grandfather was a Czarist exile. It was the dominant experience of his life and he kept it alive for years afterward, handed it down through the generations. I'm beginning to think he passed his obsession on to me, in my genes. I have always had a sense of being the alien corn."

"You feel this way even in America?"

"Especially in America."

"Strange!" She sighed.

"Am I making any sense?" he asked, unsure that he was, but at the same time enjoying the exquisite sense of unburdening himself to her.

"When this opportunity came up—" He stopped, watching her. She continued to sew, showing no signs of heightened interest. "I have this mind's-eye view," he said. "A whole landscape has been imbedded in my mind and it just seemed important that I see the real thing. So, you see, it is quite possible to hand down an obsession."

"Yes," she said, looking up. "Quite possible."

But he went on talking, carried on by his own momentum.

"You see, my grandfather was reliving the great adventure of his life and immersing his offspring in the idea of it. He was a prisoner here, a convict."

"What was his crime?" she asked quietly.

Alex smiled grimly.

"This was his crime. When he was sixteen, the head of his village's council decided that everyone who sold firewood for a living should give him a portion of wood in return for a license to do business. It was really a bribe, of course, and my great-grandfather refused. His license, of course, was withdrawn. He was forbidden to cut or sell his wood. Soon he was barely able to provide for himself and his family. Goaded by hunger and his inability to provide for his family, he soon became an object of ridicule, a kind of village character, whom no one took seriously. My grandfather was just becoming a man himself, and seeing this happen to his father made him bitter and angry. One day, he followed his father into the village and saw him go up to the head of the village council.

" 'Thief,' " his father cried. 'You steal the bread from the mouths of the starving. You pig!' "

"The councilman just looked at him for a minute. Then he cleared his throat and spat in my great-grandfather's face. My grandfather, who was standing right there, threw himself on the councilman and ground his face into the mud.

"That was all there was to it. Banishment by word, with no recourse, no trial, no chance to defend himself."

They were both quiet for a few moments. Anna Petrovna did not seem to know what to say. Alex decided to go on.

"He did knock off a few years by helping to build this railroad," he said, in a lighter tone. "When he was released, he started a new life in Irkutsk, your home town. He became a prospector and fur merchant. In 1913, he told me, he could smell what was coming and converted everything he had into gold nuggets. He sewed them into my grandmother's and my father's clothing, and they hopped the Trans-Siberian and made their way to Vladivostok, then on to Japan and the United States."

"He sounds like an adventurer, your grandfather."

"He admitted to being an opportunist, a briber, a cheat and a killer."

"A killer?"

"He may have been exaggerating."

"Everything about Siberia is exaggerated," she whispered. "That will be your principal discovery."

"How do you mean?"

She stopped her sewing. "It is considered by everyone a beastly place, hardly fit for human habitation."

"Is that an exaggeration?"

"Absolutely. Here you have an example of good Siberian stock."

"And me?"

She looked up at him with a slow smile. "The soft life may have taken its toll."

It seemed a challenge. Was it an invitation?

In a sudden burst of courage, he reached out and grabbed her hand. It was cold. He saw her lips were trembling, and he sensed that her uncertainty somehow gave him an advantage.

Bending down, he pressed his lips gently over hers, feeling the sweet tingle of her flesh, and the mounting tension in his body as he breathed in the special smell of her. He knelt beside the chair and enveloped her in his arms, and felt all his fears slip away. Whoever she was, what did it matter?

Burying his head in her breast, he felt her hands run through his hair, gently caressing the back of his neck. The surge of desire then gripped him, as if every nerve end had suddenly become kindling. Rising, he drew her out of the chair, feeling the full length of her body, his lips moving over her face and neck. She sighed, and said his name, and then drew out his shirt and her hands found the bare skin of his back.

Then, as if some secret signal had passed between them, she insinuated herself out of his arms and moved back, watching his eyes as she began to undress with slow, languorous movements. Instinctively, she knew that he loved watching her. Not a word passed between them. Even the sound and bounce of the train seemed suddenly suspended. His fingers trembled as he removed his shirt and drew his T-shirt over his head. She stood now almost naked, and he reveled in the sight of her high breasts with big pink nipples, erect now, and he watched while she removed her panties, the last barrier. He looked for a long moment, then removed his own pants, and saw her eyes dart down longingly toward his phallus. No woman had ever looked at him that way, not even Janice—certainly never Janice.

He moved toward her, pressed his lips against hers again, caressing her nipple with one hand and, with the other, dipping into the fold of her buttocks. He could feel her shiver as he held her, and knew she was already on the edge of orgasm. Then he drew her down on the lower bunk, a confined space, where they fitted themselves together in an instinctive mutuality. Her hand, with tremulous lightness, reached out for his manhood and, as if she were plunging a dagger smoothly into its sheath, brought it deep into her body. He felt himself shudder and reach into her, and she responded with the same animal sense of abandon. This was the meaning of sexuality, he told himself when it was over, still holding her, determined to keep her in his arms.

He felt as if he owned her and, strangely, as if he had long known her. He knew it was all a fantasy, a reality totally distorted by the parameters of the train journey. Here, life unfolded within a confined space and time. He barely knew this woman, had spoken to her briefly, exchanged information, some of it banal and pedestrian, and yet he could tell himself that he was in love with her. The idea was foolish, adolescent, irrational. But as much as his mind tried to brush it aside, he found himself hooked by this overwhelming sense of possession. Could she be acting for anyone but herself?

He explored her face silently, his gaze washing over her skin, absorbing all the details of her pores, the curve of her full lips, the straight bridge of her nose widening at her nostrils, and finally, above the ridge of her high cheekbones, the blue eyes with their tiny flecks of yellow and black. He had not noticed this before. Old doubts crowded back. What did she really feel? Was he imagining all this?

"Am I dreaming?" he finally asked aloud, drawing blankets around them in the tight space. The sun was higher now, throwing a cold glaring light into the compartment. Outside the landscape had changed as the train threaded through endless rows of white birch.

"The taiga," Anna Petrovna said. "That's what we call the birch forests. Millions upon millions of birch trees," she said, sighing. He followed her eyes, watching the trees, feeling the hypnotic effect of the repetitive whiteness.

"Beautiful," he said, but he could not be sure what he meant. Everything was beautiful, he decided, putting his lips to her forehead and kissing her gently, feeling the chill of her skin. "I can't believe this is happening," he said, as if it were something provocative, profound.

"You are a romantic."

"Me? A romantic?" He looked at her in disbelief. "I am the least romantic man I know."

She reached for the hairs of his chest and crushed them in her fingers.

"You must accept good things as they come," she said, smiling.

"They haven't come that often." He smiled back, but suddenly felt panicky. Was she trifling with him? Using him?

"You have been celibate?"

"Practically," he said, then, feeling a challenge to his manhood, retreated into bravado. "Well, perhaps not quite."

She laughed, showing the incredible evenness of her teeth.

He raised himself on one elbow and looked at her.

"Why do I feel I've known you all my life?" he asked.

"Because you are a romantic. You are reading more into events than meets the eye."

"And you?"

"I think of myself as more practical."

"So did I."

"You should trust more in science."

"I did. Until now."

"What do you mean?"

"I mean—" he paused, not wanting to banter, wanting to give her a real answer—"science cannot adequately explain this." He leaned over and pressed his lips on hers, caressing her tongue with his own. He felt his phallus beginning to harden again. "I can explain the body's reaction. What the body does under these circumstances. But not why."

"It is simple animal attraction," she said.

"Simple? That would imply that all men are attracted to all women, indiscriminately." He felt pedantic. If I'm not careful, we will talk it away, he told himself, his fingers roaming her body, reaching for her clitoris, caressing, feeling the need of her again.

"There is no explanation for this at all," he whispered, feeling her hands reach out for him as she moved her body to receive him. He felt the tight exquisite fit of her organs, the soft, yielding wonder of their joining.

"I love you," he said, the words coming smoothly, yet foreign to his ear. He might have said them a hundred years ago, perhaps in another life. He was not sure whether he had ever said them to Janice. "I love you, Anna Petrovna," he repeated, feeling comfortable with the words now, as his body pressed itself to hers. It was as if all the heavy years of dreariness had disappeared, he thought. It was like being born again. He was no longer afraid.

"You must love me," she said, her voice a whisper, translating the urgency of her body's needs, as she drew him into her, her hands pressing on his buttocks. He felt the beginning wave of her trembling, like distant thunder. In his mind he imagined a flash of lightning as she gasped her pleasure, her teeth biting into his shoulder.

She continued to tremble in the afterglow of their closeness and he felt his phallus shrink slowly within her.

"I am a very physical woman," she said, almost in apology. Again he felt a pang of anxiety, wondering if she took her pleasure indiscriminately. He felt vaguely humiliated. Suppose I mean nothing to her? he thought.

"Does that imply that it is always like this?" he asked cautiously.

Her eyes opened and she looked at him with indignation. "No," she said, "it does not mean that."

"You have no lovers?"

"No."

"And your husband?"

"We perform our duties."

"Duties?"

"Are you married?"

"Yes."

"Well then. Shall I ask you about your wife?"

"Please don't."

"Then what of your mistresses?"

"I'm sorry I started this."

"You should not question so much."

He was annoyed at his own jealousy, the smothering feeling of possession. She was silent, looking out the window at the passing taiga. He looked at his watch, his sense of time returning. It will soon be over, he thought, and felt her impending departure like a stab of pain. She put a hand over his watch and nestled her head on his shoulder, seeing the soreness where her teeth had dug in.

"I have drawn blood," she said, licking the small wound.

She finished her ministrations, then kissed him on the neck and closed her eyes. He watched her slip into a light sleep, her lips parted, her breathing calm, and wondered what it all meant. What did it matter? I have never been so happy, he told himself, and he felt his mind relax and sleep begin.

11

In his mind Grivetsky ran through his options. The sun was slipping beyond the edges of the taiga, but he had not noticed the changing patterns of light. The crowded compartment was thick with the smells and tension of the onlookers. The old man sat silent, motionless, his one good eye fixed on the chessboard as he waited for Grivetsky to move. But the general was carefully replaying their past games, the string of losses that had, at last, revealed the old man's strategy. He was barely conscious of the movement around him, the whispers of the spectators who watched transfixed, perhaps infused with the same obsession that had kept him at it through an entire night and a full day. When the train stopped, he had sent one of the young spectators to buy sausages and bread, which he shared with his old opponent as they continued their nonstop duel.

"He will never beat him," he heard someone say behind him, but that only goaded him to greater effort.

"They have been at it for nearly twenty-four hours," someone said with excitement as the crowd swelled and shuffled, each man trying to find a place from which to see the board.

"He will wear him down."

"Never. The old man is like iron."

Grivetsky heard the comments and willed them out of his field of concentration, with the automatic reflex of a horse's tail swatting flies on its hide. Now he had the fix of the old man's mind. It was, after all, the classic strategy of the armies of the land-rich nation. Draw in your enemy. Always trade geography for knowledge. Husband your strength while your opponent spends his. It was the classic maneuver that defeated Napoleon and Hitler; that destroyed Chiang Kai-shek. I will win now, he told himself, as his mind jumped ahead a half-dozen moves. He could feel the old man's mind clicking over the same ground, analyzing the squares and pieces, sensing the imminence of defeat.

A hush fell over the compartment as if each of the spectators had ceased to breathe. The old man's gnarled hand moved, lightly fingered his remaining bishop, then withdrew. The train bounced beneath them, making the pieces on the board jump in tandem. Watching the old man's hesitation, Grivetsky suddenly was sure of his victory. With that the tension in his mind and body relaxed.

"The old man is finished," someone said, breaking the tension in the room. The flow of life began again.

The old man raised his one good eye, and blinked. "I am defeated," he said hoarsely.

He held out a gnarled hand which Grivetsky took, feeling its roughness. The old man's pressure signaled his admiration. The joy was in the hard fights, Grivetsky knew. What was any battle without a worthy foe? He took the old man's crumpled ruble notes, stuffed them into his pocket and stood up, feeling the full weight of his fatigue as his joints refused to unlock. With effort, he pulled himself up to his full height.

"You are a great opponent," Grivetsky said in a

gravelly tone. He had not spoken aloud in over twenty-four hours.

"Now let me," a young man said, obviously thirsting for his own taste of the old man's blood. His defeat would put two more rubles in the old man's pocket, Grivetsky thought, knowing the force of will and concentration that had to be invested to defeat him. He looked down into the old man's eye and nodded. The old man smiled thinly.

Grivetsky turned and moved through the crowd into the corridor, the stiffness in his legs and back painful. Passing through the freezing space between two carriages, he discovered a soldier posted at the entrance to the next car. It surprised him, confronting the impassive young soldier with his machine gun strapped across his chest, a finger on the trigger. He looked at the insignia on the tunic, and recognized it as KGB border command.

"You cannot pass," the soldier said arrogantly, the butt of the gun jabbing into Grivetsky's tight stomach muscles. It was then that he realized that he had walked in the wrong direction and, without a word, he turned, reopened the door behind him, and retraced his steps past the crowded compartment where the chess game was being played.

By the time he had seated himself at a table in the almost empty restaurant carriage, it dawned on him that he had confronted a most unusual situation. Why had they tacked a troop carrier onto a regular passenger train, and KGB troops at that? Normal procedures were to transport the military on separate trains, except, of course, for individual soldiers traveling under separate orders.

He dipped his spoon into a bowl of borscht and fished out a potato. Why so much KGB clout? he thought. If this much was blatant, he could imagine the strength of what he could not see.

Normally the general would have put their little cloak-and-dagger games out of his mind. But this time he himself was involved in their games up to the hilt.

Dimitrov was directing the little puppet show and Grivetsky was one of the puppets. This whole exercise on the Trans-Siberian was a carefully contrived subterfuge. They were watching him, he was certain, but he could not decide the source of the surveillance. Dimitrov? Bulgakov? Others within the Army? Within the KGB?

He pushed away the stainless-steel bowl and threw down some kopeks angrily. On his way out, he stopped at the table where the restaurant manager worked. The little man jumped up, as if the seat of his pants had suddenly caught fire.

"Good to see you, sir."

"You know who I am?"

"Of course."

"Who told you?"

The little man hesitated. Under Grivetsky's glare, he began to sweat.

"That man told you." Grivetsky pointed to the empty table at which the red-haired man had sat the other night. The little man followed the direction of Grivetsky's finger, then looked up at him, dismayed.

"What man?"

"Come on. Don't play dumb with me."

"You mean the red-haired man?" The restaurant manager sat down again in anguish.

"Who is he?"

"KGB."

"No fooling. And he told you who I am?"

"No, sir."

"Don't you lie to me."

The little man patted his pockets and drew out a crumpled piece of paper. He opened it, pointing with grimy finger. "Your name is on the manifest of the soft passengers."

Grivetsky looked at it, feeling stupid, as if he had lost some of his dignity. Then he was puzzled.

"Well, then who *is* he watching?"

"Sometimes"—the little man sighed—"it seems that they are watching everybody. I don't ask. I don't want to know. I have a wife and two children and I have been working for the railroad for fifteen years. They come to me. They ask me to report. They tell me who shall not sit with whom. They drive me crazy." He had worked himself to the verge of hysteria. "And they have a trainload of troops attached to the train. What do you want from me?"

Grivetsky watched the man's lips tremble. He turned away and started toward the soft class, feeling the cold shoot through him as he opened the door between the carriages. So they are watching everybody, he thought with contempt, and certainly that includes me. He wondered if he should call Dimitrov. He could make the call from Sverdlovsk, the next stop. But Dimitrov's line might be tapped. He could call Bulgakov. His phone was almost certainly tapped, but he knew he could make himself understood by using cryptic references that came of long association with the Marshall. Or he could call directly into the protected military line, but that, too, might be tapped.

Entering the passageway of the soft class, he immediately noticed the strange-looking man with the odd walk. He had pulled out one of the spring seats that lined the passageway and was peering out into the darkness. Another KGB man, Grivetsky thought, feeling his contempt rise within him.

"What are you staring at?" he said with deliberate brutality to the seated man, who looked up at him, startled.

"I'm looking out the window," he said, equally belligerent.

"You think you are so clever," Grivetsky hissed, leaving the startled man to contemplate his meaning as he let himself into his compartment and slammed the door behind him.

He was livid with rage, a consuming anger that made him clench his fists in despair. Pulling a bottle of vodka from underneath his bunk, he took a long, lingering drink. He felt its heat immediately and leaned back against the wall. By the time he had drunk down to the bottom of the bottle's neck, the edge of his anger was blunted.

He felt his eyelids droop and his arms and legs grow heavy. Then something flickered in his mind, and his eyes opened wide again. Something was not quite right in his compartment. He searched and re-searched the room with his eyes, probing every square inch and comparing it to his recollection. Then he found what he was looking for. Jumping up from the bunk, he poked into the plastic garment bags in which his uniforms were hanging. When traveling, he always reversed the garment bags, since that was the only way he could be sure the zippers would stay fastened. Now the bags were turned rightside out, and the zippers had slipped down a few inches. Someone had come into his room, removed the garment bags and reversed them.

He opened the bags and drew out his uniforms, searching the pockets and the linings for something amiss. What am I looking for? he wondered. Perhaps a new kind of electronic bug. His fingers searched along the seams, under the collars and epaulets. Even after his careful search, he was not entirely satisfied, but he reversed the bags again and zipped them up from the inside. His mind was racing now, its iron discipline returning. Who was watching him? Bulgakov would have the most to lose from any radical change in military policy on the Chinese front. Not that he would protest the strike. What was important to Bulgakov was not ideology, or even policy, but his own prestige and position. It was essential that Dimitrov make Bulgakov feel that he was part of the decision, that he had not been skipped over. But suppose it was too late for that? Suppose Bulgakov had insinuated his own intelligence into the General Secretary's dacha, and he already knew. Unlike Grivetsky, Bulgakov did not feel that a military man should be above intrigue and ingratiation. He had built his brilliant career as much on ruthless intrigue as on his military talents. It was Bulgakov, he decided. Under that bland façade of hearty camaraderie, Bulgakov was tracking him now. Somehow he would have to warn Dimitrov. He, Grivetsky, would have to learn to intrigue.

He felt the train slow and saw through the window the beginnings of lights. They were on the edges of Sverdlovsk. He took his pistol out of his suitcase and slipped it under his jacket. Then, still feeling the stiffness in his joints, he carefully opened the door to the passageway. The squat man was no longer sitting on the spring seat. Only the younger train attendant was in the passageway, busy with the samovar under which he could see the red glow of the coals.

"Good evening, sir," she said, looking up at him with wide, pleasant eyes.

"How long do we stop at Sverdlovsk?" he asked.

"Fifteen minutes. It is normally ten, but we are five minutes ahead of schedule."

"And the telephone?"

"Just inside the station. Turn right."

"Thank you." He stretched his hands over the coals, feeling their warmth. "Where is the man that was sitting out here? The funny-looking fellow, the one who waddles."

"He went that way," she said, pointing toward the front of the train. "He parades around the passageway as if he didn't have a compartment."

"Where is his compartment?"

The attendant pointed. She moved her face closer to his.

"But he's rarely there. He just stalks up and down the passageway with his funny walk."

He looked into the woman's frank, open face. She seemed self-assured, strong. He wondered if he could confide in her.

"And the red-haired man?" he asked casually.

"In there." She pointed without hesitation.

He had forgotten the woman's name.

"After we move again, please bring in a glass of tea."

"With pleasure, sir."

The train came to a stop at Sverdlovsk. Groups of

women vendors shivered in the cold, their baskets held in the crooks of their arms. The train attendant scrambled before him and opened the door, holding it respectfully as he clambered down the metal steps. The station was nearly deserted. He dialed the operator, looking at his watch. He could hear the buzzing sound repeat itself over and over again. After nearly two minutes, he heard a voice on the other end.

"I am General Grivetsky," he said with controlled anger. "You must put this call through immediately to Moscow." He read off the number from a little book he kept in his pocket.

"It will take some time," the operator said.

"How long?"

"Maybe ten minutes."

"You must do better. I insist that you drop everything and concentrate on it. It is a matter of grave importance, an emergency."

"I will do my best, sir."

Stupid, inefficient telephone system, he thought. A bureaucratic nightmare. He looked around the deserted station. A few derelicts slept on the wooden benches. Out on the platform, passengers huddled around the vendors, stamping their feet in the cold as they made their purchases.

Impatiently, he clicked the telephone cradle, but got no response. He felt a heavy ball growing in his gut as he tried to organize his thoughts. He was not sure how to approach Bulgakov, although, as always, he leaned toward directness. He would say that he was under surveillance and Bulgakov would have to make some response. Grivetsky was confident that whatever Bulgakov said, he would be able to find in it some hint of the truth.

"May I help you, sir?" the operator said, suddenly breaking into the line.

"You must hurry on my Moscow call."

"I am working on it."

He forced himself to remain calm, looking at his watch, the minutes ticking away. Then he saw the funny-looking man again, roaming the almost deserted station, slapping his arms around himself, waddling about on his short legs. So they are still watching, he thought. With his free hand he reached inside his jacket and curled a finger under the trigger guard. In the station doorway he saw the train attendant, peering inside, signaling to him. He pressed the telephone cradle again and heard a clicking, but no other sound. He watched the second hand of his watch move relentlessly around and, raising his eyes again, he saw that the crippled man had left the station.

He waited, growing more and more anxious, wondering whether he was doing the right thing. Suddenly he heard ringing at the other end and the voice of the operator. He looked again at his watch. Less than two minutes left.

The train attendant appeared again, beckoning him, making motions of extreme panic. He heard shouting along the platform as the passengers disengaged from the vendors and climbed back on the train. Then, suddenly, startling him, he heard the sleepy cracked voice of Bulgakov coming over the bad Moscow connection.

"Maxim Sergeyevich here," the General said quickly, breaking into the babble of the operator. "I am at the Sverdlovsk station. I believe I am under the surveillance of the KGB. A trainload of their troops is attached to the Trans-Sib. Can you understand me?"

An unintelligible voice came back to his ear, the sound wavering and fading.

"Can you hear me?" he repeated, then felt an anxious tug on his jacket sleeve.

"You must come." It was the train attendant.

Looking up, he saw the train begin to move. He dropped the receiver, leaving it hanging in the booth, grabbed Tania's hand and dashed for the platform. As they reached the train, his breath coming in short gasps, the vapor pouring from his lips, he gripped the handhold of the moving train and, with a mighty effort, lifted himself aboard, pulling the train attendant behind him. They clung to the bottom step as the train picked up speed, moving past the startled faces of the vendors.

When they had caught their breath, they carefully climbed the steps and entered the passage.

"The train never waits," the train attendant said, as they arrived at the entrance of his compartment.

Grivetsky took the woman's hand and squeezed it. "You've been quite efficient. Over and above the call of duty."

"Thank you, sir."

She looked up at him, her cheeks flushed with the exercise and the sudden warmth.

"I might still be in that booth," he said. "You are quite a woman."

His admiration made her blush deeply. "You must rest now," she said gently, "while I make you a nice glass of tea."

"You're very kind," he said, opening the door of the compartment.

Once inside, he removed the revolver from his jacket and placed it under the pillow. Then he began to undress, feeling the ache in his bones as he changed into pajamas. He wondered vaguely if he had not been too precipitous. Falling heavily on the bunk, he slipped beneath the blankets and closed his eyes, his brain numb now, barely able to register thoughts. He was, he knew, on the point of exhaustion and even the opening of the compartment door did not alert him, or cause him to reproach himself for not remembering to throw the latch. Even the cool caress of a woman's hand on his forehead failed to move him as he faded into a stupor of unconsciousness.

12

Mikhail slid from the upper bunk, avoiding the steps, bounding instead in one jump to the floor of the compartment. He was hungry, the kind of gnawing, stomach-talking hunger he had felt only during the happiest moments of his life, the years at the University when he and Kishkin would stay up the entire night studying for exams, continually eating sausages and hard-boiled eggs. He had been locked in a deep sleep, and when he opened his eyes to the gray dawn, he had imagined he was in the University dormitory and had just closed his eyes for a moment between studies.

As he felt the cold seep into his bare feet, his sense of time and place slowly came back to him. He ate some sausage and black bread that he had bought from an old woman at the Sverdlovsk station. Turning, he looked at the outstretched form of his wife. She had hardly stirred since they had moved into the compartment, sitting up only once to drink some *kvas*. It did not strike him as odd that she continued to sleep. The trials of the last few months had simply exhausted her.

He was surprised to see her eyes open.

"You're up, darling! Look." He held out the sausages and bread. "I bought some delicious treats for us."

Vera blinked and smiled. He sat down on the edge of the bunk and kissed her forehead. The heat of her skin startled him. He took her cheeks in his hands.

"You feel feverish," he said.

"It is nothing."

"Nothing? You're burning up."

"I'm so tired, Mikhail," she said, her voice weak.

My God, he thought, she is sick. He hadn't banked on that. Pulling a couple of blankets from his own bunk, he covered her and pulled them up to her chin. She smiled thinly.

"Where are we, Mikhail?"

"Somewhere on the way to Omsk. We stopped at Sverdlovsk near midnight last night."

"How much longer?"

"To Omsk?"

"To Birobidjan."

"Not long."

"Really, Mikhail?"

"Only a few short days." He looked at her thin, childlike face in the whitening light.

"How many exactly?" she said, a note of pleading in her voice.

"Four days," he said. "Four days and then we are free."

"So long!" she sighed.

"Not long at all. Look, you've already slept through two days."

"I haven't been sleeping, Mikhail."

"You haven't?"

"I've been lying here thinking. Just thinking."

"You think too much," he said. "Let me do the thinking for us."

"I'm sorry, Mikhail."

"What are you sorry for?"

"For everything."

He wondered what she meant, felt her head again. It was burning. He was becoming frightened now. Opening the door, he looked into the corridor. The old attendant was busy polishing the brass window protector and a little woman with white hair was just leaving the toilet.

"Is there a doctor on the train?" he asked the attendant, who turned a mute bovine face toward him. The gray-haired woman stopped.

"A doctor," she repeated. The word in Russian was the same as in English.

"My wife is sick," he said in Russian. The little woman poked her head into their compartment and, seeing Vera's flushed face, apparently understood. She felt the girl's head and smiled down at her serenely.

"Poor dear," she said in English, as Mikhail brushed past her with a cold compress and put it on Vera's forehead.

"She needs a doctor," Miss Peterson said in English. Mikhail looked at her blankly. "A doctor," she repeated, going back to her compartment and returning quickly with a Russian English phrase book.

"Yes," Mikhail agreed. He had understood the word. The little woman held up her finger and left the compartment.

"I'm sorry, Mikhail," Vera said.

"Again? About what?"

"I want to go back to Moscow."

"You can't, Vera," he said quickly. "Things were awful in Moscow. They hounded us, persecuted us. Made us feel like lice."

"I can't do it."

"Do what?"

"I don't want to go to Birobidjan." She paused and lifted a hand to his face. "I love you, dearest, but I can't do it. I'm not made for such suffering. I haven't got your constitution."

"Nonsense. You're just feeling unwell."

"I'm not saying that you shouldn't go," she said gently. "Only that I can't. I simply can't do it."

"You want me to go alone?"

"Yes."

"You mean you want to leave me. Forever."

"Yes." Tears slid from under her eyelids and ran down her face.

"I had no idea," he said. Surely she was hallucinating.

"I'm not Jewish, Mikhail," she said. "I know that they do terrible things to Jewish people. I understand all that. But I am not Jewish. I can't bear the suffering of being Jewish. I was not made for it. I haven't got your ability to cope with it."

He got up slowly, went to the washroom and resoaked the cloth in cold water. When he returned, she had managed to bring herself to a sitting position. She waved away the compress.

"You must understand this, Mikhail. I am not going with you."

"We'll talk about it later." He was becoming genuinely panicked by her ravings.

"I will get off at the next station and take the train back to Moscow."

"You're not fit to travel alone."

"I'll be better. You'll see." But even the effort of sitting had tired her and she slipped back into a reclining position.

Mikhail could understand her words, but could not believe she meant them. Why now? All of a sudden, after months and months of bearing with him.

A knock on the compartment door startled him, and he jumped up and opened it.

"The doctor," Miss Peterson said in Russian, pointing to a tall man, his hair uncombed, his eyes still puffy with sleep. He wore slacks and a pajama top.

Without a word, he withdrew a stethoscope from his bag and warmed it in his hand. After a few moments, he thrust a thermometer into her mouth and felt her pulse.

"She seemed all right in Moscow," Mikhail whispered defensively, although inside himself he had already acknowledged that he was to blame. I should have paid more attention to her, he told himself. I was too busy with my own self-pity. Surely, though, now it was her illness talking. They had been through too much together to quit now.

"How long has she been like this?" Dr. Cousins asked.

"I don't know," Mikhail answered. "She has been quietly sleeping."

"Can I see you outside for a moment?" Without waiting for an answer, the doctor opened the compartment door and moved into the passageway. Mikhail followed.

"Is it serious?"

"She has pneumonia," Dr. Cousins said. "I can't tell what kind, specifically. Her temperature is 103. Frankly, I'd recommend hospitalization at the first available opportunity." He reached into his bag and pulled out two vials of pills. "Give her those. This one is an antibiotic. It will not cure her, only help ward off further infection. And be sure that she takes these. They're aspirin to control fever." He looked at his watch. "What's the next station?"

"Omsk. We should arrive there in a few hours."

"Good. See that you make hospitalization arrangements."

"You don't think she can make the trip if she stays in bed?"

"I didn't say that," Dr. Cousins snapped. "Only that I recommend hospitalization. She is rundown, obviously, and apparently not very strong. Why look for trouble?"

"There can be no mistake?"

"In my business there are always mistakes," Dr. Cousins replied. "I can't confirm a diagnosis of pneumonia without an X ray. But believe me, it's a pretty good bet."

The doctor seemed frank and businesslike and Mikhail, although he tried, could find no reason to doubt his words. Mikhail swallowed deeply and looked into Dr. Cousins' eyes, measuring them for understanding.

The doctor stood watching him, with the beginnings of impatience.

"Doctor—" Mikhail began. He sighed. There was a long pause.

"Yes?"

"She has been saying things," Mikhail stammered. "Strange, hysterical things. She wants to leave me." A sob gargled in his throat. He controlled himself. "What I want to know, Doctor"—he hesitated—"is it possible that the illness is making her mind play tricks?"

He watched the doctor search his mind for a proper answer, then interrupted, feeling that more argument was necessary.

"I am a Jew, you see," Mikhail said, feeling the floodgates open. But he could see that the explanation was not enough for the doctor, who seemed confused. "You are an American. I'm sorry. I know it must be strange. But you see we are having a Jewish problem at the moment in Russia. Because of it, I have lost my job. Then I applied for a visa to Israel and Vera lost her job, although she is not Jewish. Are you following me?"

"Somewhat," the doctor said. "But I really don't see, Mr.—?"

"Ginzburg."

"Mr. Ginzburg. Yes, I can understand your dilemma. If you are asking for medical advice, I'd say that you should get her to a hospital as soon as possible. As for the other, I'm not qualified to make much of a judgment, except that it's quite a stupid idea of the Russian Government to persecute anybody." Dr. Cousins turned and started down the passageway.

"And is her illness making her say things that she cannot mean?"

Dr. Cousins stopped, and turned to face Mikhail. "I cannot say for sure."

"But it is possible?" Mikhail persisted.

"In a fevered, weakened condition anything is possible. But there is no proof. I am not a doctor of the mind, Mr. Ginzburg."

Mikhail felt a sinking in his heart, a sudden dizziness.

"You must get some rest yourself," Dr. Cousins said gently, squeezing Mikhail's arm. "I'll stop in later," he said. "And if you need any help in terms of the hospitalization—"

"Thank you, Doctor."

Mikhail watched as the doctor let himself into his own compartment, leaving him alone in the passageway, then he went back inside.

The gray-haired lady had tidied Vera's bed and gone back to her own compartment. Mikhail poured a glassful of water and lifted Vera so she could drink. He put the pills between her lips and urged her to swallow the water. She gagged momentarily, then gulped and looked up at him, her eyes shining. Her lids were heavy, like little hoods.

"You must let me go back to Moscow, Mikhail," she said.

"Whatever you wish, my darling."

"I wish I was stronger, Mikhail."

"I understand."

"You must forgive me."

"Of course, my darling."

He lifted her frail figure from the bunk and held her to him, feeling the tears start, trying with every effort of his will to keep his shoulders steady so that she would not know he was crying.

3

13

Godorov stood in the frigid space between the cars and felt the cold seep into his bones. Cold seemed to ease his pain, perhaps freezing the nerves. He leaned against the frigid metal walls. Immobility always increased his misery and on the train it was compounded unmercifully. The only escape was to continue moving, walking along the passageways, never alighting in one spot for more than a few moments. But the memories of his old agony never stopped, dredged up from his subconscious, perhaps, by the movement of this infernal train. Soon he would be confronting Shmiot, and he would wipe out his debt of pain.

It gave him courage to think in those terms. He knew he had been strong and had let nothing stand in the way of that central idea. There had been false alarms, of course. Many times he had seen a face in the crowd that he was certain was Shmiot's: the shape of the head, the arch of the nose, the wide-set, cruel eyes. Sometimes he would spend days stalking a likely prospect, studying the man, wondering if his memory was playing tricks on him, and for a while, he had begun to see Shmiots everywhere. But he knew that he would have no trouble identifying Shmiot at close quarters. There was a sharp cloying smell about the man that he was sure would be the final confirmation.

The idea of Shmiot, the imagined act of revenge had given Godorov's life a goal. And the sweet cry of pain as he dug his knee into Shmiot's spine and crushed his testicles would be to him like the sound of a thousand angels welcoming him into the Gates of Heaven.

A man and a blonde woman came into the space between the trains where he stood in the frigid air, his back against the metal walls. The man looked at him briefly, then turned his eyes away, holding open the heavy door for the woman. An American, Godorov thought. The woman was tall, well-proportioned, self-assured as Natasha had been.

Natasha, too, had been one of the sustaining pillars of his life, an oasis from the desert of his hate, although his memory of her had faded with the passage of time. Sometimes, when even movement could not relieve the agony of his pain, he would find that empty place in his memory where Natasha lay buried, resummoning the images of her with great care, as if the slightest jolt might break them into a thousand pieces.

Even now, beyond the agony of his pain, he remembered his homecoming evening, the night he returned to Georgia after the war. The whole village seemed to have conspired to leave Natasha and him alone, and they walked along beside the fields that surrounded the village. The arc of the sky was full of stars, which seemed like a million candles lit especially for his triumphant return.

He spread his tunic along the edge of a stack of hay and they lay on it, looking up into the sky. It was the vision of that sky that left the strongest images in his memory and years later, in moments of his greatest pain, he could trace the exact patterns of the constellation frozen in the vast bowl of blackness.

He knew they had made love, but that he could not

relive. He remembered only that somehow Natasha's naked flesh had become luminescent. That was the apogee of his life, the one sweet irrevocable moment of joy, the beginning and the end, all at the same time.

Ten years later there was a second homecoming, and this time he limped through the town from the railroad station with a heavy, broken step. His father had died by then and his mother was ravaged by sickness and worry. She barely recognized him at first, and she had opened the door indifferently, as if to a stranger.

He had stayed around the house for only a day or so. He left as soon as he had caught a glimpse of Natasha, or someone whom he had imagined to be Natasha. She was a dull hulk of a woman in a shabby coat, holding a small, equally dull-looking little boy by the hand as they waited patiently in line in front of the store. Seeing her convinced Godorov that even this the Gulag had taken away from him. Only his hate was left.

The momentary relief from pain that the cold had induced disappeared quickly and each bounce jarred his spine again. He passed through the restaurant car, and waddled his way through the crowd waiting at the entrance. As he walked, he heard a rippling wave of laughter pass through the people in the car. All eyes had turned toward him. Godorov had grown used to ridicule. He had quickly discovered after his injury that his walk made people smile. Some of the men at the Gulag had even gone as far as to quack when he passed. At first he had been quick to take offense, getting in fistfights and putting the new strength in his arms and shoulders to good use. Then one day he twisted a man's ear right off and that won him the permanent respect of his fellow prisoners.

Now, in the restaurant car, he knew instinctively that he was being laughed at and he stopped suddenly to glare into the face of one of the diners, a foreign-looking sandy-haired man with a high-pitched laugh. He shook his head helplessly as he met Godorov's stare, unable to control himself, pointing at something behind Godorov. He turned sharply to find a little boy following him, imitating his walk. The little boy stopped in his tracks as Godorov caught him. For a moment they stared at each other. Then, turning, Godorov moved quickly out the other end of the carriage. He heard the laughter begin to ripple again, and knew that the boy had resumed his imitation.

He pushed through the carriage doors into the hard class, with its peculiar disarray and mixture of smells. Soon the laughter began again. People who stood in the passageway looked at him curiously, unable to contain their amusement; others poked their heads out of their compartments to join the fun. He knew that the boy, exhilarated by the attention, was still following him. Without looking back, he goaded his broken body into greater speed which, he knew, only emphasized the waddle and increased his pain.

Pushing into a crowd watching a chess match, he moved on quickly, hoping to lose the child in the crowd. Looking back, Godorov could see the little boy waddling along, stopping when he stopped, moving when he moved. He passed through other hard-class carriages. Still the boy dogged him and the laughter rang in his ears. Finally he reached the last carriage, only to be confronted by a fierce-looking soldier with a machine gun hitched across his chest. The young soldier looked beyond him at the boy and snickered too. Then Godorov sensed that the train was grinding to a stop. Squinting through a mud-caked window he read the word "Omsk" and saw the ever-present statue of Lenin, polished and glistening in the bright light of the station.

Painfully, he climbed down to the platform and made his way down the length of the station to where the soft-class carriage was standing. He knew the boy was still behind him. People giggled, clucked their tongues and pointed to call the scene to the attention of others. Godorov's irritation was growing now. Who among them, he thought bitterly, could possibly know how deeply abused he felt? But then, his whole life had been the same.

TRANS-SIBERIAN EXPRESS 143

As he walked along the platform, the boy waddling in his wake, his mind began to focus on a plan of revenge. He stopped for a moment and looked back into the face of the boy. Emboldened by the sensation he had created, Vladimir walked right up to him and stopped just a few feet away. Godorov forced a broad smile. The boy returned it, reassured that his little imitation apparently had won the admiration even of its victim.

Godorov turned again and headed into the station, a long, low building. Few people were inside, just the usual malingerers trying to keep warm. They slumped on benches, dozed or read papers, trying hard to look like passengers waiting for a train. They ignored the spectacle of Godorov and his shadow, and he was able to survey the station's interior. He had no fixed idea what he was looking for, only that it had become important to him to find a method of revenge. In the far corner of the station he saw a small anteroom, its door ajar. He headed toward it, followed by Vladimir, who continued to perform even though no one was watching. Godorov paused for a moment to pick up a newspaper lying folded on the floor, then he moved on. The boy followed, intent on his performance.

Once inside the room, Godorov quickly stepped aside, flattening himself against the wall behind the door. The boy followed, a lamb to the slaughter, Godorov told himself. He folded the newspaper again to increase its thickness. Then, before the boy could turn, Godorov ducked out of the room and slammed the door, at the same time inserting the newspaper between the door and the jamb. The pressure created a tight wedge. Vladimir would not be able to open it from the inside.

Godorov went straight back to the platform, where passengers clustered around the carriage entrances. A fat woman in a dirty housecoat, her hair wrapped in paper curlers, stood on the platform beside the soft carriage, searching the faces in the diminishing crowd.

"Vladimir!" she screeched.

The people on the platform stared.

"Vladimir," the woman cried frantically. A uniformed official walked toward her.

Godorov reached for the handhold and painfully hauled his squat body onto the metal steps. At the top he turned to watch the spectacle, chuckling to himself.

"Vladimir," the woman cried again, her hysteria mounting. "Vladimir!"

A fat man pushed past Godorov, shoving him aside rudely and clambering down the steps.

"I can't find him on the train," the man said.

"My God, where is my Vladimir?" the woman cried, her voice shrill. "Vladimir!"

The uniformed official tried to restrain her, but she slapped him sharply in the face and began to run, her heavy breasts jiggling under her housecoat.

"The little brat's probably hiding somewhere on the train," the young train attendant said. She stood behind Godorov on the steps.

"I tell you, he's not on the train," the fat man insisted, his pose of officiousness gone now. He knelt to check the undercarriage of the train, looking like a man at prayer.

"You must get this train moving," another uniformed man said. He had just emerged from the station and, by his bearing and attitude, was obviously in charge.

"She says her little boy is not on board," the first uniformed official explained.

"The schedule must be maintained," the man in charge said with emphasis.

Godorov watched calmly. Now there is something to imitate, he told himself, watching the jiggling flesh of the hysterical woman.

"Vladimir!" she screamed as she ran back and forth like a stuck pig. Her housecoat had become undone, partly revealing her fat and pendulous breasts.

Godorov sensed a crowd forming behind him. He saw a small gray-haired woman, the American and the blonde lady.

"They have lost a boy," the gray-haired woman volunteered.

"How unfortunate," someone said.

"Dennis the Menace," the American said, smiling.

Tania looked toward the front of the train.

"The mother is standing on the tracks in front of the engine and the engineer is furious."

The crowd thickened around the uniformed man in charge. A tall military officer wearing the KGB insignia stalked through the crowd, confronting the man in charge.

"We need your help, Major," the man said. "Could we use some of your men to help find the missing boy?"

"You must assist us, sir," the fat man pleaded, while the officer looked down at him contemptuously. Then he strode toward the rear of the train, signaling as he walked.

Suddenly groups of soldiers materialized, fanning out in all directions along the platform, machine guns banging across their chests as they moved. The train attendant darted into the crowd, then emerged to report back to the passengers huddled on the steps.

"The troops are searching the train and the station," she said.

"Suppose they don't find the boy?" the gray-haired woman asked Godorov softly.

He shrugged. What did it matter? he thought. It was something to enjoy, a rare moment of pleasure, a harbinger of what he might feel with Shmiot. Besides, something had at last bent to his will. The delay might mean a massive disruption in the schedule of trains rolling over the six thousand miles of the Trans-Siberian track. And that was no small achievement. He, Godorov, had forced his will on others.

The troops had just begun to search the soft-class carriages when a shout went up.

"They've got him. They've got him," someone yelled and all eyes turned toward the entrance of the station to see little Vladimir emerge, smiling and obviously enjoying the sudden attention. People began to applaud and the boy's mother stopped her incessant screaming and clutched him, squirming, to her ample body.

"That ends that," the train attendant said, lifting herself back aboard. The crowd hustled into the train, Godorov along with them. He felt the pain in his wracked body sputter and shift as he stretched out on his bunk. He was oddly content. It was an emotion he could barely identify, but once he had, his pain eased and he slipped quietly into a deep sleep.

14

They had lost more than a half-hour, Tania observed as she shined the samovar. The little brat had somehow gotten himself stuck in a room in the Omsk station and had been pounding on the doors, but everyone inside the station had run out to the platform to see what was happening. When a train was late, it reflected badly on all the personnel, including herself. Delays always made her work harder. Up beyond Lake Baikal the stations were few and far between. Maybe the engineer would skip them if he saw no signs of passengers.

She had just begun polishing the handrail below the window when the buzzer sounded from General Grivetsky's compartment. Feeling the beat of her heart accelerate, she lightly tapped on his door. The lock snapped back and the door swung open.

"Yes, sir?" she asked.

The general was wearing a silk robe and red slippers, and his hair, still damp from his bath, was neatly combed. He reminded her so much of Colonel Patushkin, her Colonel Patushkin.

The general let her into the compartment, then resumed his seat, crossing his legs and picking up his cigar. It occurred to Tania that his bunk needed tidying, so she began to smooth the sheets and tuck them tightly around the edges of the mattress.

"When you finish there I'd like some tea," he said, taking a long drag on his cigar and blowing smoke toward the ceiling.

"Of course, sir," she said.

She felt his presence, his closeness, and she was relieved that he had returned to his compartment, to her care.

The morning she had discovered that the general had not slept in his bunk, she had become frightened, wondering if he had left the train. His clothes were still there, but that only increased her anxiety. People who disappeared often left belongings behind.

But then, one of the attendants in the hard section told her about the chess marathon going on in her carriage. From her description of the players, Tania recognized the general, and was elated to know he was safe.

Later that day, seized by a wild, mischievous urge, she let herself into his compartment and snapped the lock shut from the inside. She had sprayed the room earlier, but she could still detect the delicious aroma of his cigar smoke and, closing her eyes, she recalled her first sight of him. She touched the chair and sat down on it herself, imagining that she could still feel his warmth along the back and seat. Then, seeing the garment bags, she unzipped one and removed the crisp uniform, holding it up in front of her, marveling at the polish of the buttons and its wonderfully clean smell. She hung it on a hook and watched it for a few moments, picturing the general dressing himself in it, feeling a surge of pleasure at the image. Then she jumped up suddenly. The chess game might be ending at any moment.

She started to replace the uniform in the garment bag, discovering in the process that the bag was actually inside out. Shaking her head, she reversed the bag, enjoying the idea that she was bringing some domestic order to the general's life. Then she had quietly let herself out of the compartment.

She knew the general's eyes were on her now as she tidied the place, then moved out to the samovar. She dared to imagine that there was a bond between them, forged at Sverdlovsk. She could still feel the strength and warmth of his hand as they had dashed together to reach the train. Moments like that brought closeness, she told herself, and she poured a glass of tea, set some cookies and sugar on a little plate and returned to the compartment.

"Thank you, Tania," the general said, his eyes level with hers as she bent to put the tea beside him on the table.

"If there is anything, anything at all, sir," she paused, "it will be my pleasure."

"Thank you, Tania," the general said again, sipping the hot tea cautiously. She wondered if her words had delivered the message of her feelings. What is he thinking? she wondered. Can he sense what I feel?

In the passageway she continued to polish the window rail, moving in the direction of the samovar. When she had finished, she put the rag in a bucket, mentally calculating that she had finished tidying all compartment interiors except for the Trubetskois' and the Ginzburgs'. She knocked on the door of the Jewish couple's compartment. She heard shuffling about inside and imagined that someone was breathing just beyond the steel door. "Can I help you?" she called.

"Go away," a man's voice said.

She shrugged and obeyed, wondering whether she should ask the doctor about the woman's health. It was, after all, the duty of the train attendant to know what was going on among her passengers. She started toward the doctor's compartment, then hesitated. She knew what was going on inside. It was impossible to hide. Clues were everywhere: the blotches of stiffness on the sheets and blankets, the odd angle at which the mattress lay on the bunk, the familiar odors and, of course, the embarrassed glances, the change in routine. The doctor and the blonde lady had not left their compartment once during the entire second day. They hadn't even ordered tea.

She looked at her wristwatch, set, as always, on Moscow time. They would be in Novosibirsk in two hours. Perhaps that would be the moment to make inquiries of the doctor. She decided to work on the toilet, and began washing out the inside of the bowl. She stopped to light a cigarette. Smoking was against the rules, so she closed the door, leaving it open just a crack so she could keep an eye on the passageway.

After a few minutes she heard the familiar click of a compartment door. Through the tiny opening she could see a flash of flowered material. It paused in her field of vision, rustled, then moved. She pushed the door open a bit more, watching as Mrs. Valentinov stood for a moment in the passageway, hesitating. Suddenly the red-haired man emerged from the compartment next door, silently crept up behind, and grabbed her around the waist, putting a hand over her mouth. In a moment the two disappeared into his compartment.

Tania sucked in her breath, sorry that she had seen anything. Somewhere along the line she might be asked to tell what she had seen and her future, even her life, might depend on the reliability of her information. They might even test her. She noted the time, the exact moment; fixed the train exactly; made note of her own movements. She was even careful to observe the condition of the toilet and the angle at which she had seen the woman. Then she went back to her own compartment, slamming the door loud enough to wake the old crone who lay asleep on her bunk. The old woman's snoring sputtered to a halt. Her eyes flickered open.

"Is it time?" she whispered hoarsely.

"No."

"Is anything wrong?"

"No. It is only seven o'clock."

Then Tania began to run the water, soaping her hands and rubbing them clean. Satisfied that she had established her whereabouts with a witness, she went to the door and peered out cautiously in either direction. The stocky man with the funny walk had pulled out a spring seat again and was staring blankly into the cloudless night. As she returned to the toilet to finish her work, Tania wondered whether Mrs. Valentinov had returned to her compartment, but knew that if she had not, she would not do so as long as the stocky man was still in the passageway.

After finishing up in the toilet, Tania started toward the samovar again, but as she passed the doctor's compartment, he opened the door and looked out in either direction. It had been about an hour since Mrs. Valentinov had disappeared.

"May I help you, Doctor?" she volunteered quickly, sensing that Mrs. Valentinov had not yet returned.

"No, thank you," the doctor said. His hair was tousled, as if he had just awakened. He seemed preoccupied.

"Have you looked in again on Mrs. Ginzburg?"

"Huh?" He seemed confused.

"The woman in the end compartment."

In spite of his preoccupation, Alex's mind turned to what she was saying. She could see his concentration gather.

"You mean they did not get off at Omsk?"

"No."

"That woman needs hospitalization."

"Mr. Ginzburg hasn't been out of his compartment. He has not even let me in to tidy up."

"You think there is some problem?" He ran his fingers through his tousled hair.

"Yes, I do." She hoped this new subject would take his mind off Mrs. Valentinov's whereabouts. The doctor looked tentatively up and down the passageway again. The funny squat man shifted restlessly in the spring seat, a brief frown of pain clouding his face. If only I could get him to move, she thought.

"I suppose I should look in," the doctor said, ducking back into the compartment and emerging again with his medical kit.

Tania led the way down the passage, stopping at the Ginzburg compartment and knocking softly. She knew there would be no answer. Looking at the doctor, she shrugged and knocked again, this time with more force.

"Harder," the doctor said.

She knocked harder.

"Go away," a voice said from inside.

"It's the doctor," Tania said.

"Everything is fine. Please go away."

The doctor moved closer to the door. "Has her fever gone down?" he asked.

"Yes," the voice said.

"Are you sure?"

"Yes."

"I think you had better let me take a look," the doctor said gently.

"Please go away," Ginzburg said, but a note of hesitation had crept into his voice.

"Can you open the compartment from the outside?" the doctor asked.

"I have a master key," Tania replied.

"Really, there is no need," the voice in the compartment pleaded.

"Please, Mr. Ginzburg," the doctor said, "if you value your wife's life, I would suggest you open the door."

There was a long pause. Ginzburg was moving about in the compartment. Finally, the snap lock clicked and the compartment door was opened. The doctor pushed it with his fingers and it gave way at his touch. Tania followed in behind him.

Ginzburg was unshaven and his face looked thinner. His eyes seemed to have sunk into their sockets. He stood aside and, sitting down in the chair, put his face in his hands. Mrs. Ginzburg was lying in the upper bunk, her eyes glazed. The doctor put his hand on her forehead.

"She's burning up," he said. "I told you that she needed hospitalization."

"She wouldn't go," Ginzburg said, removing his hands from his face.

The doctor took his stethoscope from his kit and began to warm it in his hands. Then, undoing the woman's robe, he listened to her chest.

"It is much worse," he said.

"She wouldn't go," the man repeated, distraught.

"That is absurd. You have no choice."

"I thought perhaps in Birobidjan—" he began.

"No," the woman said weakly from the upper bunk, trying to sit up. "I want to go back to Moscow."

"Of course," the doctor said gently. "But first you must get well."

"I must go back to Moscow."

The doctor turned to Ginzburg. "You must make arrangements at the next stop," he told him.

Tania edged backward and opened the compartment door, glancing into the passageway. With a sigh of relief, she saw that it was empty. The funny squat man had disappeared.

"What is the next stop?" the doctor asked.

"There is a small country stop in about an hour," Tania answered. "Then comes Novosibirsk."

"Fine. I'm told they have good medical facilities there. It should not be difficult to make arrangements."

"For Jews everything is difficult," Ginzburg moaned.

"I am not Jewish," the sick woman said with sudden strength.

"You must be still," the doctor said, patting her thin arm.

"I am not Jewish," the woman repeated.

"Please, Vera," Ginzburg pleaded.

"I'm sure it won't be as difficult as you assume," the doctor said.

"How could you know, Doctor?" Ginzburg said, his lips tightening.

"Do I have your word?" the doctor said, putting a hand on the man's shoulder.

Ginzburg lowered his head.

"Do I have your word?" the doctor repeated.

The man nodded. The doctor looked up again at the sick woman. Tears were running down her cheeks.

"You must rest," he said. With that, he snapped the kit shut and left the compartment.

Tania followed him. "Will she die?" she asked.

"She is very bad."

The doctor paused at the door of his compartment. "You have not seen Mrs. Valentinov?"

Tania walked away, pretending not to hear. The doctor lingered a moment longer, then let himself into his compartment.

15

Days and nights had begun to blur in Alex's mind, his rhythm shattered by this remarkable passion. Like Jonah in the whale, he was trapped in an environment totally foreign to his experience. He knew that the train was moving relentlessly forward, over a bouncing ribbon of steel, through the endless taiga, over bridges of concrete and stone and wood, through the blackness of tunnels. He knew there was movement, but he could not feel it. What he felt was an intensity that shattered his sense of time and space, a heat generated within himself and focused, like a single magnified dot of fire, on the body and soul of Anna Petrovna.

In her embrace he had reached the outer bounds of tenderness and passion. He felt the danger, too, but he dismissed it from his thoughts. Hardly anything mattered except the "now" of this consuming wonder. It was not uncommon to feel most alive on the threshold of death, a condition he might be sharing with Dimitrov. It did not matter to him how Anna Petrovna fit into Dimitrov's equation. All that was merely their other lives, and now they had passed through a dark tunnel to the white light of the other side.

"It is beyond my understanding," he admitted as they half-lay, half-sat crosswise across the lower bunk, their bare legs stretched across the carpet.

He looked out the window deep into the taiga, wishing that it would be more endless than it was, that the world would suddenly stop on its axis.

"All my life," he said, feeling the need to plumb his own depth, "all my life, I have considered known quantities. I have used my curiosity, the scientific method, but I have never been up against a mystery like this before. This sudden attraction between us— I can't explain it; I can't even examine it. My old habit of curiosity seems useless, even wrong, in the face of this."

"Never lose your curiosity," Anna Petrovna said drowsily. "It will destroy your work."

"I have been up against mysteries before."

"Oh?"

"But of the blood only. Why, for example, does the white corpuscle suddenly develop odd tendencies? It is an enigma within an enigma."

"If you lose your curiosity, you won't care why the white corpuscle behaves as it does. You will just accept it. And that would be a terrible catastrophe for the future of the human race."

"Who knows if it has a future?"

She put a finger on his lips. "It must have a future."

"That's the historian talking."

"If I believed that there would be no future, why would I bother to study the past?"

"Study the present. There is enough nuclear energy poised on launching pads to destroy the whole world ten times over, and all your history with it."

He felt her stiffen, then shiver.

"Are you cold?" He pulled a blanket up around their shoulders.

"You are frightening me."

"I'm sorry."

She remained silent for a long time. Then she said firmly, "We Russians will never start the holocaust."

"Nor will we Americans."

"I hope not."

"You sound so tentative."

"We did not drop the first bombs."

"You would have if you could."

"Never."

"How can you be so sure?"

It was rushing back at him now, Dimitrov, bigger than life size. They were all helpless in the face of that man's private thirst for power, for immortality.

"We are a family," Anna Petrovna said. "Because of that we have more control over our destiny. Our lives are built on comradeship, on sharing."

"You believe that?"

She turned and kissed him on the neck.

"I tell myself to believe that."

"You're denying your own history."

"I know that."

"Of all the countries in the world, you have spilled more of your own people's blood, have brutalized your own people with such passion that it's a wonder you're still under one national umbrella."

He wondered if he had gone too far. He was no expert on the subject of Russian history. What he knew he had learned more by osmosis than by design. He looked down at her tousled blonde hair, noting that the roots were as blonde as the ends. He pressed his lips to her head. But she was absorbed in her thoughts.

"We are a big country with big excesses. We are no more brutish than the rest of the human race. Surely, as a scientist, you know the lessons of the evolutionary process. Only the strong hold the land, and he who holds the land survives. You're a Siberian." She laughed. "You must understand that. The land is everything. Without the land there is nothing."

He looked down at her again, seeing the tendons of her neck tighten. "You can only see that," she said, "when you live on the edge of extinction."

"Extinction?"

She sat up and looked at him, her eyes flaming above her high cheekbones like smoldering ashes come to life. Smoothing the blankets between them, she pointed a finger and drew imaginary lines.

"There are more than four thousand miles of Chinese border. The day will come when all along this border there will be missiles poised to destroy us. At this moment there are only a few, and their range is small. But soon the range will be unlimited. Now they can probably destroy only parts of Siberia and, perhaps, the western underbelly of the Soviet Union. Soon, very soon, they will be able to destroy all of us. Here, right here, good Dr. Cousins, lies the fate of the world."

She looked at him, eyes still blazing, waiting for a response. He watched her. It was as if she had suddenly changed colors, like a chameleon. Was she an agent of Dimitrov? How much did she know? Then he saw the lines of her face soften, the hard surface of her fanaticism disintegrate, and she was herself again.

He remembered the evening he had sat quietly with Dimitrov, playing chess in a corner of his bedroom. "Even paranoids have enemies," said Dimitrov suddenly, breaking half an hour of silence.

"What?" Alex had responded with some confusion. It was, after all, a statement in limbo.

"I must be quick," Dimitrov said. Clearly his thoughts were not pleasant ones. Then, shaking himself like an old dog, he stood up, a sign that Alex was dismissed. It had, of course, been just one more piece in the puzzle, fitting into place in his mind at the right moment.

Anna Petrovna slumped back against the bunk, her fingers intertwining with his.

"I am much too serious," she admonished herself, nuzzling her lips against his ear, her breath soft, like a warm tropical breeze. He felt his body stir again.

"Apparently it's another national trait."

"What is?"

"This fast swing between joy and depression. My grandfather was a perfect example. Sometimes he would tell a joke, roar with laughter, then almost immediately disintegrate into tears."

"The Russian soul."

"Is that what it is?" he teased.

"In all joy there is sadness."

He let go of her fingers and felt them begin to roam over his body, coming to rest on his penis, which hardened to her touch.

"Now there is mystery," she said.

As if to counterpoint his body's involuntary response, he reached for her nipples, felt their hardness.

"Another mystery," he said, leaning over and biting them gently.

She drew one of his hands down and moved it between her legs. "And still another."

She bent over him, letting the blanket slip to the floor of the compartment. She kissed his chest, her hair brushing lightly against his skin as she nipped at him, moving downward over him languorously. Again, he felt the pressure of time, as if Dimitrov's obsession had suddenly taken possession of him.

Then she was kneeling between his legs, kissing him gently, her lips roaming, her tongue searching out every nerve end of pleasure as his hands played through her hair. Her body quivered beside his thighs as he stroked her, then, feeling her longing, he lifted her, moving her upward as she spread her body to receive him.

They stayed joined for a long moment. His body lay suspended in happiness. Then, with a will beyond his control, he felt his pleasure come.

Later, he could not tell how much later, since he had lost his sense of time, he felt her moving around him. Struggling up from sleep, he heard material rustling, odd movements, breathing, a sudden change of sound. Then he was awake and his eyes were open, but the compartment was empty. He reached out to where Anna Petrovna's body had been wedged against his, feeling the warmth where she had been. She must have slipped out, he thought, stretching his legs. It was dark and he could not see the face of his watch, not that it would have mattered, since it was still running on Moscow time.

Putting his hands behind his head, he looked up at the bottom side of the upper bunk, listening to the rush of wind against the steel and glass of the carriage. They were moving deep into Eastern Siberia now, into the wilderness of his grandfather's memories.

He could even recall the pitch and timbre of his grandfather's voice, deep, resonant, strong even to the very moment of his death, which Alex had witnessed, standing beside the high, pillowed bed. It was a frosty morning in midwinter, and his grandfather had turned his ashen face to the window where two glistening icicles hung from the eaves.

"Étape," he had cried, lifting a gnarled hand and pointing. That had been his last word and, like all the others before it, it was an umbilical cord connected to his past.

Étape! Alex could not remember when he had first heard the word, but it had always epitomized, for him, his grandfather's obsession. Remembering it now, he sprang out of bed and pressed his head against the icy window, peering into the blackness. He knew exactly what he was searching for, could see it in his imagination, feel the horror of it, the degradation and despair.

"Étapes," his grandfather had explained, were way stations which dotted the thousand-mile journey from Omsk to Irkutsk. They were miserable, foul-smelling shelters built by the Czars at intervals of from twenty-five to forty miles. Parties of three to four hundred prisoners of every description—including women and children, political exiles, thieves and murderers, and those like his grandfather simply banished by administrative order—were expected to make the three-month journey by foot from Omsk to Irkutsk. Guarded by forty soldiers, they snaked their way ponderously over the permafrost and through dirt roads cut into the taiga to the transfer prisons of Irkutsk.

Every day they were subjected to unbearable hardships. But worst of all, his grandfather assured him, were the nights spent in the étapes. Men, women and children, hopeless, cold, tired, hungry, would crowd into the long, low, airless building, still reeking with the stink of prisoners who had passed that way before them. His grandfather left out no detail, painting the picture with Brueghel's eye and burning the image on Alex's mind. He could smell the excrement bucket overflowing in a great horrible puddle on the permafrost floor. Since the prisoners were locked into the étape for the night, the bucket could not be emptied or removed. Sometimes his grandfather would gag on the description. Alex heard the low moans of the sick and the maimed. Cries of children urging themselves upon their exhausted mothers who were locked in a dead sleep, too tired to uncover their breasts and give suck. Men and women reaching for each other in the darkness for a moment of escape. The hardened criminals who threw the weaker of the group from the choice sleeping spots along the long low platform.

It was so unbearable that desperate escape attempts were frequent, all doomed to failure since all prisoners were forced to wear leg fetters. His grandfather's scars never completely faded, and Alex had seen them when the body was removed from the bed by the undertaker.

Now, years later, those scars were the proof that it had really happened. He had never put the question to his grandfather, but he had always wondered. Three months along that endless, bleak landscape. As he watched it now from the train window, he felt even more strongly that it was beyond the imagination. His grandfather must have invented it. Such cruelty was not possible.

All his grandfather's stories, taken together, formed the catalogue of an obsession. Alex could understand why it had been necessary for his father to grab the first opportunity to return to Siberia, as a young man in the uniform of a United States Army lieutenant. Alex had found in himself the same compulsion, which had brought him here by chance, actually against his will. Would the chain end with him? he wondered. His own daughter seemed permanently indifferent.

"Not again, Daddy. Not all that stuff about olden days."

It was a sign of a breach in the continuum, he thought. An intensity, passed down through his family's seed until now, had been lost, and he blamed it on Janice, whose view of life was so different from his own. He began to long for Anna Petrovna again. He measured her absence, not in time, but rather in yearning, a hunger growing inside of him.

Putting on his pajama top and slacks, he opened the compartment door and looked out the passageway in either direction. He saw the younger attendant come toward him with a look of consternation, and soon he was standing in the compartment of the sick woman, examining her, gathering his concentration again.

She was much worse, and it annoyed him that he had forgotten to look in on her as he had promised. But then, he had been certain that the Ginzburgs would have had the good sense to leave the train at Omsk. This time he would take no chances. He would see that they got off at Novosibirsk. There was obviously some terrible problem between them, having somehow to do with the husband's Jewishness, but he could not get involved, he told himself, slipping into the discipline of withdrawal that had been his weapon for so many years.

For a moment he stood before the door of his compartment, half hoping that Anna Petrovna might appear at the door. But the compartment was empty, just as he had left it. It seemed as if she had been gone for hours. Perhaps she was in the restaurant carriage, he thought. She was wearing a housecoat, but women were always parading around the train that way.

He set off in the direction of the restaurant carriage, certain that his redheaded shadow would soon spring out from nowhere to take up position behind him. But he did not appear. Alex stood for a minute in the glare of the half-empty restaurant carriage. He did not see Anna Petrovna.

"Is anything wrong, Dr. Cousins?" a voice said. It was Miss Peterson, looking relaxed and benign as she sat, a plate of greasy stew before her, at the first table in the carriage.

"No, nothing," he said quickly, forcing a smile.

"You are welcome to join me."

"Thank you." He hesitated. "Have you seen Mrs. Valentinov?" he asked.

"Who?"

"That tall blonde lady."

"No, I haven't," she said, a brief frown creasing her forehead.

She looked at him and smiled.

"Come join me for a glass of tea. This stew is beyond the possibility of consumption."

"Not right now," he said.

Waving good-bye, he proceeded toward the hard-class carriages, glancing quickly through each open compartment door. In one compartment he saw a heavy woman slipping into a skirt. She looked at him angrily and slammed the door. A crowd was gathered in another compartment and he looked in hopefully. But it was only a chess game. He moved on, feeling an urge to shout Anna Petrovna's name at the top of his lungs. Where could she be? he wondered, opening the next door with some trepidation, since he knew he had already reached the last car.

The heavy face of a Russian soldier confronted him.

"You cannot pass," he said arrogantly.

"Have you seen a tall blonde lady in a flowered housecoat?" he said.

The young soldier looked at him as if he were crazy.

"I'm sorry," Alex said, moving back into the passageway feeling like an idiot.

As he turned, he saw the face of the red-haired man, impassive as ever, but somehow reassuring as it watched him. That one knows, he thought. He knows everything. Alex walked faster, determined to confront him, but the man suddenly moved away with equal speed, disappearing down the passageway.

These people are all crazy, Alex thought, pushing through the crowd that was gathered around the chess players. Up ahead he saw the door between the carriages slide shut. Following quickly, he reached the icy chamber and gripped the metal handle to open the door ahead. He felt the wrench in his shoulder as the door stuck, refused to budge. He pulled hard, with all his strength. It would not move.

Gripping the metal handle with both hands, he wedged one of his feet against the door jamb and tugged. Still the door would not move. He stepped back, pushing his bruised and frozen fingers into the waistline of his pants for warmth. He kicked at the door and hammered on it with his fists.

"Open the damned door," he shouted, knowing that his voice would be lost in the din.

With a great effort, ignoring the cold and pain in his hands, he calmed himself. After all, sooner or later someone would have to pass through the stuck door.

But after a few minutes, the cold proved too much for him. His lips chattered, his shins trembled. The cold seemed to seep into his nerve ends and bone marrow. Finally he yielded to the discomfort and let himself into the carriage he had just left, searching for the attendant while he warmed his frozen hands on the coals of the samovar.

The attendant was nowhere to be seen in the crowded passageway and the group bunched around the chess game were chattering noisily. Farmer, the British diplomat, emerged from the crowd and came toward him.

"He's done it again, old chap. Simply marvelous." He looked down at Alex's hands. "I say, how did you do that?"

"The damned door is locked in the carriage ahead."

"Now there's a mystery, old boy."

The diplomat went out and looked curiously at the face of the door, bending down and feeling below the handle. Then he came back inside. "There's no trip-lock there," he reported. "Only a keyhole."

"The mechanism may have frozen," Alex volunteered, rubbing the blood back into his fingers.

"The best way to cope with this part of the world, old boy, is to suspend your sense of Western logic," Farmer said, puffing delicately on his cigarette, and blowing the smoke upward from a puckered lower lip. His eyes crinkled and the bow tie jumped below his Adam's apple as he talked. He looked a lot like Basil Rathbone, Alex thought, comforted by his easy self-assurance. The man was a calming influence. Alex felt his anxiety diminish. Surely, Anna Petrovna was back in their compartment, perhaps anxious about his own whereabouts.

"The Russians are a mass of contradictions." Farmer was warming up to his subject. "Capable of all sorts of excesses. When they are joyous, it is an endless banquet. When they are angry, it's a tantrum. Everything is an excess. Love. Hate. Suspicion. When it comes to suspicion, they are absolutely beyond comprehension. They think of themselves as a healthy body about to be besieged by a pack of enemy viruses. Don't you think so?"

Is he trying to tell me something? Alex wondered. Or trying to get me to tell him something? Looking up, he saw an attendant coming toward them, a fat, almost slovenly creature with a morbid look about her. He felt his moment of closeness with the diplomat pass.

"The door to the next carriage is stuck," Alex told her, in as neutral a tone as he could manage.

The attendant looked at them both, tight-lipped and contemptuous.

"How do you know?" she asked with a sneer.

"Try it yourself."

She watched them for a moment, then stepped outside and tried the door. Returning, she looked at Alex and shook her head, as if he were a child who had broken it deliberately.

"She is rather annoyed with us," the diplomat said. "She thinks we did it to confound her."

As he spoke they felt the train begin to slow down as they reentered the carriage. Within a few moments it was clanking to a crawl.

"A country stop," the diplomat said. "Probably for less than five minutes." The sour-looking attendant bore down on them, a toolbox swinging in her hand. They followed her into the space between the carriages as the train continued to slow, edging its way through the taiga. Watching over the woman's head, Alex could not make out any breaks in the trees. Then, as if it were an apparition, a dimly lit platform came into view. Huddled there was a single female figure, wrapped in a heavy coat with the collar drawn over her ears and a kerchief on her head wound under her chin. As the train passed, her face was briefly illuminated. She looked cold and lonely. Then Alex's car went by, but he could still look back and see her, an unvanquished figure in the emptiness. She is Siberia, he thought, the image of her imprinted on his mind.

As the train stopped, the woman attendant grabbed her toolbox and swung herself to the ground, opening the outside door to the next carriage and hoisting herself up. Alex and the British diplomat followed.

As Alex hit the ground, his attention was caught by a sudden movement up ahead. A robed figure half-jumped, half-fell from one of the carriage entrances and began moving hesitantly toward the little shack that served as the station. Anna Petrovna, he thought, his heart jumping as he ran toward the faltering figure. He could hear his shoes pounding the hard ground. Faces in the lighted restaurant carriage turned toward him, gaping.

As he ran, he saw another figure leap from the train and begin running toward the robed woman, who had paused, holding fast to a strip of metal fencing. "Anna Petrovna," he cried, but the words were swallowed even as he uttered them. It was not Anna Petrovna. He recognized, instead, the sick woman he had treated on the train.

When he reached her, she had already collapsed in her husband's arms and was gasping for breath.

"I was only gone a moment," Ginzburg cried.

"You had better get her aboard," Alex commanded. She had a raging fever.

The wheels of the train were already turning as he hoisted himself aboard and helped Ginzburg lift the woman into the carriage. Together they laid her gently in the bunk. Alex felt her pulse, a faint beat against his fingers, and put his head against her chest.

"She is leaving us," he said.

"Please, Vera!" Ginzburg cried, pulling her to him, tears streaming down his cheeks. "I can't bear it."

The woman opened her eyes, sunk deep in their sockets, her face ashen as life left her.

"Vera," Ginzburg pleaded, "forgive me. Forgive me." The words seemed an incantation.

"I am not a Jew," the woman gasped, lurching forward, the last tremor of life departing as her head fell back.

The coming of death was a common experience for Alex, but it never failed to stir him. His first impulse was to place the blame, to establish Ginzburg's guilt for this death that might have been avoided. But the man knew his own guilt, and his agony was beyond simple grief. He was moaning now, an incoherent Hebrew prayer.

Alex lifted Vera's limp arm to confirm her death officially, then, in a practiced gesture, he pushed her lids down over the staring eyes. He touched Ginzburg's shoulder, then backed out of the compartment. Tania was waiting in the passageway.

"Mrs. Ginzburg has died," he told her. "What must be done? I don't know how you handle these things here."

"They'll remove the body at Novosibirsk."

"Tough go," the diplomat said. He had also been waiting in the passageway. Then he paused. "Jews?"

"Yes," Alex replied. It seemed too complicated to explain.

"It never ends for them."

"If I'm needed, Tania, let me know," Alex said. "It's best that Mr. Ginzburg be left alone for awhile."

"Of course."

He made his way back to his compartment. It was dark, but he could tell by the faint aroma of the familiar perfume that Anna Petrovna had returned.

16

Zeldovich's impatience had turned to frustration and instead of giving him a lift, the quantities of vodka he had consumed only depressed him more. He sat in the chair of his compartment only a few feet from Dr. Cousins, but still he had not obtained the information that he required. To make matters worse he had to share the compartment with Yashenko, who rarely talked except in the line of duty.

Zeldovich shook his head, rolled a swallow of vodka on his tongue, and cursed his fate, his age, his vulnerable position. Soon I will be fifty, he told himself, feeling the vodka slide down the back of his throat. He had fastened himself to Dimitrov twenty years ago, had lapped at his ass like a groveling dog to prove his loyalty, had groped to the stratosphere of power, always at Dimitrov's beck and call. Self-pity washed over him like a hot wave.

"Can we trust him?" That was Dimitrov's refrain, to which he returned whenever a new face appeared in

the picture. "Can we trust him?" It was Zeldovich's
job to find out—to make the judgment, and to be right.
So far he always had been, and he had built his little
empire, a KGB within the KGB, on the corpses of a
thousand careers. He was the most feared man in the
Soviet bureaucracy. Dimitrov had never called him anything but Zeldovich, as if he had no Christian name,
no personality of his own. Fyodor Petrovich, you
bloody bastard—that's also my name, he had wanted
to scream. How he hated that man to whom he owed
everything!

"Can we trust him, Zeldovich?"

"No."

"Then dump him somewhere."

"Of course."

The rivers flowed with the blood they had shed,
and now the bastard was going to abandon him to the
vultures who would pick his carcass and leave his
bones in the desert. He had watched Dimitrov's energy
wane, the once ruddy face turn pale, the strong, well-
fleshed frame begin to wither.

It was Zeldovich who had arranged for the tests,
confounding the doctors and clinicians so that they
could never trace the true identity of the patient.

"Whoever has this disease is a cooked goose," one
of the doctors had told him, not daring to inquire about
the patient's identity, not even daring to think the unthinkable. And then this Kuznetsov had turned up and,
for the first time in twenty years, Dimitrov had kept
his own counsel. Doesn't he trust *me* anymore? Zeldovich wondered, jealous and uncertain. But whatever
the doctor had done, whatever magic potion he had
poured into Dimitrov's bloodstream, it had done the
trick. The eyes glistened again with their old fire. The
color rose in the cheeks.

The question that ate at Zeldovich, like acid in his
entrails, was: For how long? How much time did
Kuznetsov's magic potion provide for General Secretary Dimitrov? He had tried to pry the answer out of
the doctor, but with no success. And that was only

the first question. As Zeldovich knew, all questions were open-ended, leading only to other questions. That had been the prime discipline of the KGB, drummed into his brain when he was a young agent. Answers lead only to other questions. Other questions lead only to more answers and other questions. And there was this mysterious matter with Grivetsky, mysterious only because it had been made a mystery. He could easily surmise Grivetsky's mission. But why had Dimitrov kept the confidence from him?

In one way, all the questions were the same. At their core was fear, blind, raging fear. Dimitrov had begun it. He had taunted Zeldovich with the possibility.

"What will become of you, Zeldovich, if I were to check out?"

"Check out?"

"Croak."

"God knows," he had replied, the possibility beginning to reveal itself in Dimitrov's glazed look.

"God knows? Zeldovich, we buried Him long ago."

"I hadn't thought about it."

"Take a gun to your head, Zeldovich," Dimitrov had said, watching him, as if he were jealous of his health. "They will tear you apart like an overcooked chicken."

"Well then, you had best not check out."

Dimitrov had nodded. "I am not over yet."

But Zeldovich had developed strategies for survival before. He had an instinct for it, and he would find a way to survive after the old man's death. He had already toyed with a thousand different ways. When he had first pieced together the nature of Dimitrov's illness, he had pondered the idea of killing him. It would be quite simple, a vial of poison dumped into his soup, a little change in his medicine dosage. The problem was deciding in advance who would be the winners in the contest for succession. Then he would simply confront them and put his plans on the table.

But whom could he trust? And, besides, as Dimitrov's killer he would be a pariah. Even if his faction won out, they would eliminate him as quickly as the other side would. He needed something far more subtle, a scheme that would leave him straddling all camps, a centipede with one foot in every territory.

In trying to assemble the pieces floating in his head, he had decided that, like Dimitrov, he was running a race against time and he could hear the pendulum banging on the sides of his brain. He sensed that the most important starting point for his own campaign of survival was to know exactly how long Dimitrov would live, a timetable locked in the mind of the American doctor. Such knowledge was a golden nugget, valuable enough, perhaps, to buy back his own life.

And then there was Grivetsky. The general had come to the dacha more often lately, always arriving under the tightest security. Zeldovich had begun to wonder if Bulgakov knew about these visits. He dared not ask Dimitrov, but he filed the information for future use.

The reason for these meetings with Grivetsky was perfectly transparent, of course, at least to Zeldovich.

"Do they think I will actually negotiate with the Chinks?" Dimitrov had said to Zeldovich more than once. "What fools!" Zeldovich himself had no such illusion, but he knew that the other members of the Politburo, as well as Bulgakov, believed it.

"I will make a Chinese stew, before that moment ever comes."

No, Grivetsky's mission was plain. But knowing that secret was useless until he also knew the timetable. He had only one-half the puzzle. When he knew what the American doctor knew, he could present both halves of the puzzle in a neat package to Bulgakov and somehow receive amnesty in return.

"You must arrange for the doctor's return to America," Dimitrov had ordered. He had not even looked up from his desk, although Zeldovich had sensed a hesitation. "By train."

"Train?" Zeldovich was alert.

"To the East," Dimitrov had continued.

"The East?"

"The Trans-Siberian," Dimitrov had said, looking up at last. "It is my gift to him."

"That trip, a gift? I see." The doctor was, after all, of Siberian extraction. "He has done wonders for you, Comrade."

Dimitrov ignored the remark. He knows I am probing, Zeldovich thought.

"I want him protected throughout the journey."

"Of course."

"Which means you must go with him."

"Me?"

"I can trust no one else," Dimitrov said, his eyes boring into Zeldovich. "And he must not know you are there." Zeldovich sensed that the Secretary wished to say more, but hesitated. "And you must find a way to restrict his communications."

So he is suspected of knowing something, Zeldovich thought.

"Grivetsky"—Dimitrov cleared his throat—"General Grivetsky will also be on board."

Zeldovich understood instantly.

"The doctor will journey to Nakhodka and take the boat to Japan."

"And then?" Zeldovich felt his tension increase. Dimitrov clenched his fists, a sure sign of uncertainty.

"It is a dangerous journey. The crossing is rough. Many a passenger has fallen overboard."

Zeldovich said nothing, afraid he woud betray his agitation.

"But you must stay in touch," Dimitrov said, with an air of finality. "I may need his medical advice."

Another warning bell went off inside Zeldovich's head. Dimitrov is still uncertain about his health.

"And Zeldovich," Dimitrov called as he walked to the door. He could tell from the voice's urgency that this was not an afterthought, more an underlining of what had, up to now, been unspoken.

"Protect him well," Dimitrov said haltingly, wanting to be understood, but afraid to articulate his meaning plainly.

"Yes, of course," Zeldovich said. "He holds important knowledge."

That was, of course, the unspoken thought. Would Dimitrov see it as a probe?

"Yes." Dimitrov nodded. "I imagine his knowledge would be in great demand."

"I understand," Zeldovich said, turning to go. But Dimitrov held him. "Do not try to understand too much," he said.

It was, of course, a warning.

It came to him. The doctor possessed two bits of knowledge! The China strike as well as the parameters of Dimitrov's life on earth.

How long did Dimitrov have to live? That was the key to Zeldovich's own survival. How could one pry this knowledge out of the doctor's head during a seven-day journey? There were hundreds of ways to unlock information from the human brain. Some were blatantly mechanical—physical or psychological torture, the use of sophisticated truth-inducing drugs, all impossible under the present circumstances.

Other methods were far more subtle. The exploitation of weakness, emotional hunger, sexual inducements, the temptations of the flesh and spirit. But the doctor had not betrayed much about himself at the dacha, although there was that little episode with the nurse. Zeldovich racked his brains, rattling restlessly through the halls of the dacha, taking long walks along the river.

He had a week to work out the problem. Under any other circumstances, it would have been quite simple. Simply snatch the doctor off the train, shoot him with sodium pentothal, get the information and be done with it. In Stalin's time they would have put electrodes on the doctor's testicles and thrown the switch until he begged to be allowed to talk.

In his room at the dacha, Zeldovich lay on his bed and watched the ceiling swim as he sucked on his nightly vodka bottle and felt his world breaking into little pieces, nightmare images that no amount of alcohol could defend against.

Anna Petrovna Valentinov had emerged as a potential instrument out of his own desperation. He had called Bogach, the Chief of the Guards Directorate of the KGB, whose appointment Zeldovich had made possible.

"It is a rather odd request, Nikolai Andreyivich," Zeldovich had said on the telephone, his tone deliberately tinged with self-effacing humor. "A beautiful, intelligent, sensitive woman. Not one of those floozy types that are used to compromise those who are too weak to discipline themselves. This is a special need. You must ask your people to search carefully and it must, somehow, be kept out of regular channels."

Bogach was businesslike and eager to please. He would try. It is ridiculous, Zeldovich told himself, after he had hung up the telephone, an absurd idea. The American doctor was simply not the type. Nothing in his dossier or in his conduct at the dacha indicated that such an idea was workable. But the incident with the nurse had somehow stuck in Zeldovich's mind, the only bit of revealed information that just might provide the key to the doctor's mind. Women could be formidable interrogators under the right circumstances.

A hundred times he had decided to call the whole thing off. It was sheer nonsense, exposing himself to consequences perhaps worse than anything that might happen when Dimitrov died. But the more uncertain he became, the more he pressed Bogach.

"Anything?" he would ask, burning up the phone lines.

"Not yet."

"You must work faster."

"I assure you—"

"Faster."

He could almost hear the whir of the computers as the clerks in the Registry and Archives division plumbed their categories, the massive lists of Soviet citizens who had enlisted in the KGB's work, some for money, some for patriotism, some for adventure. And then the call from Bogach came.

He had come up with a single name—Anna Petrovna Valentinov. She met the requirements, except for one point: she had not worked for the KGB for ten years. She was at this moment in Moscow, at a seminar of history professors, and had made arrangements to return to her home in Irkutsk via the Trans-Siberian. She was staying at the faculty building at Moscow University. Zeldovich, who refused ever to write anything down, memorized her name and address.

"She is marvelous-looking," Bogach had crowed into the telephone, "with quite an impressive list of academic honors."

"And what has she done for us?"

"Surreptitious interrogation. Her file indicates that she was quite efficient, especially in the intellectual community."

At first Mrs. Valentinov had been adamant in her refusal.

Bogach had arranged the meeting in her room at the faculty building, a whitewashed cell furnished with only a bed and a chair. She had refused to be seated, pacing the little space like a caged tigress. She was full-bodied, supple, intense, with an intelligence as striking as her appearance. In her presence, Zeldovich had felt bumbling and clumsy, more like a supplicant than the powerful KGB agent whose name could strike fear in the hearts of the nation's most important leaders.

"I've done my share," she insisted, not intimidated, as if she sensed her superiority over him.

"This is a special assignment," Zeldovich said.

He was not good with women. The only way he could dominate them was by paying for the privilege.

"It's much different with me now. I can't pretend as well as I did then. Believe me, I know myself. When I was younger, I had more confidence in my own physical impression. I was vain enough about my looks to think I could do anything. Really, I don't believe I can do the job."

"Is that the only reason?" he had asked, hoping that his words would hint at further intimidation.

"Really," she said, stopping her pacing, "it won't work. It has nothing to do with ideology, or lack of commitment to Marx and Lenin and to the society which we have evolved for ourselves. No. I refuse to be defensive. It's just that I'm no longer able to carry out the charade, whatever the circumstances."

She was the perfect agent, the perfect mixture of the soft and the hard, provocative yet subtle. He wanted her for the job, and made the decision to tell her more than he had planned, in order to persuade her.

"It is a question of the Chinese."

"The Chinese?"

He had aroused her curiosity. She was, after all, from Irkutsk, where the Chinese horde was a living presence. Confrontations with the Chinese were not taken lightly in Irkutsk. He knew he had stoked the ashes of her fear.

"If it meant the possible destruction of your city, of the whole of Eastern Siberia—"

He was embroidering now.

"I don't understand."

"If it meant the obliteration of all the humanity in that part of the world—"

Was he carrying it too far? She had stopped her pacing, was suddenly looking pale.

"What are you trying to say?"

"I must have your complete confidence, your total commitment to secrecy."

"Now really, Comrade. How else would I answer a KGB agent?"

"This is beyond the KGB."

"You are talking in circles."

"I have reason to believe that Comrade Dimitrov will within a short time provoke an armed confrontation with China."

"You mean we will start it."

"Either that or we will provoke them to fire the first missile."

"My God! That's madness." She lit a cigarette and pushed the smoke out of both nostrils.

"Dimitrov is dying. It will be his final stroke, the last effort to unite all comrades under the Soviet umbrella."

"And are you sure he's dying?"

"He has leukemia."

"That is terminal."

"If it were only that simple. It seems that an American doctor has treated him successfully with chemotherapy. We don't know how long he has to live."

"You realize that this sounds like a fairy tale."

"I told you it was important."

"What am I supposed to do?" She laughed, a high, nervous twitter.

I am reaching her, he thought.

"We must find a way to stop it."

"You want me to assassinate the General Secretary?" she said sarcastically.

"You'd better curb your tongue," he said severely, almost as a reflex. He watched her, saw the brief spark of fear flicker, then recede.

"Think of your children, your family. Everything we have strived for."

"But we are far more powerful than the Chinese."

"We would, of course, win, if that is the correct definition of emerging from a conflict with thousands of square miles in total desolation, perhaps uninhabitable for years."

"Siberia?" she asked, her eyes glistening.

"Siberia has always been expendable to the Russians. It is, in their minds, the dump for their garbage."

"The bastards," she hissed. He was sure he was reaching her now. She lifted her blue eyes to his face. "What can I do?" she asked with determination.

It was the one moment of elation that Zeldovich had experienced since the onset of Dimitrov's illness.

Later, in the car returning to the dacha, he felt gloomy again. It may not work, he thought. If it did, what would be the next step? Whatever happened, she would have to be eliminated, he told himself without pity. What did one more matter?

Now they were all on the train, an interminable journey into timelessness. He had not shaved, had barely touched the fatty sausages and dark bread that Yashenko had provided, and felt only a growing anxiety as he watched the boring landscape pass monotonously before him. Keeping out of Kuznetsov's sight was not as simple as he had expected, and he was constantly confined to his compartment, where Yashenko was driving him crazy with his blank fawning stare and long stretches of silence. He thought of Grivetsky. Keeping an eye on him was fraught with potential danger. There was a tacit understanding among the top rank of the military and KGB that precluded the possibility of overt surveillance. Of course, they all knew it was an illusion, a game of mirrors, since they all watched each other in any case.

He wondered if he, too, was being watched. Dimitrov was capable of anything now that he had decided to act. What galled him was the nature of the act, so untypical of Dimitrov whose *modus operandi* was never the frontal bold stroke.

Zeldovich was frightened and because the emotion was so new to him, he knew he was acting differently. Even the requisition of an entire train of KGB guard troops provided by Bogach seemed an extension of his own fear.

For a day or two he had amused himself with the electronic surveillance device that Yashenko had attached to the speaker in the doctor's compartment. But the talk about Siberia, the sentimental flabbiness of the conversation only made him more impatient. He had not dared to monitor Grivetsky's compartment. If the general discovered a surveillance device, he would set off a chain reaction that would go right up to Dimitrov and Zeldovich's goose would be cooked. Instead, he had Yashenko keep an eye on Grivetsky and check up on him by questioning the railway personnel aboard the train.

Zeldovich lay on his bunk, occasionally putting on the ear phones, imagining what might be taking place on the other side of the steel plating. Sometimes he napped, but his mind could not sleep for very long. It raced like a mouse on a treadmill, working out scenarios of survival.

Suddenly he sat up, shocked into alertness. The sound link had been broken. There was only one reason why: Anna Petrovna had simply cut him off. He swung out of the bunk and began to pace the compartment. He looked at his watch. They had passed through Omsk, where the delay had occurred, and they were heading toward Novosibirsk.

"Bring Mrs. Valentinov to me at the first opportunity," he had ordered Yashenko.

Yashenko had whisked her into their compartment, grabbing her from behind with a hand over her mouth and an arm holding her in a vise around the waist. He stood, holding her that way in the compartment, waiting for a signal from Zeldovich as she struggled to break free. Zeldovich put a finger to his lips. She stopped squirming, and blinked her eyes in assent. Yashenko released her.

"This was hardly necessary," she said, brushing back her hair, straightening her housecoat and looking contemptuously into Yashenko's dull, obedient face.

"I'm sorry," Zeldovich said.

He signaled for Yashenko to leave, then stood up and held out the vodka bottle. Anna Petrovna nodded and he poured out a tumblerful.

"You must have more trust, Zeldovich," she said, lifting her glass.

"Trust?" he said. "I was merely backing you up."

"Do you think I'm an idiot, Zeldovich?"

"Of course not."

"Emotionally vulnerable? Is that it?"

"It hadn't occurred to me," he said. Until now, he told himself.

It was she who had raised that issue. There was no mistaking the sounds he had heard, before she had cut off the link. But emotion? He had not thought in those terms.

"What have you learned?" Zeldovich asked, deliberately refocusing their conversation.

"He is cautious."

"Of course."

"It is not so simple," she said, after a long pause.

"Do you think he suspects you?"

"Perhaps. He is not a fool."

He felt that she wanted to say more, but had checked herself.

"The question remains," she said. "What happens when we learn the truth? How can we prevent a holocaust?"

He took a deep swallow from the vodka bottle. The holocaust was not his concern. What he cared about was his own survival.

"We must take one step at a time," he said. "We will know better how to proceed when we know how long Dimitrov will be with us."

"And then?"

"Others will need to know."

"And quickly."

"So you see why I am anxious," he said, feeling the edge of his own cunning. "For all we know, there is no time left at all."

"You mustn't get too impatient. There is a delicacy here. We are dealing with a sensitive man. There is, actually, some question whether he will ever tell us what we want to know."

Zeldovich could feel again the irritation in his nerve ends that no quantity of vodka could erase. Perhaps he was being too subtle. Other methods might be far more effective. He took another swallow from the bottle. His eyes roved over the compartment. It was confining, maddening. Like Dimitrov, he craved space, big high-ceilinged rooms, a large scale. This confinement is killing me, he thought.

Anna Petrovna looked out into the darkness. "We

will be in Novosibirsk soon," she said wistfully. "We are heading home."

"It is a godforsaken country," Zeldovich said, shivering lightly. Hearing his own words, sensing her disapproval, he knew he had spoken rashly.

"Forsaken?"

"I mean it is formidable, huge, an enigma." He felt himself reaching for ways to placate her.

"The future is here." She stood up, then moved toward the door. "You will know when I know. And don't send for me again." She opened the door a sliver, paused, then let herself out.

Alone in the compartment, Zeldovich felt the full weight of his depression descend, and he emptied the vodka bottle to the dregs.

17

Tania stood on the bottom step of the train carriage, gloved fingers wrapped tightly around the handhold as the lights of Novosibirsk glowed up ahead. The icy wind against her cheeks felt wonderful, and she waved to the crowd of babushkas who lined the tracks. She felt a great sense of her own importance as she stood there on the moving train, the old women's faces looking up as if in tribute. She was sure they envied her. She was Cleopatra coming down the Nile, and these rows of babushkas were her subjects.

In her free hand she could feel the paper rubles the general had given her. She would have declined this mission for anyone else, just as she had refused countless scores of passengers who asked for similar consideration. It was against the rules, although it was winked at even by the inspectors. But since they no longer sold vodka in the restaurant concession, what was one to do when the craving became oppressive?

For many of the attendants it was regular business. They ducked off the train and went straight to the supplier, usually an ancient crone who bribed the police not to notice her as she stood in the shadows. Some attendants even stocked it in their quarters, stashing bottles in every spare bit of space. Tania found that unthinkable. But she was not against vodka. She always kept a bottle herself, and understood that, for the passengers, there was something about a train ride that seemed to induce drinking. What surprised her was how quickly she had agreed to the general's request. Not the slightest quiver of protestation had occurred to her. It was as if she had been merely waiting for him to ask her for something, anything.

She was happy to do this for the general, but she felt her mission to be an interruption of her efficiency. That made her nervous, for this was no ordinary, routine journey. There was, after all, a dead woman in one compartment, and KGB men in another, on an active mission of surveillance. She had observed the blonde woman being carried bodily into their compartment. And then there was that little brat Vladimir, and the squat fellow who walked like a duck and never seemed to sit still.

It was her duty to observe them all, and she wondered when she herself would be interrogated. As always, she was fully prepared. Suddenly she remembered one of her duties. The Jew, Ginzburg, had to get off at the next stop with the body of his wife. The general's mission had driven the thought out of her head.

Reentering the carriage, she knocked at the door of Ginzburg's compartment, and the grief-stricken face of Ginzburg appeared, his skin ashen, his eyes puffed and bloodshot.

"We will be in Novosibirsk in a few minutes."

He nodded. She looked beyond him into the compartment, hesitating, unwilling to enter. She imagined that the dead woman had already begun to smell and made a mental note to disinfect the compartment as soon as possible. The very idea of death was offensive, the epitome of uncleanliness.

"I've asked the night attendant to help you," she

whispered, as if the sound of her voice might provoke a resurrection. Then she backed away and returned to the steps of the carriage.

The platform filled with people as the vendors crowded toward the edge of the train, hawking their wares. Searching the shadows in the rear of the platform Tania saw an old woman, huddled in a huge coat, her unruly gray hair wrapped in a large babushka. Beside her was a pushcart, covered with canvas.

Soldiers in the rear train jumped off, their guns slung over their tunics as they crowded around the women, some of them flirting with the few pretty girls among the peddlers. Without looking around, Tania moved toward the old woman. Pulling off her glove, she put up three fingers and counted out the correct number of rubles. Out of the boxes in the pushcart came three bottles of vodka, which Tania quickly tucked under her coat. As she turned to depart, she was blocked by the big red-haired man, who stared impassively at her for a moment, then motioned to the old woman. Tania felt suddenly unnerved. Her knees began to shake as she ran toward the train without looking back.

On the edge of hysteria, she hurried down the passageway and tapped frantically on the general's door.

"You're as white as a sheet," Grivetsky said, taking the bottles and lining them up on the table.

She felt perspiration begin to pour from her armpits as she struggled to keep herself from trembling. "I'm sorry, sir."

"Sorry?"

"He saw me," she said, blurting the words out. Surely she could trust the general. He stood in the center of the compartment watching her, his handsome face showing concern. Being with him calmed her. She felt suddenly under his protection.

"Who saw you?"

"KGB," she said, in control again. "The red-haired man. He must have followed me."

"Did he say anything?"

"He didn't have to. He just looked at me. I know he will report me."

"I doubt that."

"I know them," Tania said. "They can make it hot for you."

"It's me they're watching," the general said, smashing a fist into his hand. "This train is infested with them."

"You?" She had assumed they were watching the American doctor and the blonde woman. It was very confusing.

The general opened one of the vodka bottles and poured her a tumblerful.

"This will make you feel better," he said, pouring out a glass for himself.

She drank slowly, two hands wrapped around the tumbler, feeling the heat of the liquid in her throat and chest.

She looked into the general's face. It was strong, kind, manly.

"Why are they watching you?" she asked, feeling the closeness grow between them.

"They cannot bear not knowing," he mumbled.

"I don't understand."

"They must know everything," the general said.

The train began to move and Tania felt her fear and anxiety slip away. A real enemy could only exist outside the world of the train. She looked at the general, the reflection of his profile etched in the window as the train moved out of the light. She felt suffused with sensations and mysterious yearnings. The general was watching her, just as Colonel Patushkin had. His eyebrows met above the bridge of his nose, his forehead was wrinkled with thought.

"We must find a way to outfox them," he said, putting a hand on the sleeve of her coat.

She wanted to place her own hand on his, to touch him. But he seemed too formidable.

"I will do anything," she said. Anything, she repeated to herself, remembering Patushkin and the agony of her disappointment. In spite of everything, she told herself, it was the finest moment of her life, never duplicated.

"You must tell me everything you see, everything you hear. There is more to this than meets the eye. This is a massive operation of either surveillance or, perhaps, interdiction."

"Interdiction?" She stumbled over the word.

"They are trying to prevent something."

"Prevent what?"

"Me."

She nodded knowingly, remembering his fine uniform, the glistening symbols of rank, the delicious smell of the crisp fabric. He had drawn the chalk line and she had crossed over to his side, irrevocably.

"Do you understand?" he asked loudly. Then he softened, and began to pour more vodka into her tumbler, which she hastily set down.

"I must be alert," she said sincerely, her sense of mission profound.

He nodded and sat in the chair again, folding his hands, a brooding grayness descending over his face. She stepped backward, out of the compartment. Except for the old attendant, the passageway was empty.

"You must tell me everything that happens tonight," Tania barked, beginning to unbutton her coat. The old woman nodded, but there was something about her manner that made Tania suspicious. That one is up to something, she thought. Perhaps she has been assigned to watch me.

"What is it?" she snapped. Long ago she had learned that these people responded only to intimidation. The old woman stopped her vacuuming and, with a wag of her head, pointed to the end of the passageway.

"What?"

"The Jew," she said, avoiding Tania's eyes. "He is still there."

"How could he be?"

"He would not leave."

"And the body of the woman?"

"Still there."

"A dead woman!"

"He would not leave."

"You should have reported it."

"I wanted to. Believe me, I wanted to. But I could not find you."

"You should have told the station master."

"By the time I realized it, it was too late."

"Katrina Ivanov!" Tania barked, hands on hips.

The old crone was trembling now. She looked down at her fingers and would not raise her eyes.

"Well," Tania urged.

"He gave me twenty-five rubles." The woman looked up. "Before I could think, he had thrust them into my hand. 'Here, old woman,' he said. Just like that. 'Here, old woman, take twenty-five rubles. We will keep her here until Birobidjan.' It had all happened so fast. I was frightened. Who knows what these Jews will do? He frightened me."

"Stupid hag," Tania cried, walking to Ginzburg's compartment, feeling the full authority of her railway service. She rapped sharply on the metal door with her knuckles.

"Go away," Ginzburg's voice whined from within.

"Open this door immediately." Tania could feel the old woman's eyes on her. The woman was goading her to great heights of indignation.

"Go away," Ginzburg said.

"Open this door," she cried, rapping more sharply now, persistent and loud, the sound reverberating in the passageway. A door opened nearby. It was the fat Trubetskoi, rubbing his pouchy eyes.

"Stop this racket," he cried. "We are sleeping."

Tania lifted her hand to knock again, then checked her swing in midair. Another door had opened down the corridor, and the red-haired KGB man was watching them now.

"Sorry, sir," she said to the fat man, who yawned, scratched his belly, and walked back into his compartment, slamming the door behind him.

Tania picked up the vacuum cleaner the crone had been using and began to push it across the carpet. The KGB man continued to watch her. She could feel his dull eyes on her. But she found her courage in the pact with the general. It is us against them, she told herself over and over, as she moved the vacuum nozzle across the carpet. She cursed the stupidity of the old woman. There was no sense creating another incident. She herself had failed on two counts—purchasing illegal vodka, and grossly neglecting the disposition of the dead body.

After a while, the red-haired man disappeared into his compartment. When he had gone, Tania turned on the old woman. She could not contain her malevolence.

"That dead woman in there," she said, waving a finger in front of the hag's petrified face. "That dead woman in there," she repeated. "She will give you the evil eye."

The woman's stifled scream hung in the air as Tania walked toward her quarters.

18

The cold seeped through the layer of carpeting on the compartment floor, chilling the bottom of his feet. A gray light revealed the outline of objects as he searched through little piles of cast-off clothing for his wristwatch. He vaguely remembered shoving it into the pocket of his trousers.

He had managed to slip out of bed without awakening Anna Petrovna. The size of the bunk had become a joke between them, and they laughed at the idea that they slept, talked and copulated in a space barely fit for one undersized human.

He found his wristwatch. It was 3 A.M., Moscow time, but he was ravenous. He tiptoed to where his overcoat was hanging, put it on over his naked body and slumped in the chair, curling his feet underneath him for warmth. Outside, the gray light brightened, picking out shimmering icicles that hung from the white birches. Sunrise was not far away.

He looked at the long strands of blond hair that lay jumbled on the pillow. He reached out and touched them, careful to keep his hand light. He sighed, feeling the weight of time. One more day and one more night, he calculated, and then Irkutsk.

"I'll get off with you at Irkutsk," he had pleaded.

She had put a finger on his lips to silence him, and he had brushed it away, holding it in his fist.

"What harm would it be?" He felt his own foolishness.

"It wouldn't be the same," she said, after a long pause.

"Nothing will ever be the same," he said. "My life has taken on a whole new dimension."

He wanted to probe, to force her to admit that she felt the same. But he could not bring himself to press her, afraid that the truth would be other than he would wish. How will it be after Irkutsk? he wondered, looking about the compartment, imagining how it would be when she was gone for good.

Already, his other life—Janice, his daughter, his work, the bland suburban life of Washington—seemed pale and insipid. In twenty years, he and Janice had not experienced what Anna Petrovna and he had found in just a few days. How can I go back, he thought, even if they let me?

He remembered the terror he had felt, searching for Anna Petrovna. Once he had imagined that she had simply fallen off the train, doomed forever to roam the frozen paths of the taiga like some of the escaped prisoners his grandfather had told him about. He had pictured Anna Petrovna as one of the spring flowers of Siberia, perfectly preserved in ice.

Finding her alive, lying on the lower bunk in the darkness, he had wrapped her in his arms.

"I looked everywhere," he had said, holding her tightly.

"I took a walk," she said, returning his caresses. "We must have missed each other."

"I was worried."

"That is silly." She reached up and playfully traced his nose with a forefinger.

"You can't imagine what I was thinking."

"Was I kidnaped by a Russian bear?"

"Worse."

"Brutally abused, raped, garrotted and tossed off the train?"

"Given the history of your countrymen, it is quite possible." He leaned over and kissed her deeply on the mouth, grateful that she was safe.

"See how propaganda in your country creates stereotypes."

"The rape part was quite plausible," he said, reaching between her legs with his hand, kissing the breast that had slipped from her opened robe.

"I can't get enough of you," he whispered, lying down beside her. "I can't envision living a single second away from you."

"Please," she responded, then closed his mouth with her own in a long, deep, lingering kiss.

"I love you, Anna Petrovna," he said, pulling away.

"You mustn't say that." But she drew him to her, caressing him, as he unzipped his trousers and kicked them off to the floor.

"Do you love me?" he blurted, his passion rising, the words exploding in the darkness.

She gripped him tighter, drawing his body into hers. Was the fury of her response meant as an answer, he wondered.

"Do you love me?" he asked again, his urgency increasing as he felt her body rise, writhing in the throes of a powerful force within her. He felt his own blood pound as the pleasure surged upward from his legs to the tight focus of his nerve ends. Words lost their meaning, and he accepted her body, joined to his, as the answer he had to have.

Then he lay still in her embrace, her body slack beneath him, her eyes closed, her breath even, her heartbeat caught in the same rhythm as his own. He watched her eyes open languorously, and was surprised to see two giant tears roll down each cheek.

"Are you crying?"

She shook her head. She stirred, insinuated herself away from him and sat up, leaning against the wall of the compartment. He pulled himself up, slumped beside her, and covered them both with a blanket.

"Why are you here?" she asked suddenly, her directness startling.

"On the train?"

"No. In Russia?"

"I was asked." He paused, searching her face, the old caution surfacing, then quickly dissolving. "Must you know?" he asked gently, wanting to tell her, but holding back.

"Yes."

"Why?"

"The perspective is important."

"The historian again."

"It is a habit of mind. Perhaps the circumstances might help explain the result." She looked at him. "Please explain."

"It is official business."

"That explains nothing."

"Confidential business."

"You're teasing me."

"The knowledge has risks."

"Everything has risks. Perhaps the risks are greater if the knowledge remains in the shadows."

He wanted to tell her, felt the need to share everything with her. Perhaps that was part of the mystery of attraction, the hunger to be, not alone, but part of someone else. Yet she was a stranger, at least in a conventional sense, although he believed that he had always known her. It was inconceivable that she would betray him.

"Perhaps I am prying beyond my province," she said softly.

Then he knew he would tell. It is a test of my trueness, he told himself. She was suddenly his whole world; the idea of boundaries between them was unbearable.

"I have been treating Dimitrov."

"Dimitrov? The General Secretary Dimitrov?"

"Yes."

"For what?"

"Leukemia."

"I don't understand. Why you?"

"I was ordered here by the American President. He wants to keep Dimitrov alive. It has been a rather odd assignment, one in which I had little choice."

She seemed puzzled. He hesitated now, the full weight of his knowledge an impossible burden. Could he tell her that, by successfully treating Dimitrov, he had doomed Eastern Siberia, her home?

"And will Dimitrov live?"

"Not forever," he whispered, barely audible.

"For how long?"

He felt himself slipping into his doctor's role again, the old mantle comfortable and reassuring. He cleared his throat.

"It's hard to tell. He is being treated with chemotherapy, and the results have been good. He has responded. But one can never be sure. He lives almost from day to day."

"How long does he have?"

"He could die at any time. Or he could live for five years."

"Well, which is more likely?"

"You sound like him," Alex said, feeling somehow unburdened. "I can't make a prediction. I'm not God." He heard the echo of his own words in the dacha. Any prediction was pure speculation.

She frowned, closed her eyes, became pensive. But the door had been opened. Should he tell her more? he pondered.

"That is the principal difficulty about this whole business. Everybody asks me the same question, as if it were a death watch. Zeldovich—Dimitrov's right-hand man. He was always asking, always obliquely, the same question: How long? How long can Dimitrov live?"

"Perhaps he had good reason," Anna Petrovna whispered.

He brooded over her words, turning them over in his mind. Shall I tell her? Can she help? He wanted to share everything with Anna Petrovna, to smash all the barriers that had been constructed between himself and everything. He watched her, his hand moving over the wonder of her body as he searched for more and more of her. They had no right to take this from him.

"It cannot end," he whispered.

"It will never end in the mind, the memory."

"That's not enough, not now."

"It is sometimes far more potent. Look at you, carrying the memories of your grandfather's Siberia with you. The intensity is there, the flame is still hot."

"That's different. This passion is more complete." He kissed her deeply, feeling the cycle begin again in both of them.

"Our lives are totally different."

"Tributaries of the same river."

"For a scientist you are an impossible romantic."

"Is that what it is?"

"What?"

"This desire to spend every moment with you, to capture you, to surrender to you. For the first time in my life I am a ship without a rudder, drifting in your wind. It is a terrible responsibility."

"I don't want it," she said quickly.

"It's too late."

"Then it's gone too far," she said, stroking him tenderly.

"I'll never let you go, ever." At the same time that he was drifting, he felt his strength, a new power over himself.

"I will get off at Irkutsk and that will be the end of it." Her breath quickened as she kissed his eyes, his nose, his lips, while he smoothed her hair.

"There will never be an end to it."

Then the words had stopped and he felt his life begin again as they embraced.

Sitting now in the gray light, in the circumscribed world of their compartment, he marveled at the energy that had passed between them, the waves of sexuality that had sent them thrashing about the compartment, from upper bunk to lower bunk, in a whole range of classic configurations, as if they had tried to create new ways of reconstructing the primary act of procreation.

Now, as he sat in the chair watching Anna Petrovna sleep, the sun was rising. It was the face of his watch that told him how much the rhythm of his life had changed. By every ordinary measure, his energy should have been spent, his mind clouded with fatigue. But he felt alive as he had never felt alive before, and for the first time he began to share Dimitrov's appreciation of the finiteness of time.

Finally the light broke through the grayness and the sun bathed the compartment's interior. Anna Petrovna turned over onto her stomach, blinking into the sun, squinting and rubbing her eyes.

"Morning?" she asked.

"Theoretically."

"Was I dreaming?"

"If you were, I would have liked to be in it."

"If I were, you would be." She reached out and touched his thigh.

Then she lifted her head and looked out of the window. "I love this," she sighed. The sky had turned deep blue and each white birch seemed etched in the landscape. "It must stay like this forever," she said.

"It's done pretty well for itself up to now."

"It could disappear in a single poof."

He stiffened.

"Damn your Russian sense of guilt," he said cautiously. "Isn't it possible to feel joy without balancing it with gloom? Where do you get the idea the taiga is in danger?"

"It is," she said emphatically.

"From what?" he asked. Were they crossing another Rubicon?

"Splitting atoms."

She knows, he thought. By God, she knows.

"Would you save it if you could?" she asked suddenly.

She watched him, the light shining into her blue eyes, the pupils little pinpoints of fire.

"If Dimitrov were planning to unleash a holocaust, would you destroy him?"

He continued to watch her, unable to respond.

"If you knew in advance that he was going to order the first shot of a nuclear war, and if you had the power to destroy him, would you?"

She is one of them, he thought. It was an instant judgment, but even as he made it, he could not bring himself to believe it. Then guilt nudged at his throat. He had had the power to destroy Dimitrov. Perhaps he still had. But he had not acted. Was it because he lacked the courage? The logic seemed crystal clear— one life exchanged for tens of thousands, perhaps millions.

"Would you, if you knew?" she pressed.

"I am a healer, not a killer," he stammered, his thoughts cloudy.

"You would let millions die?"

The question was delivered with such wide-eyed innocence that he became cautious again. They are trying me, he thought.

"It is beyond my frame of reference," he told her.

"Then you would destroy Dimitrov?"

"I didn't say that." He felt calm again, cerebral, under control.

"If you knew in advance, for sure, that he was to be the instrument for killing millions?"

"I would have to be very sure." It was his place of refuge.

"And if you were?"

"Then I would ponder the alternatives."

"Does that mean you would kill him?"

"I didn't say that."

"If you had known in advance that Truman was

going to deliberately kill millions in Hiroshima and Nagasaki, would you have destroyed him?"

"There the choices were different," he said angrily. "Truman thought that by illustrating the horror of the ultimate weapon he would save tens of millions. He wanted to show the futility of war as an instrument of change."

"And do you think the lesson was learned?"

He almost smiled, delighted at the way she was parrying his attempts at logic.

"Probably not."

"And if you had the power to destroy Hitler in 1938?"

"How could I know what was being contemplated?"

"He had told everyone."

"But how could I be sure?"

She fell silent. He watched her grope for words, her lips trembling.

"I would destroy him," she said. "The possibility would be enough."

"Then you would be God."

"I don't believe in God," she said. Her decision had been made; she was sure of what she said.

"I couldn't," he said with equal finality. He had come to the core of it. Not cowardice, but a respect for life.

"A single life is nothing, including mine. Especially mine," he had added. Alex had thought it mere bravado in the face of death. "You must read your Marx, Kuznetsov."

"I have, but I can't remember the reference."

"It underlies everything he tells us. We are one family with a single objective, the organization of our resources for the cumulative good of the whole family."

"You had better take your pills and go to sleep."

"You are a nonbeliever, Kuznetsov," Dimitrov had said with weary humor.

"Cousins."

"Kuznetsov."

"All right, have it your way."

"It is the only way. The blood is the blood."

Alex watched Anna Petrovna, her skin pink in the brilliant sunlight now filtering through the compartment. "I am not God," he whispered, reasserting his passivity in the face of everything. Besides, he thought, his hand reaching out to touch hers, what do others matter? He would not ask for the source of her knowledge.

19

Like a magnifying glass focusing a single sunbeam to white heat, Godorov's mind focused on the dominant obsession of his journey, the ultimate act of retribution, his impending murder of Shmiot. Planning it offered a counterbalance to his pain, as an act of imagination so compelling in its intensity that it could act as an opiate on his nerves. It suggested that the act itself would remove, by a magic that defied logic, the burden of his physical hardship. He dared not dwell on this thought, although he had begun believing in his heart that even before Shmiot's body grew cold, his own back would miraculously straighten, his legs would quiver with sudden strength and the whole direction of his life would change. The possibility of such a metamorphosis seemed to increase in his mind as the train moved toward Krasnoyarsk.

Platinov had carefully described the station, a wooden shell in which one might still see some of the trappings of Czarist Russia, including a Byzantine cupola and a broken carving of the Imperial crown.

"I watched him for a long time," Platinov had said. "I missed my train. He seemed as lazy as ever, sitting there in the little office drinking tea and twirling his mustaches while others did all the dirty work."

The mustaches were new. Could Platinov be sure? Godorov had prodded, over and over again.

"One could hardly forget Shmiot."

It was confirmation enough and Godorov had had to paste a mustache on the face in his memory. Somehow it contributed to his hatred, warmed his blood. Only that kind of passion could have sustained him on the journey in the bouncing train, where each movement of wheel over rivet created new agonies in his body. The solace that he had derived from locking little Vladimir in the room at Omsk had now dissipated, although it still made him smile to think about it.

In his mind, the little brat symbolized all the meanness of Russian authority, the ridicule that one could suffer at their hands. It was not a child over whom he had scored a victory, but rather the monster of humiliation that had plagued him from the moment he had been sent away from his old life.

The euphoria of his little victory had been tinged with a slight uneasiness, since he had half-expected the boy to accuse him. Godorov was prepared for that —in the face of the boy's brattiness, witnessed by everyone on the train, his accusation would be seen as just another silly tantrum. But the accusation had never come. *He knows it was me,* Godorov told himself. *Why is he silent?*

He imagined that Vladimir's parents had confined him to his compartment. Perhaps the boy had even been beaten. Godorov was fascinated by the idea, imagining over and over how it would feel to perform the deed himself.

Once he had seen the boy's slovenly mother emerge from her compartment, her fat bouncing in tandem with the train as she moved toward the toilet. *Where is the little bastard?* Godorov was tempted to ask.

From time to time he would dart into his compartment and throw himself on his bunk.

At Omsk the gymnast had departed and an old man had joined him, his age somehow affecting his perception and he had insisted on conversing, hardly bothered by Godorov's practiced rudeness. He was the only passenger who had not yet gotten the message that Godorov was not disposed to transient friendships, or even to conversation.

"I am going to see my grandchildren in Irkutsk," the old man had begun, describing each child in detail, then progressing upward through the genealogical tree in an endless soliloquy. No calculated rudeness could shut him off.

Godorov lay on his bunk gathering his concentration, focusing on the details of his act, the old man's drone fading into the din of the train's movement. The sunlight that streamed into the compartment was somehow disconcerting, as if the deed Godorov contemplated required a more somber setting. In his imagination, he had seen snow as a backdrop, great heavy whiteness from which he would emerge with a drop of wet blood—Shmiot's—dripping from his finger, a dab of scarlet on the white starkness.

Most important, though, was making Shmiot feel the same degree of pain and terror that he had felt. It was an impossible dream, he suspected, since he had to compress into less than seventeen minutes—the length of the stopover in Krasnoyarsk—thirty years of pain, the waste of more than half his lifetime. He wondered what Shmiot had done with the last thirty years. It was the first time he had asked himself that question. The first time he had let himself believe that Shmiot had had any mission in life other than escaping Godorov's avenging wrath.

What would these thirty years have been for him, if he had held his temper on that fateful day, if he had simply given up his package without a murmur, as others had done, or if he had never entered the prison train?

Godorov had long ago lost the ability to imagine such a life. Even Natasha and their moment of love could not be summoned up for a hint of what that life might have been like. For that night on the train had also been the death knell of his sexuality. No one, not even the prison doctors, knew this. There was no physiological cause, and at first he had convinced himself that it was only some psychological trauma that would fade in time. But years passed and nothing changed. Besides, soon he was convinced that his injury had left him so repulsive physically that he would never again perform the sexual act.

Once, long after he had faced up to the reality of his predicament, he did attempt to test his sexual response. He was in Moscow, shortly after his release, and it was not difficult to find a partner. Prostitution was officially a crime punishable by imprisonment, but that did not stop prostitutes from openly soliciting on Gorki Street, and he had seen policemen nod knowingly to them as they passed.

It was summer, warm for Moscow, and the streets were never empty even in the middle of the night. Perhaps it was the huge glistening canopy of stars, the full moon, a reminder of his night with Natasha long ago. He had been walking behind the woman, not by design, and had not noticed her until the crowd thinned and her high heels tapped along the sidewalk ahead of him, echoing loudly in the silence of the streets.

It was not uncommon for him to spend the entire summer's night out of doors. Anything was better than the stifling top-floor room which he shared with four other men. That summer he had taken to spending his nights out of doors, usually in a public park or on the grounds of public buildings, or even in cemeteries, where the flat ground sometimes caught the breeze which wafted off the Moscow River. Tonight he was heading for the grounds of Lenin Central Stadium.

The woman turned sharply off Gorkogo onto Yulius Fuchika, past the Czechoslovak Embassy, then turned again toward the Zod. Godorov was only aware that he was consciously following her when she turned again onto Klimaskina and he found himself going in the opposite direction from his destination.

The streets were growing quiet, although people sat in the open windows of the seedy apartments that lined Klimaskina Street. Occasionally a catcall broke the stillness as some drunken man would try to attract the woman's attention. Sometimes she would shout an obscenity back at the harasser, confirming what Godorov had already suspected from the woman's suggestive walk and dress.

He kept his distance, his anxiety growing as he contemplated how he would approach her. On Khodynskaya Street, near the Vogankovskoye cemetery, she slowed down and stopped to light a cigarette, the brief flash of light revealing a heavy face thick with makeup. She puffed deeply, blew out the match and turned suddenly to Godorov who was just a few feet behind her.

"Store's closed," she said, smiling contemptuously. Her indifference gave him courage.

"I have money," he said. He dipped his hands into his pocket and felt his paper rubles. He always carried his money with him, never trusting it to the locker in his room.

"Pussy is tired, gone to sleep," she said, laughing at her own joke.

He pulled out his pile of rubles and flashed it in front of her eyes. In the moonlight he could see her eyes glisten, and he smelled her breath as it mixed with the cigarette smoke. She had been drinking.

"Perhaps I can wake pussy up," she said.

He peeled off ten rubles, making sure she saw the denomination.

"Pussy needs a bigger push," she said, giggling drunkenly.

Godorov felt his palms sweat as he peeled off another ten-ruble note. "The cemetery?" he asked.

"Why not?"

She reached for his arm and moved with him toward the pillars between which stretched a single chain. They ducked under it and passed through, threading past the gravestones on the gravel road, the smell of grass and newly turned earth heavy in the air. They stopped in a little clearing near a freshly prepared grave.

The woman looked into the gaping dark hole. "Getting ready for the stiff," she said. Then she sat down on the grass and looked around her.

Someone had recently put a bouquet of flowers at the foot of a gravestone within her reach. She picked it up and handed it to Godorov.

"Now you can pretend I am your sweetheart," she said, giggling again as she lay back. "My God, I am in heaven," she laughed, folding her hands on her chest. "Come lie down and see heaven."

He dropped down painfully beside her, looking upward, the memory of the night long ago with Natasha vaguely recaptured. He remembered the peace he had felt, his last moment of tenderness.

"The money," the woman said.

He handed her the rubles, moist from his hands. She took them, unfolded the bills, checking the denominations. She refolded them and put them into her brassiere. Then, businesslike, she reached for his pants, unbuttoned the fly and reached for his penis.

He let her, feeling himself heavy and dead, totally lacking in sexual response.

"So you want me to earn my money tonight," she said, bending her head over his soft phallus. He could feel the coolness of her tongue as it mechanically caressed him. He lay back and looked at the sky, feeling only disgust and misery.

"What's going on?" she said.

He looked down at her, saw the saliva shining on her lips and chin. Then she lifted her dress and quickly removed her underpants, spreading her legs.

"Here, play with pussy," she said, lifting his hands and rubbing it between her legs. "Come on, it won't bite."

She bent over him and tried again with her tongue. "I haven't got all night," she said impatiently.

His hand dropped away from her flesh, his fears confirmed, his hate rising as he watched her bobbing head over his groin. Then he lashed out with a clenched fist, feeling its heel strike the side of the woman's head. Without a sound, she rolled over on the grass, a big crumpled doll, her soft belly glistening in the moon's light.

He stood up and looked down at her. He could not tell whether she was still alive, nor did he care. In the distance a voice called, a horn honked, crickets clicked rhythmically. For a brief moment he had forgotten Shmiot, his mission, his need for retribution. He heard the woman sigh, then bent over and gripped her throat with his hands, feeling his strength as he crushed her windpipe.

Then he dragged her over to the open grave and tossed her body in, hearing the soft thud as it struck the earth. Taking a shovel from the pile of fresh dirt, he sprinkled a layer of earth over her, then pushed the shovel back into the dirt.

Even now, twenty years later, the incident was no more than a motion picture in his mind. He sometimes wondered whether her body had ever been found or was simply covered by a casket. Occasionally, he thought of her in connection with Shmiot. He had given the woman a swift death, but Shmiot would not be so lucky.

The train was slowing. Godorov stood up quickly and pressed his face to the window, trying to see ahead of the train. Log cabins dotted the landscape now, with thin straggly plumes of white smoke disappearing into the deep-blue sky. He felt his excitement rise. Soon, he thought, trying to be calm, mentally picturing the station again. The old man babbled on.

The train chugged slowly into the station. On the westbound side was a stretch of wooden platform on which a group of babushkas, swathed in layers of clothing, their noses red with cold, stood staring indifferently at the train. Moving to the space between the carriages, Godorov pulled open the door and watched the station come into view, exactly as Platinov had described it, only shabbier. He jumped to the platform and a stab of pain sliced through his back. In his impatience he had stepped down before the train had stopped moving.

The pain throbbed downward toward his legs, making each step more difficult, but he pressed forward. Groping through the crowd of vendors, he moved into the overheated station. His heartbeat accelerated as he paused to get his bearings, his eye searching for the little office that Platinov had described. He felt a moment of panic when he could not find it, then realized that he was looking on the left instead of on the right. There, indeed, was the train agent's office, the door half-opened, and through it he could see a man in a railway uniform. Moving slowly, he realized that one of his legs was dragging, and the other was barely able to support the full weight of his body.

When he reached the office, sweat began to pour down his back. A wooden nameplate over the door confirmed that he had reached the culmination of his long journey.

"Shmiot" the name read. Godorov's body shook uncontrollably at the sight; his head pounded as the memory of thirty years ago returned in a rush, focusing the full power of his hate. He pushed the door open the rest of the way and stepped into the office, closing the door with a movement of his shoulder.

A gray-haired man with pink cheeks sat behind a desk.

"You are Shmiot?" Godorov asked, his voice tremulous and uncertain. Was this really the cruel visage that was etched in his mind? Behind the mustache, the spectacles, the pink cheeks and gray thinning hair, the man actually looked benign, kindly, hardly the object of a sustained hatred.

"Yes," the man said, his eyes calmly searching Godorov's face. Godorov stood staring at the man, waiting to be recognized. Know me, you bastard, his heart cried.

"Well," the gray-haired man said with disdain, a hint of the old arrogance.

"I am Godorov."

"Yes?" The shoulders shrugged with indifference, the old Shmiot emerging, recognizable.

"You don't remember?" It was the first illusion to explode. How could he possibly remember me? Godorov reasoned, his mind strangely calm and alert. It was dark. I was merely another victim.

"I am Godorov," he repeated, his voice strong now. He felt a charge of strength, savoring his power, goading Shmiot toward the revelation. He could see the man reaching back in time, searching his memory.

"Do I know you?" he said, his curiosity engaged.

"I am an old friend from the days in the Gulag," Godorov said, his face cracking into a smile. Shmiot's body relaxed. He sighed. The word "friend" seemed to give him a sense of security.

"Some days," Shmiot said, smiling. My God, he looks back on them with joy, Godorov thought, the good old days.

"Where did we meet?" Shmiot asked, like an old general searching for a point of reference with a private who had served in his command.

"In the Stolypin."

"When? What year?"

The hatred simmered. Godorov watched as Shmiot stood up and held out his hand. Godorov took it, squeezed, felt the warmth of the flesh. The man walked from behind his desk, still clasping Godorov's hand. His body was fit, lean and strong. Godorov felt the full weight of his hatred return, the rhythmic throb beat in his blood.

As Shmiot stepped forward, Godorov tightened his grip on Shmiot's hand, focused all his strength in one knee and swiftly jammed it into Shmiot's groin. Another throb of pain washed over him, delicious now, as Shmiot fell to his knees, gasping, his hand still clutched in Godorov's. He shook the hand off and let it fall to the ground, stamping on it with his foot, feeling the bones smash and hearing Shmiot's grunt as his glasses fell to the ground.

Shmiot was now on all fours, off balance because his crushed hand could not support him. Godorov came up behind him and groped between his legs, finding the testicles, squeezing with every ounce of strength, then lifting his fist and smashing the heel into the small of Shmiot's back, in the exact spot where his own spine had been broken. Shmiot's body crumpled under the blow, but Godorov continued to strike him, beating out the blows in a businesslike rhythm. As he had dreamed, Godorov felt his pain disappear: a miracle of transference.

Shmiot lay on his stomach, his breath coming in short gasps. Godorov knelt awkwardly and lifted the head by the hair, looking into the gray eyes that pleaded their helplessness.

"Do you remember, Shmiot?"

The eyes closed. A trickle of saliva rolled down Shmiot's chin. Then the eyes opened and the mouth made gurgling sounds. He was unable to talk.

"May you have a long life," Godorov hissed, struggling to his feet, using the desk for support. He looked down at Shmiot's broken body, seeing the uncontrolled tremors in the legs, which indicated that he had shattered the nerves in Shmiot's spine. His own pain had returned.

"Now you will remember," he whispered, moving backward toward the door, savoring each second as he watched Shmiot's eyes roll in their sockets.

Godorov turned finally. The door behind him was open, and staring in, his lips turned upward in a broad knowing smile, was the cherubic face of Vladimir. The boy giggled, then disappeared. By the time Godorov closed the door behind him, the boy was running swiftly through the station toward the train.

Vladimir ran blindly, not watching where he was going. As he reached the metal steps of the train he ran headlong into Tania, scattering the pail of charcoal she was carrying all over the platform. He stopped for a second and looked at her. Then he looked back over his shoulder and, seeing Godorov coming after him, he bolted up the steps and into the train.

20

General Grivetsky had been sitting immobile in the chair for hours. The changes in the landscape and the weather had made no dent on his consciousness. All his energies were applied to considering the essential details of Dimitrov's plan. Dimitrov had revealed nothing, asking only that Grivetsky take command, get his fingers on all the strings of command. But what was to happen next was obvious. From a military point of view, the options were narrow. The essential ingredients were full preparedness, alertness, vigilance.

He reviewed again the first strike capability of the missiles in the arsenal. The Chinese second strike potential was hardly a threat, in terms of either range or power. And he would order the Air Force into a full strategic alert, which meant that more than half the planes in the command would take to the skies as a protective shield against enemy aircraft. He was pleased with the weaponry that the technological people had developed and the factories had produced. Nothing had been spared to achieve this state of readiness and sophistication. The machines had been tested and re-tested, checked and double-checked. No other products made in the Soviet Union got such care.

The only possible malfunction was in the area of human response. There could be no such thing as a totally automated war, he thought sadly. They must still depend on human beings, the most fallible cipher in the equation. Hundreds of mistakes were possible—an error in timing, pressure on a wrong button, an optical illusion, a sudden stroke, a cardiac arrest, psychological paralysis, an emotional blockage. He himself, of course, was fully prepared, mentally and emotionally, to react to the ultimate order.

Grivetsky admitted to feeling a little uneasy about Bulgakov. Dimitrov, it was clear, had chosen to circumvent Bulgakov in the line of command. Grivetsky dared not question why. Private judgments were not his province. The fact was that Dimitrov was the ultimate leader, the power source. The Politburo might number sixteen members, but Dimitrov was the leader. Let them keep their illusions of collective leadership. Dimitrov could charm them, terrorize them. Dimitrov! He was cunning. He had bamboozled them all. Let them quibble over the fine points of leadership. If Dimitrov gave the order, Grivetsky would obey. They would all obey. The only question in his mind, the thing which made him restless, was who had set the KGB to watch him. Were they operating under Dimitrov's orders, acting as insurance of his trustworthiness? That was too insulting. Besides, Dimitrov would not have confided this mission to him if he had not had absolute faith in his loyalty. Or was it Bulgakov? That was the one possibility that could not be reasoned away. Yet Bulgakov would not confess insecurity about one of his generals to the hated KGB, who would relish any hint of Bulgakov's vulnerability. Or was it that the KGB was working on its own? It was quite conceivable. Perhaps they had not been fooled by his ploy of taking the train to throw off any suspicion that a military decision was pending.

Grivetsky picked up the vodka bottle and poured himself a stiff drink, downing it in one long swallow. At least he could count on the solid loyalty of the train attendant, Tania. She had popped in and out of his compartment all day, bringing him tea and cookies. He was vain enough to understand the meaning of her offerings and old enough to be gratified by it. In return, he valued her as he would an English sheepdog that was obedient to a fault.

During every visit Tania would report her observations, growing more and more chatty with each exchange. During the last visit, she had given him a rundown on each of the passengers, laced with her own observations.

"There is another man in the compartment with the red-haired KGB."

"Have you seen him?"

"No. He is always in the washroom when I clean up. They also have electronic equipment and guns."

"Guns?"

"I have yet to see a KGB without guns."

"Of course."

"And the American doctor and the blonde woman have not left their compartment for the entire day. Occasionally the KGB man darts out, walks up and down the corridors and goes back into the compartment."

"And the funny-looking squat man, the cripple?"

"Something very strange has happened. He got off at Krasnoyarsk and barely made it back to the train again. He looked pale and sick when he got on. I saw him walking down the passageway, holding onto the handrail as if each step was a chore. Then he went into his compartment and has not come out since, which is strange, since up till now he was hardly ever in the compartment."

"And the soldiers?"

"Still on the train. They piled out at Krasnoyarsk, a usual, to buy things from the women."

"When will we be in Irkutsk?"

"In the morning. At 7:31 A.M., providing we make up the half hour we lost at Omsk."

"Will the snow slow the train down?"

"Never," she said proudly. "We have beat the snow on this run for more than seventy years." It was the proud railway employee talking. "There will be plenty of workers ahead to clear the tracks."

"It is an extremely efficient operation."

She blushed, taking it as a personal compliment.

"You will wake me before we get to Irkutsk. I must use the telephone again."

Something she had said had triggered his curiosity, set his mind going in a different direction. Why was another KGB man hiding in one of the compartments?

"You say you have never seen that other man?" he asked gently.

"Who?"

"The other KGB man."

"No."

"It is unusual for them to stay out of sight like this?"

"Yes. Normally they are visible. Unless he is a technician using the equipment. But even then one man usually relieves the other. I have never seen one holed up like a squirrel."

"Do you have a passkey to the compartments?"

She hesitated. He smiled at her benignly.

"Yes."

"Could you lend it to me, Tania?"

He watched her flush, her eyes darting uncomfortably around the compartment. His half-conceived plan became clearer as he pressed her. It was a necessary countermeasure, he decided. Sooner or later he would have to force a confrontation and, if the surveillance was inspired by Dimitrov himself, it was better that he knew it right away. If Bulgakov had ordered it, that, too, was better brought into the open. And if it was the KGB acting alone, that should be immediately communicated to both Bulgakov and Dimitrov.

"Would you lend me the key, Tania?" he asked

again. He watched as she twisted and untwisted her fingers.

"I am afraid," she whispered.

"A great deal depends upon my knowing who is behind this," he said, speaking gently, as if she were a child.

She shook her head. "I am afraid," she whispered again, her words barely audible.

He moved toward her. She stepped back, but there was not far to move and her back pressed up against the compartment door. He reached out and caressed her cheek. Her hand went up and covered his, pressing it to her skin. She closed her eyes, and he felt the strength of his power over her.

"You must give me the key."

She opened her eyes, looked into his.

"I am afraid for you."

"For me?"

"They are cruel," she said. "I have seen them—" He placed a finger over her lips.

"You must," he said, drawing her body against his. He felt the outlines of her big body, the press of her heavy breasts, and heard her breath come faster. It was a subterfuge on his part. He felt no stirring for this hog of a woman. He brought his lips close against her ear.

"Later," he said. "Tonight."

She pressed her body harder against his. Should he kiss her? he wondered, detesting the idea. She spared him the necessity.

"I will come," she said with obvious excitement. The skin of her cheeks had grown hot.

"And the key?"

"It is in my quarters."

"Get it now." She pressed herself tightly against him, kissing his cheek. When she was gone, he poured himself a stiff vodka and gulped it down.

He had already relit his cigar when she returned with the key on a metal ring.

"You must be careful," she said, grabbing his hand and lifting it to her lips.

"Yes," he said, not allowing himself to snatch his hand away.

"I will see you tonight," she reminded him.

"You must tell me when he is alone."

"Yes," she said. "But you must promise to be careful."

"I promise," he said quickly, mechanically, like a small child promising to always be good. This is ridiculous, he thought.

When she had let herself out again, he poured himself another stiff drink and looked out the window. Heavy snow rattled against the glass, the crystals clinging on impact and sliding slowly downward. He bent down and slid his suitcase out from under the bunk. Clicking it open, he moved his hand around the inside edge until his fingers touched the smooth leather of a holster. The gun was cold as he removed it and checked the magazine.

21

Alex straightened his tie, feeling Anna Petrovna's eyes on him as she lay in the lower bunk, propped against the pillows, the blankets drawn to her chin. He had shaved, patted cologne on his cheeks and carefully combed his hair. He could not remember when he had taken so much care with his grooming.

"There," he said, turning to face her, reminded of a time long ago when he had primped for the approval of his mother.

"You look lovely," Anna Petrovna said, a touch of wistfulness in her tone.

The words were a caress. His love for her had taken away his fear and, with it, his caution. Otherwise, he might have reacted quite differently to her strange interrogation. As it was, he put Dimitrov out of his mind. She is an innocent, he told himself—not a neutral, merely an innocent—and that was enough for him. If I am to live only two more days, I would spend it with her, just like this.

"Come with me to Nakhodka," he said.

"It is impossible. You're being an adolescent school-boy. I have another life, children, a husband." She paused, turned away from him. "You don't know about me."

"I know enough to love you."

"That's not enough."

"It is for me. I also know that you love me."

"How do you know that?"

"I feel it."

"Sentimentality." She sighed, patted his head, reached for his hand.

"You must control your emotions."

"Why?"

"It is not scientific." She was teasing now, playful.

"You are making a joke of it."

"It is a joke."

He decided then not to think about her leaving, hoping that the train would somehow hurtle endlessly through the snow.

"We will have the best feast the Russian railway can devise. Champagne. Caviar. Extravagant delicacies." She giggled like a young girl, and he wished that he had known her sooner, had grown up with her, had loved her since the moment of her birth. He was jealous of every lost moment. The thought of her conceiving children with another man was unbearable.

"Get dressed," he ordered. "I'm taking my best girl out for dinner."

"You go," she said, a shadow falling across her face. "I'll have to put myself together." She put out her cigarette and watched him for a moment. He imagined that they both felt the same sadness. Tomorrow they would be in Irkutsk.

"I'll meet you in the restaurant car." She lifted her head from the pillows and smiled at her reflection in the window. "I have a lot of work to do before I can be seen in public."

He bent and kissed her forehead.

"You are the most beautiful woman in Siberia."

She pushed him away. "What do you know of Siberia?" she said.

"Only all the lies my grandfather told me."

"Lies?"

"It was all a figment of his imagination. As you are a figment of mine."

With that, he reached for the blankets and yanked them down to the foot of the bunk. He marveled at the whiteness of her skin in the light, the soft, youthful curve of her belly, the thatch of pubic hair, shades darker than the hair on her head. She relaxed under his gaze and stood up.

"You're magnificent," he said with unabashed admiration, feeling the glorious sense of possession.

"And you're crazy."

She reached for her flowered dressing gown, hanging on a hook, and slid gracefully into it.

"You go," she said again. "I'll fix myself as quickly as humanly possible."

He enveloped her in his arms, kissed her face, and buried his lips in her hair. She caressed the back of his neck.

"We'll go later."

"The restaurant will close."

"You're right. I'll get the best table in the house. I'll bribe the maitre d'."

"It's against the rules."

"You Russians and your rules." He kissed her hair again. "Fuck the rules," he said in English."

"What?"

"It's an English obscenity."

"Say it again?"

"Fuck."

"Fuck," she repeated, pausing. "It is beautiful. I must remember it."

He laughed, and started to unbolt the compartment door. "I'm off."

"Yes, go," she said, and pushed him firmly out into the passageway.

*　　*　　*

The restaurant car, glistening with light, was a cozy oasis in the thick blizzard. Alex took a seat at an empty table, directly behind the British diplomat and the Australian.

"Two bottles of your best champagne and double orders of caviar for starters," he told the waitress.

"A celebration, is it?" Farmer said, his bow tie bobbing on his Adam's apple.

"Of sorts. Are you enjoying the journey?"

"It's driving me round the bend," the Australian said. "Never again."

"You should have flown," the diplomat said. They had obviously reached the outer edge of tolerance as roommates. The red-haired man appeared at one end of the car and was watching them carefully.

"Someone said it would be exotic," the Australian said bitterly. "They're full of bull. This is one boring experience."

"It's isolating for anyone who can't speak the language," Farmer said, with exaggerated superiority.

"These Russkys have nothing to say anyway. They're a morbid lot. We should have kicked their asses in when we had the chance."

"He doesn't think much of them," Farmer explained to Alex.

"Can't understand why the British keep an Embassy at Ulan Bator. It's the middle of the end of the world," the Australian said.

"Precisely the reason," the diplomat said. He was getting off the next day, to transfer to Ulan-Ude. "It could very well be the place where the world ends." He looked up quickly to see if anyone else had heard. Then he pointed to his eyes and ears. "We watch and listen. It is like being between the devil and the deep blue sea." He took a deep breath, then leaned toward Alex. "We are trapped there, of course. They know everything. Not a word. Not a letter. Not a telephone call escapes their surveillance." He looked at Alex to see if he understood. Alex nodded. Even if he could have brought himself to trust Farmer, this avenue was obviously closed.

"The Mongols who live out here are in the middle," the diplomat said. "They've survived wars, disease, famines. They're tough, beyond feeling. Even if the whole country becomes one big Gobi desert, they'll be the first to dig themselves out of the ashes."

"Descendants of Genghis Khan," Alex observed.

"They once controlled most of the civilized world," the British diplomat said.

"Yesterday's dishwater," the Australian retorted.

"He has no sense of history," the diplomat said.

"They're nothing more than savages." The Australian threw his spoon into the bowl of borscht. Little red flecks spilled over the tablecloth.

"No more than we are," the diplomat said, looking with disgust at the mess the Australian had made.

Alex listened to their chatter, losing the thread as his mind turned inward. In its way, his life in Washington had been a simplification of himself. His time with Janice and Sonia was merely a rote exercise. His only real life was lived deeply in the mind, and his work consumed him even more because of the emptiness of his other life. And now he had found Anna Petrovna, the perfect balance between the life of the mind and the heart. Just a few days ago he would hardly have understood what the heart meant. It would have been far from any familiar frame of reference. The fantasy of romantic love that blared out in popular songs, movies and books, all that sentimentality that he had detached himself from was suddenly a burning relevancy. And that it should happen in Siberia, on the Trans-Siberian Express, compounded the mysterious joy of it. In the very conception of Anna Petrovna, Alex thought he had acted out the idea his grandfather had planted in his head so many years ago. He had come home.

The Alex Cousins who had stood in Yaroslav station only a few days before had been a different man, detached and indifferent. What had Dimitrov mattered to him, except as an extension of his work? Now Anna

Petrovna had split open his mind as well as his heart and he was beginning to piece together what it all meant.

"If Dimitrov was on the verge of unleashing a holocaust, would you destroy him? Would you save him?"

For Alex, the question had created a new set of possibilities.

Suddenly the waitress plunked two plates down on the table, bringing him back to his surroundings. It was the caviar, surrounded by little piles of neatly trimmed toast. Then she returned with the two bottles of champagne, placing them on the table in a stainless-steel bucket. Instead of ice, the bucket was packed with snow.

"How practical," Alex said.

"As you can see, we have plenty." For the first time, the waitress smiled, showing a flash of gold tooth.

Alex slid his knife into the caviar and spread some on a square of toast. I should have let him die, he thought. Knowing what I know, how could I have possibly let him live?

22

Zeldovich rubbed the bristles on his chin. He had not shaved in five days, nor had he changed his clothes. He had never been a fastidious man, but his mother had impressed on him the importance of changing his underwear and wiping his nose, and to this day he could not feel comfortable unless he changed his underwear daily and carried a clean handkerchief. Cooped up in this compartment on the Trans-Siberian, Zeldovich felt that he was wallowing in slime.

He closed his eyes, felt the lids burn, and listened to the sound of the moving train. He took another deep gulp from the vodka bottle. Watching the wall that separated him from Dr. Cousins and the blonde woman he imagined that he could see them, locked in an obscene embrace. All hope rested in Anna Petrovna's hands, he told himself, convinced that what she would discover would be enough to set things straight. Moments before, Yashenko had stirred, opened the compartment door a sliver and looked into the corridor.

"He is leaving," Yashenko had said, putting on his jacket and slipping out of the compartment with the practiced silence of a big cat in the jungle.

Zeldovich might have dozed. He could not tell. The distinction between wakefulness and sleep had become blurred. Vaguely, as if from a distance, he had heard a clicking sound, but he had neither the will nor the inclination to become alert. There was a burst of light as the door opened, and he opened his eyes to see the silhouette of a big man entering the compartment. Then it was dark again and he squinted into the blackness, hearing the sound of the man's breathing.

The light clicked on and he blinked, unused to the brightness.

"You," he heard the man say. The voice was vaguely familiar. Then he opened his eyes again and saw General Grivetsky, gunmetal glinting in his hand. Zeldovich reached for the vodka bottle, lifting it in a mock toast, and drank slowly.

"Well?" Grivetsky said, holding the barrel of the gun steady a few feet from Zeldovich's face.

"You should have a drink, General. Good for long journeys." He lifted the bottle toward Grivetsky, who struck it with his free hand. It hit the carpeted floor and spilled, rolling to a stop against the foot of the lower bunk.

"Dimitrov?" Grivetsky asked, his eyes flashing with hatred.

Zeldovich began to laugh. The tears came to his eyes and rolled down his cheeks. He felt the barrel of the gun against his forehead, the chill of the metal. He felt no panic. Let him shoot.

"It will make a big mess," Zeldovich warned, laughing again, but starting to fight for concentration.

Grivetsky moved the gun away. "Why?" he asked bluntly.

"Why what?"

"Why this surveillance?"

"Surveillance?" Through the fog of alcohol, Zeldovich could not follow Grivetsky's meaning.

"Drunken bastard," the general hissed. Suddenly Zeldovich understood.

"You think you are being watched?"

The general shifted his weight nervously. "There is no other explanation."

"You think that?"

Grivetsky held the gun steady, but he seemed uncertain, an uncommon posture for the general, Zeldovich thought.

"KGB troops attached to the train. KGB agents crawling all over the place. You." Grivetsky pointed with the gun barrel. "Dimitrov's shadow. Holed up here like a stowaway. Even the most inefficient intelligence analyst could reach only one conclusion."

"It is not Dimitrov," Zeldovich said, looking into the barrel of the gun. He finally realized his danger.

"You expect me to believe that?"

"What does it matter what you believe?" He felt his hands shake and the overwhelming need for a drink. He sensed Grivetsky's anger.

"You must be calm, General," he said. "We are actually two peas from the same pod."

"What is that supposed to mean?"

"That our interests are not in conflict."

"Our interests?"

"We are both pawns in Dimitrov's game." He saw Grivetsky's reaction immediately. The gun barrel was lowered slightly.

"Why do you always talk in riddles?"

"Because we are locked into a riddle." Zeldovich now knew he had the general's attention.

"What riddle?"

"The riddle of Dimitrov's longevity." Grivetsky blinked. "We both need to know just how long Dimitrov will live."

"Is he dying?"

"We are all dying."

"Riddles again."

"Dimitrov may be dying faster." Zeldovich paused. "He has leukemia. Apparently the American doctor has saved him temporarily. The question is: For how long?"

The general sat down, letting the gun rest on his lap.

"You see the effects of such an enigma on yourself."

"What do you mean?" the general shot back. Zeldovich watched his fingers tighten on the gun, but he did not raise it.

"What effect would the death of Dimitrov have on your mission?"

The general looked around the compartment, as if he were seeking some escape hatch. Zeldovich knew he had struck home.

He had never been truly certain about Grivetsky's role until now, trusting the clues that Dimitrov had dropped. During the thunderstorm, Dimitrov had said weakly, "That is Lenin, cursing the infamy of mortality. Vladimir Ilich, ranting up there. He is crying for the lost moments. He had only five years. The lousy cheats. I hear you, Vladimir Ilich. I will not let them take me until the work is done. They will not cheat me as they cheated you. I'll finish it, Vladimir Ilich." Finish what? Zeldovich had wondered. Hints of answers emerged as he watched Grivetsky.

He let the silence hang heavy as Grivetsky's mind groped for some understanding of his predicament. Finally the general stirred.

"Then what is the point of this exercise?"

"The need for knowledge."

"What knowledge?"

Was this supposedly brilliant general obtuse? Zeldovich wondered.

Slowly Grivetsky's puzzled expression cleared, as he began to understand.

"The American doctor?" he asked.

"He is the one. Only he knows what we must know."

"Of course," Grivetsky said, taking a deep breath. "I hadn't realized." He pointed in the direction of the compartment occupied by the doctor and the blonde woman, and raised an eyebrow. Zeldovich shrugged.

"The method is rather primitive, but considering the options, it seems to have the least number of risks."

The general smiled, then put his gun in the belt of his pants.

"And if it doesn't work?"

"I might have to resort to stronger methods."

The general thought it all over.

"And this is strictly your own operation?"

"Totally."

"No one knows?"

"Not even my friends at the KGB who have supplied the troops."

Grivetsky was watching him closely, searching his face. Zeldovich knew what was on his mind, the central mystery, the heart of the enigma. Let him wonder, Zeldovich thought. For the first time since the general had arrived, Zeldovich felt the strength of his position. Bulgakov could not know about Grivetsky's mission. He filed that bit of information in the inner recesses of his mind. It might someday save him.

The tapping on the door roused them both. They looked toward it, the general standing up quickly. Zeldovich put a finger over his lips and pointed to the washroom. Grivetsky stepped inside, leaving the door open a crack. The tapping persisted, urgently. Zeldovich stood up, felt a surge of nausea, and grabbed the upper bunk for support. "Who?" he whispered.

"Comrade Valentinov."

He opened the compartment door and Anna Petrovna moved inside quickly. Impeccably dressed, she looked about her, grimacing at the sloppiness.

"This is a pigsty," she said, sniffing the stale air.

Zeldovich bent down and picked up the overturned bottle.

"You look like you've been enjoying your work,

Comrade," Zeldovich said. Bending down had made
him dizzy again.

Her eyes flashed angrily. "If you are looking for a
definite answer to the central question, forget it. There
is none."

She stood stiffly in the center of the compartment,
waiting for a reaction. Zeldovich said nothing.

"There is only a statistical prognosis," she continued. "He could live anywhere from five minutes to
five years. There is no way of knowing."

"You believe this?"

"Implicitly. I am certain the doctor is telling the
truth."

"Certainty, Comrade Valentinov, is quite concrete.
There is not the slightest doubt in your mind?"

"Not the slightest."

Zeldovich sensed her stubbornness, her determination to be believed. But he was unwilling to accept her
answer. It was not his way to live with uncertainty.
The prospect of five years in limbo was very distressing.

"You realize what this could mean?" He put the
question loudly, so Grivetsky would be sure to hear
him.

The woman frowned, her eyes revealing her confusion.

"It is unthinkable." Anna Petrovna sighed. "Inconceivable."

"I assure you it is quite a real possibility."

"I've been thinking about what you said." Anna
Petrovna lowered her voice as if her words were too
distasteful for her own ears to hear. "No one could
have so little respect for humanity. That is insanity.
Unless you are telling me that Dimitrov is insane. And
if he is insane, he should be removed."

"You've become sentimental over the past few days,"
Zeldovich said with contempt. He distrusted this philo-
sophical softness.

"I assure you—"

"Don't assure," he interrupted. "The information you

have provided is totally inadequate. I must have more definitive parameters, something more positive."

"But there isn't anything more."

"There must be."

"Would you rather I lied?"

He could wish that, yes, he thought. At least then he could calculate a course.

"If this is not stopped in time, it will be on your head." The remark seemed absurd, plumbed from the depths of his youth. But he could tell by the woman's expression that she felt its impact. "We can take stronger measures."

"I don't understand."

"There are other ways to elicit information."

"I absolutely forbid it."

"*You* forbid it."

"You can't extract infomation that doesn't exist," she argued desperately.

Her coolness had disintegrated. I am hitting home, Zeldovich thought maliciously.

"At least we would be sure."

"You would torture him?"

"It is an option."

"It would be useless." She paused. "I tell you there is no information beyond what I have told you." Panic was gripping her now.

"Who can be sure?"

"I am."

The woman was glaring at him. He rubbed the bristles of his beard. His threats were intimidating enough to cause the woman anguish, but he knew that he was helpless. She was telling the truth.

"People must be told," she said, after a pause, her voice stronger now. "Surely if we tell people, they will put a stop to it."

"Tell who?"

"Others." She looked about the compartment like a trapped animal. "The Americans. The Chinese."

"Then they will move first."

"Our own people then. Surely there is someone who will see the madness of it."

"Who?"

"You are taunting me." She paused again, reaching for Zeldovich's arm. "You are KGB. You have people everywhere."

"And what shall we tell them?"

The train jounced over a particularly rough spot on the track. The snow beat against the glass.

"There is one course of action we have not yet considered," she said hesitantly. Zeldovich shrugged. What did it matter? he thought, feeling for the first time his own exhaustion.

"We could tell him the truth."

"The truth?"

"I'll tell him everything. Tell him what you have told me. Tell him why I am here." The train bounced again, and she reached out to the upper bunk for support. "It will be a blow to him," she whispered. "But he is a good man. He will understand. He will tell the American President—"

It is out of control, Zeldovich thought, remembering Grivetsky's presence. He looked toward the window again, powerless to shut off the words.

"This has gone far enough," Grivetsky said. Zeldovich turned, saw Anna Petrovna's face pale under the makeup, the eyes wide with fear above the high cheekbones. She stared at Grivetsky's imposing figure, the gun visible in his belt. She turned finally to Zeldovich, her eyes pleading for some explanation.

"This is General Grivetsky." What else was there to say?

"He has been listening?" she asked, more as a reflex than out of any recognition of what that would mean.

"It is all right," Zeldovich said, surprised at his own gentleness. "He is aware of the situation."

"Whatever happens to Dimitrov," Grivetsky said, addressing himself to Zeldovich, "no one must know of my mission outside the Soviet Union." He was every inch the military man now, secure in his decisiveness. "It is quite obvious that such knowledge can never leave this room."

Zeldovich watched the general's fingers as they touched the gun in his belt.

"I don't understand," Anna Petrovna said. "Does he know?"

"Know?" Zeldovich stalled the answer, not taking his eyes from Grivetsky.

"About what is intended. What Dimitrov is planning."

It was, of course, too late to retrieve his credibility with Grivetsky. Anna Petrovna turned to the general.

"He is planning to launch a nuclear attack on the Chinese," she said, her voice quavering. "Zeldovich said he has gone mad. You must help us."

He watched Grivetsky's finger move closer to the trigger of the gun. All else seemed trivial.

"I must reach Dimitrov," he heard Grivetsky say, seeing the gun barrel glint as the general drew it out of his belt. Anna Petrovna stopped talking. She turned pale and stepped backward, suddenly afraid. Zeldovich felt the paralysis of hesitation. Then he saw the question of his own survival written in the deep lines of Grivetsky's drawn brows. His eyes searched the compartment, falling on the knife that he had used to slice sausages. At the same time he saw Anna Petrovna jump backward, and her shoulder hit a sharp corner of the bunk, making her cry out in surprise. As Grivetsky glanced her way, Zeldovich scooped up the knife and plunged forward. The knife moved in an arc, upward, catching the general in the neck. Zeldovich felt the blade falter, blocked briefly by the sinew; then it moved forward, cutting deeply. The general dropped his gun to the carpet, clutching the spot where the knife had entered. A jet of arterial blood spurted from the wound across the length of the compartment.

Anna Petrovna felt she was watching a film in slow

motion as the general's body sank, the knees buckling, the eyes rolling backward in their sockets, a gasping sound gurgling in his throat. Then the general was on his knees, the blood running in rivulets between his fingers, over the back of his hand, down his sleeve, onto the carpet of the compartment.

Zeldovich watched, fascinated by the sight of someone else expiring. He was conscious of nothing except Grivetsky's fight for breath as his life slowly ebbed. Then suddenly his body crumpled, and he lay dead along the length of the compartment.

It was only then that Zeldovich looked at Anna Petrovna, frozen against the compartment door. He felt in command of himself again, as if Grivetsky's death had somehow given his own life a sense of renewed purpose.

"It had to be," he said, looking down at the body. "He was the instrument."

"Instrument?"

"It was he whom Dimitrov had sent to take over the Red Banner Armies in Chita. It was he who was to carry out Dimitrov's plan for nuclear attack."

He heard her sigh.

"It was horrible," she said.

"Compound it by millions and you will get a sense of what they were up to." His head had cleared, his sense of cunning returned. She was believing him and he was discovering how close he had come to the truth.

"Say nothing," he said. "We have bought only time. Others will come."

"How much time?"

His answer came to him in a flash of insight.

"That depends on what you learn from Dr. Cousins."

She looked at him for a moment, her lips tightening, as she turned and reached for the bolt of the compartment door.

"Say nothing," he repeated. "I will take care of this."

He was already contemplating ways to get rid of Anna Petrovna. He held her at the half-opened door.

"And you cannot get off at Irkutsk," he said.

She watched him for a moment, her eyes narrowing. Then she turned and let herself quickly out of the door.

23

Tania lay on her bunk, imagining the moment when she would find herself in General Grivetsky's arms. She had proved herself worthy of the general's attention, she thought defiantly. By violating the rules she had risked her career, her medals for outstanding achievement, her future security, everything she held dear, for love of the general.

Before she lay down on the bunk, she had scrubbed herself until she was thoroughly cleansed and sweet-smelling. She laid a freshly starched uniform across the covers of her bunk, then lay down to wait for the right moment.

What she was contemplating, of course, was another violation. Cohabiting with the passengers was a grievous infringement of the rules and she wanted, above all, to keep the secret from Katrina Ivanov. She had enough on Katrina Ivanov on the matter of the Jewish couple to have her removed from the Railway Workers, but it was best to trust no one. The old woman had accepted a second bribe from the Jew, this time promising to help him carry out the body at Irkutsk and put it in the baggage car, which was like an icebox.

The sooner the better, Tania thought. If the body began to stink and was discovered by an inspector, it would only create more problems for her.

When she thought of the key she had given the general, she admitted to some uneasiness, but she was sure the general would confront the KGB men and soon put matters straight. A general had more power than a KGB man anyway, she thought, remembering the pleasure she had taken in feeling the material of his uniform, caressing the insignia.

The train began to slow and she hopped out of bed. Quickly she took off her robe and put on her clean starched uniform, buttoning it with nervous fingers. Then she stepped into a half slip, giggling as she took her cotton panties and, instead of putting them on, neatly folded them in the pocket of her uniform. She felt wicked, a trifle silly, as she stood poised against the compartment door. Then the train jerked to a halt and she moved swiftly down the hall to the general's compartment.

She tapped lightly and waited for his response. It was past midnight and in the sudden silence of the train she could hear faint stirrings, coughs, whispers, hints of life behind each door. She tapped louder. Perhaps he is sleeping, she thought. She tapped again, feeling her giddiness recede. Then the train began to move and she heard Katrina Ivanov's cackling voice.

"He is gone," she said. She had been outside to fetch pails of charcoal, and her nose was red and running snot. Melting snow dripped down the sides of her coat.

"That is ridiculous," Tania said, panic rising. "The manifest has him ticketed to Chita."

"Just the same, he got off three hours ago." She thought a moment. "In Angarsk."

"You stupid old woman," Tania said with contempt. "I promised I would shine his shoes."

"Well, then you can go back to sleep. He is gone."

Tania grabbed the old woman and shook her angrily. Lumps of charcoal rattled in the pail.

"I tell you he is gone."

"You old crone. You liar."

"See for yourself."

Tania hesitated. She had given Grivetsky her key, and now had none of her own. Not to be delayed, Katrina Ivanov put the two pails of charcoal on the floor and produced her own master key. Tania unlocked the door.

"See," the old crone said. "I cleaned it myself. The red-haired man packed his things."

"The red-haired man?"

"The one in that compartment."

Tania felt her anger rise as she looked about the compartment. The bunks had been neatly arranged and all signs of the general were gone.

"I brought the baggage to the top of the stairwell. I think he got off with the red-haired man."

"At Angarsk."

"Yes."

"But it's only a tiny hamlet. In the middle of nowhere."

The old woman shrugged.

"And you saw them get off?"

The old woman looked at the ceiling, hesitating.

"Did you see them get off?"

"No. I was too busy. They were ready to get off. What does it matter? They come and they go."

Tania kicked the door shut in the old woman's face and stood in the center of the compartment. He would not have left without a good-bye, she thought bitterly, swept by frustration and disappointment. Her hand smoothed the pillow he had slept on. How could he? She walked into the washroom. Surely there was something, some sign, some remembrance. On the floor under the stainless-steel sink she found a toothbrush, which she picked up tenderly, as if it were alive. She placed it in the pocket where she had thrust her panties and went back to her own compartment.

The train had started again, moving relentlessly through the heavy snow. He was gone, lost forever. Just another passenger on the way to somewhere. She sank heavily into the chair, feeling a terrible chill crawl up her bare legs, moving upward like an icy skewer. She waited deliberately, knowing that it would soon reach the heart of her, chasing the last vestiges of her warmth.

24

Alex sipped the champagne and dabbed caviar on the toast.

The snow was melting fast in the shiny bucket. The British diplomat and his Australian roommate finally disappeared, still bickering, through the restaurant-carriage door. It was a relief not to have to listen to them. The restaurant was emptying, but the red-haired man still lingered over his tea. Alex was beginning to grow concerned over Anna Petrovna's absence.

At last she came into the restaurant car. He waved, his heart lurching at the sight of her. She seemed preoccupied, and he felt a stab of longing. He could not bear to believe that she lived a life without him. He rose as she reached him, kissing her on the lips without embarrassment.

Sitting down opposite him, she looked out of the window at the falling snow. He took her hand and found it cold.

"My God, you're freezing." He poured her a glass of champagne and refilled his own. "To Siberia," he said, lifting his glass and clinking hers as she lifted it. Her hands were shaking and she spilled her champagne as she lifted her glass.

"What is it?" he asked. "Would you rather we went back?"

She shook her head, her lips trembling.

"I'm being silly," she said, throwing her head back, the hair shifting like silk. He sensed that she was terribly upset, but determined to hide it.

"What is it?"

"You must trust me," she said, the yellow flecks in her eyes clear against the deep blue. She pressed her face against the window and, shielding her eyes from the interior glare, peered into the snow-filled night.

"What can you see?" he asked.

"A white world."

"Perhaps the train will get stuck," he said hopefully.

"Never," she replied, her breath making a puddle of vapor on the window.

Suddenly, Anna Petrovna picked up the champagne glass and tossed off its contents in one gulp. Alex reached into the bucket and filled their glasses again.

"I must not be gloomy," she said, smiling. She drank the champagne and again he refilled their glasses.

"Are you hungry?" Alex asked, pointing to the caviar.

Anna Petrovna shook her head. He felt her anguish.

"What is it?"

"I want to go back."

He dared not question her further. Tomorrow the train would arrive in Irkutsk and the spell would be broken. He had vowed to himself not to think about it.

"Give the rest of the champagne to that idiot there," he told the waitress, pointing to the KGB agent. But when they rose and started back toward their compartment, the red-haired man rose instantly to follow.

"Bastards," Alex hissed.

"What?"

"Nothing," he said as they walked through the icy vestibule. "It was a lousy celebration," he said, opening the door of their compartment. He felt the half-digested caviar, a heavy glob bloating his stomach.

Anna Petrovna sat down on the lower bunk. "Perhaps it was because there was nothing to celebrate."

She began to shake, burying her face in her hands. The size and strength of her body only added to the image of despair; a frail woman could not have looked so desolate. He sat beside her. As their bodies touched she moved into his arms. Kissing her cheeks, he could taste her tears.

"We are heading to oblivion," she whispered, sobbing.

Then, after a while, she stood up.

"There will be nothing, not a trace of memories anywhere. Only nothingness."

She rested her head against the door, then pounded it with her fist.

"Alex, if only I could say—if only I could make you understand."

He stood up and moved closer to her, kissing her hair, whispering in her ear.

"I can understand."

"Will you forgive me my deceit?"

"Your deceit?" They were the words he had told himself he would never hear.

"You will never forgive me," she said, moving to the other end of the compartment. She faced him. Behind her he could see the snow smashing against the window.

"You have something to tell me," he said, his heart racing.

"I have been working for the KGB," she said quickly, the words a bullet aimed at his brain. He felt his tongue freeze in his mouth and a sudden heaviness in his legs. Of course, he told himself. Had he had any illusions? "I knew," he wanted to say. But it wasn't true.

"It is not the first time I have done so," she said. "But the last time was years ago."

He must have looked as if he were about to speak.

"Don't. Let me go on," she said. "For the love of

an ideal you are sometimes willing to suspend what
you might call personal integrity. You do it for your
country. I do it proudly for mine. We have a viable
experiment here. We are trying to provide a better life
for everyone, all the people. I live by that concept.
Considering man's greed and selfishness, it is no small
achievement that we have gone even this far. There
have been abuses, I admit that. But I am not ashamed
of having helped to root out our enemies. I was quite
prepared to give anything to such a cause."

She paused, clicked open her handbag and shakily
lit a cigarette. For a moment, he thought she might
collapse into tears again. Her speech had been ridiculously formal, lines from a bad play. He felt her pain
and his own despair. It was all a charade, after all.

"Alex"—she paused—"my darling Alex," she said
softly. He wanted to cry himself. "You have information locked in your head that could have consequences
for millions." Dimitrov had said, "Be careful. They are
clever."

"Dimitrov is planning a nuclear strike against the
Chinese," she said quietly.

"I know."

He watched the confusion in her face. Her body
tightened as if it had been struck. Which of them, in
the end, had engaged in the greater deception?

"You knew?"

"Yes."

"In his dacha? Then?"

"Yes."

"And you did nothing?"

"That again." He paused. "I am not a killer." Then
it occurred to him that Dimitrov could have sent her.
If not Dimitrov, then who?

"You must be one of the jackals." He spit the words
through his teeth. "What is it you want from me then?"

"Will he live long enough to do it?"

"Who wants to know? Who hired you to find out?"

"Zeldovich."

"Zeldovich?" It was less clear than ever. "But he is Dimitrov's lackey."

"I know his reputation."

"He's the hatchet man. He does the dirty work. Everyone knows that."

"It doesn't matter. Our goals are the same."

"Goals?"

"He is trying to save lives—Chinese and Russian."

"You believe that?"

"Yes. And you have confirmed what Dimitrov intends."

"Cross cross and double-cross," he said in English.

"What does that mean?"

"It means"—he paused, remembering suddenly what they had shared—"it means that we are both cooked geese. It means that we possess information that cannot contribute to our longevity. It means—" A thought intruded, pulling him up short. "But you are getting off at Irkutsk."

She slumped against the door as if she were about to faint. "No," she said weakly. "He has asked me to stay."

"Asked?" Alex shook his head. "With a trainload of troops and that red-haired goon and God knows who else?"

"You're wrong," she said. "He is trying to prevent a horror, a crime against humanity. He is acting out of morality." She was shouting at him now. "There's one man, at least, with the courage to act."

"Then why didn't he put a bullet in Dimitrov's brain? He was with him every day. He could go back to Moscow right now and do it."

Anna Petrovna's upper lip trembled.

Of course, Alex thought, Zeldovich would do it if he could get away with it. But what was Zeldovich without Dimitrov?

"He is trying to save his own skin. He wants to know how much time Dimitrov has so he can chart his own course. If Dimitrov goes on for years, so does Zeldovich.

If Dimitrov is to die quickly, so does Zeldovich—unless he finds a way out."

She was cowering now, all defenses crumbled.

"You are his dupe," he said gently, thinking about himself and his feelings for her. He wanted to draw her into his arms. "And a marvelous actress," he said bitterly.

"Alex—" she began, a hint of tenderness in her quivering voice. Then she pulled herself back to the danger.

"I saw him kill Grivetsky. The general from the restaurant car."

"Zeldovich?"

"Yes. In his compartment. Next to ours." She pointed to the common wall.

"He knew about us. Of course, he knew." Alex felt unclean, disgusted.

"Grivetsky was to be Dimitrov's instrument. He was going to take command of the operation."

"And he was killed for that reason?"

"What other reason? He would have killed Zeldovich. And me. Nothing, no one was to stand in their way." Her courage seemed to be returning. "We have delayed the plan. At least for the moment."

"And now?"

"I don't know."

"I do."

"What?"

"You are the witness." He wanted to hurt her at the same time that he wanted to protect her. "Anna Petrovna," he said firmly, "if Dimitrov dies, you are Zeldovich's insurance. He will be able to say he killed Grivetsky to prevent the actions of a madman. It will be his reprieve."

"And if Dimitrov should live?" The question did not need an answer. If only she meant nothing to him. Was it too late for that? His anger rose as he thought of Dimitrov, the charming monster. Could he bring himself to kill him for Anna Petrovna's sake when he could not do it to save countless anonymous thousands? Or even to save himself?

"We have both been made fools of," he said, thinking of how she had betrayed him.

"No." She was emphatic, her voice rising in protest. The train was slowing for another brief stop. "You must not think of yourself that way," she said in a whisper.

"It is not important how I think of myself. That's not the main question."

"When Dimitrov discovers that Grivetsky is gone," she said quietly, "he will send someone else. It is all a matter of time."

"Time again," Alex thought aloud.

"How long will Dimitrov live?"

Was she thinking now of her own life? he wondered.

"I told you."

"You gave me possibilities. Nothing definite."

"What if I can't be any more definite?"

She shrugged. "You must get word to the Americans, to the President."

"From here?"

He looked at her, felt her anguish. And his own. He felt no compassion for either the Russians or the Chinese. He was not politicized like Anna Petrovna, or Dimitrov, or the President, or the Secretary of State.

"How long will Dimitrov live?" Anna Petrovna asked, her voice a whisper again.

"If you put a bullet in his brain you would know to within a millisecond. That is much simpler."

"How long?"

"I told you."

"Please. Tell me again."

"Anytime—from now, this minute, or months from now, or years. That is the simple statistic. The odds get better as time goes on. As of four days ago, the disease was in remission. If the cells suddenly multiply again, he will begin to droop like a marshmallow over a fire. The end could be quick or slow, painful or quiet. He is sixty-nine years old. Anything can happen at that

age. In any event, if there is a problem, he knows exactly where to find me."

His voice rose well above the din of the train. The
compartment seemed to have shrunk; he felt it caving
in on his head. Suddenly it was all too much. He
reached for the door handle and escaped into the passageway, walking swiftly in the direction of the hard-
class carriages. In the space between the carriages he
paused, letting the cold seep into him. He had to get
off the train, he told himself. That, above all. This was
a claustrophobic nightmare, and he was afraid for his
sanity.

Walking through the darkened restaurant, he smelled
scoured pots. The little manager was slumped over a
table, snoring loudly. At the end of the carriage, in the
faint light, Alex squinted at the timetable hanging in
the glass frame. He compared it with his watch, which
was still running on Moscow time. The train would
reach Irkutsk in a few hours. Irkutsk, the name had
once brought back the richness of his grandfather's
stories, the feeling that a piece of his life was there to
be retrieved. Now it represented a dividing point, a
chapter's end. He had had quite enough of the Trans-
Siberian Express, with its illusions of time and space.
Looking behind him, he waited for the footsteps of the
ubiquitous red-haired man, but he was not there. Alex
walked on.

In the passageway of the hard-class carriage he took
comfort in the noise and smells of the surrounding
community. The never-ending chess marathon was still
in progress. He felt the warm breath of the men as they
watched intently, the old man still in the same position,
all eyes concentrating on the chess board.

"He has won continuously for the past three days,"
someone whispered in Alex's ear.

"He has retrieved his respect," another said.

Pushing past the crowd, Alex looked into each compartment as he passed. He finally found an empty spot,
in an upper bunk near the door of the last car, the one
before the troop carriage. Again he looked behind him,

searching the passageway for the red-haired man. Then he slipped into the compartment and climbed onto the empty bunk, feeling the hard wooden surface against his spine.

Could he excuse her betrayal? He wanted to forgive her. After all, she too had been betrayed. Pawns in a terrible game. Both of them had been used and humiliated. If only he could stop the flow of his anger. Conversations drifted across his consciousness, bits of reality that could not find understanding in his overheated brain.

"Dimitrov is our man," the President had stated— the President of the United States—and he, Alex, had accepted the contention as easily as if he had been watching a deodorant commercial on television. "He is committed, apparently, to a more moderate stance toward the Chinese," the President had said, and that time Alex had heard the hedge—"apparently." So even the President wasn't sure, Alex thought, his mind grasping the possibility like a drowning man reaching for flotsam. Could he be convinced, even if Alex could get the word out? More than likely they would think him a raging idiot.

"You don't believe in this thing we have created, Kuznetsov?" Dimitrov had said. Alex could remember the exact place in the woods near the dacha, the river rushing below them, the winter sun setting as they walked slowly along a gravel path. Dimitrov's cheeks glowed slightly with the exertion. He is responding, Alex remembered thinking. He was hardly listening to the conversation, his concentration focused on Dimitrov's physical reactions, the spring of his step, the measure of his energy, his alertness. Only now, as he played the conversation back, did it hold his interest.

"This system we have created—this reorganization of life—this recalibration of man's aspirations."

"What recalibration?"

"We've reset the dials on man's greed, the drive to exploit other men. Before Lenin, a few men in every country, more ruthless and talented than the others,

would acquire an inordinate share of the world's resources and with it the ability to manipulate other
men for their own personal gain. We have changed all
that, Kuznetsov. It had never been done in the history
of the world. We did it, in my generation, in my lifetime."

Alex remembered now that he had thought of responding, but didn't feel it was worth arguing. You don't
trust your own people, he might have said. What kind
of paradise is that?

"Nothing would have been achieved if we had let
everyone pull in different directions. We had to impose
discipline. Given the circumstances, one might excuse
Stalin." Dimitrov had looked back over his shoulder at
Alex. "History will tell us if he was right. All opposition to the central idea had to be rooted out, destroyed."

"And was it?"

"The struggle will only end when we are all put
under one umbrella. Coexistence is a myth. That is the
truth of it. Hegemony is the only objective."

He had walked on quickly, surprisingly energetic.
He is growing stronger, Alex had thought at the time,
ignoring the actual words spoken.

"It took two thousand years for the weeds to grow.
They cannot all be pulled out overnight." Dimitrov had
sighed. "If only there is time."

"For what?"

"You are not listening, Kuznetsov," Dimitrov had
admonished mildly. He had opened his left hand and
made a plucking motion with the fingers of his right.

"There must be time to pull out all the bad weeds.
They are persistent. We pull them. They grow. We pull
them again. Someday we will pull them out and they
will never grow again. But only if we have the will to
keep on plucking." He made plucking motions again
and again in his palm.

So Dimitrov didn't believe a word of this détente
business, as the President so blandly assumed.

"And the Chinese?" Alex asked himself the question,

recalling still another conversation with Dimitrov. It was another day at the dacha. He was taking Dimitrov's pulse, feeling the steady beat against his two fingers, counting mentally as he watched the face of his wristwatch, as always only half-listening to the words.

"The Chinks." Dimitrov would never grant them more than coolie status. The Russian word was guttural, offensive. "They are peasants, simplistic and naive. They must be taught a hard lesson."

Alex had felt Dimitrov's pulse surge.

"Stop teaching such hard lessons. It is making your pulse push too fast."

"You feel it, Kuznetsov? You feel the passion?"

"I don't know what it is. But I feel it."

"It is strength you feel, Kuznetsov. Soon they will feel it."

"Who?" he had asked absently.

"The Chinks."

"Can't you say Chinese?"

"Someday maybe. Now they are Chinks."

"When will they change?"

"Soon."

Clues were everywhere now, rushing to Alex's mind. "Do I care what they think?" Dimitrov had said one evening when he had worked for fifteen hours straight and had to be forced to go to bed. The question was meaningless to Alex, since it was the first sentence the Secretary had spoken when Alex had entered his bedroom.

"History will be the vindicator," Dimitrov had continued, looking into space as Alex removed his slippers. "A leader must have the courage to act."

"Without rest, you won't have the strength or the courage."

Dimitrov smiled, acknowledging for the first time Alex's presence.

"Do I look like a barbarian, Kuznetsov?"

Alex had hesitated. He is tired, he remembered thinking. He must be humored.

"Of course not."

"Believe me, Kuznetsov," he had said. "If there was another way, another path, I would go in that direction. But all roads are closed. They will not bend of their own free will. There can be no sharing."

Alex had tried to draw up the bed covers, but Dimitrov had resisted.

"You Americans are such children," he had said.

"Does that mean you're ready to acknowledge that I am an American, not simply a Russian refugee?"

Dimitrov smiled. "Naive and innocent," he had whispered, his eyes closing. "We will not need to use our bombs on you."

The remembered conversations were coming to him like sunlight filtered through a prism in his mind. They had not been conversations at all, he saw now, hardly dialogues. They had been monologues, continuous and consistent, and although he had been a bystander then, he was a participant now. If only he could go back and relive the lost moments, probe the mystery of Dimitrov's mind with the same zeal that he had probed his blood. It would have been simple then to send Dimitrov to his reward. And now Anna Petrovna stood to be martyred by his passivity. Himself as well.

Perhaps, after all, he deserved to suffer for his lack of action, condemning half a continent to death. How could he possibly live with the knowledge that he might have prevented it? He shivered, bunching himself into the fetal position for warmth. There was no blanket on the bunk. He pushed his cold hands under his body, feeling the pain where the door handle had bruised the skin. He must get off the train, communicate with the outside world. Tell anyone who would listen. And yet, he could not, still, bring himself to forgive Anna Petrovna, not in his mind, although he yearned for her and continued to feel the power of his longing. It annoyed him that he could not shake the feeling. The urge to run to her, to throw himself in her arms seemed overpowering, although he lay still, forcing himself to remain where he was, as if imaginary chains were wrapped around his body.

He might have dozed. He could not tell, except that a change in the rhythm of the train suddenly triggered his alertness. The compartment was dark, but he could sense bodies moving around in it, heard heavy breathing, the sound of energy.

"Irkutsk," someone said. He sat up quickly, bumping his head against the ceiling. Climbing down from the bunk, he stood for a moment recovering his sense of space. A young man stood beside him buttoning a uniform tunic.

"Nearly home," he said. "I hope my mother and father will meet me at the station."

Edging himself out of the compartment, Alex moved into the passageway, crowded with people preparing to depart. Outside, men and women trudged through the snow. He saw horse-drawn sleighs, their drivers bundled snugly. Plumes of smoke moved upward through the chimneys of log cabins. Then, as the train moved slowly forward toward the bright lights of the city, the landscape changed. Huge blocks of apartment houses could be seen, and tan brick smoke stacks belching yellow smoke and showers of red sparks.

He remembered how Anna Petrovna had talked lovingly of Irkutsk. To him, Irkutsk was merely an idea, a sentimental heritage handed down by his grandfather. To Anna Petrovna it was home; her roots were embedded in it. Was it possible that Irkutsk was on the edge of extinction?

The train chugged to a halt. "It is Irkutsk I," someone said. "Only a five-minute stop on the outskirts."

Passengers had started to debark when Alex saw through the windows an unusual sight. Running soldiers, their heavy boots crunching in the snow, their machine guns at the ready position, were deploying along the length of the station. As passengers left the train, the soldiers stopped and interrogated them as they stood shivering in the snow. When they had answered satisfactorily, they were allowed to pass through the checkpoints the officers had set up at the edge of the platform.

"KGB troops," someone whispered behind Alex. A pall of fear had fallen on the crowded hard-class carriage. "Who are they looking for?"

Alex would not let himself dwell on the idea of it.

"How long before the main station of Irkutsk?" he asked someone next to him.

"Twenty minutes," an old man said with authority, his eyes still leveled at the soldiers. "They must be preventing someone from leaving the train," he said, loud enough to be heard through the passageway. The fear in the crowd became tangible. Alex felt a brief weakness in his knees. He had decided to dash off the train at the main Irkutsk station and run for a telephone. He wondered if the KGB would repeat their blockade there, and if he was really the target of their vigilance.

The train moved again. Back in the compartment where he had bunked, Alex looked about him in the semidarkness. The only other occupant was a big man, snoring in one of the lower bunks. Moving quietly, listening for any break in the rhythm of the snoring, Alex struggled to open the window. The upper portion was designed to move up and down, but it seemed to be jammed. His fingers shook with strain as he stood on his tiptoes and pushed downward with all his strength. Taking deep breaths, he tried to control his panic. Then he pushed downward again, still listening to be sure the other man was still asleep.

The train picked up speed, moving through what appeared to be a huge railroad yard. Electric lines crisscrossed overhead, layers of white snow weighing them down. The city was just awakening. Truck traffic flowed, and horse-drawn carts moved freely among the motorized vehicles. A slice of icy air cut through Alex as the window moved at last, making a sharp noise. The snoring man gurgled, then resumed his rhythm. Curling his fingers over the top of the window, Alex pulled downward, hanging on with his entire weight, feeling the window give finally and move slowly downward.

Bringing the chair close to the window, he stood on it and stuck his head out, measuring the possibility of moving his body through the opening. The space was wide enough, but as he stood poised, waiting for the train to slow down for Irkutsk, the futility of escape from the train struck him. He was, after all, in the dead center of Siberia, with three thousand miles between him and the Sea of Japan. The irony of it did not escape him. Like his grandfather, he would have to traverse half the great Siberian land mass. It was formidable, impossible. But, like his grandfather, he had to try. Poking his head out again, he could see the lights of what he assumed to be the main Irkutsk railroad station. Lifting himself to the edge of the window, he slid his body halfway out, gripping the window edge with one hand and reaching downward toward the lower ledge, waiting for the train to stop. Until it did, he would be dangerously conspicuous.

The moment the train stopped, he pushed himself out, falling like a rock onto a soft layer of snow. Then he moved, crouching, keeping close to the train, moving past the hard-class carriages, crouching lower as he passed the restaurant car. As he reached the soft-class carriages, he began to feel the physical strain, and he paused to catch his breath. Peering under the train, he could see feet moving, the lower torsos of the soldiers, the butts of their machine guns glistening in the harsh light of the platform.

He felt absurd. Mild-mannered Dr. Alex Cousins, crouching in the snows of Siberia, freezing, moving toward an inexorable fate. It was ludicrous. Then he felt his rage rise, and with it his determination. He was going to get word to the President, no matter what it took to do so.

He moved forward again, reached the windowless baggage car, then moved around the engine, straightening as he looked upward into the single electric eye of the engine's beam. He walked through a crowd of babushkas who were patiently waiting for the train to pass.

He calculated quickly. It was perhaps twenty yards to the ornate railway station building. Farther down, troops were intercepting the departing passengers as they stepped off the metal stairs. Their drawn guns were ominous. He tried to calculate his route and the timing. Then he started to move casually. He would stay close to the train and make his break for the station when he was parallel to the baggage car. The soldiers were standing with their backs to him, a human corral funneling the debarking passengers to the check-point.

Suddenly soldiers were running, calling loudly to each other. Alex froze, then saw that the soldiers had crowded around a man and an old woman who seemed to be carrying a heavy object between them. Alex stepped back into the shadows and listened.

"You must let me through," the man said. Alex recognized his voice instantly—it was the Jew whose wife had died. It was the body of his wife, then, that they were holding between them, bundled in the train's blankets and tied with string like an Egyptian mummy.

"You must let me through," Ginzburg pleaded.

"What's in there?" one of the soldiers asked, jabbing the bundle with the butt of his machine gun.

The arrogant brutality of the act seemed to Alex perverse and unnecessary. The Jew exploded in a burst of rage, kicking the butt of the gun and lashing out with one free hand while the other still held his end of the bundle. In a moment the soldiers had kicked him to the ground. The attendant dropped her end of the burden and stood dumbly looking about as if she were just a disinterested observer.

"Jew haters," the man screamed, squirming and kicking as two soldiers lifted him to his feet and pin-ioned his arms. The soldier whose gun Ginzburg had kicked away from the bundle drove the butt into the Jew's midsection.

Alex watched, hypnotized by the sheer brutality of it.

He stood rooted to the spot, torn between the necessity of reaching the station and the temptation to intervene on Ginzburg's side.

As Ginzburg retched and gasped, his body limp, his eyes bugging out, the soldier who had hit him knelt down next to the bundle and took out a long knife. He slit the rope and sliced carelessly through the blanket, then parted the edges with his blade.

"A woman," he said. The knife had sliced into her flesh, leaving a long black line down one side of her face.

Somehow Ginzburg recovered his breath. "Bastards," he screamed at the top of his lungs.

The soldiers laughed as he screamed and struggled in their viselike grip. The commotion attracted the attention of the major who had been supervising procedures at the checkpoint. He walked directly over to Ginzburg, who was still struggling.

"What is this?" the major asked, looking down at the mutilated body.

"A dead woman," the soldier said. "They were carrying the body in that direction." The soldier turned and pointed directly at Alex. The major looked where the soldier was pointing, then turned back to Ginzburg, as if Alex had been invisible. Ginzburg was silent. The major then looked questioningly at the old woman who stood trembling beside them.

"She died." The old woman shrugged.

"That is quite obvious," the major responded.

"What were you doing?" he demanded of Ginzburg.

The Jew stopped struggling, his eyes roving from his wife's lifeless face to that of the major. From where he stood, Alex could see the glare of hate in his eyes.

"Quickly, I have no time." The major glanced at his watch briefly, then looked back at Ginzburg. For a moment they stood glaring at each other, vapor pouring from their mouths, their faces a few inches apart. In the split second before it happened Alex could see it coming, could forecast its happening. The muscles of Ginzburg's neck moved and in the next moment he spit into the major's face. The major struck him one quick open-handed blow across the face, a conditioned reflex. Then he reached into his tunic for a handkerchief.

"You swine," the major said. He poked at the body with the tip of his boot. "Remove this garbage," he ordered the soldiers.

Alex stepped forward. "I would suggest you stop this stupidity," he said. All eyes turned toward him.

"Doctor," Ginzburg cried, struggling again in the grip of the soldiers.

"Doctor?" the major asked.

"You realize that you are being ridiculous."

The major watched him curiously, his eyes narrowing.

"We were carrying Vera's body to the baggage car," Ginzburg said, surprisingly calm now. "She must be buried in Birobidjan."

"Is there any harm in that?" Alex asked.

"You are Dr. Cousins?" the major asked coldly.

"Will you please release this man?" Alex said.

The major hesitated, then nodded at the soldiers. Ginzburg dropped to his knees over the body of his wife and quickly brought the ends of the blanket together. He retied the bundle with great gentleness, as if the woman were still alive.

"Now will you allow them to proceed?" Alex asked.

The major hesitated again, then looked into the face of the trembling old woman.

"Make it fast," he commanded.

Ginzburg lifted one end, the woman the other, and they proceeded toward the baggage car. One of the soldiers ran ahead and opened the carriage door.

Alex turned to the major. "I demand to be taken to a representative of the American Government."

"There is no one in Irkutsk."

"Then I demand to be flown to Moscow immediately."

"I can't allow that."

"Then I demand to communicate directly with General Secretary Dimitrov."

The idea had come to him suddenly. He would tell Dimitrov about the murder of Grivetsky.

The major seemed startled for a moment. "I can't allow that."

"I am his physician."

"I have my orders."

"From whom?"

The major did not answer that. "My orders are simply to see that you do not disembark," he said. "I mean you no disrespect."

"You have no right," Alex said. "I am a United States citizen. I am General Secretary Dimitrov's personal physician. Do not interfere with me in any way."

Alex started to walk toward the ornate railway station, his body stiff with expectation. The major followed, obviously uncomfortable in his role.

"I cannot allow this."

"You had better."

"I have orders."

"You can tell Zeldovich to piss on a stick."

The major hesitated, then caught up with Alex again.

"You must come back to the train."

"Kiss my ass."

The major darted in front of him, barring his way.

"Let me pass."

"I have my orders."

"Fuck your orders."

The major continued to bar his way. The line of soldiers was watching. Alex had issued his challenge. Now he was waiting for the moment when the major would be forced to act.

"Let me pass," Alex hissed at the major.

The major called his bluff. "Escort this man back to the train," he shouted to one of his officers.

Alex was instantly surrounded by tall, grim-looking soldiers, machine guns at the ready, ungloved fingers curved around the triggers. He felt oddly exhilarated. His sudden aggressiveness was as new to him as his feeling for Anna Petrovna, and, in its own way, as exciting. Finally, irrevocably, he felt drawn in at last, a player not a spectator. He was in the game now.

He suddenly pushed with both hands against the midsection of one of the soldiers, feeling the icy barrel of the machine gun.

The soldier struck Alex a glancing blow to the side of his face, making him reel backward into the snow. As he struggled to rise, the major bent over him.

"You must not resist," he pleaded.

"Go fuck a duck," Alex said in English.

He got to his feet and started again for the railway station, his feet sliding in the snow. Another soldier stepped in his path, barring the way, and Alex barreled into him.

"Don't . . ." he heard the major shout. He barely felt the blow, only the sensation of disappearing into an endless void.

25

If there was one thing Zeldovich had learned from Dimitrov it was decisiveness. Looking down at the lifeless body of Grivetsky, he had the comfort of knowing that he had made a commitment. He had set a policy and there was no turning back. He had not consciously planned to destroy Grivetsky. But as the perpetrator of the deed, he had suddenly given himself two interesting new options. He could now pose as the savior of millions, the man who had forestalled a holocaust. That could be his ticket to political asylum in the West. On the other hand, he could also pose as an ally of Bulgakov, claiming that he had executed Grivetsky as a traitor to the high command of the Red Army. Anna Petrovna would make a reliable witness.

There was, of course, a third option, one for which he had to be prepared. If Dimitrov was going to live, he had to keep Dimitrov from ever learning what he had done. For this option, all witnesses had to be eliminated. He was thankful now that his head had cleared, that his mind was racing, that the weight of indecision had been eliminated from his brain. He lay back, felt his body relax.

Someone knocked on the door. Yashenko! He could tell by the timbre and rhythm of the knock, casual yet urgent. He sprang from the bunk and let him in. At the sight of Grivetsky, the usually impassive face of the red-haired man registered astonishment. Zeldovich shrugged.

"It was necessary," he said. His casual tone seemed to placate Yashenko.

"We must get rid of him," Zeldovich said. "All traces. You must empty his compartment."

Yashenko nodded.

"Bring his coat in here and his baggage to the carriage entrance."

Zeldovich looked at his watch, and fished in his pocket for the timetable.

"There is a three-minute stop in Angarsk," he said. "We will tell the attendant that the general is debarking in Angarsk."

While Yashenko was gathering the general's belongings, Zeldovich washed, changed his clothes, and felt, for the first time since he had boarded the train, a delicious sense of well-being.

When Yashenko returned, they propped up the body of Grivetsky and dressed him in his coat and fur hat, being particularly careful to keep the coat from dipping into the pool of blood on the carpet.

"We must clean this up," Zeldovich observed. They laid Grivetsky's body on the bunk and both he and Yashenko, on hands and knees, proceeded to scrub at the stains on the carpet.

Then Zeldovich opened the compartment door a sliver, put his cheek against it and observed the passageway. As far as he could see, it was empty. Opening it further, he saw the old attendant, her back turned toward them, lazily shining the samovar.

"Quickly," he whispered and they moved into the passageway, the body of Grivetsky supported between them. The body was a dead weight, and their muscles strained to keep it erect between them. They did not have far to go.

Yashenko quickly slid open the door and they hurried into the freezing space between the carriages, leaning the body against the steel walls. Opening the outer door, Zeldovich peered into the snowy darkness, feeling a stab of chill as he drew his breath. Grabbing a handhold, he swung outward to get a full view of the area ahead, lit by the beam of the engine.

The train was moving along a river bank. Zeldovich could hear the heavy gush of water, the crackling sound of ice floes. He smiled into the darkness, seeing the river below him, feeling a sense of deliverance. Ducking into the train again, he grabbed the sleeve of Grivetsky's coat and yanked as hard as he could; with Yashenko's help the body began to move and fell away from the train. Looking back, Zeldovich watched the body fall, a dark hulk hurtling toward the river and oblivion.

"Now the baggage," Zeldovich said, stepping into the train as Yashenko picked up the baggage and positioned himself at the entrance. Zeldovich carefully calculated the distance. He was deliberate now, businesslike, feeling nothing. He reached for the wall to brace himself, then moving backward, lifted his leg, aimed it toward the small of Yashenko's back and struck. Yashenko's body flew outward without a sound. This time Zeldovich did not look backward, but quickly reached for the remaining baggage, flung it off the train and slammed the carriage door. He took a deep breath, feeling the tension in his fingers ease as he opened the inner door to the corridor and slipped quietly back to his compartment.

The train was slowing down now, moving into the tiny Angarsk station, a mere speck in the endless journey. He pulled out his timetable again. They would reach Chita tomorrow. It was unlikely that Grivetsky would be missed by Dimitrov until then.

He had no set plan in his mind, but at least he was moving again, his brain turning over, his despair purged. Reaching into a leather bag under his bunk, he drew out a pistol, checked the clip for bullets, and put it in his belt. Then he stepped into the passageway. The old attendant was busy shining the handrail along the corridor. She looked up dully, nodded, and continued her work. Zeldovich went to Anna Petrovna's and Dr. Cousins' compartment and knocked. The door opened almost immediately.

"You," Anna Petrovna said. She was alone in the compartment.

"The doctor?"

She shivered, drawing her dressing gown tighter. Her broad face was anxious and tear-stained.

"Gone where?" he asked firmly.

She had obviously been waiting for some time. The ashtray beside her was filled with the short butts of cigarettes. Without looking at Zeldovich, she waved her hand in the direction of the passageway.

"You let him go?"

"What should I have done? Stuck a knife in his neck?"

"Did you tell him?"

"Tell him what?"

"About Grivetsky."

"No," she shot back quietly.

He wondered if it were the truth. It was obvious that the woman was in an emotional state.

"I'll be back," he mumbled, as he let himself out of the compartment.

He walked quickly through the train, headed for the troop car at the rear. Above all, he must prevent the American doctor from leaving the train. He gave the major Alex's name and description. "Dr. Cousins must not be harmed," Zeldovich told him. Then he returned to the soft-class carriage.

Anna Petrovna answered his knock after a long delay. Inside, he inspected the doctor's belongings.

"His coat is still here," he observed.

Anna Petrovna looked up at him, her feelings for Alex clearly written in her face. Emotional involvement,

Zeldovich had found, was the shortcoming of all female KGB operatives, of women in general.

"He is probably sulking," Zeldovich said, hoping for a reaction.

"No one likes to feel betrayed," she said. He watched her eyes fall on his belt, where his fingers touched the butt of his revolver.

"You must not harm him," she whispered.

"We will do what must be done," he said, deliberately posturing. Was there anything to be gained by threatening her? he wondered. Then she stood up, reaching out to pat the linen dust cover of the bunk, her features betraying her uncertainty.

"There would be absolutely no point to it," she said slowly, watching him, her eyes occasionally dropping to the gun at his beltline.

In the end there is only fear, he thought.

"What is the point? He has told us everything he knows."

"Are you certain?"

"Totally."

"Then what is to come is irrevocable," he said, feigning a sigh. He knew he had pressed the right button from the beginning. Fanatical idealists, Zeldovich told himself, with contempt. Easily manipulated.

"We have at least bought some additional time," he said to Anna Petrovna. "But we have got to use it wisely." He was being deliberately soft, lulling.

"Dr. Cousins could be the instrument," she said quickly, emboldened by his manner. "He could get word to the American President. In three more days the doctor will be in the Sea of Japan. Then in Yokohama. There he could communicate with the United States without obstruction." She was becoming excited now. "They are the only ones who could stop it."

"How?" American intervention had never been, in his mind, a viable alternative. Dimitrov had destroyed for him the idea of American will.

"They have power," Dimitrov had said, "but no goals. They are soft, flabby. They showed us in Vietnam. We could push them out of half, perhaps three-quarters of the world, before they would have the will to resist us and then it would be too late."

In any case, this was the least appealing of Zeldovich's options. There was, after all, still Bulgakov. It all came back to the question of Dimitrov's longevity.

"It is ironic that going to the Americans may be the only possibility of stopping this madness," Anna Petrovna said, pausing to pull a cigarette from a pack on the table. "Isn't there anyone in this country in a position of leadership to whom we could take this information?"

It was laughable, naive. Who would believe Zeldovich? He had left too many carcasses around. They would think it was some new intrigue of Dimitrov's. Members of the Politburo spat at the mention of his name. Although he was only Dimitrov's instrument, Zeldovich was the one they hated.

"You are a remarkable man, Zeldovich," Dimitrov had told him.

"Remarkable?"

"You have a universal appeal among all the Politburo members. You are universally hated and distrusted." Dimitrov roared with laughter.

"I have just taken orders, Comrade Dimitrov, from you."

"It's not so easy to hate me. I'm too powerful. They must have someone to hate in my place. You are perfect for the role."

How Zeldovich hated Dimitrov now, and cursed his mortality. Mrs. Valentinov was looking at him and he was having difficulty concentrating on the conversation.

"Is it possible that the Army will not obey when given the order to strike?" she asked.

"Soldiers not obey? Bulgakov perhaps, but certainly not Grivetsky."

"And now that Grivetsky is dead?"

"Dimitrov doesn't know he is dead."

"But he will soon."

"He will only be able to surmise. They will have to

fish him out of a Siberian river, an extremely remote possibility." He paused, searching her face. "He has gone swimming with Yashenko."

"Yashenko?"

"Our red-haired KGB friend."

He watched her shiver.

"What will Dimitrov do when he discovers that Grivetsky is missing?"

"He will find someone else. There will always be others."

"Is it possible that he can make such a decision alone?"

"A decision like that would be impossible to make in a committee. They would talk it to death. Dimitrov's method is to act, then debate. If he is dying, why should he care what the Politburo thinks afterward?"

She was a mass of questions, Zeldovich thought wearily, wondering if his explanations were satisfactory.

"If Dr. Cousins told the American President, would he believe him?"

"Perhaps."

"But certainly he would ask Dimitrov about it."

"And Dimitrov would deny it."

"Then what would be accomplished?"

"Perhaps nothing."

"Then it is all futile." Anna Petrovna puffed deeply on her cigarette. It began to look as if there were no way out.

The light in the east was growing and the snow continued to whip against the windows as the train bounced forward relentlessly. Zeldovich watched the snow as it swirled in an uneven cascade against the windows.

"We will be reaching Irkutsk soon," Anna Petrovna said, a catch in her voice.

"Did you tell your people you would be arriving on this train?"

"I sent them a postcard from Moscow."

"Will they be at the station?"

"Yes. My husband and my two children. I have been away from home more than a month."

He could see that she was holding herself stiffly, under tight control. There are always unseen complications, he observed with resignation. He remembered his early days at the KGB. The people who rose within its system were those least encumbered by family, friends, emotional ties. It had been the primary lesson of his own career. Human involvements were a disaster in objective intelligence work.

"And what will they do when you do not arrive?"

"They will worry."

"Then we must get word to them."

He reached out to touch her forearm, but she recoiled. He could not care less whether her family worried or not. The problem was that they would undoubtedly make inquiries, create difficulties.

"Write them a note. Tell them you have been delayed in Moscow and that you will get word to them as soon as you know when you are coming."

Her disappointment was quite visible.

"Just let me speak to them for a moment," she pleaded.

"It is out of the question."

"What harm could it do?"

"I am not really sure, but we should preclude the possibilities. Sometimes information is transmitted inadvertently."

"But I might never see them again—" She hesitated. Did she sense her danger? He thought he had reassured her. But she was the only living witness to the murder of Grivetsky. And she knew it.

She looked at him, her eyes coming to life with hatred. "You are a cold man, Zeldovich."

He reached into an inner pocket, found a ball-point pen, then looked for a piece of paper. Anna Petrovna removed a small notebook from her purse. He motioned her to sit down, holding the pen toward her. Taking it, she sat down and began to write as he stood watching the snow beat against the windows. Through the snowflakes, he could see the beginnings of civilization again. Trucks and sleds moved along the roads. Electric lights beamed through the blizzard.

Watching her writing, her head bowed low over the table, he felt his own sense of decisiveness falter. Perhaps the simplest solution would be to eliminate Mrs. Valentinov and Dr. Cousins and fly back to Dimitrov. But then he would be tied to Dimitrov's life-span, exactly the situation from which he was trying to extricate himself. Or should he contact Bulgakov? Tell him everything. Cement the alliance. Was there future security in that? Or seek asylum? Simply get on the boat in Nakhodka with Dr. Cousins and let him explain the situation to the American President.

He felt the wheels of the train slow. Outside, the perennial army of babushkas leaned over their shovels.

"It is the first station in Irkutsk, the outskirts," Anna Petrovna said looking up, her eyes glistening with tears.

"I will be back," he said, letting himself out of the compartment.

From the passageway he could see the soldiers dispersing outside along the length of the train, running beside it as it slowed. Satisfied, he went into his own compartment and pulled on his coat and fur hat, drawing on his gloves. Whatever happened, they would have to search the train after Irkutsk for Dr. Cousins. After Irkutsk, there would be fewer passengers.

Before he left the compartment, he looked around again, noticing that the bloodstains were brownish now, but barely distinguishable. He put an extra packet of bullets into the side pocket of his coat. As he let himself out, the train began to move again, heading for the heart of Irkutsk. He reentered Mrs. Valentinov's compartment.

Anna Petrovna stood now, waiting. She held the folded note in her hand.

"I want to see them, to point them out."

He took the proffered note and opened it.

"Must you?" she asked quickly.

"Of course."

"Darling," the note began, "I'm sorry I could not arrive but unforeseen delays have kept me in Moscow. As soon as I know when I can return, I will let you know. Please forgive me. I miss you all very much and send my love. You must take good care of each other. Mother."

Something in the note disturbed him. Perhaps it was the way she signed it. Would they detect something amiss?

"Why do you sign it 'Mother'?" he asked.

"It is addressed primarily to my children."

"And your husband?"

"He will understand."

"Understand what?"

"That it is addressed to the children."

He pondered its meaning for a moment, sensing the relationship, accepting the explanation, but still troubled.

"This last sentence seems to indicate a finality, a farewell."

"I am being realistic."

"Could you alter it?" he asked, forcing himself to speak gently.

"To what?"

"Perhaps 'You must all take good care of each other until I see you again.'"

She shrugged. "What does it matter?"

Taking the note from him, she leaned over the table and quickly scribbled the additional phrase. "There. Are you satisfied now?"

"Yes."

"I wonder if I ever will see them again."

"That is the whole point of this exercise."

"I suppose," she sighed, slumping heavily into the chair and watching the early morning activity of Irkutsk through the window.

"What a lovely morning!" she whispered.

"Lovely?"

"To a Siberian, snow can be as lovely as sunlight. One could not imagine Irkutsk without snow. I always felt sorry for people who lived in the south, who had no snow."

"I have never been in Siberia before."

"That is obvious." She turned to the window again.

He leaned against the bunk, watching her profile against the glow of lights.

"Summer, too, is lovely here," Anna Petrovna said, talking more to herself than to Zeldovich. "The flowers in a Siberian summer are brighter than anywhere in the world. Sometimes in the winter you see it in your mind's eye and long for it." She paused, then shook her head and turned to Zeldovich. "Is it possible that there are people who would want to deliberately destroy this?"

"Without a tear."

She watched him. He could feel her eyes boring through him.

"And you, Zeldovich, does it really matter to you?"

He hesitated a moment, feeling the iciness of his own indifference. He did not care about the snow or the flowers, or anything other than his own survival.

"I am not sure," he lied, knowing that it was as close to the truth as any words he had ever uttered.

The train slowed again, moving through the rail-yards. Zeldovich opened the compartment door and Anna Petrovna followed him. They watched the soldiers jump to the platform and form a line along the length of the moving train.

"Soldiers," she whispered, her breath warm against his cheek.

"A precaution. For his own good."

In the passageway a procession began of passengers for Irkutsk. Anna Petrovna peered onto the lighted platform, searching the faces of the crowd. Suddenly she gripped his arm.

"There," she pointed, ducking behind Zeldovich. "They musn't see me. There. The two little boys with red woolen hats." She began to sob.

"Get back into the compartment," he ordered firmly.

"Please," she said, clutching his arm.

"They will see you," he said, wrenching free and pushing her back toward the inner wall of the passageway.

"Oh, my God!" she said, tears streaming down her cheeks.

"If they see you, I will shoot them," he hissed. In the end, it was only threats that worked, he told himself, disgusted at his earlier feelings of sentimentality. "Do you understand me?" he whispered. She nodded, and stood back against the corridor wall.

Zeldovich rushed through the corridor and stepped into the snow, walking quickly in the direction of the major.

"Keep a close watch," he said.

"No one can get through," the major answered, walking by his side through the checkpoint. Zeldovich looked around and spotted the red hats. He walked up to the two small boys, and the man who had to be their father. He was holding each boy by the hand and looking toward the train.

"Mr. Valentinov?"

The man looked up anxiously. Zeldovich could feel the children's eyes on him.

"I have a note." He watched as Valentinov read it.

"What is it, Father?" one of the boys said, seeing the disappointment on his father's face.

"Your mother is not on the train."

"Not on the train?" Zeldovich watched tears well in the boys' eyes. The older one turned to his little brother and said, "Stop crying."

"But the party."

"They had planned a welcoming party," the father said.

Zeldovich shrugged. He did not want to become involved in their disappointment. He fingered the barrel of his gun, the metal icy against his fingers, and looked toward the train again. From that distance, Mrs. Valentinov was not visible.

"Comrade Zeldovich," a voice spoke from behind

him. Startled, he spun around, his fingers tightening on the gun.

"The major pointed you out," the man said. He was dressed in the uniform of a telegraph agent. "I have a wire for you. It just came in."

Zeldovich looked at the man suspiciously. "Let me see it."

He knew he had the ability to intimidate and used it now, taking the wire roughly from the man's hands. With it came another envelope with a familiar name on it. "Grivetsky."

"I know him," he said, pointing to the name on the envelope that he had accidentally grabbed. "I will deliver it and save you the trouble."

The train agent rubbed his chin. "I'm not sure—" he said.

But Zeldovich, hardly listening, was opening the envelope addressed to himself.

"The doctor must call at once. D."

What did it mean? he wondered. Was Dimitrov ill again? He is so clever, Zeldovich thought contemptuously, trying to be so casual, using the public wire system as if his message were a mere telegram of congratulations. The old fox was so clever. He replaced the message in the envelope and looked again at the troubled telegraph agent. He pulled out a wad of kopecks and stuffed them into the man's breast pocket.

"I am not Zeldovich."

"You're not?"

"Do I look like Zeldovich?"

"But the major said—" Then it dawned on the telegraph agent.

"Tell them that you missed the train."

"But the time is on the wire."

"Then change it." Zeldovich pulled his KGB identification out of his pocket and waved it in front of the man's face.

"Yes, sir. Of course, sir." The man bowed obsequiously and hurried away.

When he had gone, Zeldovich read the wire to

Grivetsky: "No confirmation on matter discussed." It was unsigned.

Zeldovich felt the beginnings of a new annoyance. The sudden elation he had felt on reading Dimitrov's wire dissipated with the knowledge of what was in Grivetsky's. He repeated Dimitrov's message to himself. Why only call? he wondered. If Dimitrov was ill, why would he not be asking for the doctor's return?

As he walked back to the train, the major came toward him, an anxious expression on his face.

"We found him."

"Who?" For a moment Zeldovich felt himself disoriented. He had been thinking of Dimitrov's wire.

"The doctor." The major fell in step beside him as Zeldovich walked quickly toward the train.

"He is injured," the major said quickly.

Zeldovich stopped. "I warned you."

"He wouldn't obey," the major said. "It was the only way he could be restrained."

"Where is he?"

"We brought him back to his compartment. He is unconscious."

"Ass!" Zeldovich snapped, running toward the train now. He noticed that a new engine had been hooked up, a huge yellow diesel. The information passed in and out of his consciousness as he gripped the handrail and lifted himself up the stairs. The train began to move as he opened the door to the passageway.

26

Mikhail Moiseyevich lay on the unfamiliar bunk and stared at the ceiling. He had been lying there for hours, nursing his humiliation. Only yesterday he had sat in the other compartment, the body of Vera peaceful and quiet below him, and had vowed to himself that nothing they could do would ever move him again. He would feel no pain. No anger. No joy. Nothing. If they wanted to hate Jews, let them. Whatever was to confront him in Birobidjan, he would not let it make a dent on his inner life. Perhaps Vera was right. There was no physical escape from them. Geography alone was not enough. He must withdraw from them mentally. The incident at Irkutsk had confirmed it. Vera knew. The final escape was death. Short of that, he was determined to try his own method. He would never let them glimpse his inner life. They had taught him what he had long denied, that his Jewishness was important.

But while he vowed to live only within his mind, he was having considerable trouble following the plan. It was not easy to learn to be pliable. The train had barely

left Irkutsk when the attendant, the younger one, had
knocked at the compartment door.

"You are being transferred to another compartment,"
she had said.

He had wanted to protest, feeling the anger begin
again inside him. Then, remembering, he replied politely. "Of course," he had said, forcing a smile. He
quickly gathered up his baggage and put it into the
passageway. The attendant picked up the bags and
proceeded down the passageway, stopping in front of
a compartment and knocking. Hearing no response she
turned the handle and slid open the door. Mikhail
recognized the squat man who had been at the Yaroslav station. He was stretched flat on the lower bunk,
eyes open, ignoring them as they arranged the suitcases
in the place set aside below the bunk. The attendant
looked at him, shrugged, and left the compartment.

It was strange being at such close quarters with
another man. Mikhail climbed to the upper bunk and
lay down. The man below him groaned. At first,
Mikhail ignored him. Under his new method he did
not have to pay attention to anyone else's pain.

The man groaned again, moved, then sat up. Mikhail
lay still, watching the ceiling and listening. Suddenly
the man stood up, gripped the edges of the upper bunk
and hissed with pain. Then he sat down on his bunk
again. Mikhail could hear him breathe heavily, then
groan again.

What did that man's pain matter to him? Mikhail
thought. He was surprised at his own reactions. He felt
unburdened, set free. Vera's absence, far from filling
him with remorse, was a relief. He had felt her presence
during those two days that her lifeless body lay still on
the bunk. He had sat beside her and patted her hand,
although her skin felt cold and clammy to his touch.
In the end he had forgiven her the denial of her Jewishness. It was true, he had told her, that she had not
been born a Jewess. But heredity and blood were not
all. Through her marriage, she had cast in her lot with
the idea of Jewishness. What was it, after all, except an

idea? The idea of being a Jew was based upon the assumption that someone must be blamed. How could anyone possibly exist on this earth, especially in the Soviet Union, without having someone to blame? It was a law of man. It was a privilege, if one thought about it. If people were in misery and pain, starving, suffering, unhappy, diseased, they could feel hope in having someone to blame. The worst possible thing would be if people blamed themselves. Thus, he had told her, the Jews had to be invented to be blamed. The reason that Vera had not been able to bear it was that she had not been conditioned, as he had, to take that blame.

He had never experienced such clarity of thought as when he had sat beside her still body on the bunk, explaining to her what it meant to be a Jew. It was the reason he felt unburdened now, freed by his own eloquence. Now, lying on the upper bunk, staring at the ceiling of the bouncing train, he felt the need to share this knowledge with others. He heard the man below him groan in pain.

"I am a Jew," Mikhail said suddenly, quite pleasantly he thought. He propped himself up on one elbow and looked down at the sweating face of the man below him.

"I am a Jew," he repeated.

The man stopped groaning for a moment, looked up, and shuddered.

"I am a Jew," Mikhail repeated. Was it possible he wasn't being amiable enough? The man looked up finally and grunted.

I will give him time to understand the consequences of what he has just learned, Mikhail thought. The compartment suddenly brightened as the sun burst through the clouds. In the distance he could see water, incredibly blue against the whiteness. The man below him sat up on the edge of the bunk.

"You up there," he said suddenly. Mikhail shook himself alert.

"Me?"

"You are a Jew?"

"Yes."

There was a long pause, a groan and a restless movement as the man thrashed around in his bunk.

"I am a murderer," the voice said from below. The voice sounded cracked, the words spoken with a great effort. Mikhail felt his heart pound.

"A murderer?"

"What do you think I said, you idiot?"

"I'm sorry," Mikhail said. It was part of his new plan to apologize at all times. "I was not prepared for such a revelation."

"Well then, prepare yourself," the voice said. "I am a murderer. Actually, I am sure I murdered a woman, a damned prostitute. But I'm not as sure about Shmiot. Frankly, I hope he is still alive. It would be a pity if he is dead."

"Why?"

"Because dead is dead."

"There is no question about that." Mikhail was trying to be pleasant.

"If he is alive, he will know what pain means."

"Yes, that's undoubtedly true."

"He was an excellent teacher," the voice said.

"A teacher?"

"He taught me how to endure pain."

"Yes."

"What do you mean 'yes'? That's a stupid answer."

"I mean I understand."

"How could you understand?"

"Because I'm a Jew."

"What has that got to do with it?"

"You don't know?"

"And I don't care."

The man thrashed about some more, then sat up again. Mikhail delicately turned his eyes to the ceiling. He didn't think that the man would want him to see his face.

"My wife is dead," Mikhail said.

There was a long pause.

"Did you kill her?"

"Kill her?" It was an interesting concept, Mikhail thought. He could feel the man's intensity.

"Did you kill her?" the man repeated urgently.

Mikhail did not wish to be hurried; he wanted to think about the proper answer.

"Perhaps," he said at last.

"You don't know?"

Why was he pressing him so hard? Mikhail thought. He wanted to ask the man to define murder, but felt that might be presumptuous. And yet he did not want to avoid answering the question. It warmed him to imagine a kinship with the strange man writhing in pain below him.

"In a way," he answered finally.

The fact was, Mikhail wanted to say, that Vera had died because she was not programed for endurance as he was. And he had, after all, forced her, by marriage, to accept conditions intolerable to her makeup.

"Yes," he said to the man.

"Yes, what?"

"I am guilty. Of murder."

The man lifted himself upright beside his bunk and looked at Mikhail. Mikhail saw the thick features, glazed eyes, the low forehead and short cropped hair. It was the kind of face that threw fear into the hearts of every Jew in the Soviet Union, a reminder of Stalin, the promulgator of modern, more subtle pogroms.

"I thought so," the man said.

"You did?"

The man squinted into Mikhail's face, his eyes two glistening coals of hatred.

"You are just as guilty as I am."

I just admitted that, Mikhail thought. It was obvious that the man was looking through him, through the steel walls of the moving train, into the heart of the Siberian waste, seeing what was only visible to himself.

"I was innocent," the man said. "Totally innocent. I am sure of that, dead certain. I shouted it at them. I am innocent, I cried. You are guilty, they assured me. When they tell you this over and over again, your resolve cracks and the knowledge of your innocence becomes unsure. Innocent of what? Guilty of what? You can hardly distinguish between them. In that train, I tried to protect my innocence. I didn't really care about the suit or any of those silly possessions. I was trying to protect my innocence."

The man groaned again and slipped into a kind of trance.

"Shmiot had no right to take away my innocence," he cried. "No right."

Mikhail had no doubt that he was listening to some sort of confession and he tried to look sympathetic. At some point the man was sure to come to himself, and it would not do for Mikhail to look hostile, not after receiving such information. Mikhail was, after all, judging his own act philosophically. The murder of Vera was not a crime against society, not punishable by the laws of man. The threat of retribution was not to his person, only to his soul. But this man was a self-admitted criminal in the traditional sense, and the punishment for his crime was confinement in their unspeakable prisons. He shivered, feeling a cold chill ripple through him.

"I had every intention of killing him," the man below said, breaking the long pause. "But the idea that the man had no memory of what he had done made it suddenly important that he stay alive as long as possible in a condition that might bring back the old memory."

Mikhail bent over the bunk. The man's eyes opened wide. He shook his head and looked at Mikhail as if he knew him.

"In the case of the prostitute," the man said. "There was no justification whatsoever. I killed her out of pique, sheer anger. Did I think she would make me a miracle? It was a physical impossibility—a lost cause. I felt no pity for her. No remorse. Nothing. In fact, I rarely thought about it. Besides, if you are finally convinced of your own guilt, what does anything matter? You might as well be guilty of the most unspeakable

crimes. Guilt is guilt. There is no such thing as guilti-
est."

Yes, Mikhail told himself, he could understand that.
He could also understand why the man should choose
to unburden himself suddenly to a complete stranger.
He felt the bunk shake below him and, looking over the
top, he saw that the man had turned over on his
stomach and his shoulders were heaving with deep
sobs. Mikhail watched him for a long time, then reached
down and touched the man's back, feeling the wracked
body heaving. The man's shoulders quieted. Mikhail
looked about him, searching for Vera's approval. It
did not take him long to realize that it was futile. Vera
was gone. All that was left of her was a mutilated body
in the dark baggage car. He was suddenly disgusted
with her for not having had the will to survive, and he
felt his grip tighten on the man below him.

27

As Alex lay warm and secure in his own thoughts, the memory of Irkutsk station began to intrude. He had been trying to contact someone, the American ambassador, anyone. He thought of Dimitrov as he had first seen him, his first words.

"This indisposition is an absurd joke."

"Believe me, it is no joke," Alex said.

"We will attack and destroy it. I will do exactly as you ask," Dimitrov had said.

"It is between us. Live or die."

"Of course."

"You must pledge me."

"How does one do that?"

"By your word. There is nothing more important than one's word."

Alex opened his eyes. Faces were watching him. Anna Petrovna was dressed in a blue skirt and white turtleneck sweater, her blonde hair hanging loose to the shoulders. The light was failing, but the color of her eyes shone clearly—a royal blue with flashes of yellow. She was sitting on the chair and Zeldovich was sitting at the foot of the bunk. She must have seen Alex's eyes flutter open. She leaned over and squeezed his hand.

"Alex," she said.

"How do you feel, Dr. Cousins?" Zeldovich asked.

He lifted his head, felt the pain where the blow had struck, and rubbed his palm on the bump.

"Was this really necessary?"

"I can only offer my apologies. They were over-eager." He stood up. "But then, so were you."

Alex could feel Anna Petrovna's eyes on him, but even though he still clutched her hand, he didn't turn toward her.

"Why am I being detained?" he asked stupidly.

"You know why."

"Are you planning to keep me bottled up here forever, riding back and forth on the Trans-Siberian Railroad?"

Alex let go of Anna Petrovna's hand and stood up, feeling dizzy and weak in the knees. Slight concussion, he told himself. Walking shakily, leaning on the walls for support, he went into the washroom and slapped icy water on his face. Dipping a towel in the water, he pressed it against the back of his head. It did not show any blood.

With the towel against his head, he walked back into the compartment.

"Would you like some tea?" Anna Petrovna asked gently.

"The Russian panacea," he answered, nodding, watching her press the button for the attendant.

In a moment the younger attendant came in. Anna Petrovna ordered three glasses of tea.

When the attendant had gone, Zeldovich said, "Mrs. Valentinov told me that she had explained to you the importance of the information you possess."

Alex looked quickly at Anna Petrovna, who lowered her eyes in embarrassment. He imagined her suffering, the conflicting emotions churning inside of her. Yet he could sense the bond of alliance between her and Zeldovich. Be cautious, Kuznetsov, he told himself.

"She also has that information," Alex said, watching Anna Petrovna twist and untwist her fingers. "The General Secretary's health is stable. The leukemia is in a state of apparent remission. Beyond that, there is no predicting how long he will stay that way."

He recited the facts mechanically. Hadn't he given this summary a hundred times?

"Could this condition change suddenly?" Zeldovich asked.

"Yes."

"Or could the change be gradual?"

"That, too."

"It is unpredictable?"

"I have been trying to explain that to anybody who would listen. Including Dimitrov." He had blurted out Dimitrov's name without thinking.

"Then he also knows?"

"Yes."

"That he could topple over quickly?"

"Or go gradually."

"It is positively exasperating," Zeldovich cried.

"I have tried to explain that to you," Anna Petrovna pleaded. "You cannot find specifics where there are no specifics."

Alex looked at Zeldovich, could feel the man's cruelty.

"You, Zeldovich," he began, feeling his voice faltering. "A man obviously without the conscience of an ant."

"Alex, please—" Anna Petrovna said.

"You think his motives are the same as yours?" He was furious with her for unwittingly sharing a moral position with Zeldovich.

"Does it matter?" she asked softly.

"You needn't be so self-righteous, Dr. Cousins," Zeldovich sneered. He stuck a thumb in her direction. "She saw me kill a man who would have carried out Dimitrov's orders without blinking an eye. On the other hand, you preserved a life that will soon be responsible for the death of millions. We should compare acts, not motives, Dr. Cousins."

So they were putting him on the defensive now, he thought, feeling the guilt begin again.

There was a knock at the door. Tania set down the tea and departed. Zeldovich looked at his watch.

"It is midnight at the dacha," he said, lifting the tea and blowing on it.

"There is bread and sausages," Anna Petrovna said, opening a newspaper and spreading it on the table.

Their actions seemed so banal. The sausages tasted delicious, but Alex felt uncomfortable, as if he had no right to this enjoyment. It was not the simple act of eating that disturbed him, but rather the camaraderie that it implied, as if he and Zeldovich were old friends. Did Zeldovich think they had captured him now, that he was part of their joint action?

Wiping his fingers on his pants, Zeldovich pulled out a piece of paper from his coat pocket and handed it over to Alex.

"What does this mean?" he asked.

Alex read Dimitrov's message, then looked back at Zeldovich. He could not deny his doctor's instincts. What Zeldovich had only suspected, he felt with certainty. Something was wrong with Dimitrov, or going wrong, despite the casual tone of the request.

"When did this arrive?"

"I picked it up in Irkutsk hours ago."

"You waited this long to tell me?"

"You were not conscious, remember?" Zeldovich burped and patted his stomach. "Besides, we will not be near communications until we reach Ulan-Ude." He looked at his watch. "At nearly four in the morning. We will decide what to do later," he said, standing up and looking toward Anna Petrovna.

Had they communicated something in that exchange of glances? Alex wondered.

"There will be a guard posted at the door," Zeldovich said, letting himself out.

When he had gone, Anna Petrovna busied herself rewrapping the leftovers in the newspaper. Alex watched her movements, graceful yet efficient. He knew she was acting out of nervousness. The window was a black mirror in which her white sweater and blonde hair appeared almost translucent.

"Ulan-Ude," he said stupidly. "What an odd name."

"It is the point where the Trans-Mongolian Railroad intersects. It is the road to Peking."

She sat down on the chair and faced him. He loved her. He was sure of that, no matter how many doubts about her assailed him.

"It was heralded twenty years ago as the great railway to friendship. The Chinese built a connecting link direct to Peking in the same gauge as ours. Then they tore it up again and rebuilt it in the standard narrower gauge. That is what happened to friendship."

They were silent for a long time.

"So you have complied with their request that you stay," he said at last.

"Yes."

"You had no choice."

"I am aware of that."

"You would not have stayed if you hadn't been forced?"

"No." She looked away. "I saw my sons at the Irkutsk station, and my husband. It was a cruel moment."

"I'm sure it was." He waited a moment. "If you had gone, would you have given me a moment's thought?"

"Of course."

"With longing?"

She looked uncomfortable. Her eyes would not meet his eyes.

"This sentimentality disturbs you?"

"Yes," she whispered. "It is—" She could not find words.

"Incongruous."

"Certainly that." She found her poise again. "Alex,

with the world on the brink of destruction, it seems so pointless."

"And selfish."

"That, too."

"I'm sorry, Anna Petrovna," he said, reaching out, taking both her hands in his. "I love you more than my own life, more than the dead millions. Beside what I feel for you, everything else is trivial."

"This is absurd," she said.

He drew her up from the chair, his arms enveloping her, feeling the heat of her skin, the perfume of her body. A shiver ran through her. He felt his loneliness vanish, felt a sense of purpose that had never seemed to exist before.

"I would never have breathed without a thought of you," he whispered, feeling the joy of her response as she pressed closer to him. He put his hands under her sweater and ran his fingers down her back to her hips. Then he drew her downward to the lower bunk and pressed his lips onto hers, feeling her breath in his mouth.

Is there more than this? he wondered.

"You are everything," he said.

They sat up. Silently, they removed their clothing and he held her. She began to shiver again and he drew the blankets over them.

"I'm frightened," she whispered.

He was full to bursting with the joy of her nearness. It was the sweetness of reunion, which he had never experienced before. His emotions were like fireworks in a dark sky.

"Yes," she said suddenly, a dam within her breaking, the fury of her yearning seeking an escape as she reached out for his hard manhood and plunged it into herself, her body sinking under his. She cried out, and he heard that cry as a confession, her admission that she understood life's meaning now, beyond the fear of death and nothingness. For an endless moment they were together in their understanding. Then the tidal wave seized them and crashed them to the ocean floor, and they lay in each other's arms, time suspended. He had been outside of himself, he was certain, for the first time in his life. And not alone. He lay in a haze, hardly knowing whether he was asleep or awake.

The train began to slow down. Artificial light poured through the windows. Then the train halted. He turned his head, saw a tiny building and against it a dark figure huddling in a coat, holding a red railroad flag stiffly in the air. Then the train began to move, the metal shivering forward, beginning again the interminable invasion of the Siberian wasteland.

"Misavaya," she whispered. "The other side of Lake Baikal. I was here once with my mother, one summertime."

"It is a lonely place," he said. "It is hard to believe that people live here."

"I have never been lonely," she said.

It was the answer he had expected, but not wished for. She was revealing the essential difference between them, the cultural anomaly. It made his romanticizing seem pathetic.

"Never?" He was immediately sorry he had pressed the point. He half-expected her to say: It was not allowed.

"It is an indulgence," she said.

"You have never felt cut off from other people?" He slid his hand between her legs, fingers probing gently.

"Only as an individual," she said, her words precisely spoken. "I never feel cut off from the group."

"Why must everything be objective?" He removed his hand.

She raised herself on her elbow. "Poor Alex," she said, rubbing the hairs on his chest.

Her pragmatism was maddening.

"You think I'm a child," he said.

"In a way. Mostly ignorant."

"Ignorant of what?"

"Of social values, of the practical considerations necessary in providing for people's needs. Sooner or later all society must be structured along those lines."

My God, she is propagandizing me! he thought.

"And Dimitrov's intentions," he said, moving his head away. "How do you explain that?"

"An aberration."

"And Stalin?"

"Another aberration. We self-corrected that."

"Only after millions died."

"He was impatient, indulgent of his own sense of power."

"He was a paranoid, like the bunch of you."

He was trying to insult her. He found her glibness offensive. Why should I love her? he asked himself. He was certain she felt the same dichotomy.

"Dimitrov is impatient, too," she said, ignoring his remark. "He is impatient with the historical process. He is trying to force evolution. If he were twenty years younger and healthy, he would be reacting quite differently."

"Are you really against his intentions?" Alex asked.

She looked up at him. He could see her confusion.

"Not in the abstract," she answered.

He was coming to the nub of her anxiety now, and knew it.

"A nuclear strike is not an abstraction. Ask the Japanese."

He understood now how her naiveté had been manipulated, her convictions played upon. At that moment he forgave her the part she played for the KGB. Who is the child here? he asked himself.

"What you fear is the destruction of Siberia," he said. "Your Siberia. You know it will mean nothing for him to sacrifice it."

"Siberia must be protected." Her body began to shiver again.

"It is all that matters to you," he said. "Beyond everything. Beyond me? Beyond yourself?"

He lowered his body onto hers again, feeling her drawing him into her again.

"We must destroy Dimitrov," she whispered between short gasping breaths.

"We?"

"I will do anything you ask of me, Alex. I will go wherever you wish me to go. I will never leave your side."

He felt her body compelling him, pleading with every nerve end. When he looked up again, the train was still moving through the darkness and he could see his reflection in the window.

28

A freezing mist hung over the station at Ulan-Ude. Zeldovich burrowed deep into his fur collar as he walked toward the gloomy stone station that straddled the border between the Soviet Union and Outer Mongolia. Here at Ulan-Ude a charade of customs and visa surveillance took place, since the Mongolian People's Republic was little more than a vassal of the Soviets. The railroad was heavily trafficked by the Soviet military who manned the network of missile bases and military camps along the line. Many of the soldiers who had traveled in the hard-class sections of the "Russiya" were lined up at the exchange point. Zeldovich was disgusted by their lack of military bearing.

He watched them now, their tunics unbuttoned, their hats awry. He spat onto the hard ground. The American doctor walked at his side, looking ashen in the pale afternoon light. KGB soldiers marched in front and behind the two of them, their machine guns strapped to their shoulders, trigger fingers at the ready, conscious of the smartness of their military demeanor.

Zeldovich looked at his watch. The Ulan-Ude lay-over was seventeen minutes and he hoped to do his business in that time. The KGB troops would block the path of the engine, so there was no chance that the train would leave without him. But unless it was abso-lutely necessary, he preferred not to interfere with the railroad's timetable. To do so seemed an affront to Russian pride.

As they walked briskly toward the station, a tall, thin man suddenly came toward them. The soldiers moved to intercept him, but Zeldovich motioned them away. The tall, thin man never even noticed. He stood before the American doctor and put out his hand.

"I'll be leaving you here," he said in English. "Too bad we couldn't spend more time together."

"Quickly," Zeldovich hissed impatiently at Alex.

"Mr. Farmer is quite fluent in Russian," the doctor said, smiling at Zeldovich.

"No tricks," Zeldovich mumbled.

"Are you in trouble?" the thin man asked in English. He kept his face from showing alarm or concern.

"In a manner of speaking," Alex said.

"Who is this man?" Zeldovich asked.

"I am with the British Embassy in Ulan Bator," the thin man said in Russian. Zeldovich had only the vaguest notion of where Ulan Bator might be. But he was prepared to be cautious. He motioned to a soldier, who quickly stepped between Dr. Cousins and the British diplomat. The tall man started to protest, but the soldier stood his ground and Zeldovich hurried Alex away, holding him by the arm.

"I was only saying good-bye," the doctor said. He waved toward the tall man, who responded in kind.

"It is pointless to be difficult," Zeldovich said, walk-ing faster.

It was warmer in the station. An old-fashioned pot-bellied stove glowed in the center, with a group of slovenly old men drowsing around it. Zeldovich saw a door marked "Station Master" and strode in without knocking, startling the bald man who was sitting with his feet on his desk. Ignoring the man completely, Zeldovich looked around for the telephone, which stood on a table behind the bald man.

The bald man was so frightened by Zeldovich and the KGB troops that he moved quickly out of the way, obviously assuming the invaders were on official party business. Zeldovich nodded to an unarmed soldier carrying a metal suitcase. The soldier opened it and drew out wires, tools and earphones. Working quickly, he began to fiddle with the telephone connection in the wall.

"We will only be a few moments," Zeldovich said to the bald man, finally acknowledging his presence. "Please wait outside."

Apparently relieved, the bald man quickly left the office. As the soldier worked, Dr. Cousins leaned against the desk, wiping his nose with his handkerchief.

"How much more company will we have on the line?" Dr. Cousins asked.

"None. I will be calling a number that will automatically scramble at this end."

Zeldovich would say no more in front of the troops. He had learned long ago to distrust even the most common soldier, especially those under KGB command.

"It is done." The soldier who was working with the wires held one earphone to his ear while the lieutenant whispered into the instrument behind the bald man's desk.

"Please wait outside," Zeldovich said to the soldiers. Everyone but he and Cousins filed out of the room. Zeldovich opened his coat, deliberately revealing the revolver stuck in his belt.

Dr. Cousins smiled. "Really, Zeldovich," he said.

Zeldovich shrugged, removed the earpiece of the old-fashioned stand-up telephone and jiggled the cradle impatiently. He waited, hearing only the odd whishing sounds of the instrument. The Soviet telephone system was a constant embarrassment. Dimitrov would sometimes get so furious he would rip the wire out of its wall connection, continuing to shout expletives into the dead phone. Zeldovich could feel the beginning of his own fury now as the instrument refused to respond.

"Apparently you are better at running trains," Dr. Cousins said. Zeldovich ignored him, listening to the whish of the ocean's waves in the earpiece.

Dimitrov had tried everything to improve the telephone system, Zeldovich remembered, constantly bringing the heads of the telephone company to the Kremlin for a dressing down, firing them, replacing them, perpetually reshuffling personnel. Three top officials of the system had been sentenced to hard labor for negligence. At one point Dimitrov suspected saboteurs, but even the assignment of a special team of technicians to the Kremlin telephones had not solved the problem.

Dimitrov had even told the American Secretary of State that a prime condition of détente would be that the Americans redesign the phone. "If it is the last official act of my life," Dimitrov had vowed, his face florid with anger, "I will fix the flaws in the Soviet telephone system."

Zeldovich felt the irony of the remark as he waited, with Dr. Cousins watching him.

Finally Zeldovich heard an operator on the line, then a long pause, and he tried to get the operator back by shouting into the telephone his identity and his official capacity.

"I am Zeldovich, KGB. This is an official call to General Secretary Dimitrov. I must have absolute priority." The operator faded out, then in again, then connected him to someone else.

"You idiot," Zeldovich finally said, when it was apparent that someone with authority was at the other end.

"I'm sorry, sir," the voice said.

Zeldovich debated whether service would improve if he tried to intimidate the voice, but instead he barked out the number in a tone that he hoped would be persuasive. He heard a series of buzzes and clicks that seemed to go on interminably. Finally he recognized the familiar voice of one of the operators at the Kremlin who put through calls to the dacha. The phone began to ring and another familiar voice answered. Zeldovich announced himself.

"One moment, please." His hands trembled as he waved for the doctor to come and stand next to him.

"Zeldovich?" a voice said. It was unmistakably Dimitrov. He sounded hoarse, tired. It could be distorted in the line, Zeldovich thought—they were about four thousand miles apart.

"Yes, Comrade Dimitrov."

"Where are you?"

"Ulan-Ude."

"My God."

"I have Dr. Cousins here beside me."

"I was expecting his call last night," Dimitrov said testily.

Zeldovich was sure now that the hoarseness was not due to the connection. He moved aside and handed the phone to Alex, quickly moving to the earphones that the soldier had connected. He drew his revolver and pointed it at Alex's head.

"I am here, sir," Alex said. He listened to a series of harsh coughs, followed by an expectoration.

"Kuznetsov?"

"Yes. I am here."

"I've caught this damned abomination," he said. Zeldovich noted the sudden lightening of his attitude.

"Have you any fever?" Alex asked.

"Slight."

"Exactly?"

"Two points above normal."

"And your bowel movements?"

"I hadn't noticed."

"Are you constipated?"

Zeldovich felt his lips break into a smile. The doctor's demeanor was one of stony professionalism.

"No." There was some hesitation. "No. I am sure of it. I went just before I went to bed."

"Was the stool hard or soft?"

"I didn't notice." There was a pause. "Was it important?"

"Any other symptoms?"

"This damned cough."

"Have you looked at the phlegm?"

"Just a moment." There was a silence, then Dimitrov's voice returned. "It is yellowish."

"Thick?"

"Yes, slightly. What does that mean?"

"Is there nasal congestion?"

"Occasionally. When I lie down."

"Are you in bed?"

"Yes."

"Stay there."

"What does it mean?"

Was Dimitrov feeling more than routine anxiety? Zeldovich wondered. Was he beginning to panic?

"Have you been following the regimen, the exact doses recommended?"

"To the letter."

"Do you feel weak?"

"I have felt better," Dimitrov said. "I have not had a cold like this in years."

Alex hesitated, turning his face from Zeldovich, who was watching for a reaction.

"Is it a recurrence?" Dimitrov asked. The timbre of his voice seemed weaker.

"It is probably a bad cold, maybe a grippe," Alex said.

Zeldovich thought the response was being forced.

"Not the other?"

Alex hesitated. "No," he said flatly.

"You're sure?"

"It is a bad cold," Alex said.

Zeldovich noted that the doctor was perspiring, although the room was chilly.

"Get me one of the nurses. I'll give you a prescription."

"I have sent them all away."

"Why did you do that?"

"I felt better. There was no need. I was feeling fine. It only came upon me yesterday."

"I was going to prescribe some antibiotics. They should make you feel better faster."

"And if not?"

"It will take longer."

"Are you sure it is not the other?"

Alex hesitated again. "If I thought it was, I would ask for transportation immediately."

"Well then, that's a relief."

"I don't like the idea of no nurses," Alex said.

"They were all so ugly." Dimitrov's good humor was returning, his anxiety dissipated.

"I will call you tonight. If there is any change, contact me. If you feel that I should be with you, let me know."

"I feel better already."

"Good."

"You like our trains?" Dimitrov asked.

"They are quite interesting."

"And have you found Siberia interesting?"

"I have found something, but I'm not quite sure it was what I might have expected."

Zeldovich felt his stomach tighten. He prodded the doctor's temple with the barrel of his gun.

"I hope that Zeldovich is not heavy-handed. I sent him along to watch over you."

"He is doing an excellent job."

"Good."

"I will call you later." Alex paused. "If you need me, you know exactly where to find me."

Dimitrov chuckled. There was a click. Zeldovich felt his stomach relax as he replaced the gun in his belt. He watched the doctor run his sleeve over his forehead, wiping away the perspiration. The soldier who had worked on the telephone came back and began dismantling the work he had done.

They moved outside of the station house again, into the cold misty rain.

Zeldovich deliberately held back his questions as they

walked quietly toward the waiting train. All the windows of the carriages had misted and people were writing words and drawing pictures in the moisture. In one of the windows of the soft carriage, Vladimir was writing the word "shit."

As they neared the train, they heard the sounds of an argument. The driver of the huge engine had climbed down from his cab and was holding a big round watch in front of the major. The KGB troops stood in front of the engine, blocking the tracks.

"We are thirty minutes behind schedule," the engineer cried.

The major towered over him, trying to ignore him, but the engineer went on, pointing furiously at the watch.

"Do you know what it means for us to be thirty minutes late? There will be delays along the entire six thousand, four hundred and twenty-seven miles of this track. Supplies, troops, passengers. This is a deliberate crime against the Soviet people!"

At the sight of Zeldovich, the major barked an order to his men and they immediately moved back to the troop train. Triumphant, the engineer lifted himself up the metal stairs to the cab. The attendants who had stood on the platform hoisted themselves back into the carriages. Zeldovich stepped aside to let Alex climb up first, following quickly.

As the train began to move, Zeldovich followed the doctor along the passageway. Vladimir looked at them briefly and continued his writing with long unhurried strokes. The sandy-haired Australian was sitting on a spring seat watching the boy.

"I taught him that," he said in English to Alex, who paused, watching the boy at work. Zeldovich could not make out what they were saying.

"He is expressing exactly my feelings about the trip," the man said. "And about these Russian bastards."

"What is he saying?" Zeldovich asked, feeling awkward, wanting to prod the doctor back into his compartment.

"I have been sitting here and telling him dirty jokes," said the Australian, pointing to the guard posted at Alex's door.

"And does he laugh?"

"Hello, you dumb prick," he said to the guard. "You've got all your brains in your ass. See?"

"Yes," Alex said.

"What did he say?" Zeldovich asked.

"He said that the guard has all his brains in his ass," Alex translated.

"He's probably right." Zeldovich smiled, relaxing a little.

"He says you are probably right," Alex said.

The sandy-haired man smiled.

"I'm going to have the kid write 'asshole' in English on all the other windows," he said.

They were silent for a moment, watching the train slide away from the station.

"Did you see laughing boy get off?" the sandy-haired man asked.

"You mean Farmer?"

"My roommate. The voice of doom and gloom. He said good-bye as if he was going to see his Maker. He insists the whole world is going to blow up, beginning right here." He waved his hands wildly about him.

"He may be right."

"They should blow each other's balls off, the bastards."

Zeldovich was getting uneasy about the length of the conversation. "He is drunk?" he asked Alex. "Or crazy?"

"What did he say?" the sandy-haired man asked.

"He wants to know if you're drunk or crazy."

"Tell him to go jerk off."

"What did he say?" Zeldovich asked.

Before Alex could answer, Vladimir came running up and tugged on the Australian's arm.

"Good?" he asked in Russian, pointing at his handiwork.

"How do you say cocksucker in Russian?" the Australian asked Alex.

"The word is too long to fit on the window."

Zeldovich squeezed Alex's upper arm, indicating that it was time to move on. Does it all come down to that? Zeldovich wondered, whether the stool is hard or soft? He followed Dr. Cousins into the compartment.

29

Tania recognized the chief inspector as the train slid into the Chita station. He was standing in a crowd of waiting passengers, mostly young soldiers and rough farmers from the big agricultural communes that stretched through this part of Eastern Siberia. He was watching, Tania imagined, his small pig eyes looking for reportable violations of procedure. He was a dumpy, heavy man, with puddles of chins that shook as he moved. He looked jolly, but that was a false impression. He was a dour, serious man, whose ruthless pursuit of violators had earned him the post of chief inspector for this section of the line. With him was another man, taller, with a mane of white hair that stuck out from under his fur hat. They stood motionless in the freezing cold, watching, waiting for the crowd to disperse.

Tania grabbed the handrail and hopped off the train. The American doctor and the KGB man rushed past her, followed by a group of armed soldiers. The crowd watched them with great interest, as did the inspector and his companion. Tania, uninterested, was surveying the debarking passengers for any sign of the general. He had, after all, been ticketed for Chita and, although she had inspected every inch of the train, she still hoped that the old crone had been lying and he was hiding somewhere. Hadn't he confided his fears, and pressed her for information about the KGB men and the strange cripple? She might have been more thorough in her search for the general, but the sight of the inspector made her remember her lost master key. Was it possible that the general had reported her? she wondered. It made her bitter to think about it.

She felt a sudden tightness in her throat, as the inspector and his companion moved toward her. Was it possible? Why had they singled her out? When they reached her, she bowed obsequiously to the chief inspector.

"Comrade Romoran," the chief inspector said, nodding, the puddles of chins shaking like jelly as he spoke.

"Comrade S-Sokolovich," she stammered.

"This is Comrade Voikov of the Railway Police."

The presence of a policeman startled her, adding another dimension to her fear.

"Comrade," the white-maned man responded pleasantly, showing a set of yellow teeth. He extended his hand and she took it gratefully, feeling a little relieved.

"We will be traveling with you, Comrade," Sokolovich said.

He talked in a low, even voice that was deliberately noncommittal, expressionless. One never knew what he thought of one's performance until he actually sent his memorandums, which were frequently scathing.

Tania picked up their suitcases and carried them into the train. They followed her along the passageway to the compartment formerly shared by the Jew and his wife. Hesitating at the door, she wondered if the old crone had done a good job of clean-up. She had meant to inspect it, but never had. The stench of death had always sickened her, made her afraid. It was a superstition from her childhood. She was thankful that at least she had wiped away the obscenities the Trubetskoi brat had written on the misted windows.

She watched the men look about the compartment while she placed the suitcases under the bunk. Removing his hat, Voikov ran his fingers through his thick white hair and removed an envelope stuffed with papers from an inside pocket. He sat down and began to read while the chief inspector moved into the passageway, motioning Tania to follow. He peered into the well-lit station.

"This is not a routine inspection," Sokolovich whispered, turning to face her. "We are investigating a brutal attack."

Tania was silent. Somehow, she was sure, it was related to the general. Her knees shook. She cursed her own weakness.

"The railroad and its personnel are frequently the target of hooliganism, the work of dissidents who choose to vent their spleen on the railroad."

The inspector shook his head, the chins rippling with anger. They are not after me, Tania thought, reprieved.

"The latest incident is by far the most serious we have encountered," Sokolovich intoned, boring into her with his little pig eyes. "One of our train agents in Krasnoyarsk was brutally attacked. His spine was deliberately broken and he is paralyzed."

She tried to look sympathetic and compassionate. He was, after all, talking about one of their own.

"All of our people are on the alert," Sokolovich said, his face expressionless. It occurred to her that the "Russiya" was being singled out for the inspector's personal attention. Again she felt her security in jeopardy. She wanted to inquire, but kept her silence. Long experience had taught her not to speak except in answer to a question directed specifically at her.

"There is a possibility," Sokolovich continued, his little eyes fixed on her face, "that the culprit might be on this train, since we have fixed the attack at the exact time that the 'Russiya' was at the Krasnoyarsk station."

She felt like a pendulum swinging between guilt and

innocence, fear and hope. Could it have been one of her people? Would she somehow be penalized if it were found that someone on her carriage had perpetrated the attack? "Voikov is our best man, Comrade Romoran," Sokolovich whispered. "He will be asking for your full cooperation, as well as the cooperation of all of our personnel on the train."

"Of course," Tania said.

She knew that the outward investigation would be secondary to Sokolovich's own observations. He would always be watching, she knew.

He turned from her and peered again into the brightly lit station. The crowds around the vendors had thinned. Some of the women had already begun to pack up their goods. Tania could see Sokolovich squinting in the direction of the station, watching the soldiers. She knew he would not make inquiries. The special KGB train was sure to be the subject of rumors all along the six-thousand-odd miles of track. The official explanation was surely known to Sokolovich and it was the unwritten code of all railroad workers not to question KGB affairs.

But despite the cooperation between the KGB and railway workers, some of whom were covert agents themselves, Tania was conscious of considerable rivalry between the two groups. The railroad workers were a powerful entity in their own right, a privileged group in the Soviet Union.

"We are a nation within a nation," a railway official had once said at a meeting. The idea had frightened her, for it hinted at separation from the goals of the State. That had been early in her railway career. Now she knew the official's real meaning: the railway was an entity answerable to its own hierarchy, a powerful bureaucracy with its own interests, including a special police force and a surveillance system that was both part of and separate from the KGB. "The Railroad washes its own linen," was their slogan.

Sokolovich squinted at the station clock, checking it against his own silver pocket watch. It was one thing to cooperate with the KGB, but when they interfered with the railroad timetable, that was quite another matter.

"Bastards," Sokolovich mumbled.

The Chita stopover was scheduled for fifteen minutes. It was now five minutes overdue. Voikov came out from the compartment and joined them in the passageway.

"We are late," he said, looking at Tania as if she were responsible.

The two men stood in the passageway, their eyes fixed on the station entrance, as if they could not begin their investigation until the train was moving again. As they watched, the blonde woman came out of her compartment and joined them in their watch.

At last the American doctor and the KGB man reappeared. The soldiers re-formed at the station entrance and moved quickly back toward the train.

"Ten minutes behind now," Sokolovich observed. The blonde woman glanced at him and returned to her compartment.

When the train had begun to move again, Sokolovich went into the toilet while Voikov rubbed his chin and looked at Tania. Under his thick white hair, his face was ruddy and veined. He beckoned Tania into the compartment and sat down again on the only chair, putting on his glasses and looking over his papers.

"Shmiot. The man's name was Shmiot. Did you know him?"

Tania shook her head.

"It seems to have been totally unprovoked. He was seen just five minutes before the train arrived at the station and was discovered by one of the switchmen less than five minutes after the train had left. All roads lead to the 'Russiya.'" Voikov paused. "The only logical conclusion is that someone slipped off the train, attacked Shmiot, then came back on the train."

"I was sleeping," Tania said, calculating that Krasnoyarsk was a late night stop, nearly midnight local time.

"It is not an easy assignment," Voikov said. "Our people are interrogating everyone who debarked within the last two days. We are handling those who remained on the train since Krasnoyarsk—about a hundred people."

Tania shrugged. She was trying to appear intelligent and concerned, but she was still afraid that somehow this investigation would uncover her intrigue with the general.

Sokolovich came back into the compartment. Voikov removed his glasses and stood up.

"Thank you, Comrade Romoran," he said. "We will start at the hard class and work our way back here. The important thing is not to alarm the passengers or alert our killer. Judging from the condition of the victim, our man may be a psychopath."

Tania excused herself and left the compartment. Her head ached and her uniform was soaked with perspiration. She opened the door to her quarters and was immediately assailed by the stench of the old crone who lay on her bunk, snoring heavily. Soon Tania would have to wake her to take her shift. The idea of the old crone answering questions filled Tania with dread. Who knew what stupidities might come out of her mouth, inadvertent remarks that could reflect on Tania's own actions. She changed her clothes quickly, deciding not to wake the sleeping woman.

When she returned to the passageway, it was empty except for the dull soldier who leaned against the door of the doctor's compartment. She began polishing the samovar, determined to win back her sense of pride in her work. Never again would she allow herself to be corrupted by her emotions. She would distrust them forever, she vowed, if only she might escape detection now.

She polished the samovar until she felt she might be rubbing through the metal. Then she attacked the toilets with an attention to detail that startled even herself. That done, she carefully scoured the filigreed cup holders and polished each metal curlicue until they sparkled in the light like the crown of the old Czarina that she had once seen in Leningrad. She scrubbed the windows in the corridor and promised herself that as soon as the train stopped again she would drop everything and start work on the muddy outside windows. She could finish the job by Skovorodino if she hopped out to the platform at every fifteen-minute stop, washing one window at each station.

The prospect of further chores energized her, spurring her sense of purpose. Even the corridor carpets got an extra effort as she sat on her haunches, ignoring the curious glances of the guard, and loosened the encrusted dirt with her fingers before running the vacuum. She would show Sokolovich what it meant to be a railway worker.

Sokolovich and Voikov returned to the carriage just before dawn. The train was running along the Amur River, very close to China. Both men looked somber in the early light, and the eyes of the chief inspector showed strain and fatigue.

"Wake us in two hours," Sokolovich said as they went into the compartment. Tania had already turned down their bunks and puffed their pillows.

As the men closed the door behind them, the door to the Trubetskoi compartment opened and the fat woman, her hair in curlers, walked drowsily to the toilet. A few moments later a fierce-looking Mongolian, who was the sandy-haired Australian's new roommate, came out of their compartment, heading for the occupied toilet. He tested the door. It was unlocked. As he swung it open, Mrs. Trubetskoi's scream of outrage echoed through the passageway. Rising from the seat, she banged the door shut on the startled Mongolian's hand. The scream brought Trubetskoi dashing out in the passageway, the gap in the front of his pajamas wide open. He banged on the toilet door and called to his wife inside.

"That Mongol pig," she screeched. "He opened the door."

Trubetskoi glared at the Mongolian, who was mumbling, "I'm sorry. I'm so sorry," in heavily accented Russian.

"Filthy foreigners," Trubetskoi growled. He turned on Tania. "You should not allow them in the soft-class compartments. I will report it to the railroad authorities."

He had regained his arrogance, and was happily unaware of how ridiculous he looked with his testicles exposed through the opening of his pajamas.

The inspector's compartment opened and Sokolovich, chins quivering, came out into the corridor.

"They allow these disgusting Orientals in the soft class," Trubetskoi hissed, obviously mistaking Sokolovich for an ally. Sokolovich squinted in the direction of the man's crotch, then turned to look at Mrs. Trubetskoi, who was finally emerging from the toilet. Little Vladimir had awakened and crept out to stand beside his father. The door of the doctor's compartment opened a crack and Tania could see the dark face of the KGB man watching the scene.

Mrs. Trubetskoi, gathering her dignity, had started moving down the corridor, when she suddenly noticed the display of her husband's genitalia.

"These Orientals are pigs." Trubetskoi was still raging at Tania and Sokolovich. The Mongolian stood wringing his hands and appeared not to understand.

"Papa," Vladimir cried, pointing to his father's crotch. Not comprehending, annoyed at the interruption, Trubetskoi took a wide swing at the boy, who instinctively stepped backward, escaping the blow but upsetting a bucket of charcoal. At that instant Tania remembered the incident at Krasnoyarsk, the boy rushing past her, spilling the charcoal.

"Krasnoyarsk," she said, pointing to Vladimir.

Sokolovich, instantly alert, looked from Tania to the boy, then turned to the father, whose anger was still gathering momentum.

"We should not permit these filthy barbarians to contaminate the train—"

"Will you please cover yourself?" Sokolovich said calmly.

The man paused in his diatribe and looked questioningly at the inspector. His wife, flushing a deep red, reached downward and pulled the sides of her husband's fly together. Trubetskoi was suddenly speechless. The Mongolian quickly ducked into the bathroom, slamming the door behind him. Doors closed all along the passageway. The incident was over.

When Mr. and Mrs. Trubetskoi had departed, Tania explained to Sokolovich the circumstances at Krasnoyarsk. The inspector looked at Vladimir, who was playing with the charcoal he had spilled. Then he went into his compartment and roused Voikov. Tania repeated her story.

"It may be nothing," she said, a hedge against such a possibility.

"Bring in the boy," Voikov ordered.

Tania went out into the corridor and bent down beside Vladimir. She detested the boy.

"Those men would like to talk with you, Vladimir," she said. The boy continued to play with the charcoal, not even looking at her.

"Vladimir, if you come they will give you a nice present."

He stopped and looked up, his little face suspicious. "A present?"

"Yes. A present."

He got up from the floor and rubbed his dirty hands on his shirt and trousers.

"You are making yourself dirty," Tania scolded.

He looked at her, then at his blackened hands, and ran them down the front of her uniform. The dirty little bastard, she thought, leading the boy into the compartment where the two men waited. Vladimir stood in the center of the room and put his hands on his hips defiantly.

"Where is my present?"

The men shrugged and looked at each other.

"Do you like candy?" Voikov said pleasantly. When

he smiled, he looked grandfatherly, reassuring. "I have a little boy that likes candy."

"What kind?" the boy snapped. He seemed to be playing with them, enjoying his newfound power.

Voikov poked in his suitcase and brought out a bar of chocolate. Tania sensed his embarrassment at having to reveal his own extravagance. The boy's eyes opened wide as he put out his hand. Chocolate was an expensive delicacy and even Vladimir's indulgent parents did not buy it often. But Voikov drew the chocolate back.

"What were you doing inside the Krasnoyarsk station?" Voikov said with a practiced blandness.

"Krasnoyarsk," Vladimir repeated, not taking his eyes off the candy.

"He was running as if he were frightened," Tania said. She felt hesitant suddenly. Vladimir was a brat, but he could not have committed such a violent crime. He did not have the strength. But, perhaps, he had seen something. The connection of events meant something, she was certain. She was proud of her memory and hoped it might mean another commendation.

"What were you running from, Vladimir?" Voikov said.

"Give me the candy," Vladimir demanded.

"Perhaps you saw something," Voikov urged. He looked up at Sokolovich. "Although he doesn't look as if he is capable of fear."

Voikov undid the wrapper and broke off a piece of the thick, shiny brown chocolate. "Would you like a bite?" he said.

Vladimir rubbed his lips with the back of his hand, and Tania could see all the gluttony of his heritage.

"If he saw such brutality," Voikov whispered, "he would remember."

"Are you sure he was there, Comrade Romoran?" Sokolovich asked. Tania thought hard. Her own credibility was in question now. She remembered the boy coming at her, looking backward over his shoulder. When he had collided with the charcoal bucket, he had stopped for a brief moment, looking up at her in panic and pointing in the direction from which he had come. The picture came to her clearly now. She knelt quickly and grabbed Vladimir by the shoulders.

"He will come after you now," she hissed. "He will do the same to you." She had acted on impulse, but it worked.

"You must not let him," Vladimir cried, his lip quivering.

"See," Tania cried, exhilarated by her vindication.

"What did you see?" Voikov asked.

"The funny man." He enacted an attack, flailing his arms in the air, twisting and gyrating, enjoying his own exhibition.

"Who?" Voikov asked. He was still patient, gentle, the candy bar poised in his hand.

Vladimir stopped and looked at the floor. Then he slowly lifted his head and pointed toward the compartment door, smiling and reaching out his little hand for the chocolate. Voikov broke off a piece and put it in his grimy hand. Vladimir stuffed the entire piece in his mouth.

"Now you will show us," Voikov said.

The boy darted into the passageway. He stopped outside the compartment shared by the Jew and the cripple. Then he put out his hand.

Voikov gave him the rest of the chocolate and the boy skipped away down the passageway.

"Miserable brat," Tania whispered.

"We will bring him back later," Voikov said.

"The key," Sokolovich whispered, touching Tania's arm. She felt her heart stop, her throat constrict.

"One moment," she managed to say. She rushed to her quarters and violently shook the old woman awake.

"Your master key, please."

The woman automatically patted her pockets, then looked up warily.

"Where is yours?"

"Give me the key or I shall tell them that you took bribes from the Jew."

"Who?"

"Chief Inspector Sokolovich. He is outside."

The old woman reached into her pocket and drew out her master key. Tania tore it out of her hand and ran back into the corridor. Both men were poised at either side of the compartment. She eased the key into the hole and stepped back. Sokolovich turned it slowly, then threw the door open and burst into the compartment.

The two men inside looked up in surprise, then immediately turned to each other. Tania felt certain that in that glance, some message passed between them. One of them was surely the culprit, she told herself. It hardly mattered which one.

30

The train bounced forward, rattling the glasses and agitating the borscht in its stainless-steel bowl. Zeldovich, Anna Petrovna and Alex were in the almost deserted restaurant car. Alex squinted into the declining sun, missing the warmth as the sun sank over the horizon. The train moved along the river's edge, through tunnels, over bridges, past stations with odd incomprehensible names—Ksnevkskaya, Mogochur, Amazar, Yerofey Pavlovich—names that hung on the tongue like thick syrup.

Time was topsy-turvy and his watch, still running on Moscow time, was useless. They had spent the day, or was it night, sitting in the compartment speculating and debating. He felt as if he were in the dead center of a prism, so that with each new position he took, he saw the world in a different light.

He sat facing Anna Petrovna. Her skin was glowing in the suffused light, growing softer as the sun dropped below the horizon. He had been watching her face all day, studying it as if his eye had been a microscope, watching the ripples of sunlight wash over it. Yet it was Dimitrov who dominated his thoughts—Dimitrov!

Was Dimitrov dying? Alex's conversation with him at Chita had hinted at what his own intuition told him. He had felt Dimitrov's strength ebbing and, over the distance of thousands of miles, had sensed the imminence of death.

"What do you think?" Zeldovich had persisted.

"You heard him," he had answered testily.

"His voice was weak."

"It is probably a flu."

"Probably."

"How can I be sure? He's thousands of miles away."

"Only a flu, eh?"

"Must I repeat it all day?"

"It is essential that you be accurate. You are not holding something back?"

"You are one pain in the ass," Alex said in English, exasperated by the probing.

He had held out throughout the day and night while Zeldovich probed relentlessly, demanding a prognosis. A quick death for Dimitrov would save Anna Petrovna's life, at least over the short term. Eventually, after Zeldovich used her testimony, they would have to destroy her. Like Alex, she simply knew too much of Zeldovich's machinations.

Alex had no illusions about himself. Certain death. They would never let him go back to America and alarm the President and his Secretary of State with tales of Russian intrigue. His only chance of survival was to alert the Americans somehow, to telegraph his danger. Sighing, he felt helpless.

He speculated on the condition of the blood, the diminishing red corpuscles, the invasion of white blood cells, weakening the body's defenses. Tomorrow, he knew, Dimitrov would have no more illusions.

He should, of course, be back at the dacha easing

the way for Dimitrov's last passage. That was an essential part of his ministry, and he recognized his own abdication of responsibility. The old fox would certainly understand, even appreciate his unwillingness to return. They would use his presence, he knew, perhaps to make the United States a viable suspect in the General Secretary's death. That he could even think of such a strategy confirmed his suspicion that he was becoming as paranoid as the Russians. Sorry, he apologized in his heart to Dimitrov. There is really nothing I can do now, anyway. But he could not shake his sense of guilt. It was ironic. He might be letting Dimitrov down, but a good case could be made for his heroics. Wasn't he saving a continent?

Dimitrov would not think so. "Power is absurd," Dimitrov had told him one day as they strolled on the dacha's grounds. "It needs constant illustration since it is based primarily on fear."

"Fear?" Remembering the conversation, Alex was ashamed now of how unwilling he had been to act.

"What good is a nuclear arsenal if people do not remember what it represents? People must be reminded of its terror, of its force. Power rests with those who have the will to use it. The day is coming when the weapon itself can be carried on the back of a single man. In a knapsack or a suitcase. Every conflicting ideology in the world will have an arsenal capable of destroying millions of people. That will be the ultimate chaos. The end of order."

"What do you suggest?"

"One system. One order. One power to administer the world, the uniting of mankind under a single banner."

"Whose?"

It was intellectual gymnastics, speculation. He remembered his surprise at Dimitrov's answer, which came slowly, after he stood for a few minutes watching the river's flow.

"Those who have the courage to accept the responsibility of world domination, the courage to display their power, the courage to use it."

"And who has that?"

Dimitrov had continued to look into the river. Then he looked up. By an odd reflection of light, Alex could see the river's flow in Dimitrov's gray eyes.

"I have," he had said. It was the final confirmation of what Alex had begun to suspect. The memory shocked him back to his sense of place.

"What is it, Alex?" Anna Petrovna asked.

"Nothing." But it was hardly nothing. He felt a sudden chill and reached for a glass of tea that stood cooling on the table. He sipped it, but felt no warmth.

"Are you all right?"

"Yes," he lied. He reached over and took her hand. He sensed Zeldovich's discomfort in seeing the uncommon display of emotion. Pretending to ignore the gesture, he dipped his black bread into the gravy of a greasy stew and hunched over the plate.

The restaurant was coming to life again. The noise level began to increase as new people entered. Alex heard silverware tinkling on plates, the cacophony of voices speaking different languages. Behind him, he could hear the pedantic voice of Miss Peterson sharing her knowledge of the railroad's history with an elderly American couple who had recently boarded the train.

"It is the longest railroad in the world," she was intoning. Turning sideways, he could see the elderly couple listening eagerly. Apparently Miss Peterson's fund of facts had not yet become boring.

"Czar Nicholas turned the first spade of earth in Vladivostok in 1891. This is the second time I have come this way."

"Has it changed?" the elderly man asked.

"Yes," she said primly, obviously relishing his attention. She had found her audience at last, grist for her mill. Alex was glad for her.

Anna Petrovna's eyes peered through the window into the darkness.

"What do you see?" he asked.

"China. It is just beyond those hills."

He wondered again what her real motives were. Was it really compassion for all the possible victims, the innocent millions, or only the instinct for self-preservation?

"Is it possible that what he intends is the right course?" Alex whispered.

He could see Zeldovich's fork stop in midair. A flush, like round dabs of rouge, mounted to Anna Petrovna's cheeks.

"That is utterly preposterous, inhuman," she said.

"Is it?"

"I can't believe it is you saying this, Alex. The idea is unthinkable."

Zeldovich grunted, looking about him, his instinct for secrecy operative. Apparently everyone was absorbed in other matters, food, conversation. The little man in charge of the restaurant was talking to a tall, thin man, whom Alex recognized vaguely as someone he had seen in the hard-class carriage.

"He has an unbroken streak since his defeat," the man was saying loudly.

"He rides back and forth on the train. I have never seen him sleep," the man in charge of the restaurant said.

"He has won back his right to be the champion," said the other man.

The train bounced through the declining daylight. Alex could begin to see their images in the mirror of the window. He studied his own reflection. Was that really him? He appeared remote, unconcerned. Was it because, in the end, he could not go against his grain? As a doctor, as a scientist, he was not conditioned to consider any factors except the prolonging of life. Despite all that they had told him, all that he had deciphered for himself, all the passion and commitment that he felt for Anna Petrovna, all the visible and invisible evidence of an impending holocaust, he persisted still in his narrow interest, the life of his patient. He·had followed the progress of the disease and knew Dimitrov's condition to be hopeless, yet he saw his duty clearly.

But Zeldovich would never let him leave, unless he could persuade him that his objective was to speed Dimitrov's death. Would Zeldovich trust him?

"I must go back," he whispered. Zeldovich's fork stopped again in midair.

"Where?" Zeldovich asked, putting down his fork, bending his head lower to assure the privacy of his words.

"To him," Alex said firmly. "He is failing."

"Dying?" Zeldovich asked, the word barely audible. His face was ashen.

"Perhaps swiftly. I cannot tell without tests. It is a good bet that the condition has returned. In the absence of confirmation, I can only guess what is taking place."

All pretense was over now. Zeldovich rose and placed a handful of kopeks on the table, nodding at the manager who nodded back nervously. As they rose, Alex saw the soldier at the end of the train stiffen and reach for his machine gun, turning his back to prevent the diners from observing the weapon. Alex waited for Anna Petrovna, then followed her in the direction of the soft-class carriage.

Zeldovich led the way, the soldier following behind. As they passed through the icy space between the cars, Alex saw the boy Vladimir in the shadows munching greedily on a piece of chocolate. His hands were filthy and his lips were stained brown. As they passed, he turned away quickly like an animal, as if afraid they might snatch away his feast.

"You'll freeze out here," Alex muttered in the direction of the boy as they moved through the door.

Back in their compartment, Zeldovich threw the bolt and confronted Alex.

"When did you decide this?" he demanded, a droplet of spittle showing at the side of his mouth. Anna Petrovna stepped toward him, touching his arm.

"In the restaurant, at the moment it was expressed."

"Why did you wait so long?"

"That is my business."

"You think you can save him?" Zeldovich asked.

"I didn't say that."

"Then why would you go back?"

"I owe it to him."

"You owe him nothing," Anna Petrovna said.

"I'm sorry," he said gently. "I must go back."

"Are you serious?" Zeldovich sputtered.

Alex could remember the pride with which he had taken his oath, his absolute belief in its rightness. It exactly fit the way he viewed the world and his role as a doctor.

He looked at Anna Petrovna, felt the strength of his love for her. Its power over him was enormous, beyond all the conditioning of his previous life. And yet, he could not be commanded by it. One life for a million, perhaps millions.

"Is it possible that we are all mistaken?" he asked suddenly.

Zeldovich looked at him, then shot a glance at Anna Petrovna. "What does it take to convince him?" he said with annoyance.

"Surely there are checks," Alex said.

"In theory, yes," Zeldovich responded. "I grant you that. Others are supposed to be consulted. There is a definite procedure. Quite different from your own country where the nuclear trigger is in the hands of a single man who cannot be countermanded. But don't let that lull you into believing that Dimitrov would not be able to find a way to do it."

"But you have destroyed his instrument."

Zeldovich looked sharply at Anna Petrovna. Damn, Alex thought. This time I am the betrayer.

"So now we are all in it together," Zeldovich said,

turning to Anna Petrovna. "You might have spared him the knowledge. It could be bad for his health."

"You wouldn't dare," Anna Petrovna said indignantly.

Pulling out his gun, Zeldovich put the barrel against Alex's chest.

"So pull the trigger, you son of a bitch," Alex said, surprised at his own show of courage.

"It would be simple," Zeldovich said with obvious bravado. "Puff, and I will throw your carcass to the Siberian wolves."

"Then you will have to kill me as well," Anna Petrovna said. "Then who will save your ass?"

Zeldovich smiled and put the gun away.

"In due time," he said, chuckling. "Do you really believe that Grivetsky's death will stop Dimitrov? I know him well. He controls the Politburo, although if he had to, he would act without them."

"If he lives," Anna Petrovna said.

"Which is highly unlikely," Alex interjected.

"Then why are you so anxious to go to him?"

"I am a doctor."

"Even if it meant that he would live long enough to release his missiles?" Anna Petrovna asked.

"Even if that."

He knew he was trying her patience.

"I don't understand," Anna Petrovna pleaded. "This man has it in his mind to murder millions and can conceivably find the power to do so. By prolonging his life you will be a party to it."

"I am not God," Alex said, but the context seemed all wrong.

Zeldovich watched the exchange, looking from face to face as one might watch a tennis match. Was his desire to return to Dimitrov just a sop to his own ego, an academic vindication of a self-righteous moral position? Whatever happened, this experience had marked him.

"Do you really think there is the remotest possibility

of your ever returning to Dimitrov's bedside?" Zeldovich said slowly, his lips pressed tightly, as he looked
at his watch.

So it was out of his hands, Alex thought with relief.

31

From the moment when the two men burst into the compartment Godorov sensed that this might, indeed, be the beginning of the end of his life. Not that it mattered. He felt no pain now. He was stretched out in the lower bunk, floating, it seemed, on the bounce of the train. He wondered whether he was feeling joy, since he could barely remember what it was like.

Perhaps he had been sleeping, was still sleeping, or had been transported back in time to his old home and he was lying in his own warm, soft, quilted bed, his head on the oversized feather pillow. He could not summon the barest personal memory of the past thirty years of his life. It was as if all that misery had happened to someone else, a man for whom he could feel only some vague pity, like a blind beggar who had sat perpetually on the wooden steps of his little village's only store. Occasionally his father would fling a kopek into the man's lap. Godorov was always envious of the gift, but he had been ashamed of his greed. It was that sense of shame, of wanting to do good, that he could recall in himself now, which tranquilized him and made that other Godorov, that hateful, miserable, murdering Godorov, seem a figure beyond reality.

The other man in the compartment, the Jew Ginzburg, had jumped to the floor, obviously startled by the two men's sudden entrance. They stood in the center of the compartment, feet planted firmly as they hesitated momentarily, their eyes darting from one man to the other.

"Krasnoyarsk," the man with the white hair said. "Which one of you got off at Krasnoyarsk?" Oh that, Godorov thought, remembering the old Godorov, that limping wretch who had paid a little visit to Shmiot. That one. What does he have to do with me? he thought. He rolled his eyes away from the two men and looked into the Jew's face. It was twisted into a defiant grin.

"I had better get the boy," the man with the quivering chins said. He started to move toward the door. The white-haired man put a hand on his chest, postponing his exit.

"Make it easy on yourself," he said to both men at once. "The boy will identify you in any event."

Godorov remembered the small face of the boy watching the other Godorov, mimicking the silly walk of the other Godorov. He smiled. It was a good likeness, a perfect replica. In his mind he could see the boy, staring as the other Godorov sweated over the body of Shmiot, cracking the bones as if they belonged to a doll.

"Well," the white-haired man said.

Godorov felt the eyes of the Jew on him.

"Yes, Krasnoyarsk," the Jew whispered.

"You admit it then," the white-haired man said gently, looking at Ginzburg.

"The boy will know," the man with the quivering chins said.

"That's why it would be better to admit it," the white-haired man said, looking at the Jew. Godorov felt himself merging with the other Godorov again, but only in body, since he was certain that his spirit had moved elsewhere. He could not muster any pity or compassion for Shmiot. It all seemed to have occurred quite outside of himself.

"You might as well tell him," Godorov said.

It hardly mattered. It was of absolutely no importance. He was trying to remember what hate had been like, what pain was.

"That is good advice," the white-haired man said to the Jew.

His manner seemed vaguely familiar, Godorov thought, recalling other interrogations. At the beginning of these affairs there was always politeness, he remembered. He knew he had returned to the essence of himself again, and he was almost giddy with delight. Tell them what I did, he told the Jew silently.

"Tell them," he said aloud.

"Your passports, please," the white-haired man said. He was polite, soft-spoken. Ginzburg reached into the suitcase that lay under Godorov's bunk. Their eyes met. The Jew's eyes flickered briefly. It is all right, they seemed to say. I am used to such matters.

"Mine is in the inner pocket of my coat on the hook." Godorov pointed.

"Well, then, stand up and get it."

Godorov chuckled. "I can't walk."

The officials looked at his legs.

"He is crippled," the man with the white hair said.

"That is the long and short of it," Godorov said.

The heavier man dipped fat fingers into the pocket. He removed the passport and looked into Godorov's face, confirming his identity.

"Godorov, Ivan Vasilyevich," he read.

But the white-haired man was obviously more interested in Ginzburg, who rummaged through his suitcase and withdrew a packet containing two passports. He handed them over.

"Mikhail Moiseyevich Ginzburg." The white-haired man intoned the name, looking sharply into Ginzburg's face.

Ginzburg nodded. The white-haired man held out the opened passport for the man with the quivering chins to see. Godorov watched him nod conspiratorially. Now that the pain was gone, he felt more lucid, almost clairvoyant. Ginzburg looked at him again, the hooded eyes transmitting information clearly. I know them, Godorov imagined the eyes said. He blinked in affirmation.

"And this other passport?" the white-haired man said, looking around the compartment.

"My wife."

"Where is she?"

"In the baggage car."

The two officials looked at each other. Godorov smiled. I am being deliberately obtuse, Ginzburg's eyes said. His silence seemed a deliberate affront.

"What is she doing in the baggage car?" the man with the quivering chins asked. "There is no heat or light in there."

"I am taking her to Birobidjan," Ginzburg said, not even bothering to explain.

"What does he mean?" the white-haired man said to Godorov.

Godorov shrugged. Could they possibly understand? He could feel their politeness ending, their exasperation and cruelty starting.

"You can stop all this Jewish cleverness," the white-haired man said. Ginzburg was standing up, his bare feet cold on the icy floor. The white-haired man grabbed a handful of his flannel undershirt and, lifting, forced Ginzburg to rise up on his toes.

"I am talking about you, you little Hebe."

Godorov watched as Ginzburg took the abuse without resistance. The man with the quivering chins had joined the attack, grabbing a handful of hair and roughly tilting Ginzburg's head back.

"We have a witness," the white-haired man said. "It is useless to claim your innocence. It will go better with you if you confess."

"Confess?" Ginzburg whispered. "I killed no one," he said with mild indifference.

"He is so clever," the white-haired man said. "These Jews are so damned clever."

Ginzburg watched them, expressionless.

"He knows damned well he didn't kill him," the white-haired man said to his companion. "He didn't try to kill him. He wanted to maim him beyond hope of recovery." He turned again to Ginzburg. "Isn't that right, you little Jew bastard?"

Ginzburg refused to respond. I'll handle them, he seemed to say, looking briefly at Godorov.

"What did he do to you, this Shmiot?" the white-haired man probed. They still held Ginzburg by the shirt and head. "Try to rape your precious Hebe wife? Something like that, Ginzburg?"

"She wasn't Jewish," Ginzburg said in a tone of indifference. The white-haired man released Ginzburg's shirt and opened the passport of Ginzburg's wife.

"Russian," he said with disgust.

"And in the baggage car?" said the other man, with heavy sarcasm. "If she was in there since Moscow, she'd be dead by now."

"She is," Ginzburg said calmly.

"Killed her too?" the white-haired man said.

"Perhaps."

"The man's a psychopath," the white-haired man said.

"You are all absurd," Godorov said calmly. "It was me."

The two officials looked at each other and smiled.

"They are both crazy," the man with the white hair said. "A man who can't walk could hardly be a suspect."

"I'm telling you. It was me," Godorov persisted, but the officials ignored him.

"I'll get the boy for a formal identification," the man with the quivering chins said.

"That will close the matter," the white-haired man agreed.

Ginzburg settled into the only chair. Clasping his hands in front of him, he seemed like a small child showing his good behavior. The man with the quivering chins let himself out, leaving the white-haired man scowling at Ginzburg.

"They are very clever, these people," the white-haired man said, speaking to Godorov. "You cannot imagine how brutal the attack on Shmiot was. The man is literally a basket case. You can never tell about motive. Jealousy. Greed. A fit of temper. Could have stemmed from a simple argument over some trifling subject. You never know about these people." He seemed to warm up as he continued. "They have these hidden aggressive tendencies, all disguised under a bland humble exterior. Look at him sitting there." He tapped his own head. "You'll never know what goes on in their heads, some plotting and deviousness, no doubt." He opened Godorov's passport and studied it again. "You Georgians know what I mean." He winked at Godorov. "Although I'll never understand why you wanted to take the rap for him."

It was a game they were all playing, Godorov thought. Very soon the boy would arrive and the little charade would be over. He wished it could be prolonged. The idea of humiliating these officials was titillating, especially to him, who had been deprived of such amusement for so long. He felt younger, stronger, clearer in mind than he had felt since his youth, as if the balloon of his anger had burst and all the horror had sputtered out in one continuous exhalation.

"Did you really think you could get away with it?" the white-haired man asked Ginzburg, who looked up at him blankly.

Godorov turned his head quickly when he heard the latch of the compartment click. In the doorway, filling it up, the man with the quivering chins held little Vladimir by his upper arm. The little boy's face was a mass of black and brown smears, from the charcoal and the chocolate, and he was squirming in the man's grip.

"It will only take a moment, you little brat," the

man with the quivering chins said. Godorov watched as the little eyes darted from face to face, coming to rest on Godorov. He is a stupid little fellow, Godorov thought, wondering how he could have harbored such hatred for him. He is just another ridiculous little boy. Godorov prepared to rise from the bunk and submit to the two officials. But although he pictured the movement in his mind—the actual act of rising, then sitting, finally standing—he could not move. He touched and squeezed his thighs, but the flesh was unresponsive. Summoning all of his will, he again made an effort to move, only to find that it was impossible. He traced downward with his fingers from his neck to his hips. That far he had feeling. Beyond that point was only soft flesh without feeling and without pain. He saw the eyes of the boy meet his own, the little mouth twisted in a sticky smile. He raised himself on one elbow, conscious that he was grimacing with effort. Only the little boy noticed.

"Well?" the man with the white hair said impatiently. The boy looked at Ginzburg, who smiled back at him, his face glowing with contentment.

"Well?" the man with the white hair said again, trying to be more patient.

The old Godorov might have felt despair in this predicament. But the new Godorov continued to be calm, savoring the joy of painlessness, the absence of any anxiety whatsoever. The old Godorov might have felt the biting desperation of a wasted life, while the new Godorov felt only tranquility and fulfillment. He lay back again on the bunk and waited for the boy to accuse him.

"Dammit," the man with the quivering chins said, shaking the boy like an oversized rag doll.

"Just point out the man you saw in Krasnoyarsk," the white-haired man said.

"Tell him, you little brat," the man with the quivering chins said.

"Let me." The white-haired man knelt beside the boy.

Vladimir stared imperiously down at him. For a moment Vladimir looked away, glanced at Godorov. Then he looked down again.

"Would you like some more chocolate?" the white-haired man said. The boy's eyes opened wide. He nodded his head.

"Then just point out the man you saw in Krasno-yarsk." He pointed his own finger at Ginzburg. "Just point your finger," he urged.

Godorov did not wonder about Ginzburg's silence in the face of the accusation. Between them there was a kinship of understanding. What did it matter to either of them?

"Well, you little monster? Point," the white-haired man said.

"Point," the man with the chins echoed, shaking the boy again.

"He is the one," Vladimir said at last, turning abruptly and pointing to Godorov.

"You little bastard," the man with the quivering chins said. "I'll see you are severely punished."

Godorov chuckled to himself. Even Vladimir must be intimidated by now, if that were possible.

The white-haired man stood up slowly and, with a sweeping motion of his arm, struck Vladimir across the cheek. The boy yelped like a kicked dog, then stepped back and kicked the white-haired man in the groin. He doubled up, clutching his genitals. The man with the quivering chins grabbed Vladimir from behind and pinned his arms against his sides. But the boy continued to strike out with his feet.

The white-haired man slowly straightened, conscious of his lost dignity and obviously angered by the general refusal to cooperate. He turned to Ginzburg and grabbed him again by the shirt, lifting him from the chair. "I warn you for the last time."

Indifferent, Ginzburg turned his eyes away. The white-haired man pushed him back in the chair, turning again to the boy.

"One last time," he shouted, "before I lock you up."

He pulled out a ring of keys from his pocket. Obviously he was a policeman of the old school, a wielder of the carrot and the stick.

At the sight of the keys, the boy quieted. They were always dangling their keys, Godorov remembered. It was their greatest weapon of intimidation. The old Godorov had dissolved in paroxysms of fear at the mere sight of those keys, swinging ominously on huge metal rings. It was not at all odd to Godorov that the boy would understand the meaning of the keys. They were the perfect symbol of power.

"We will lock you up forever," the white-haired man said. "No more chocolates. No more good things to eat. No more fun. No more mother and father. No more play."

"It was him," the boy said suddenly, pointing at Ginzburg, who looked at him blankly.

"Are you sure?" the white-haired man said.

The boy looked at Godorov, who turned his eyes away. What difference did it make?"

"Deny it," Godorov said to Ginzburg.

"Deny what?"

"That you did that."

"Why?"

"Because you didn't."

"He did," the boy said, pointing again at Ginzburg.

"I did it, you idiots, I did it. It took me thirty years to find him."

"Take him out of here," the white-haired man said. The man with the quivering chins began to drag the boy from the compartment.

"What about the chocolates?" he asked.

"I'll give you chocolates up your ass," the white-haired man said. He dragged Ginzburg to his feet and snapped on a pair of handcuffs.

"Deny it," Godorov repeated.

"Why?"

"How can he deny it?" the white-haired man said.

Ginzburg smiled. "It is much better this way," he said gently.

"Why?" Godorov asked.

"It is something specific. At least if I am guilty of something, it is something specific."

Godorov could understand that. He could remember his own unspecific crime. How it confused him.

The white-haired man opened the door of the compartment. He stopped for a moment and looked down at Godorov.

"Why would you want to save this Jew?" he asked. Then, as if expecting no answer, he stepped through the doorway.

Godorov lay back again and looked up at the underside of the bunk above him. What did it matter? he told himself. He was quite content to lie there without pain, without anger, without hope, heading nowhere.

32

It was like holding a chunk of ice against his ear. Zeldovich stood in the bleak emptiness of the Shimanovsk station, listening to the crackling sounds of merged voices. The KGB troops were blocking the engine's way again and, from where he stood waiting for the connection to be made, he could see the engineer muttering to himself, occasionally shaking his fist at the guards. Then the voice of Bulgakov came through, distorted by the static, but familiar to Zeldovich. He had used the special military line, the privacy worth the distortion in sound caused by the security scrambler.

"Zeldovich here," he said. "I am in Shimanovsk."

"Shimanovsk?"

"Siberia. Near the Amur."

He had no need to offer further landmarks. The Amur was the dividing line between the Soviet Union and China. He could sense the tension at the other end of the line.

"Grivetsky is dead."

"My God!"

335

"You must come at once."

"How did he die?"

"I cannot explain. Please. I am on the 'Russiya.' We are one day out of Khabarovsk."

There was a jet airport at Khabarovsk where military aircraft could land.

"And Dimitrov?"

Bulgakov was well aware of Zeldovich's connection to the General Secretary. He felt a slight difficulty in speaking. His throat constricted. It was the moment of decisiveness.

"Dimitrov is dying."

"Will you repeat that?"

"Dimitrov is dying."

"And Grivetsky is dead?"

"Yes."

There was a brief pause. Zeldovich was willing to bet that the Marshall was evaluating the link between the two men, speculating on the consequences.

"I will meet the train at Khabarovsk."

The connection was immediately broken. Zeldovich continued to hold the earpiece to his ear, pleased with his decision.

Dimitrov was dying. The doctor had confirmed it. Each man must chart his own course through the thicket, Zeldovich thought, sensing that he had taken the only turn in the road available to him. The death of Dimitrov would have meant the death of Zeldovich, unless he had acted in his own interest. He put the earpiece in its cradle and moved quickly toward the waiting train. At his signal, the troops boarded their carriage and the train began to move, the wheels turning slowly over the rails.

Satisfied that the doctor and Mrs. Valentinov were well guarded, Zeldovich made his way into his own compartment and dropped into the chair. He was exhausted, and feeling that sense of rootlessness that had gripped him at the beginning of the journey. He poked under his bunk and found a bottle of vodka. He took a long drink, feeling the heat in his chest. He took a cigar from the case in his inner pocket. It had been Grivetsky's cigar case, and it had fallen to the floor as Grivetsky stumbled, his fingers gripping his mortal wound. Zeldovich puffed deeply, watching the smoke jet from his mouth, filling the air around him. He felt calmer now, his thoughts clearer, less agitated.

It was beyond his conception to think of life without Dimitrov. For thirty years now, he had been the moon to Dimitrov's earth. For them death had had no meaning except as a method of eliminating rivals. In that context death had many forms. It was removal from the power structure, by banishment, by intimidation, by humiliation, by ridicule, and, only as a last resort, as he had eliminated Grivetsky, by stifling life itself. Not that he personally had always been the instrument of these political murders. He had only carried out three or four over a period of thirty years, which was not a bad record considering the number of people who had had to be removed from Dimitrov's path. This did not include, of course, the contrived "legal" deaths of persons by accidental means, death by third parties, in prisons, in hospitals. Dimitrov himself had been a pallbearer in a number of funerals of men who had been eliminated by his own order. And yet even these orders had been oblique, never direct, since the suggestion of elimination was all that Zeldovich ever needed.

If there were accusatory whispers, Dimitrov would put them to rest by invoking the specter of Stalin.

"Thank God we have seen the last of those methods," he would say and all in earshot would nod in agreement, their innards congealed with fear.

The process of elimination earned them, in those later years, long stretches of calm. Dimitrov had, at last, reached the pinnacle of unassailability, and although Zeldovich still stood as a symbol of implied terror, they both knew that that period had passed. Few dared to offer opposition, except in the most subtle ways, and differences of opinion were usually allowed as a kind of escape valve for bruised egos.

But age and rumors of Dimitrov's illness had resurrected the smoldering ashes of ambition. Dimitrov, with his infallible sense of his own power, could detect the striving for power among those around him.

"My life is your ransom, Zeldovich," Dimitrov had told him. "You will be their first course at my funeral."

"They will choke on me," he had said, and Dimitrov had laughed at his bravado.

Zeldovich knew that Dimitrov resented his need of him. And he was often abused, credited by Dimitrov with a capacity for cruelty that he did not feel was justified. He would characterize himself more accurately as a professional, whose job was to protect the goals of the state, as embodied by Dimitrov. It had been hard for him to bear being ridiculed by Dimitrov, and made the subject of his sarcasm.

Why was he thinking these thoughts now? Zeldovich wondered. Dimitrov would forgive him. It was not, at least in Zeldovich's mind, a betrayal. Surely Dimitrov would understand that he had had to find some way to survive. Besides, he knew that Zeldovich was totally without commitment to anything beyond the person of Dimitrov. He had no interest in ideology. Lenin was merely a statue. Marx was a book. Communism was simply the approved doctrine. The party was nothing more than an organization, as were the Army, the KGB and the myriad of other agencies, too numerous to ever remember. Dimitrov was the only object, person, ideology, that had given any meaning whatsoever to his life. Dimitrov and he had discussed what would happen after his death, the adulation, the memorials. "If I do not stop the Chinks they will piss on my grave. History will destroy me for my lack of courage," Dimitrov said.

Zeldovich felt his resentment engulf him like a wave. How dare Dimitrov be mortal, a rotten lump of flesh? It is you who are betraying me, Comrade Dimitrov, he railed, feeling the acid rise in his chest, the anger trigger the explosion inside of him. He puffed deeply on the cigar, annoyed at his own search for justification.

Zeldovich stood up and paced the compartment. Was

it his own survival that really mattered? he wondered. Death was so commonplace an incident in his world that it hardly seemed worth fearing. There was no God, no unknown, nothing to fear. There was only nothing-ness, wasteland, like this bleak country. The mind grew blank. The body cold. And that was that.

He felt the wheels begin to slow beneath his feet. Through the window, he could see a faint glow of lights and figures moving like phantoms along the tracks. Shielding his eyes, he could make out squat forms mov-ing slowly, shovels and brooms on their shoulders, a work gang of babushkas.

Then the wheels clanked to a halt, the din of move-ment receding as the great train stood silent in the glow of the station. He read the faded letters on the sign that hung from the eaves of a dilapidated wooden station. Belgorsk. It held no meaning for him. He could make out only a few odd-shaped houses where weak lights glowed. In a nearby window a woman was filling a samovar while a man in woolen underwear sat at a table drinking from a large cup. They seemed familiar, like his own mother and father, whom he had not thought about for years. Zeldovich flicked a cigar ash to the floor.

A sharp knock on the compartment door startled him. His fingers automatically went to the butt of the gun tucked in his belt.

"Sir?" a woman's voice said. He recognized it as that of the younger attendant and opened the door. She stood, puffy-eyed, in the passageway, holding out a small brown envelope.

"A message," she said, obviously curious. Taking it from her, he slammed the door and tore the envelope open.

"Call at once. D."

He could imagine Dimitrov lying in his bed in help-less uncertainty, his strength and confidence ebbing, his paranoia mounting. He smiled as he imagined the man suffering, thrashing in frustration. Grivetsky's con-firmation of arrival in Chita had not come. The American doctor had not called again. He could see Dimitrov reaching for the telephone, stirring the flunkies on his staff, none of whom dared to imagine his consternation, his mounting frustration. He looked at the message again.

"Call at once. D." Then he tore it up and flung the pieces against the window like confetti.

33

Anna Petrovna had been sitting motionless, looking out the window, watching the vague forms of the passing landscape. Occasionally a pinpoint of light could be observed in the distance, or a thin wisp of smoke rising from a lone chimney. She might have been sitting there for a few moments or hours, her blonde head hardly moving, as if she had turned to stone.

You must understand, he begged her silently. He felt no agitation or impatience. To him now the world was only the compartment and the arc of landscape visible outside. I love you, he wanted to say, and draw her into his arms. He detested his own intransigence. What he had chosen could only be, at best, a pyrrhic victory for his conscience. Could he possibly expect to escape from this surveillance and traverse what must be more than five thousand miles to reach the bedside of the failing Dimitrov? It was like standing at the base of a vertical incline and making the choice to scale it, without a single climbing tool, without rope, without hope. What satisfaction was there in that, except perhaps in

some secret corner of the mind where the pure ego lay
trapped in its cell?

He didn't even have the power to save the man, not
now. At best the chemotherapy that he had prescribed
could only postpone the end. The disease was still the
master of the flesh, although he had given his lifetime to
thwarting it. It was resourceful, ingenious, a mixed bag
of disguises and surprises. He could admit defeat as
he had done thousands of times in the past, with grace.

"We will beat this thing together, you and I," Dimitrov had said.

"It is formidable."

"Everything is formidable."

The impossible is only impossible because of igno-
rance, he told himself, still holding out the idea of somehow getting off the train and heading back to the dacha.
But he was offended by his own smugness. There is no
escaping now, he admitted, watching the landscape
slide by. A small boy slogged along the track with a
heavy package on his back, his face raised to the passing train. A stray dog barked a greeting, his spindly
hind legs stiff with effort, yearning for recognition from
the train, which moved on relentlessly.

He imagined he understood what Anna Petrovna
might be thinking. That he had somehow failed to
understand the implications of what she believed. To
him it was only a piece of the earth flashing by outside
the window. To her it was ground hallowed by her
vision of life. In her mind the boy, the dog, the pinpoints of light in the distance, the lines of babushkas,
the train, the taiga, the rivers gorged with ice, all would
be atomized, sacrificed to forces beyond her control.
And he was committed to prolonging the life of the
man who would command those forces.

Was it possible that he agreed with Dimitrov, that
somehow he sanctioned the act? Was he a victim of
Dimitrov's magnetism?

"Two powers," Dimitrov had said, that day in the
oak forest near the dacha. "Two opposing systems
would be quite acceptable. Not three. Not more than

two. America and the Soviet Union. We will divide the world up and disarm everyone but ourselves."

He had looked at Alex and pointed a blunt forefinger. "You will take half and we will take half, like two halves of an apple."

"Why not take the whole?" Alex had said.

"That would not do. One must have the example of the other. What good is the critical faculty if there is no one to criticize? Everything is like the earth. Two poles. Two sexes. The competition would be healthy."

"And would people choose between the two?"

"Of course." He put his arm on Alex's shoulder. "And which would you choose, Kuznetsov?"

He had not answered.

"In the end there are only two basic choices," Dimitrov had said.

The memory faded. Alex stirred again, stood up and put his hand on Anna Petrovna's hair, stroking it, feeling the softness against his fingers.

"I've disappointed you," he said softly.

Apparently she had been waiting for him to speak. She turned toward him, her eyes hard, her lips tight. "You are either a fool or a coward."

"Probably both." He thought a moment. "But not a murderer."

"A murderer?" Her cheekbones flushed. "One life for millions. You have a distorted view of morality."

How could he explain it to her? She continued to let him stroke her hair. Perhaps she was just indifferent.

"It would have been quite simple," she said. "It would have required little effort. An overdose of something. Who would have been the wiser? You knew what was contemplated. Now we have to continue this stupid uncertainty. I would have gladly changed places with you." She paused again, breathing deeply. "If it was your land, your home, you would have reacted quite differently, I am sure."

"Perhaps." He admitted the possibility to her, but not to himself. She would think I was smug, self-righteous, pompous.

"He will probably die in any event, and quickly," he said.

"Perhaps not quickly enough."

She moved her head away from Alex's hand.

"In any event, you would have had his ear. You might have reasoned with him."

"With Dimitrov?"

"Of course."

"Then you don't know him."

"You could have done something. You could have found a way. If you hadn't told Zeldovich what you knew about Grivetsky, we might have convinced him to let you go back now."

"That is absurd. Zeldovich would never allow it."

"We could have persuaded him."

"How?"

"If you had sworn to destroy him. Your silly moral posturing was counterproductive. Zeldovich would have responded. He would have arranged for your return."

So, even at this late hour, she was still clinging to the purity of Zeldovich's motives. It was ridiculous. Zeldovich would never have let him return. Even his announcement of his desire to return had been an empty gesture.

"But I had no intention of destroying him. That was not my purpose."

"Your purpose is to save lives."

"His life."

"And the others?"

He looked at her and shook his head.

"You really think it is moral posturing on my part?"

"Of course. If you were actually with Dimitrov, you would have made the only decision possible."

"You think I would have killed him?"

"Yes. Or how could you live with yourself?"

He sighed. It was useless to debate the issue now. Despite the feeling of perpetual motion that vibrated his bones and rattled his teeth, and seemed now a permanent condition of his environment, the end of the journey was almost in sight. He lay down on the lower bunk and tried to calculate the remaining hours. His own watch read three o'clock, but it could have been early morning or midafternoon. The light was a uniform greenness that merged into the horizon. They had just passed Belgorsk.

"How much longer?" he asked quietly, talking to the underbelly of the bunk above him. He listened, felt her stir in the chair.

"In two days *you* will be in Nakhodka. *You* will have to change in Khabarovsk." He caught the emphasis on the second person pronoun. "Foreigners must change there," she said.

"And then?" He whispered the question, feeling the impending loss of her. Could the question have disturbed her?

It occurred to him then, as it must have occurred to her, that the whispered question had no logical answer. And then? What then? Would Zeldovich simply let them debark and go their way? Whatever Zeldovich's motives might be—and Alex knew they were hardly in the general interests of mankind—he would not be foolish enough to let them go, not as long as Dimitrov was alive.

"We've got to get the hell off this train," he said.

He sat up and looked at Anna Petrovna's face silhouetted against the gray window. A cloud of smoke rose from the shadows, as she expelled cigarette smoke. She seemed resigned. He got up, walked past her and tried the window. It would not budge.

"This is obviously their specialty," he said. His fingertips were numb from the effort. She did not respond. "They are experts in keeping people in. In the art of imprisonment." He stood facing the window for a moment. It darkened suddenly as the train roared through a tunnel.

"We could bust out this window at the next stop," he said.

She stirred. "And then?"

Could she be mocking him?

"I'll get a message through somehow."

"To whom?"

"The Americans, of course." He paused for a moment, watching her. The train came out of the tunnel into the grayness. She was looking up at him, her eyes curious.

"And Dimitrov?" she asked.

"By now he is obviously reacting to the realization that he is gravely sick, perhaps dying."

"You are still doubtful?"

"My place is with him."

"Your place?"

He could detect the beginnings of renewed anger. Was he being self-righteous? He felt the affliction of loving her, yet not possessing her. You are hung up on geography, he wanted to scream out at her. What is so precious about your Siberia? It was time, he thought, to step out of his grandfather's fantasy. It was vanity, pure vanity, an insidious brainwashing that his grandfather had undertaken on an unsuspecting innocent young mind.

"You don't think that man in there"—he was pointing at Zeldovich's compartment—"gives a damn about your goddamned Siberia?"

"I am fully aware of that."

"You saw him kill a man. Do you think he would hesitate to kill me—or you?" He hesitated, stepped back from the edge of hysteria.

"Zeldovich is of no consequence," she said calmly. "We are talking of a man who has the power to kill millions and fully intends to use that power. In the face of that, what is all this nonsense about Zeldovich? Or you? Or me?"

"You have no right to use me as the instrument of his murder."

Had he misstated his conscience? he wondered. He admitted his confusion. The man was obviously dying now. Why persist? he wondered. The disease was terminal. In reality, the choice had been made for him. Perhaps that was the core of his resentment. He felt the full extent of his helplessness.

"You have no right to condemn those millions to death," she said calmly, the chasm between them widening. They were investing him with the guilt of it. The pores of his body seemed to open, and perspiration soaked his shirt, his socks, the seat of his pants.

"And suppose the missiles were pointed in your direction? In the direction of America? Would you be such a martyr to personal integrity?"

He imagined that he could deduce the answer if he searched far enough in his mind. If only he were researching something other than himself. He was a scientist, he told himself. He could not draw conclusions so swiftly. They are only questions, he decided, feeling his own impotence. He climbed into the upper bunk and lay down.

"We all live in Siberia," he shouted to himself, hoping that his grandfather might hear him.

34

At Kundur, Tania hopped from the metal step to the station platform and removed the suitcases of the inspector and the railway policeman. Between them, they guided the pale-faced Ginzburg down the steps. His hands were handcuffed behind him, making it difficult for him to balance himself as he shuffled downward.

Ginzburg's teeth chattered, his lips turning blue quickly in the immense cold. A crowd of passengers surged toward the hard-class carriages, while debarking passengers fought their way outward, opposing armies filtering through each other's lines. A statue of Lenin, finely polished, gleamed in the faltering light of late afternoon.

Sokolovich stepped aside and contemplated the two suitcases standing on the platform. He picked them up and balanced them in either arm as Voikov began to prod Ginzburg to movement. But Ginzburg resisted, angering the policeman.

"Please," Ginzburg protested. His eyes rested on Tania, who looked away.

"Get along, you bastard," Voikov said.

"Please," Ginzburg said.

Tania stole a glance at him. He was looking toward the baggage car.

"You must let her off in Birobidjan," he shouted, as the railway policeman dragged him away. But the instructions from Voikov were quite clear. Tania looked at him as if to reassure herself that she had understood correctly.

"At Khabarovsk, send her back to Moscow." He had written out the instructions and handed her the woman's passport. "Arrange for a box. She'll stink up the place if you don't. I'll wire Moscow to find her family."

Ginzburg had been sitting glumly on the lower bunk, handcuffed to a metal support. He had appeared not to be listening, lost in his own thoughts. Now she realized that he had heard it all.

"At Birobidjan," Ginzburg shouted as Voikov dragged him into the station. They disappeared inside and Tania grabbed the handrail and lifted herself aboard. As she stood on the steps shivering, a little man came running out toward her. In his hand she could see the familiar envelope of a telegraph message. Another message, she thought. It was the third one. She had already delivered two of them to the KGB man, who sat brooding in his compartment.

"Zeldovich?" the little man asked.

"I'll take it."

The little man hesitated a moment, shivering violently. He had rushed out without his coat.

"It is urgent," he said. "They are burning the wires from Moscow. The bosses are accusing us of inefficiency. There will be hell to pay if the message is not delivered. You will promise that he gets it?"

She watched him turn and run back to the warmth of the station. Holding the message in her hand, she continued to stand on the lower step as the train moved sluggishly out of the station.

She looked at her watch. They had finally made up the lost time. Loss of time reflected on all of them.

Despite everything, she mused with satisfaction, they were adhering to the schedule. The idea had a calming effect, and she sensed that she had begun to make peace with herself over her indiscretions.

She had tried very hard to please Sokolovich and felt that she had won his approbation. He had even taken her aside after Ginzburg's arrest and shared a confidence. She had been at the samovar, loading the charcoal from the pail to the heating bed. At first he had loitered around, waiting for a passenger to pass. Then he had touched her arm, startling her, but the unusually benign expression on his face told her that he was about to say something of special meaning.

He looked toward the KGB soldier, a brief glance. But Tania had seen it, and knew that what was coming was for her ears only. "We clean our own laundry, right, Tania?" He had even used her first name.

She understood at once, although she had, of course, shown no emotion. He could have been a KGB agent and, as she knew, he was capable of great subterfuge. She merely nodded her head to indicate that she had caught his meaning. And she had felt great pride in it. The trains move in spite of them, in spite of their foolishness, she might have said, but she kept silent.

In the passageway, she saw little Vladimir, standing with his eyes glued to the window as they pulled out of the station. He had been the instrument of Ginzburg's arrest, and it frightened her to see him. She did not dwell on the matter. It is not my business, she told herself, even though she knew, from her own careful observation of the passengers, that Ginzburg had not left the train at Krasnoyarsk.

As Tania walked toward Vladimir, he looked up, then ran away and hid in the toilet at the far end of the carriage. She wondered if the boy sensed that she knew he had lied.

She passed the guard, deliberately ignoring him, and knocked on Zeldovich's compartment door. She waited, tapping the envelope against the metal door, hearing someone stir within.

When the door opened, she was startled by a sudden surge of familiarity. Something was reminding her of Grivetsky. She handed Zeldovich the message, all the while looking beyond him, over his shoulder into the compartment. It was the smoke. She smelled the same peculiarly rich cigar smoke that had filled Grivetsky's compartment at their first meeting and which still lingered there. Zeldovich slammed the door in her face, but not before she had confirmed the aroma. Somehow she had felt the general's presence, as if the smell were not just a reminder, but a personal message to her. She shook off the idea that the general was in Zeldovich's compartment, sitting relaxed in a chair as she had first observed him. Actually, this reminder was more annoying than anything else, since she had managed to forget Grivetsky and, with him, the entire record of her sordid indiscretions. The raw wound of her humiliation was now opened again, and once again she could not believe that Grivetsky had used her so badly. Again she felt the tug of suspicion about Grivetsky's hasty departure. She went into her quarters and shook the old crone. The woman gasped, swallowed in mid-snore, and opened her eyes.

"I am going to tell them about the bribe you took from the Jew."

The older woman blinked, not understanding.

"I am going to tell the inspector."

"What?"

A nerve palpitated in the old crone's cheek and her eyes narrowed with fright.

"The inspector. Sokolovich. I am going to tell him that you were bribed by the Jew."

The woman gasped.

"Please—" she began, but it was happening too fast and she could not think of what to say.

"I want you to tell me the truth about General Grivetsky." Tania gripped the woman's shoulders and raised her to a sitting position.

"It was not my business," the woman said, trying to shake loose.

"Quickly," Tania hissed. The smell of the cigar smoke was still in her nostrils.

"They had him between them," she whispered, her resistance gone, her body limp. "His head was bobbing. I thought he might be drunk. I should not have looked."

"Looked where?"

"Out the window. They pushed him out of the door. It was all very fast. He rolled into the river. Then they threw off his bags." She looked up at Tania, pleading.

Tania felt the tears begin, then run down her cheeks.

"I did not want to look," the woman whispered urgently. "I turned away quickly and put it from my mind. It is not my business."

Tania pushed the woman back on her bunk as if she had been holding something unclean. "You must not report me," the old woman pleaded, her chest heaving. She repeated it over and over again like a litany.

"Shut up," Tania snapped, wiping the tears away with her sleeve.

The woman continued whimpering, but Tania's mind was drifting. How proud she had been of the general's interest in her. He had not abused her. Now she could mourn a lost love.

"You will not report me?" the woman whined.

It was an intrusion, angering Tania again. "Get out," she snapped.

When the old woman had gone, Tania undressed. Carefully, she laved her body in the sink, soaping herself, scrubbing as hard as if she was peeling away old skin. Rinsing off the soap, she patted her skin until it tingled, feeling the sweetness of her own cleanliness. Then she tightened the sheets of her bunk and slipped between them.

The initial chill made her shiver, and she lay stiffly, waiting for the warmth which came moving upward from her feet, over her legs and thighs, to her breasts. The train bounced beneath her reassuringly, and she listened contentedly to the sounds of her world, the tiny click of metal wheels on the track rivets, the clank and heave of metal couplings, the whoosh of the freight cars that passed heading westward.

She felt a drowsiness descend, an uncoupling, as if her mind were being let loose to roam. Her thoughts turned happily to the general, the neat cut of his uniform, his elegant carriage and, best of all, those moments in which he confided his anxieties. What had seemed indiscretions only a few hours before were now, in her mind, heroic deeds. She had sacrificed a bit of herself, endangered her status on the railroad, the most meaningful thing in her life. She recalled the anticipation which she had felt in those moments of preparation, before he was taken from her, and her hands began to stroke her thighs. Her nipples came erect, rubbing against the cool cotton of the sheets, and she felt herself reaching out for him. Her hands were his hands and they were greedy for the touch of her. He pursued her, his fingers caressed and reached inside of her and she felt his ardor, the relentlessness of his passion, and heard him whisper words of devotion in her ear. Waves of surrender engulfed her as she drowned willingly in the pleasure of it, feeling his pleasure as well, his release, his fulfillment.

Whether she had slept or fainted or both, she could not recall, except that now she was being shaken awake and was resisting with all her will. Then she was sitting up, slowly recovering her sense of time and place, and there before her was the wrinkled face of the old crone. The window was pitch-black.

"He wants to get off at Birobidjan," the older woman said.

"You woke me for that?" Tania said angrily.

The old woman flicked a switch and the little bulb on the wall behind the bunk lit up. Tania gathered the blanket around the naked upper part of her body.

"You must forgive me, Tania Revekka," the older woman pleaded.

Tania smiled thinly. The woman was simply stupid, worse than a child.

"So let him off," she said, forgiving now, remembering what the woman's confession had given her.

"He can't move his legs."

"Who?"

"The man who was in the compartment with the Jew."

Him again, Tania thought, a sudden image of the pale, squat man flashing through her mind. She lifted the clipboard with the list of passengers from its place on the hook near her bunk.

"He is ticketed to Khabarovsk."

"I know. But he wants to get off at Birobidjan. He has been making a great racket about it."

Tania remembered the general's fear of the man, and the little brat mimicking his walk. Still shrouded in the blankets, she slipped out of her bunk onto the cold floor. She lifted the woman's thin wrist and peered at the face of her watch.

"I will be right out," she said. "We are forty minutes out of Bira. We will only have a minute or two."

Godorov was sitting on his bunk. Beside him on the floor of the compartment was a battered cardboard suitcase, its frame dented, the clasps broken, held together by rope. Somehow he had managed to pack and dress. The collar of his coat was turned up and his little eyes peered out. Tania was startled at his appearance. Whereas he had once appeared sinister, he was now frail. The look of the hunted dog had vanished and in its place was an enigmatic indifference. His legs trembled as they hung over the side of the bunk, his battered shoes tapping lightly and helplessly on the floor.

"You will please carry me off the train at Birobidjan."

Tania wanted to ask why, but he was too obviously determined. It is not my business, she told herself, stifling her curiosity about the man's condition. The old crone picked up the cardboard suitcase and moved quickly through the passageway.

"And the body in the baggage car," he began. "I have been charged with its burial."

"You, too?" Tania said flippantly.

Was he joking? She was under orders to return the body to Moscow.

"I have money," he said, taking a wad of rubles from his coat pocket.

She turned away quickly, wondering if the guard who stood in the corridor was listening. The compartment door was open.

"Put that away," she said.

His proposition was insulting. Did she look as if she would be receptive to a bribe? Human garbage, she told herself, feeling the train begin to slow.

Godorov suddenly reached out and grabbed the edge of the upper bunk and, grunting with strain, hoisted himself to a standing position. Tania tried to support him, but his weight was enormous. The old crone came back and let Godorov edge his other arm over her shoulder.

"He is like a ton of lead," Tania said as they moved him out into the passageway. The guard looked at them curiously, then turned away. Not your business, eh? Tania thought, as they struggled ahead.

In the space between the cars, Tania opened the door and let Godorov sink to the steps as she squinted into the distance. Ahead, she could see the sparse lights of Birobidjan. Of all eastern Siberia, Birobidjan had always appeared the most desolate place of all. Years ago, when Tania had first started on the railroad, she had been told that Stalin had chosen it as a place for the Jews.

"It is a rotten place," someone had said and it had stuck in her mind. "A perfect place for them." It was the kind of stop along the line that seemed an afterthought.

Godorov looked up at her.

"Just leave me on the platform and remove the body from the baggage car. I will give you the rubles when the job is done."

Tania looked down at him contemptuously. The old crone turned away.

The train pulled into the station. Half the lights were out, and the others barely lit the platform. Not a single person was in sight. A banner, frayed by the wind, hung limply between two poles.

Tania stepped over the seated figure and stood waiting at the foot of the steps. Godorov reached out and lifted himself by the handrail, while the older woman supported him and Tania braced herself to receive his weight. She looked around in the darkness for a place to leave him, and spotted a wooden crate standing against a brick wall near the edge of the platform.

"Hurry," Godorov said.

The two women, bowed under his weight, carried him across the platform, his lifeless legs dragging behind. Puffing with effort, they deposited him on the crate. Even in the bad light, Godorov's ashen face glowed with sweat.

"Now the body," he urged.

Tania looked back at the train. The empty restaurant car cast the only light in the deserted station. Not a single passenger had debarked and both ends of the platform ended in total blackness. Godorov removed the rubles from his pocket and waved them in front of the two women.

"Hurry," he said. "You will not get this until you do it."

Tania looked down at him with disdain, remembering how he had once struck fear in the heart of the general. She looked at her watch. A man appeared in the dark doorway of the station house and waved at the engineer. Tania and the old attendant moved toward the train, still watching the man, who sat helplessly on the crate.

"Hurry," he shouted.

"Stupid man," Tania hissed, turning quickly and running for the train, which had already started to move, the old crone hobbling behind her.

They watched from the metal steps as the man

slipped off the crate onto the platform and tried to crawl forward, like some strange reptile. He was shouting something, but Tania could not hear. She watched until he faded out of sight, a black blob passing finally into invisibility.

35

The train halted with a violent jerk, toppling the vodka
bottle from the little table in Zeldovich's compartment.
It was empty and made a dull thud as it dropped to the
floor. Zeldovich opened heavy eyes, rubbed them and
looked out of the window. The lights of his compartment were off and he had been sleeping in the chair
for what might have been hours or minutes.

Something was happening along the track. Soldiers
armed with machine guns were running along the westbound track. They seemed to be taking up skirmishing
positions along the length of the train. He rubbed his
eyes and strained to see the insignia of the troops, some
sign of their command. They were Red Army, definitely
not KGB.

Although the train had come to a dead halt, there
was no sign of a station. Drawing out his wrinkled
timetable, he placed it flat against his knees and flicked
on the light. By his calculation, they were twenty
minutes outside of Khabarovsk. Outside the compartment, he heard the heavy thud of footsteps.

He opened the compartment door cautiously, gripping the butt of his revolver, which he shifted from his belt to a side pocket. The KGB guard outside the doctor's compartment had disappeared and at either end of the carriage he could see Red Army soldiers in pairs, their feet planted across the space of the doorway, machine guns at the ready. He looked out of the window on the eastbound side and saw the shadowy shapes of Army trucks. Above his head he heard the rhythmical clunk of footsteps. Soldiers were also on the roof. They were everywhere.

A compartment door opened and a sandy-haired man appeared, rubbing his eyes.

"What now?" he said.

The gray-haired woman, her face still puffy with sleep, was observing the activity from a vantage point near the toilet door.

"We are apparently being captured," she said cheerfully. "By the whole Red Army!"

Zeldovich pressed his face against the icy window and watched as the KGB troop car was shunted to a siding. Three trucks were lined up, their axles chained to the troop carriage, which was moving slowly forward.

"You see," Dr. Cousins said, from behind him.

Zeldovich turned quickly, reaching into his pocket, gripping the butt of the revolver. Behind Cousins stood Anna Petrovna.

"See what?" Zeldovich asked, his throat tight and dry.

"Power belongs to him who has the guts to take it."

Zeldovich smiled. So the doctor thinks Dimitrov is behind this.

"Did you think you could stop him?" the American doctor asked.

He looked smug and Zeldovich felt a brief tremor of uncertainty. It was true that Dimitrov might get the Red Army to move, but not without explaining his request to Bulgakov first. Which was why he had sent Grivetsky to Chita in the first place, to circumvent

Bulgakov and isolate the function of command. Had he miscalculated, based upon the American doctor's assessment? Was Dimitrov really dying? This exercise of power required health. If Dimitrov were visibly failing, he would have had difficulty getting these orders carried out. The jackals would be at his throat.

"You couldn't possibly have expected him to hold out forever without taking some action," Dr. Cousins continued. "A man as thirsty for life as he is. And with his nose for intrigue."

Outside an Army staff car approached, its lights throwing eerie shadows along the road, and Zeldovich saw for the first time the extent of the convoy and the unusually large concentration of troops. The staff car stopped at the entrance of the soft class. A driver and two armed guards hopped out and the driver opened the back door of the car. A heavy figure emerged, an overcoat slung over his shoulders. Bulgakov. Zeldovich watched as he gripped the handhold and lifted himself aboard.

"Who is that?" Dr. Cousins asked.

"Bulgakov," Zeldovich whispered. He wanted the doctor to feel his sarcasm, his contempt. The doctor blinked, not comprehending the irony.

The Marshall, his face flushed, lumbered into the passageway. The cold had made his face ruddy, the jowls beet red. Squinting in the sudden brightness, he saw Zeldovich and proceeded toward him. Under his veneer of charm, good humor and pomposity, he was a cunning man. It was no secret that the Marshall had expensive taste in food, uniforms and women. Was it the wives of the Politburo members who had assured his rise to eminence? Zeldovich wondered.

Suddenly, Dr. Cousins stepped forward, blocking the Marshall's path.

"I am Dr. Cousins," he said, putting out his hand. "The General Secretary's personal physician." Bulgakov looked at him curiously, then smiled broadly.

"Yes," he said pleasantly, gripping the doctor's hand. "I have just come from your patient." He looked at his watch. "About eight hours ago, I would say. This is a miserable hour, isn't it, Zeldovich?"

Anna Petrovna hung back, watching nervously.

"And how was he feeling?" Dr. Cousins interrupted.

The Marshall turned slowly to face him. "He is failing swiftly."

"And has he sent for me?" Dr. Cousins asked.

Bulgakov ignored the question. Zeldovich smiled. They are so obtuse, he thought. Bulgakov's watery eyes moved, shifted from Zeldovich's face to the doctor's, then to Anna Petrovna's. She was pale, her lips pursed.

"He is far gone," Bulgakov said quietly. Suddenly he rubbed his ungloved hands together and pulled a silver flask from the pocket of his coat, offering it first, in a courtly gesture, to Anna Petrovna. She refused. Zeldovich shook his head and the Marshall sipped the contents, smacking his lips.

Dr. Cousins turned to Zeldovich. "So there is your answer at last."

Bulgakov frowned, obviously surprised that the American doctor was in Zeldovich's confidence.

"I would suggest you leave us now, Doctor," Zeldovich ordered, motioning to the guard.

"What does he mean?" Bulgakov asked as Alex was led away.

"He is bitter about his medical failure," Zeldovich replied, ushering the Marshall and Mrs. Valentinov into his compartment.

An officer who had come in with Bulgakov addressed the passengers who now filled the passageway.

"You will please return to your compartments. There is no problem here. You will soon be under way again."

The passengers obediently went back to their compartments. The train began to move again, the metal couplings straining as the wheels began to click over the rivets.

The Marshall took the one chair and sipped again from the flask, his eyes examining Anna Petrovna's figure.

He thrust out the flask. "To a lovely lady."

It is the moment, Zeldovich thought. "She has been invaluable," he said.

Bulgakov's eyes lingered on Mrs. Valentinov.

"About Grivetsky, we had little choice, Comrade. He was the instrument of your betrayal. To say nothing of his participation in the plan for a first strike against the Chinese. It was Dimitrov's last mad gesture."

Zeldovich felt his hands grow clammy, his breath short. Bulgakov remained impassive.

"I suspected. But I was not certain. Finally he confirmed it himself." Zeldovich's words seemed to cascade from his lips. "I knew something was up back at the dacha. Dimitrov did not confide in me. It was strictly my own suspicion. I think he was going mad. Grivetsky must have sensed we were watching him." Was there a flicker of confirmation in Bulgakov's eyes? "In the end there was no choice but to kill him."

Zeldovich turned to Mrs. Valentinov. It is your turn, you bitch, he thought.

Bulgakov's eyes rested on Anna Petrovna, who lowered hers.

"It is true," she said. "I saw it. The general would have killed us first. There was no choice. He is correct."

"I called you directly," Zeldovich went on. "You had to be told. We three are the only ones who know about this."

Anna Petrovna kept her eyes down. "There is no chance he can send someone else?" she asked.

The Marshall smiled. "He is too far gone."

"You are the only one who knows about Grivetsky, Comrade," Zeldovich said, again driving the point home. But Bulgakov's mind seemed to be wandering.

"You look like hell, Zeldovich," he said, chuckling.

"It has been a tense journey."

Bulgakov nodded. Was the Marshall being faintly contemptuous? Zeldovich's hands began to shake and he thrust them in his pockets.

"Too bad about Grivetsky," Bulgakov said wistfully. "He was a fine fellow, a competent officer, and above all a friend." He replaced the flask in a pocket of his coat.

"It had to be done," Zeldovich said cautiously, watching Bulgakov's face for some reaction.

"I'm afraid so, Comrade," Bulgakov said.

He is thinking of himself now, Zeldovich thought, sighing with relief. He knows I have saved his career.

"That's exactly the way I saw it," Zeldovich said, hesitating, his body relaxing, the tension subsiding.

"Are you sure about Comrade Dimitrov?" Mrs. Valentinov asked suddenly.

"He is finished," Bulgakov said.

"Does he know you are here?" Zeldovich asked.

"I'm afraid not." The Marshall patted Zeldovich's arm. "We are monitoring all messages now. He seemed rather anxious to get that American doctor back to the dacha. But it is even too late for that."

"And the others?" Zeldovich said meekly. The Politburo! Would Bulgakov understand?

"They will be fully informed"—Bulgakov cleared his throat—"before the meeting."

"And you will explain my role?"

Had he detected a faint smile around Bulgakov's eyes, a bit mocking?

"Of course." Bulgakov looked directly at Mrs. Valentinov.

"I had no choice," Zeldovich mumbled, then regretted it. He must not overkill his position.

"You have done well, Comrade," Bulgakov said.

He reached out and touched Mrs. Valentinov's arm, stroking her bare skin gently. Zeldovich saw her cringe, then control her anger.

The Marshall turned toward Zeldovich. "Both of you. I'm in your debt."

"As Comrade Zeldovich has suggested, there was little choice," Mrs. Valentinov said, moving away a few steps.

Seeing Bulgakov's interest in Anna Petrovna, Zeldovich tensed again. Somehow he must dismiss her, he thought. There were loose ends to tie. He must be alone with Bulgakov.

"There is more to be said," he whispered. Bulgakov turned, his eyes narrowing. "Between us."

Anna Petrovna immediately turned to go, her fingers reaching for the door handle. She seemed anxious to leave. The color had drained from her face and her fingers shook. Bulgakov nodded, and she slid the door aside and let herself into the passageway.

"Most attractive," Bulgakov said, his eyes lingering on the closed door.

He drew out his flask again and, head back, poured another shot down his throat, his eyes tearing. Zeldovich watched him, the huge relaxed bulk, unruffled, sure of his own worth. He was, Zeldovich felt, a man in repose, an odd condition for someone who had very nearly been toppled from his exalted position.

"Grivetsky would not have hesitated for a moment," Bulgakov said. "Always the consummate technician. The operation would have worked like a clock."

"Dimitrov knew that."

The Marshall shook his head and, smiling, turned the full strength of his concentration on Zeldovich.

"We are both students of survival, Comrade." He sighed. "It is quite grim out there." He paused. "We should be getting to Khabarovsk shortly." He patted his stomach. "And I am getting hungry."

It was all so casual, so disarming, not at all as Zeldovich had imagined. Was Bulgakov really grateful? Would he save him?

"The poor fellow was quite bad off," Bulgakov said, his thoughts drifting. They might have been in the living room of Bulgakov's apartment, philosophizing before a crackling fire. "He senses what is happening to him. The death of life is one thing. The death of power quite another." He slapped his thigh. "I liked the fellow and he damn near pulled it off."

Could Bulgakov be trusted? Zeldovich wondered. Had he miscalculated on the key to his own survival? I am at his mercy, he thought, a detestable condition to be in. If I had not killed Grivetsky, you would be hanging by your thumbs, he thought.

"The lines around Moscow are red hot." Bulgakov chuckled. "The KGB is quite busy as well. It is very amusing, eh, Zeldovich?"

"It is a serious business," he responded. "And there are many loose ends."

"Yes, loose ends," the Marshall said. He looked at his watch. "I am absolutely famished."

It was quite confusing. Zeldovich felt his knees grow weak, and he thought suddenly of the gun in his pocket.

"There are all sorts of considerations, Comrade," he said, wondering if the Marshall could see his panic. Was it possible Bulgakov had not thought of the consequences?

"She knows everything," Zeldovich continued.

"That's quite obvious."

"And, perhaps, the American doctor as well."

Bulgakov did not seem interested. "We are now drifting into your field, Comrade."

Was that it? The stamp of approval?

"Yes, that is your area, Zeldovich," Bulgakov said, looking at his watch again. "It is dinner time in Moscow."

He is doing this deliberately, Zeldovich thought.

Bulgakov removed the flask from his tunic again and upended it, smacking his lips as the last drop poured into his mouth.

"You can count on me," Zeldovich said, the sweat beginning to pour down his back. "And I am depending on you."

"Of course."

It was barely an acknowledgment, infuriating Zeldovich.

Bulgakov looked at his watch.

"You understand the consequences of this, Comrade," Zeldovich said, his voice rising as he felt the immensity of his fear.

"My dear Zeldovich, do you really believe that I

would travel all the way to this godforsaken place for my health?"

It was the first hint Bulgakov had given of any serious motives. Zeldovich felt momentarily relieved.

"They will have to be dealt with."

"Of course," Bulgakov said.

Zeldovich waited for some further words, but none came.

"I have a plan, Comrade," he said.

Bulgakov slapped his thighs and stood up. "I'm sure you will be quite thorough," he said. "You have a fine reputation for these matters."

"We must arrange a funeral for General Grivetsky with full military honors," Zeldovich said maliciously.

"Absolutely," Bulgakov responded. "He will be quite difficult to replace, a marvelous technician."

Is he listening? Zeldovich wondered.

"His body is lying at the bottom of some river in the middle of Siberia."

"That does create difficulties." Bulgakov seemed only mildly interested.

"A detail," Zeldovich said. An idea had just come to him. He felt an odd surge of pride. "I have a body."

"You are remarkable, Zeldovich."

He could not tell if Bulgakov meant it sarcastically. Bulgakov was, indeed, an enigma. I will simply have to get used to it all over again, he thought. Dimitrov, too, had hardly bothered to hear details. "Do what you have to do, Zeldovich."

It will be the same, Zeldovich thought. Only the faces change.

"I will need your cooperation, of course. It will have to be a sealed coffin, heavily guarded to the moment it is buried."

"Done," Bulgakov said.

"There is this body in the baggage car, a woman—"

"That is good, excellent," Bulgakov said. He patted Zeldovich on the back. "You are a most remarkable fellow."

He will see how valuable I am, Zeldovich thought.

"You will simply announce that he died of a heart attack on the Trans-Siberian Railroad."

"A pity. Poor Grivetsky." Bulgakov clicked his tongue.

Zeldovich watched the Marshall's face. "That will leave only two loose ends." He jerked a thumb in the direction of the compartment next door.

"You have a plan for them as well?"

He is reacting, Zeldovich thought happily. It was like the old days with Dimitrov.

"We will have to arrange an accident. Something credible, of course. The doctor is, after all, on direct orders from the American President."

"It is your specialty," Bulgakov said, his eyes dancing merrily.

Is he ridiculing me? Zeldovich wondered. But Bulgakov's face suddenly changed expression, the façade of boredom disappearing. The smile became a snarl.

"That is the essential business," Bulgakov said, jabbing a stubby finger into Zeldovich's chest. "Not a single word must ever get out about Dimitrov's China plans. There must be no leak to the Americans. Not now. I hold you responsible."

"And the Politburo?"

"Leave them to me."

Then the bland façade reappeared, and Bulgakov's eyes were twinkling again. So he is plotting his own course, Zeldovich thought, the intriguing bastard. He is thinking now only of his own skin.

36

What an exercise in futility it had been from the beginning, Alex thought, going through the motions of packing, watching Anna Petrovna take her clothing from the hooks and stow it neatly in her bags. Did she really believe that they would let her return to Irkutsk?

Zeldovich continued to watch them, sitting in the chair, casual, putting on a good-humored front.

"In a few hours it will be all over," he had told them after the Marshall left. "The adventure will be over."

"And none too soon," Alex responded, playing along. It was no good voicing his suspicions, he thought, not now. Zeldovich was obviously ebullient, almost playful.

"The good doctor will be on his way to America. And the lovely Mrs. Valentinov back to Irkutsk and the children. For some it is a happy ending, eh, Kuznetsov?" Alex tried to ignore him, sensing what was coming. "As for romance, of course, it's a genuine tragedy."

Zeldovich was enjoying himself. Anna Petrovna remained silent.

"But think of the lives of all those Chinks we have saved. Not to mention our own hardy Siberians." He looked out of the window. "Not that they have much brains living out here in this hellhole."

There was no need for pretense now. Zeldovich's maliciousness was quite apparent and Alex wondered how Anna Petrovna felt now about her ally. Between her and Alex there was a great distance. But in spite of everything, she had opened his heart to a new way of seeing, of feeling. He loved her. Nothing could change that, no matter what happened next.

Alex snapped shut the clasp of his suitcase and swung the bag of medical journals to the floor of the compartment. Along the tracks, ramshackle houses were coming into view. A heavyset signalwoman stood stiffly at a crossroads waving a flag. They were moving into a city now, Khabarovsk. It was nearly midnight.

In a few hours he was to have changed trains and boarded the Ussuri Line to Nakhodka, where the ship waited to cross the Sea of Japan to Yokohama. At least that had been the original plan. He no longer expected such a simple end to the journey.

Sitting down on the bunk, he watched Anna Petrovna. The train began to slow, picking its way through the railyard. Beyond the yards, he could see rows of high-rise apartments stretching into the distance.

"Quite a town." He sighed.

"Our largest city," she said. "It would have been the first to go." She pointed south. "China is just a few miles away."

"Yes, China." He turned from the window. "I must say I have been greatly impressed by your compassion for the Chinese."

She looked at him and shook her head. "You still don't understand. Poor Alex!"

"Poor all of us."

The train ground to a halt in the Khabarovsk station.

Across the eastbound tracks, he saw crowds of passengers huddled in their coats, peering down the line for the westbound train to appear.

"I suppose you'll be happy to get home," he said gently. His anger was gone now and all he could think of was her impending departure. I have lost her, he thought. It is all over. He wondered if she really believed that she was heading home.

Zeldovich jumped up and slid open the door. They followed. The passageway was empty except for little Vladimir who stood watching them from a distance. Through the windows Alex could see the non-Russian passengers, their luggage hauled by burly women, walking into the large new station.

Tania made her way into their compartment and carried out their luggage. Alex stood for a second on the top metal step watching the confusion—passengers crowding onto the hard-class carriages, Russian naval officers lining up outside the soft class, waiting for the signal to move in.

Alex stepped down to the platform and gave his hand to Anna Petrovna. She took it and he felt an electricity from the cool touch of her flesh. Squeezing her hand, he imagined he felt her return the pressure, but when he sought her eyes she turned away.

Zeldovich hovered about them as Tania carried the luggage to the platform. His good spirits had faded and he seemed nervous, checking his watch, looking around the station.

"They make it damned inconvenient for foreigners," a voice said. Turning, Alex saw the scowling face of the Australian. "They and their bloody naval base. Just because of that we've got to kill a few hours, waiting to pass inspection. It's a bloody business."

"What did he say?" Zeldovich demanded.

"He said you're all a bunch of paranoids," Alex said, deliberately exaggerating.

"Tell him to move on," Zeldovich ordered. It seemed an overreaction.

Through the open door of the station Alex could see

Miss Peterson and her new American friends taken in tow by a uniformed Intourist guide whose volubility seemed to have subdued even the irrepressible Miss Peterson.

The Australian, apparently unaware of Zeldovich's irritation, continued to complain.

"They don't even have a goddamned bar in this place," he said, the smell of alcohol heavy on his breath.

Zeldovich bent over and whispered in Alex's ear.

"You better get rid of him before I have him arrested," he said.

Alex looked him full in the face for a moment. Zeldovich was not dissembling. His meanness was right on the surface.

Alex gripped the Australian's upper arm, hoping that would underline his urgency.

"He wants you to move on. He is KGB and has threatened to have you arrested."

"Tell him to shove a bloody dildo up his bloody ass," the Australian said, looking fiercely at Zeldovich, who scowled back.

"Please," Alex said. "I can assure you he means business."

The directness, perhaps the tone, of Alex's warning seemed to sober the man. He swallowed hard, and the bombast which had sustained him through the journey seemed to forsake him.

"Thanks," he said, then disappeared quickly into the station house.

"We are still in isolation," Alex said in English to Anna Petrovna. She hesitated, glanced at Zeldovich, and said nothing. But Zeldovich, sensitive to the strange language, reacted as if they had been conspiring in whispers.

"Speak Russian, speak Russian! I warn you, Kuznetsov—"

Alex would have tried to explain, but his attention was attracted by the arrival of two columns of Russian troops. They marched toward the baggage carriage, the crowd parting before them, and ceremoniously arranged themselves as a few of their number peeled off from the formation and climbed aboard. The crowd at the station seemed to freeze and a silence fell as they saw the object of the exercise. The soldiers reappeared carrying a wooden casket between them, draped with the Soviet flag. At the edge of the baggage car, they handed it down to waiting hands, as two photographers, one military and one civilian, popped flashes at the event. A number of Russians removed their hats and a few older women crossed themselves.

On the platform, soldiers lifted the casket to their shoulders and stood stiffly between the two columns. From somewhere beyond Alex's line of vision a drumbeat moved down the platform, away from Alex and Anna Petrovna. The photographers followed, lights flashing as they recorded the event.

At the far end of the platform, the procession paused in front of a tall bulky man who drew himself up in a stiff, formal salute. Photographers' flashes popped repeatedly. The drumbeat began to fade as the procession moved out of carshot and Bulgakov disappeared into the darkness at the edge of the station.

"Who is it?" Alex asked, as the crowd began to move again and activity at the station returned to normal.

Zeldovich ignored him, a faint smile playing around his lips.

"Who is in the coffin?" Alex persisted.

"A great military hero," Zeldovich said, his eye roaming over the crowd.

A young soldier moved toward them. Zeldovich waved him forward and the young soldier came running.

"Comrade Zeldovich?"

Zeldovich nodded. "You have the car?"

"Yes, sir. I have been instructed to take you to the airport."

He lifted the luggage, while Alex retained his bookbag and Anna Petrovna her small suitcase. They followed the young soldier through the thinning crowds. Behind them, the train began to move. Alex could see the young attendant watching them. He waved goodbye and felt an odd pang of sadness. The attendant waved back.

The train moved slowly past them. The restaurant car was dark, but the lights still blazed in the hard class. Alex caught a passing glimpse of the crowd still huddled around the compartment where the marathon chess game was still in progress.

"We must hurry," Zeldovich said, tapping his shoulder. "The plane is waiting."

A car waited at the side of the station, its motor running. The young soldier stowed the bags in the trunk, shutting it with a loud metallic slap. He opened the car door and stood at attention, waiting for them to get in.

Anna Petrovna started to move, but Zeldovich held her back.

"The doctor first," he said. Alex hesitated, shrugged and with a glance at Anna Petrovna's puzzled face, crouched and moved into the car.

"We will be back in a moment," he heard Zeldovich say and before he could respond, the door was slammed shut behind him, and the soldier had jumped into the front seat, his gloved hands resting on the wheel. Alex watched as Zeldovich and Anna Petrovna moved back into the shadows, Zeldovich's hand gripping her upper arm.

Alex leaned back in the soft warmth of the large car. Too much had happened. He had reached the outer limits of fatigue, and felt shaky and uncertain. He felt the eyes of the young soldier watching him in the rearview mirror. He was caught in a maze beyond his understanding. The strange procession, the clicking cameras, the beating drum, bubbled in his brain.

"Who was in the coffin?" he asked himself aloud.

"Sir?"

"The funeral," he said. "In the station."

"General Grivetsky," the young soldier said. "The old man himself came down."

"Grivetsky?"

"He was one of our most brilliant military leaders—" the soldier began cheerfully. Then he suddenly jumped out of the car again, and opened the rear door. Anna Petrovna got in next to Alex. He felt the warmth of her body, her closeness somehow reassuring, but when he looked at her face, it seemed drained and bloodless. And she was shivering. Something had happened.

Zeldovich sat heavily on the seat beside her. The door was slammed shut and the young soldier leaped into the front seat and gunned the motor.

The streets were empty and the car raced past the factories, houses, and high-rise apartments of Khabarovsk. The homes and apartments were dark, but the factories were lit by giant floodlights and they seemed to be in full operation. Great clouds of smoke leaped from their huge chimneys.

Then the young soldier maneuvered the car through a series of turns and shot out into what appeared to be an open road. Houses grew sparser as the car moved swiftly into the darkness. Soon they were moving along a highway. "To Airport," a sign read in Russian.

"It was supposed to be Grivetsky," Alex said suddenly in English.

He felt Anna Petrovna stir beside him, imagining that her leg had moved closer to his. Zeldovich said nothing. He sat stiffly watching with concentration through the front window.

"They are passing it off as Grivetsky," Alex said again in English.

Zeldovich stirred. "You will speak Russian," he snapped.

"It is probably the body of the woman who died. Or a bunch of stones," Alex persisted in English.

Anna Petrovna's hand, which had been lying in her lap, suddenly covered his. His heart began to beat wildly.

"What is happening?" he asked in English.

"Tell him to please speak Russian," Zeldovich ordered.

"What is it, Anna Petrovna?" Alex said, again in English.

The highway was running parallel to a river. Zeldovich squinted into the darkness ahead.

"Here," he said suddenly, tapping the soldier on the shoulder. He had removed his revolver from his belt and was holding it in his other hand. "Stop here."

The soldier looked back curiously for a moment, then slowed the car, running it slowly to the shoulder of the road. Below they could hear the rush of the river and the creak of the breaking ice floes.

"What is it?" the young soldier asked. "The airport is up ahead." He gestured at the lights in the distance. "There—" he began, but before he could continue Zeldovich swung the butt of the revolver in an arc and brought it down on the back of the young man's head. The crushing force of the blow thrust the boy forward against the wheel, and the horn blew sharply. Then the soldier slipped sideways and fell, lifeless, onto the front seat.

"You knew," Alex said, turning to Anna Petrovna.

Zeldovich edged his way out of the car.

"Out," he said sharply. Anna Petrovna let go of Alex's hand and slid sideways on the seat. Alex reached over and grabbed the boy's wrist, searching for the pulse. He could not find it.

"You've killed him," he said.

Alex had no firsthand knowledge of violence, so he was oddly unafraid of Zeldovich's revolver. It was Anna Petrovna who concerned him most and he watched her shivering in the darkness, unable to keep her teeth from chattering as Zeldovich stood impatiently at the side of the road urging him out of the car.

"True to form, eh, Zeldovich?" Alex said. "Just a petty little murderer, after all."

Zeldovich glanced at the river rushing below them.

"We are going swimming in Siberia," Alex said in

Russian, surprised at his own fearlessness. Then he said in English, "Did you believe it could end any other way?"

"It is not necessary," Anna Petrovna said suddenly. She took a step forward, confronting Zeldovich, who stepped backward quickly to avoid too close a proximity. "It is pointless now. Dimitrov is finished. You told us that yourself." She was pleading, speaking with great effort.

"There is no choice."

"I don't understand," she said. "What harm could he do now? It is all over."

"It is not my choice."

"Not yours?"

"The little bastard is trading my life for his," Alex said. It suddenly made sense.

"I don't understand," she said again.

"I know too much. They are afraid I will spill the beans back home. Once I tell what I know, the Americans will not trust the Russians anymore."

"Is that true?"

"I am a servant of the State," Zeldovich said.

"Please, Comrade," Anna Petrovna said haltingly. "There is no need."

"He is cold-blooded. He is interested only in his own skin. He was never interested in anything else."

Zeldovich stood facing them, the barrel of the revolver dark and threatening.

"Come here," he ordered, addressing Alex.

"I am not very far. Shoot me from there." Alex spread out his arms. Zeldovich moved quickly. In a smooth fluid motion he reached out and grabbed Anna Petrovna from behind, holding her as a kind of shield. He put the barrel of the revolver to her forehead. Suddenly all movement stopped and for a moment the two men faced each other. Anna Petrovna seemed on the edge of collapse.

"Don't harm her," Alex urged.

"Get down on your knees," Zeldovich ordered.

Alex dropped to his knees. Zeldovich took another

step forward, but as he did so Anna Petrovna's body began to sink. Zeldovich was forced to bend over, since he could no longer hold himself erect and grip the woman at the same time.

Then he gave up the struggle and, pushing Anna Petrovna away from him, he lunged forward, swinging the gun in a wide arc. But his balance was not secure and the intended blow landed on Alex's shoulder. He grasped Zeldovich around the legs, feeling the bulky body totter and begin to fall. Zeldovich dropped his gun and gripped Alex's throat with both hands. Alex thrashed and struggled, but could not pry the iron fingers loose. He felt the blankness descending, his strength ebbing.

On the brink of helplessness, he heard a shot ring out, then three more. Zeldovich's body arched above him in a spasm. Slowly the fingers loosened and Alex was gasping for air, watching Anna Petrovna, the smoking gun still in her hand, the sharp smell of gunpowder in the air. Zeldovich's body fell like a stone beside him.

The blood had drained from Anna Petrovna's face and, although she still held the gun, she seemed on the verge of fainting. Alex staggered to his feet and took her in his arms. She let the gun drop. Her body was quivering, her cheeks wet.

"It's all right, my darling," Alex whispered.

Her quivering abated slowly as she clung to him. "It was to be an accident," she whispered.

"Another fraud. Like Grivetsky."

"Can you forgive me, Alex?"

"For what?"

"For entertaining the possibility of helping him."

"Another appeal to your patriotism?"

"He insisted it was my duty."

"Perhaps it was," Alex said.

When he was satisfied that she could stand alone without his help, he released her and knelt over the body of Zeldovich, feeling his pulse. The bullets had blown away part of his head. "He is quite dead."

Looking up at her, he said, "Now what? I'd say he was going to drive the car into the river. The idea, I suppose, was to make it appear as if the driver slid off the road. It was necessary to leave me relatively unmarked. That's why he wouldn't shoot me. He reckoned on everything but you." He held out his arm. She came toward him and took his hands. "Later he would have finished you as well."

"I know," she said quietly.

"I wish I had his sense of intrigue," Alex murmured. "I would know what to do now."

In the distance, he could see the lights of the airport. The car was well off the shoulder of the road, beyond the lights of the other cars which sped by at infrequent intervals.

"If only the American authorities knew you were in danger," Anna Petrovna said.

"In the middle of Siberia. How the hell do I get word out?"

She shrugged, turned toward the rushing river. He looked down at it again, straining to see through the darkness. The alternatives seemed grim. If he reported himself to the Soviet authorities, they would know what to do. He would become a non-person. Making people disappear was their specialty. A missing American, especially one with his mission, could, of course, be an embarrassment. But considering what he knew, the risk of embarrassment would seem to them the lesser of two evils. Alex felt suddenly put upon, used by both sides. I will not roll over, he told himself. We will outfox the dirty bastards. He could feel his adrenaline surge.

The first thing to be dealt with was the two dead bodies. He reached into the car and dragged the body of the young soldier from the front seat by the lapels of his coat. The body was heavy, deadweight, and Alex could barely manage him. He realized how absurd he must look. What was he doing here? Dimitrov would be laughing at him now.

"The essential business is to survive with our goals

intact," Dimitrov had told him. He had been barely listening. Talk, talk, talk. The man refused to be quiet.

"Survive what?"

"Enemies inside. Enemies outside."

"With you, everything is like a confrontation," Alex had said impatiently, wanting to discourage conversation.

"That is life."

"I don't agree."

"You should read your Darwin." Dimitrov had smiled, then changed the subject to the state of the weather.

Now Alex knew what Dimitrov had meant. He dragged the body of the young soldier down the slope to the river's edge and pushed it into the swift current. It slipped beneath the ice floes and disappeared in the foamy darkness. Dead was dead, he told himself, the manner of burial irrelevant. Somehow the thought gave him courage.

Groping his way up the slippery slope by handholds on exposed roots, he reached the road again. Anna Petrovna had watched him ascend, reaching out to help him up. The strain had tired him and he sat for a moment on the ground, fighting for oxygen in the thin freezing air.

"It is the Amur," Anna Petrovna said listlessly, watching the river.

"What?"

"The Amur," she repeated. "The widest river in Siberia. The bridge across was the last link in the railroad. It was finished in 1916."

She sounded like Miss Peterson. The historical information was incongruous under the circumstances, and Alex hoped that Anna Petrovna was not losing control. When his heart had stopped pumping madly, he stood up, walked to the body of Zeldovich and began to drag it to the slope.

At the edge, he rolled it over like a log, watching it gain momentum, stopping short on the river's edge. He followed the trail downward cautiously, stopping when he reached the body. Zeldovich's eyes were still open, looking blankly into the darkness.

He pushed the body into the river, heard it slip into the water, a tiny note in the rushing symphony of the river's movement. Then, without a glance back, he started his ascent again. A jet plane screeched overhead, the flashing red lights on its wings an eerie apparition in the lonely black expanse. Of course, he told himself, remembering Miss Peterson's remarks on that very first day when his alertness had not yet been dulled by her avalanche of information. Miss Peterson will be at the airport.

"At Khabarovsk, I'll go directly to the airport and pop back to Moscow and on to London," she had told him.

Grabbing Anna Petrovna's hand as he reached the road, Alex pulled her toward the car. They got in and he turned the ignition and gunned the motor.

"At least these damned shifts are universal," he said, moving his foot heavily onto the accelerator. The large military car shot forward. As he drove, he felt his mind clearing.

"How long does it take to get from here to Moscow by air?" he asked.

"Ten hours."

"And to Nakhodka by train?"

"Sixteen."

"Good."

Pulling up at the edge of light that ringed the airport building, he cut off the motor and they both got out of the car.

"Hurry," he cried, grabbing Anna Petrovna's hand as they rushed in the direction of the airport entrance. A line of passengers was moving through the luggage-processing operation. He could see the big jet on the apron, its silver wings gleaming in the floodlights. A group of passengers had begun to scramble up the entranceway.

He searched the crowd, hoping that Miss Peterson had not yet boarded. They walked down the line of people. Then her voice, sweet but audible, drifted above the voices of the Russians. She had apparently found a polite English-speaking couple and was initiating them into the history of Khabarovsk, with which they were surely already satiated.

"Oh, Dr. Cousins," Miss Peterson said, turning from her victims, who looked at him thankfully. "We said good-bye. I had no idea your plans had changed."

"Please, Miss Peterson, I must see you."

She seemed confused at first, looking at him strangely, as her eyes drifted from his face to his mud-speckled clothes.

"Please," he said again, as he moved away from the line of people.

She turned to the English-speaking couple. "Would you please mind my place?"

They nodded, stealing glances of obvious relief at each other. Alex knew they were being watched as he moved toward a kiosk. He bought several magazines, gave them to Miss Peterson and smiled for the benefit of the observers, whoever they might be.

"You must help me." He felt the incongruity between his words and his grin. Miss Peterson opened her mouth to respond. "Please be casual," Alex said quickly, watching her absorb his meaning, a nervous smile form on her lips.

"You are the only person who can help."

"May I ask, what trouble—"

"You are entitled to an explanation, I know." He looked at his watch. "The time." He pointed for the benefit of anyone watching.

"What is it you wish?" she said, catching the sense of conspiracy.

"Do you know the American Embassy in Moscow?"

"Yes, indeed."

"You must go there immediately upon landing."

She frowned briefly, then remembered to smile. "But I'll miss my London plane."

"Please. Surely the Embassy will help you."

"Not likely," Miss Peterson said with the authority of experience.

"My life is in your hands."

"My God! Your life?" She seemed to warm to the idea. Her eyes became animated.

"You will go?"

She bent closer to him. "In this place we Americans had better stick together," she whispered.

"Talk only to the Ambassador. Insist on it."

She straightened, indignation rising in her diminutive body. "I can be quite insistent, young man."

It was dangerous, he knew. He wanted to warn her, but felt the limitations of their communication. Were they listening? Were they watching? Could she be trusted?

"Tell him that Dr. Cousins—Dr. Alexander Cousins —will be arriving—" He hesitated. Was it possible that he might simply board the plane? Hardly! Until the American authorities were notified, and his whereabouts exactly pinpointed, he was a non-person, easily removed from the face of the earth.

"Tell him I am on the Khabarovsk-Nakhodka train." He remembered that it was scheduled to leave in a few hours. "Yes, tell them I am on that train." The little woman looked at him.

"And will you be taking the *Khabarovsk?*"

"The *Khabarovsk?*"

"The boat that crosses the Sea of Japan. You will be quite seasick."

"I have no plans beyond Nakhodka," Alex said, wondering if he would even get that far.

"All right," Miss Peterson said, "I will tell him you are on the train to Nakhodka."

"Tell him, too, that he must inform the Soviet authorities as well. They must know that I am on that train. And—" Alex looked about him to be sure he was out of earshot of everybody—"and he must inform the President of my whereabouts—immediately."

"The President?"

"Yes, of the United States."

The little woman smiled broadly. "Now that is something." She paused. "You must be quite important."

"Not as important as you are, Miss Peterson." He kissed her on the cheek and handed her the pile of magazines. She went back to her place in line and blew him a brief kiss.

"Will she do it?" Anna Petrovna asked as they moved slowly, with a cautious air of casualness, through the airport to the entrance.

"Lord help us if she doesn't!" Alex said in English.

They drove in silence over the nearly deserted road. Occasionally another car, its headlights glowing, would pass them in the opposite direction speeding toward the airport. They passed the spot where they had dragged the bodies off the road.

"If only they can stay under for the next few hours," Alex whispered.

"It is a wide river," Anna Petrovna said. She had moved close to him, tucking her arm under his, leaning her cheek against his shoulder.

Speeding along the strange highway, Alex felt for the first time the elation of danger and with it a kind of macho heroism. He felt strong and protective. It was exhilarating, he admitted, wondering how long it would last. In the distance, the faint light of impending dawn silhouetted the tall buildings as the car moved closer to the city.

Finding the station again was not an easy task. He made a number of wrong turns before he recognized a landmark that he had seen earlier, a floodlit statue of a bearded man.

"Khabarov," Anna Petrovna said idly. "The famous explorer who founded this city." Then she sat up and pointed. "There." They could see the station at the end of a well-lit street, a huge portrait of Lenin hanging on the station's façade.

He pulled the car over to the side of the road, opened the trunk and removed their baggage.

"I'll have to hide the car somehow," he said. "Make the ticket arrangements. I'll meet you on the platform."

She nodded, picked up her suitcases, leaving his on the sidewalk, and moved toward the station. Alone on the deserted street, he felt a stab of loneliness. Getting back into the car, he drove it to the first cross street, turning off in the direction of the tracks, his eyes scanning the dark rows of low-slung buildings. He drove the car through a dilapidated alley. It was remarkable, he thought, how quickly one adapted to conspiracies when one's life was at stake. He spotted a pair of wooden double doors standing open, loose on their hinges, and drove the car through them. The structure was, apparently, a musty abandoned warehouse filled with the rubbish of a hundred years. Getting out of the car, he felt the chill, sniffed the heavy smell of disintegration. He ran back through the alley to the main street.

He saw Anna Petrovna sitting on a shiny plastic seat in a dark corner of the huge station. She seemed fatigued, her eyes heavy and glazed. Sitting beside her, he put an arm around her shoulders.

"He deserved to die," she said, her voice tense.

"Nobody deserves to die."

"I am a murderer," she said, her eyes wide.

See, he wanted to tell her, taking a life is no small thing. But it was too late now. He felt her anguish and, above all, his love for her.

37

The train was called the "Vostock" and it originated in the Khabarovsk station. The carriages were still icy, although the attendants had apparently stoked the charcoal heaters earlier and a pleasant warm red glow was coming from the brazier under the samovar. A mannish attendant, with thick legs and a heavy growth of black hairs on her upper lip, took their luggage and ushered them through the soft-class passageway. Alex had thrust a pile of bunched-up rubles into her hand.

"Together, please," he whispered.

The "Vostock" was even more Victorian than the "Russiya." Mirrors were everywhere and polished brass fittings were reflected in the heavily varnished wood paneling. Beside each mirror were two glass globe lamps etched with poppies. The windows were partly covered by red velvet tasseled curtains. The compartments were slightly better equipped than the "Russiya's." A bathroom adjoined the compartment. Both the top of the toilet and the floor of the bathroom were carpeted. A gleaming shower head lay on the sink.

The bunks were arranged one above the other as in the "Russiya," but the pillows seemed fluffier, more inviting.

"Goose feathers," Anna Petrovna said, smiling as she sank her hands into the softness.

With the compartment door closed, Alex felt safe, transported to another place, without danger, warm and friendly. Anna Petrovna removed her heavy coat and hung it on a metal hook. She went into the bathroom and he could see her looking in the mirror.

"A witch," she said.

Removing his own outer clothing, he joined her in the bathroom, crowding his face into the mirror. He rubbed his cheeks. He needed a shave.

"And the beast," he said, nibbling her ear. They were a honeymoon couple, he imagined. Perhaps a little long in the tooth, but even that could not dampen his spirit. He felt the strength of his love for her.

Anna Petrovna pushed him gently out of the bathroom and closed the door, leaving him alone in the pleasant compartment. In the background, music was playing, an American tune, "Home on the Range." He hummed along, half-remembering the long-forgotten words. He felt himself in a totally private world, far removed from any sense of the present.

The sun had begun to ascend over the high-rise buildings of the Khabarovsk skyline, throwing spears of light into the compartment, taking the edge off the chill. Earlier he had felt fatigue. But here in this Victorian world, he felt only a sense of impending good fortune, a world without worry.

Under him the wheels began to creak, turning reluctantly at first, then easily as the train gained momentum. He deliberately avoided looking out of the window. The city itself could remind him of their ordeal, and he did not want to linger over such memories. He would respond only to the reality of the moment in this special envelope of time. Next to his love for Anna Petrovna, all else was trivial. Nothing was more powerful. Compared to it, death and danger seemed unreal.

The train was picking up momentum now. The familiar bouncing movement began again and, with it, the disorientation of his sense of time. He removed his watch and slipped it into his pocket. Time was an enemy now, as it had been to Dimitrov. He could think of Dimitrov now without guilt, merely another victim of fate like Zeldovich, like the young soldier, like the young woman who had been passed off as Grivetsky.

Anna Petrovna stepped into the compartment again. He reached out to her and she came into his arms. His lips sought hers.

"You are my life," he whispered, burying his face in her hair. Stepping back, they began to undress each other. He loved the sight of her tall, well-made body. Was she seeing him, too, as a gift? What had gone before between them now seemed prologue' as they stood there in the unreality of the Victorian compartment facing each other. What was happening was beyond science, beyond logic, an immutable mystery.

He moved toward her and they reached out and joined, flesh to flesh, in an act as ancient as life. They lay motionless, feeling the power of it, the gift of it to each other. He wanted to speak, but could not find words, knowing that he was speaking to her without them and listening to her as well.

He was certain that she felt the same wonder in it, although she said nothing. It was this feast of her that moved him, gave him a life beyond himself. He had no questions now, but the fears were returning as he thought of the future, and he became even hungrier for her flesh, entering her again, drowning in the warmth of her. They lay still, but the movement of the train beneath them provided the rhythm of nature. He imagined that they had become part of the train, had merged with it, not resisting its power.

He must have drowsed. He could judge how much time had passed by the change of light in the compartment. The sun had mellowed. Dashes of pink filtered through the brightness. Lifting his head and squinting out the window he could see a brown barren landscape, low hills dotted with scraggly, leafless trees. Anna Petrovna stirred against him, her lips swollen with sleep, her breath shallow.

The train slowed, and Alex thought of his grandfather, speaking of his own train journey nearly sixty years before. He could see the aged face, the eyes glowing like coals.

"In Siberia, the journey is never over," his grandfather had said. "No one ever arrives." Now Alex felt the same panic, the same anguish of the journey.

We are all cast from the same clay, he thought. But the Russians did not accept that. They had such a vain sense of their own separateness.

"They cannot live with our foreignness without wanting to conquer it," Dimitrov had mused one day.

"Who?" Alex had asked.

Dimitrov's eyes had narrowed. "All of them. They are not content unless they can get their fangs into us, and bleed us into submission."

"Who is them?"

Dimitrov had looked at Alex for a long time.

"Not you, Kuznetsov." He had paused. "Them." He had moved his head, implying someone else's presence in the room.

"Who is *them?*" Alex had asked again, beginning to feel idiotic.

"Everyone who is not us," Dimitrov answered finally, and Alex had shivered as if the words were a cold chill.

"These people are all crazy," Alex whispered out loud. He felt Anna Petrovna stir.

"What?"

"I just made a social comment," he said, drawing her close to him.

"I heard you say 'crazy.'"

"You heard correctly."

"Whom did you mean?"

"All of us," he answered quickly. "Do you think Dimitrov is dead?" he asked.

"You are uncertain?" She seemed startled. She rose

on an elbow and looked at him. Her lips began to tremble.

"Of course I am uncertain," he said, meaning more than the state of Dimitrov's condition. "Would he really have done it?"

"You still have doubts?"

"Yes."

"And do you think he would have let you leave the country alive?"

"Yes, I think he would."

"Before the strike?"

"He trusted me."

"With his body. Not with his secrets."

He wanted to tell her he was not afraid to die, that he was afraid only for her, and, most of all, for the end of what they had found together.

"What does it matter now?" he said.

Anna Petrovna sighed and closed her eyes. He felt his own drowsiness. I will not think of it again, he promised himself, yawning and falling into a deep sleep.

When he opened his eyes, Anna Petrovna was already dressed, sitting stiffly in the chair as her hand moved swiftly over some writing paper. He watched her for a moment, then swung his legs over the side of the bunk, feeling the chill seep into his feet.

"I am writing to my children," she said quickly, raising her eyes.

He stood shivering, naked, looking out into the passing landscape. They were apparently traveling on a high plateau. It was raining. Below, a wooded valley, the tree barks shiny with wetness, spread downward into the mist.

Dressing quickly, he turned occasionally to watch her, deeply intent on her composition. Her pen moved swiftly, her hand balanced carefully against the train's motion. Perhaps they would really escape, he thought, and this is a sign she is coming with me? He dared not pursue the issue further, afraid to be disappointed. He would postpone thinking about that for the present;

there were too many uncertainties. If Miss Peterson
had somehow failed to notify the American Embassy,
their chances of leaving Soviet soil would be consider-
ably reduced. He smiled at himself in the mirror as he
scraped off a two-day beard. He was more aware of
himself, physically, than he had ever been. Anna Petrovna had given him that.

"Hungry?" he asked, putting on his jacket.

She looked up from her writing and smiled absently,
nodding. Behind her the rain beat against the window
of the train. He waited while she folded the letter into
the envelope, sealed it and put it into her pocketbook.

In the passageway, the heavyset attendant looked up
from stoking the furnace and glared at them.

"About an hour," she shouted. "Be ready please with
your baggage."

The restaurant was in the next carriage and they
passed through the familiar freezing space. The restaurant carriage was nearly deserted. The manager, a
woman with an ugly birthmark on her cheek, greeted
them with an obviously insincere smile.

"Breakfast?" she asked, then added quickly, "We
are nearly shut down. We have only tea and eggs." She
ushered them to a table. At the far end they could see
the Australian from the "Russiya." Across the aisle
were two Mongols. Alex watched as Anna Petrovna
looked at them and turned her eyes away quickly. He
knew what that meant. Sitting down heavily in his chair,
he studied Anna Petrovna's pale face across the table.

"Them?"

"I'm afraid so."

"They are watching us?"

"Yes. They must have gotten on at one of the stops
during the night."

"How can you be so sure?"

"Is the Pope Catholic?" she said in English, startling
him and making him smile. Again he dared not think
beyond the moment, especially now.

The manager of the car brought two plates of eggs

bathed in grease. Another plate contained soggy pieces of black bread.

"Nothing is going to ruin my breakfast," he said. "Not even the food."

The manager brought a pot of tea. Alex felt the pot. It was cold.

"The hell with you, you fat whore," he called after her.

Anna Petrovna smiled as she broke off a piece of soggy bread and dipped it into the yolk of the egg.

"The food tastes like shit," the Australian yelled across the carriage. The manageress turned and glared at him.

Alex raised his fist without turning around to face the man. "Right on."

"What's that mean?" Anna Petrovna asked.

"It means something like 'Give them hell.' "

"Right on," she said, lifting her fist in imitation. But her eyes were misty and her lip trembled. Reaching across the table, he squeezed her hand.

"The best time in Washington is in the spring. The cherry blossoms bloom around the Tidal Basin and the tourists make it seem like it's one big party."

"We have lots of tourists in Irkutsk," she said, holding back her tears.

"The Paris of Siberia."

"They tell me it's an exaggeration."

"Everything in this place is an exaggeration." He lifted her hand and kissed her fingers.

"It's nearly the end of this fucking train ride," the sandy-haired man yelled. As always, Alex could not tell whether he was drunk or simply mean with boredom. He looked out of the window. The train was passing through the outskirts of a town. In the distance, he could make out the inevitable high-rise apartments, stamped out of the same architectural pattern.

He pushed his plate of eggs away uneaten and gulped down his tea. The loudspeaker system was playing "Auld Lang Syne."

The sandy-haired man stood up and started unsteadily down the aisle between the tables, stopping at theirs.

"They can shove their goddamned trains up their ass."

Alex looked up at him. He could smell his breath. Both drunk and mean, he thought.

"You've been damned consistent," Alex said, smiling.

"They're a filthy lot," he mumbled, moving on. Except for the two Mongols, Alex and Anna Petrovna were alone in the carriage now. Outside, a gloomy city came into view. School children bundled in wet slickers and heavy galoshes moved along the wet asphalt streets. Anna Petrovna's lids brimmed with tears.

"What are their names?" he asked, feeling guilty suddenly, as if he had stolen something.

"Pyotor and Ivan," she whispered.

"Fine names." He tried to remember what she had told him about the children, but he felt his throat constrict. He kept swallowing, holding back his own tears. They stood up and he put a handful of kopecks on the table.

"Thanks for nothing," he said to the manageress.

As they began to move up the aisle, the two Mongols rose. Alex could feel them plodding after them.

In the soft-class car the attendant had already brought their bags out and was watching the train slide into the Nakhodka station. In the pouring rain, it was a dismal scene. People huddled together for shelter under the eaves of the station house. When the door opened, Alex could smell a faint salt tang in the air. Even now, as they followed the attendant through the passageway, down the metal stairs onto the slippery wooden platform, he told himself to think only of the moment. Don't anticipate, he pleaded with himself. The attendant left the bags on the platform and clambered back inside. The two Mongols stood beside the train, waiting, their fur hats soaking in the heavy rain. Alex turned to Anna Petrovna. Drops of rain rolled off her hair onto her face and down her cheeks like a great river of tears.

"Dr. Cousins?" A man holding a big umbrella came toward them.

They waited until the man reached them. He was tall, neatly dressed in a dark raincoat and wore an expression of eager ingratiation.

"He is KGB," Anna Petrovna whispered.

Well then, Alex thought, it is all over. They have finished their game with us. He squeezed Anna Petrovna's hand, more to find courage than to give comfort.

"Karakosov," the tall man said, holding out his hand. Alex took it, feeling its strength. "Welcome to Nakhodka." He winked. "A beastly place." The man spoke English with a British accent, and he had obviously tried to cultivate a kind of British charm.

Perhaps it is a smoke screen, Alex thought, searching the man's face for answers. Had Miss Peterson delivered her message? Or had they found Zeldovich's body? Or had Dimitrov reached him at last. Or—?

"This way," Karakosov said, taking Anna Petrovna's elbow. She looked at him briefly and brushed some of the moisture from her face. They walked down the rain-drenched platform into the station house. The two Mongols carried their luggage.

Inside, Karakosov snapped the umbrella closed and rubbed his hands together.

"Damned chilly," he said.

"Yes," Alex replied. His teeth had begun to chatter. Anna Petrovna clung to his hand.

"The important thing is to get you quickly on your way," Karakosov said, still smiling.

"On my way?" Trust no one, Dimitrov had said.

"The *Khabarovsk* is waiting. Beastly old tub. But there is no airport here. You'll be in Yokohama tomorrow morning. Even your Embassy agrees—"

His words spun on, so casual and disarming, but Alex could think only of Miss Peterson's bland schoolmarm face which masked her determination and courage. In his mind, he embraced her. But the euphoria passed in a moment. What about Anna Petrovna?

"After the train, a sea journey might be interesting." He turned to Anna Petrovna whose face seemed paler in the dull light. "Don't you think?"

The smile on Karakosov's face revealed the cruelty that lay beneath the Oxford patina.

"Mrs. Valentinov goes with me, of course."

"Alex, please," Anna Petrovna said weakly, trying to disengage her hand. The tall man's eyes narrowed as he watched her.

"She goes or I don't."

"You mustn't, Alex—"

"They don't intimidate me," Alex said, his anger rising.

"Really, Dr. Cousins." Karakosov turned to Anna Petrovna. "I'm sure she would prefer to return to Irkutsk, to her children." He paused, to emphasize his sarcasm. "And her husband."

"I will not go without her," Alex persisted, feeling his knees weaken.

"Listen to him," Anna Petrovna said.

"I will not go without you," he said again.

"You must explain to him," Karakosov said quickly to Anna Petrovna in Russian.

"I want to speak directly with the American Ambassador," Alex said, marveling at his ability to maintain his calm. Karakosov's eyes darted from Anna Petrovna's face to his own. That was reassuring. He was obviously "handle-with-care" cargo. It confirmed his bargaining position.

"She goes with me," Alex said.

The tall man hesitated, then forced a smile.

"You will excuse me," he said, moving to another part of the station, where two men stood in the shadows. They watched as he spoke to them with animation.

"God bless Miss Peterson," Alex said, putting an arm around Anna Petrovna's shoulders.

"You mustn't, my darling," Anna Petrovna said, her face drawn now. He started to speak, but his attention was suddenly deflected by another man who ran into the station and hurried over to where Karakosov was standing with the two men. They listened and Karakosov glanced at them briefly, then returned.

"Dimitrov is dead." He sighed as he stood before them. He seemed genuinely saddened.

So it had all been futile, Alex thought, knowing that even Dimitrov would have been amused. Time had deceived the old fox. His old antagonist, the disease, had once again prevailed. Now there is poetic justice, Alex mused, watching Karakosov. The game had no victors. Except himself, he thought stoutly. He had found Anna Petrovna and she had helped him find something in himself.

"She goes with me," Alex demanded.

Karakosov nodded and signaled to the two Mongols to pick up their luggage. They walked through the gloomy station. The perennial hangers-on slumbered on the wooden benches. A line of babushkas huddled at one side of the station warming their wrinkled hands on a potbellied stove. Turning backward for a moment, Alex watched the glistening train slowly move out of the station.

A group of cars waited in the rain. The Mongols loaded the baggage in the trunk of one of them while Alex and Anna Petrovna slid into the back seat. Karakosov got in the front. The two Mongols took the car behind them.

Their fingers were locked and he could feel Anna Petrovna's tenseness. He leaned over and kissed her cheek. Karakosov, with an air of diplomatic delicacy, turned away.

"It will be fine," Alex said.

The cars began to move through the wet deserted streets.

"A miserable, gloomy town," Karakosov remarked.

"It's the rain," Alex responded.

"Yes, the rain."

They drove in silence. It was not a long ride. In the mist ahead he could see the docks and the half-formed outlines of ships.

"It's an old tub." Karakosov smiled. He had regained his former lightness. "You'll dock at Yokohama. Your people will meet you there."

As they neared the docks, Alex again felt constrained. He would not think about the future, their future, until he had untangled them from their present circumstances. Despite what he knew, Dimitrov's death filled him with sadness. He realized now how much he had felt for the old man. Somehow, and he could not rationalize it, the horror of what Dimitrov surely intended had still not touched him. He was grateful that he had come through. I am not a killer, he told himself. And I am not God.

"You are a good fellow, Kuznetsov," Dimitrov had said. It was the morning of his departure. Dimitrov had turned to him with tears of sentiment in his eyes. "I thank you for the time," he had said. Did he finally grow to hate me for my failure? Alex wondered.

The cars came to a stop along the dock. The great hull of the *Khabarovsk* towered above them. A crowd moved slowly up the gangplank. Alex recognized the Australian among them, still scowling. A group of young European students in jeans and knapsacks crowded up the gangplank behind them, oblivious to the rain which had become even heavier. They waited in the car as the last passenger straggled up the gangplank.

"My grandfather hated this part of the journey," Alex said suddenly. "He hated to see the land slip away." He paused, watching the rain drip down the car window. "It didn't matter. He never really left anyway." He sensed that he was really talking to himself. He turned toward Anna Petrovna, but she was looking stiffly ahead. Later they would talk, he assured himself, and he would make it right.

"Let's go," Karakosov said.

They filed out of the car, huddling under the umbrella, and started up the gangplank. A group of tough-looking Russian sailors in shiny slickers watched them.

The Mongols followed with their luggage. When Alex reached the deck, he paused, then spat over the railing.

They were led to a stairwell on the deck, and descended the flight of wooden stairs. The ship smelled of oil and urine. Alex felt the ship's roll as they followed the Mongols. One of them came to a halt before a cabin door, while the other moved ahead.

"Mrs. Valentinov's cabin is just down the corridor," Karakosov said.

Alex shook his head, still amused at their odd sense of morality. One of the Mongols deposited her baggage in the assigned compartment. Alex continued to hold Anna Petrovna's hand. His cabin was larger than the train's compartments, but more primitive. There were no carpets on the floor and the bunks looked narrow and uninviting.

Karakosov gripped Alex's hand and shook it vigorously.

"I hope you will have a pleasant journey," he said. He nodded toward Anna Petrovna, bowed and let himself out of the compartment. When he had gone, Alex drew Anna Petrovna to him, enveloping her in his arms.

"My darling," he said, feeling a sob shudder through him. He had to fight to hold back his own tears. He held her quietly, feeling her breath against his cheek, the soft touch of her fingers on the back of his neck. "I'll make it right," he said. "Things change. We'll send for the children." He felt her stiffen. When she moved away, she was clear-eyed.

"We'll talk later," she said. "But first I would like to freshen up."

"Then we'll search this tub for a bar. We'll find some champagne."

"Wonderful, darling," she said. The idea seemed to cheer her. He moved closer, kissed her lips.

"My heart is full," he said.

She left the cabin quickly. The sudden sound of the ship's vibrations steadied him. Soon this abominable mysterious land would disappear, and he would look

ahead to a new life. The past was dead. The present
was slowly expiring. For the first time in his life he
felt joy in the future, his own future. Time, he agreed
with Dimitrov. Time was everything.

The rumbling of the ship's engines grew louder.
Pressing his face to the porthole, he tried to see through
the mist. The windows were too filthy. Disappointed,
he decided to go topside, to see for himself the last of
Siberia. He did a clumsy tap dance on the wooden deck
of the companionway, and a young man in jeans smiled
at him as he passed. He felt good, wonderful, in fact.
One of the Mongols slouched against a bulkhead. So we
will continue to have company to Yokohama. To hell
with them!

"Hello, moon face," he called. The man looked at
him blankly. Alex stopped in front of Anna Petrovna's
cabin and knocked lightly. He waited for a moment,
looked at the Mongol, and knocked again.

"Knock, knock," he said to the Mongol. "Remember
the old knock-knock jokes?"

He put his ear to the door. "Anna," he called, enjoying the sound of it, the Americanization. "Let's go
on deck and see the action." He grabbed the door handle
and turned it, pushing open the door.

"We're going—" The words stuck in his throat. He
felt the blood balance in his body change, as if it had
all congealed in the pit of his stomach. The cabin was
empty, the suitcases gone. He felt the sudden emptiness
like a blow to his head, stunning him. But he understood quickly. He turned, but the Mongol blocked his
way.

"Please, Dr. Cousins," the Mongol said in pidgin
Russian.

"You bastards. You dirty bastards." He could taste
rage on his lips as he swung out and gave the Mongol
a hammer blow to the chest. The man doubled over in
pain.

Alex took the stairs four at a time, charged by anger
and loss. Behind him, he could hear the heavy step of a
pursuer.

On deck, he felt the whip of salt spray mixed with the heavy rain.

A few passengers had lined the railing, braving the weather for a last look at land. He ran to the railing, squinting into the mist at the barely distinguishable figures that lined the dock. Was it her blonde head he saw, or only his own imagination giving him one last look at her?

"Anna," he cried into the rain, a lost wail ending in nothingness. His hand gripped the handrail, and he braced himself to jump overboard. But strong hands held him back and, as the ship slowly pulled out, the descending mist engulfed the land in an impenetrable cloud.

"Anna Petrovna," he cried again and again. The hands gripped him, locked him into his position at the railing. They held him as the strength went slowly out of his body and his hold on the handrail loosened. After a while, even the rage was gone. Then the Mongol gently nudged him along the deck, down the stairs into the cabin.

He could not tell how long he lay in the lower bunk, his mind blank. He knew that he had lost any sense of time or place. Then it was dark in the cabin and he was conscious of the roll and pitch of the boat. He swung his legs to the floor, and the lights immediately went on in the cabin. The Mongol was there, his flat face expressionless.

"What planet is this?" he asked.

The Mongol grunted and left the cabin.

Across the room was his bookbag. He dragged it over to the single chair in the room. There was a reading lamp against the bulkhead above the chair and he flicked the switch. It threw a beam of thin yellow light on his lap. Opening the bag, he extracted a medical journal. His work. He recognized the familiar medical terms, his mind searching for a point of reference as he struggled to lift himself from the pit of emptiness. As he flipped through the pages, an envelope slipped out onto his lap. He sat staring at it a long time, gathering his courage. When it came, he carefully tore open the end and tapped the folded paper out of the envelope:

My Darling Alex: They will never let me go now. Nor would I ever leave if I could. We are not very good among strangers. I am grateful for the moments we did have together, but there is more than geography between us. We are different and there is nothing that either of us can do to help that. I do not know what the future will bring, except that I do know we must not keep locked up what we know. Someone must tell them. Surely there is reason left somewhere. I hope you will not forget me and I can assure you I will never forget you. If that is sentiment, then I am not ashamed of it anymore. Good-bye. Anna Petrovna Valentinov.

He read it swiftly, greedily, pausing only over her signature. The words seemed brittle. Tell who? he wondered.

"They are all crazy," he whispered, placing the letter in the folds of the journal.

Then he began to read the article on the open page, forcing himself to understand.